Incident in Patagonia

INCIDENT IN PATAGONIA

Isabel García Cintas

©2016: Incident in Patagonia (Incidente en la Patagonia)

Amancay Ediciones/Isabel Garcia Cintas
®All Rights Reserved

US Library of Congress
TXu 2-016-114
ISBN: 978-0-9838523-0-8

Cover: Author's design over a Mycovermaker stock image.

Author's website: www.isabelgarciacintas.com
Author's email: isabelgarciacintas@ymail.com

To my husband Tomás,
for everything

Buenos Aires – New York

I did a quick check, and all was in order. My small carry-on luggage pieces were sitting next to the door, and the apartment's gas line turned off. Before unplugging the computer, I looked at the mailbox for new messages, just in case. One of the three still unopened emails caught my attention. The sender was Sergio Brauer, Alicia Rivera's widower and a dear old friend. In his usually concise way, the message read in Spanish: *Dear Lina, Mariano told me you would be in New York in a few weeks. Call me when you get here. Need to see you. It's important. Hope you can have dinner with me at home. A big hug. Sergio.*

I read it twice. It was still early to get to the airport. I had planned to get there with enough time to do some paperwork while waiting for the flight to San Francisco. I paused with a sigh before typing the answer. And I thought of her.

Alicia.

The memory of what happened still hurts, even after all these years. I wasn't there to support Alicia when she needed me. At the time of the events, I had not heard from her or Susana for a couple of years. Nonetheless, I still feel guilty for not having tried harder at keeping in touch with both of them. Even though I still wonder if they would have trusted me with what was going on. They certainly wouldn't confide by phone or letters. I was far away, living my personal experiences and enjoying the Brazilian beaches while everybody else at home survived under siege. We were close friends, so I still carry this lingering guilt and uneasy feeling when I think of them.

I wrote back, accepting the unexpected invitation. Later, during my long trip and between stops, we got to set a date to meet. That evening I caught the subway in Manhattan and got off in Brooklyn. If it were daytime, I would have loved to walk around and enjoy the beautiful neighborhood's buildings at leisure, but on my tight schedule, I had no time to spare. Sergio said he would be waiting for me at the exit gate.

When we met, I almost did not recognize him. He had grown a short beard, and his light auburn hair was nearly white. We embraced tightly for a while, unable to say a word. Then, we sighed while looking at each other, smiling. He took my arm, and we walked under the old, tall trees, finally able to catch up.

The apartment he had bought and shared with his only son was only a couple of blocks from the subway station. Pablo had just graduated from pre-med college and was getting ready to enter an M.D. program, "It's cheaper than renting," Sergio said, "But of course, now he's moving to Boston," he added, smiling.

When we got to the lovely red brick house, Pablo came down the stairs to meet us. The son was taller than his dad. He greeted me with a kiss on my cheek, Argentinean style, and left after a brief, polite exchange. I commented that American youngsters do not kiss when they meet or go, and Sergio looked back at me, amused.

"Well," he said, "he wasn't born here, and he still identifies with our customs from back home." The tone of his voice had a familiar ring that made me feel comfortable.

He had prepared roast beef, which was almost ready, potatoes, and salad. Then he opened a bottle of good red wine, and we dined chatting about this and that. Over coffee, I thought, nostalgic, *it's almost like in old times when we used to have those lengthy and lazy after-dinner conversations.* But then Alicia and Hugo, my ex-husband, shared the table and laughed with us. Now, neither one was around any longer.

Sergio faced me and said with a sudden change in his voice, "I bet I surprised you with my email."

I nodded. "Well, yes, the truth is, although I did not expect it, I'm happy you did it after so long."

He gestured with his hand, and I understood it as meaning it was about time. Then, without a word, he stood up, and from a cabinet topped with books and a laptop, he took a ream of paper box out.

"Lina, I want you to take this with you," he said.

"What is it?" I asked, intrigued.

"It's a manuscript written by Alicia during the months, maybe the whole year before she died. I got it from the wardens, but I was unable to touch it for a long time. Then, finally, when I found the strength to face her words, I understood many things that I didn't know or couldn't see before."

I looked at him, wondering what all this had to do with me, but I didn't ask. Then, as if he read my mind, he put the box on the table in front of me. "You are in the publicity business in Buenos Aires," he said, "I am sure Alicia wrote this manuscript for the world to be aware of it. These pages tell her whole story, so much so that even the names are unchanged. I want to honor this last wish of hers. It may need editing. But please, don't change the meaning of her message. See if you can find a publisher. I would appreciate it very much."

I couldn't refuse. I was too moved and brought the box with the manuscript home.

Here are Alicia's memoirs, just as she left them.

Alicia's story should be known and remembered. We owe her that much.

Lina Figueroa
Buenos Aires, 2004

Traveler,
There is no road ahead.
We make the path through walking
And when we look over our shoulder
We see the trail that nobody
Will ever walk again.
Traveler,
There is no road ahead,
Just ripples on the surface of the sea.

Antonio Machado (1875-1939)
Spaniard Poet

I

Bariloche, Patagonia Argentina, Wednesday, March 31, 1982

The two-way road meandered around Lake Nahuel Huapi's coast, following the lower Mount Otto's incline curves. Some areas were shady with trees close to the shoreline, and others had just the right space for a walking path before the steep slope to the narrow beach below. Alicia shifted to first gear, drove her old and bouncy Citroën 2CV cautiously out of the plant nursery's driveway to Ezequiel Bustillo Avenue, and headed West. She would then check the rear mirror at the curves; three vehicles were behind her. It was getting dark, and Alicia put the lights on with a sigh. It had been a long day, and she was ready for a warm dinner at home.

The incoming traffic was limited to an occasional car here and there. She reduced the speed and tried to find an FM radio transmission from Chile. Down at the distant Georgia Islands, things were getting worse by the day between the military junta governing Argentina and the British government over Islas Malvinas' sovereignty. The military junta seemed prepared to recover them. Still, the news was sparse, and other than a commando action by the Navy in the Georgias, not much was clear. Like all other media in the country, the local LRA30 was under martial rule and censorship, but Chile was sympathetic to the Brits, so maybe she could learn something new, she thought, trying again without success.

Suddenly a car right behind her, now also with the lights on, caught her attention. Although it kept a steady distance from the Citroën for a while, it was now trying to pass her. It was an almost impossible task in the narrow two-way winding route.

What the heck is he doing? She thought, surprised. They approached an area where the road's shoulder broadened between the pavement and the lake, a popular lookout point. The car suddenly passed her on her left, maneuvering and forcing Alicia to go off the roadway onto the graveled edge.

It was a dark green Ford Falcon, and she instantly felt a rush of adrenaline, her underarms itching as they did when she felt threatened. Green Ford Falcons belonged to the government's secret service. She often heard that they were spotted when kidnappings and disappearances happened in the last few years. The car was forcing her to the shoulder of the road.

Her heart pounding and confused by the unexpected maneuver, she lowered the speed, headed toward the parking area, and finally stopped. The large car cut across in front of hers, under the trees, in the shadows. A couple of vehicles passed by quickly. Alicia felt a weight right above her stomach and sat there, paralyzed by fear, looking at the other car, registering the opening of the back doors and the two men that came out in slow motion. She could not see their faces. The palms of her hands felt cold and wet on the wheel. If these guys wanted to do something, anything, she wouldn't be able to get away. Two other individuals stayed in the car, in the front seats.

The men walked toward her, their faces still blurred. She knew her body would not move even if she tried. The whole thing seemed unreal, as if she were looking at the scene from a detached place while *being in it.*

One of the men stood in front of her door. The other walked around toward the passenger's side. She opened the window, and he bent toward her. His angular face was clean-shaven, and she felt a faint smell of cheap cologne as if he had stepped right out of the shower. "Let's see your ID," he commanded, looking at her with sharp, light eyes that seemed almost animal in their alertness. As she expected, he did not identify himself.

Alicia registered the command in her brain, grabbed her purse, slowly pulled out the small brown leather wallet, took the plastic Federal ID out, and handed it over. He examined it for a few minutes, taking his time to enjoy her fear and savoring his power.

"Turn off the engine," he snapped. Alicia obeyed.

The other man stood motionless in front of the passenger's door. Through the foggy window, she could see only his thick jacket. He had his hands in his pockets and stood sideways, facing the road. The man on her side lowered his head, and the whiff of after-shave hit her again. Getting closer to her face, he handed over the card. She held a corner and tried to pull it with shaking hands, but the man wouldn't let it go. Still keeping the ID card, his face dimly visible by the reflection of the car's lights, he said in a deliberately and threatening way: "So, *señora* Alicia Rivera de Brauer." He kept silent for a few seconds. "If I were you, I would be very cautious when choosing acquaintances. Not to mention that I would refrain from offering unsolicited opinions." He shook his head, admonishing. "And you have a young kid, don't you?"

She held her breath, still connected to the man through the card both were holding.

"Consider yourself lucky," he added with a scornful shrug, letting the ID go. "As I said, if I were you, I wouldn't make waves." He had a pronounced accent, but she couldn't identify where it was from, maybe from the Northwest. Like many from the provinces living now in Bariloche, he tried to mask it under a *porteño* accent. Still, it made his voice even more intimidating. "Now go, go home, but be a smart girl, eh?"

Alicia felt drops of sweat rolling down her back while watching the men turn around and stroll toward the green Falcon. After they got into the car, now darker in the fading light, the vehicle turned around and headed back toward downtown.

After the Falcon drove away, Alicia put the first gear and left the shady area, entering the asphalt road. While clasping the wheel with shaky hands, she mustered the strength to close the window and concentrate on the fact that the men were gone. Her heart was still beating fast, and the lights of other cars seemed distorted through the tears in her eyes. She felt a knot in her throat while she tried to concentrate on keeping the vehicle steady on the road she could hardly see. Taken by surprise, now she felt frightened at the thought of what had happened.

Light snow was falling now. Tiny flakes dissolved on the windshield as soon as they touched it. Alicia remembered to have seen a flock of parrots in the morning, flying down from the hills, a reliable snowfall signal. She felt the unstoppable flow of tears again while approaching home.

She was relieved at the brick house sight, nestled in a corner shaded by old, sheltering trees. It was a small dwelling on a large piece of land, looking bright, with its amber, welcoming light showing through the windows behind the voile curtains she had sewn.

Alicia parked the car in the driveway and walked to the entrance, shivering under the cold, icy rain. Sergio was already opening the door for her.

"What's wrong?" he asked, holding Pablo in his arm while closing the door.

"Two men stopped me on my way home," she said, and her voice broke. Her eyes were red, and she looked distraught.

"What men?" Sergio sat Pablo on the high chair at the table and turned to her, arms open. Alicia rested on his chest for a few minutes, sobbing. He patted her back softly. "Calm down. Calm down and tell me everything, every detail," he said, helping her to get her coat. "What did they do?"

"They didn't do anything to me; it was a threat," she said, trying to sound coherent. Then, noticing that Pablo was moaning, uneasy at the sight of his mom crying, she picked him up, and he calmed down, delighted to cuddle with his mom.

"Why would they stop you on the road? Do you know them?" Sergio wondered

"No," she said, "never saw them before. They are not from this area, but they knew me well. This guy even mentioned Pablo."

"It's weird. Everybody knows who you are here, that's why it is so surprising. What did those men say exactly?"

Slowly she repeated almost word by word the exchange with the men, and when she finished, they looked at each other, unsure of what all meant.

Sergio was the first to talk. "There is nothing you can do now. Just relax and let's have dinner," he said, knowing what would calm her down, sitting Pablo back in his high chair. He led her toward the hallway.

"Yes. I need a shower now," she agreed.

"Go ahead. Take your time."

The shower was pleasant and energizing. *It was a nightmare, and it's over*, Alicia kept on saying to herself, and the mantra helped her regain a sense of balance. When she came out of the bathroom, a delicious aroma of basil wafted from the kitchen. Sergio had set the table, and poured fresh cut tomatoes over the steaming bowl of pasta. At the sight of him, a warm, reassuring feeling took hold of her.

"Smells wonderful. Yummy," she said, looking appreciatively. "I love you. Everything is ready and perfect. Thank you," she said impulsively. He turned to her, feigning surprise.

"Wow. You are welcome. I hope it's not a hint for me to cook dinner every night from now on."

She smiled. "It wouldn't be a bad idea... A chef for a husband."

They managed to create a certain degree of normalcy at dinner, even though their minds lingered in the thought of the unusual encounter. Alicia felt as if she had crossed a threshold tonight and was suddenly walking on uncharted territory. It was a scary feeling. She had a new awareness of the fact that she could have found herself in another place right now, not knowing why it might have happened.

Shuddering at the thought, she focused again on her family. She now appreciated details anew, like the soft yellow-orange light of the Tiffany lamp on top of the table that gave the dining room and the faces a warm glow. It felt right, as it should be. Even Pablo was unusually chatty tonight, rehearsing new words from his vocabulary while noisily slurping his noodles as if he joined the celebration of being together. After dinner, Sergio took him to bed. Alicia followed them for the nightly ritual of reading at the bedside. Soon after Alicia started the first page of his favorite Smurf book, he fell asleep. She tiptoed back to the living room to sit next to Sergio.

He watched TV on the couch and put his arm around her

shoulders in a protective way. The volume was low, and neither of them paid attention to the screen.

Sergio broke the silence.

"Early tomorrow morning, I'm going fishing with the guys. We want to go back down the Rio Manso's coast, where we had a good catch last week."

She knew he was making conversation, giving her space to get back to what dominated her thoughts.

"That's a nice area... Are you going close to the lake, near the camping site we went to last time?" Alicia tried to sound natural.

"We'll go further into the woods now to explore a couple of new uphill streams. The guys say it's a good spot. We'll see."

She felt forced to answer, appreciating his effort.

"Hum... I hope that's a good spot," she said, feigning interest, but he knew her too well.

"Are you okay? Sure, you're feeling better now?"

"Yes," Alicia sighed, managing a faint smile. "I'm okay now, here, with you."

His arm was still on her shoulder; he caressed her affectionately.

"Want to go to bed? I'm tired, and you have an early day tomorrow," she added, unconvinced.

"Yes, you look tired," he said tenderly, stroking her hair. Neither of them moved. They stayed silent for a few minutes until Alicia asked, almost to herself: "What am I going to do now, Sergio? What happens if they return?"

He stood up and walked a few steps to turn off the TV.

"Nothing," he said. "You shouldn't do anything except go on with your normal life. You haven't done anything wrong, and we don't know who sent those guys or who they are," he added, walking toward the kitchen.

Watching the dimly lit street from the window, she heard him filling the kettle with water.

"Let's make a cup of tea; it will make you feel better," he said from the kitchen door. They habitually drank tea or coffee before bedtime, usually while listening to music or watching movies.

Sergio returned with a glass of water and aspirin for Alicia, and stood next to her, knowing she needed to talk about it again, elaborate on the situation more than once to calm down. That's how she coped with her crisis.

"I'll never forget the smell of that cheap after-shave cologne." Alicia felt the tears coming back. "I never thought something like this would ever happen to me." She wiped her face with an already wet linen handkerchief. "I'm angry and scared, but I don't want to just cry about it, although, what could I do? It still shakes me."

"I know." He looked at her, and she thought she saw a worried look flashing through his eyes. "You may not want to talk to anybody about this on the radio or the paper."

"Of course not. There's nobody there I could tell something like this..." Then she added: "I'm petrified. I thought it was over; I thought they were no longer following people and taking them away."

"I know. It worries me too. But it does not mean that what happened tonight is what you are thinking."

"I'm not so sure of that. The man said I should be careful with the friends I have. Which one? Martina? If he was talking about her, this whole thing might have to do with our Sunday radio show. Lately, I have heard comments that we putting wrong ideas on women's heads. Feminist ideas, I have mentioned this to you before. Ideas that, to me, are only common sense..." She hesitated before adding, "Signs that something was brewing were all over. I should have seen it coming. "

"You do not know if that's the reason. So don't blame yourself."

Alicia seemed not to hear his words.

"Martina and I talked about this many times, about the censorship, the limitations we have, and how we try to be careful. But, then again, if we cannot say anything meaningful in our program if we don't talk about what's essential to women and families, what differentiates us from the other recipes-and-beauty-tips programs they have already in the afternoons? Who wants more make-up lessons? Other women are covering those topics. For example, take our program on the illiteracy of women and girls working at the *estancias'* remote posts. Many did not like it. Another topic was the scantly clad women ads shown next to products like cars or drinks. Again, many hated it while most listeners agreed with us."

"I know, you should say some things frankly. But, on the other hand, if they cancel your program, you and Martina will not have any outlet left to talk about what you both really care. And I think you are doing an important job here."

"Thanks... I wish others saw it like that, particularly sponsors like Schneider."

"I don't want to see you in trouble. Just keep your eyes open. I'm not so sure this came by way of the show."

The kettle's whistle startled them, and Alicia jumped from the couch and turned quickly to the kitchen. Sergio followed and stood at the door while she prepared the cups and brewed the tea. The sweet smell of chamomile filled the room.

"You are right; even if I don't like Schneider and what he represents, we need sponsors, so we cannot afford to lose his support," Alicia said.

"So, try to keep it."

"Yeah, but it's not so easy to do. Martina and I are torn between giving a public service and the fact that we need his sponsorship. Besides, I don't trust him. To tell you the truth, after tonight, I hardly trust anybody in this town."

Schneider, the owner of a ski equipment store, had pioneered the mass tourism business in the area and was a reliable sponsor of the snow sports in Cerro Catedral, the nearby ski resort. In addition, he was a co-founder member of the local mountain club, a stronghold of traditional families and from his perch he openly exerted his influence on its members and the local press.

"Well, wait and see. Schneider is heavy on the conservative side, but who knows? He may even be flexible," Sergio ventured.

"Hum...I don't think so; he was almost threatening. You talk about him being reasonable because you only know his social side. You met him as your parents' friend, so your image of him is a nice beer-drinking, happy member of the Club. However, I see him wearing a different hat. I hope I'm wrong."

"I know exactly where he comes from. I'm only saying that sometimes you have to negotiate if you want to get somewhere. Don't forget what is going on all over the country."

"Yeah... we are all going to hell in a basket. That's what's going on."

He couldn't avoid a smile. Alicia was again her usual self.

She offered a cup to him, and they walked back to the living room. She sipped her tea, and the comforting smell of the familial herb made her feel better right away, like the food and the lights earlier at the table. She needed her senses to reassure her that everything was normal, that her world had not gone out of control, that she was still living in her country, the place where she was born and always called home. Because things had changed, and there was no more a sense of normalcy around them.

They sipped tea in silence for a while, and then the news of the day about the Georgia Islands came up briefly, but she did not pay attention.

"I'm sure everything will turn out to be less serious than you think now." He tried to be comforting, and Alicia nodded. She desperately wanted to be soothed by his words. They always enjoyed and welcomed a certain degree of adventure and risk. Still, tonight the sudden realization that their world might have been built over more unstable terrain than they had expected was a sobering experience. Old ghosts they heard of or read about, shadows that had chased other generations, and remote people now seemed a tangible presence.

The mood was gloomy, and they remained in silence, awake for a long time before falling asleep, Sergio holding her tight.

The alarm went off at four a.m. They had only slept a few hours. Sergio quietly dressed and gathered his things. Right before going back to sleep, she heard the front door closing and his car leaving the driveway in the pre-dawn silence.

At eight o'clock, the alarm woke her up again. She was surprisingly alert, not like her regular sleepy morning self. The night's thoughts hit her, and she made a conscious effort to put them aside. She lingered in bed for a while, enjoying the warmth. She pictured Sergio in the freezing woods since dawn, waiting for the first light, in search of a few hours of fly-fishing, and smiled. Nothing short of an emergency would take her out of her warm bed at those wee hours of the morning. Sergio had described to her the hours of pre-dawn more than once. The solitude and peace in the forest with words that, were she less aware of his agnosticism and utter logical thinking, she would define as his spiritual experience. He needed those quiet moments, and she, searching for her inner peace, had tried meditation a few times but without success.

Finally, Alicia pulled herself out of bed, stepping on her slippers and shivering in the cold air of the bedroom while grabbing the warm chenille robe lying on a chair nearby. Sergio and the others should be driving back toward town and going to their businesses and jobs by now. But instead, from the bathroom, she heard Pablo calling for his breakfast.

The coals in the living room's fireplace were cold. After raising the heat in Pablo's bedroom gas heater, Alicia dressed the playful and energetic child. Now he was waiting for her in his crib, moaning and holding the rails, ready to claim his delayed breakfast. She hurried up. Jacinta was about to arrive if the public-transport bus that ran every hour between the city and the Llao-Llao Hotel was punctual today.

Alicia was finishing with Pablo's breakfast when Jacinta knocked on the door softly, as she always did when she thought the child might still be sleeping. When Alicia opened, a cold, dry gust of wind rushed in with Jacinta. Following a brief welcome, she closed the door after the woman, who hung her thick parka next to the entrance. Then, she walked toward the kitchen. Their occasional dialogs were very much to the point and short on words. Alicia had learned to read her moods, and she liked the woman's straightforward ways. Jacinta seemed satisfied working a few hours every day at several houses in the neighborhood, which meant a full-time job earning at the end of the month.

After pouring another coffee, Alicia put the portable electric typewriter on the dining room table and took her folders from the briefcase. Pablo was perched on his high chair nearby, surrounded by crayons and loose pieces of paper on his side of the table. He was busy drawing large circles and lines, absorbed entirely by his work. She smiled affectionately at him and focused her attention on her writing, and at times trying to catch glimpses of the news.

Unable to concentrate on her job, Alicia walked to the window, fixing her attention on the front lawn. The bare branches of the trees and the season's last buds of roses wavered in the wind under the pale winter sun. Yesterday's evening snow had melted as it touched the ground, but the grey clouds were still up there, even thicker than the day before.

A small bird landed on the yellowish lawn, and she watched his search for food distractedly. Then her thoughts went back to when she was twelve and read The Diary of Anne Frank for the first time. It was a birthday present from Aunt Marga: "This is the story of a girl during the war," she had explained. "It's a terrific story."

When adult people said *the war,* it was understood that they talked about World War II. Alicia had devoured the soft-cover, economy edition's pages and could not put it down until the last one. Then, overwhelmed by emotion, she had walked, still with the book in her hand, to the kitchen where her mother was cooking.

"Mom, I can't believe that nobody would help these people! Why didn't anybody do something to help?"

Her mother had turned to her, looking sad and confused.

"We did not know what to do, to be honest with you." Then she added: "We read all the news and sympathized and worried about the people at war. We did not even know they had concentration camps, let alone all those killings. We heard rumors, and some people did charity functions to collect money and clothes to send. We did not know how to help otherwise. Argentina was not at war."

After a pause, her mother added with a sigh, "It's not easy to explain. Nothing is clear-cut in life, Alicia. Things are complicated; you are too young, but one day, when you grow up, you will understand."

"I'm not too young, Mom. I want to be a writer. I want to know why people kill other people just like that."

"You will, but you still have a lot to learn."

Alicia felt frustrated. She mourned Anne Frank for a long time. How could the rest of the world have looked the other way or just let it happen? She talked about it with Carla, her younger cousin, and the one that followed her as a sister. Still, she was too young to comprehend Alicia's sorrow. She read a few crucial parts of the book to her, but the little girl got bored.

"So you see, Anne finally was taken away and killed with all those millions of people that were herded away by force," said Alicia, looking for some reaction.

"Then I won't call Anne the new doll that I'm asking the Three

Wise Men to bring me on January sixth. I don't want my doll to be taken away too. So now let's play mom and dad. I'm the mom today."

"That's a good idea." Alicia sighed and patted her head.

At the time, the only thing she could think of doing to relieve her hurt teenager's feelings was to sit and write a long, mournful letter to a friend that had moved to Rosario. She wrote back, visibly moved by Alicia's words and the poetry of her prose. But that was not what Alicia needed. In her response, there was no mention of Alicia's thoughts on the Holocaust, the horror of war, or the tragedy of Anne Frank. Instead, she felt disenchanted at her friend's indifference. She imagined her rising heroically in similar circumstances to defend anyone in danger.

Now, many years later, her country was living a similar, albeit less dramatic, experience. Things were not so clear-cut, just like her mother said. Bad things were happening to others, but she was afraid for her safety and looked the other way, pushed by forces that she could not control. There were rumors here and there about secret prisons and people that searched for family members and did not get any response from the military government. Nobody dared to speak openly about those rumors, afraid to be considered a subversive, a guerrilla sympathizer. But, what did it mean to be *subversive*? Just to ask questions about what was going on made a person a guerrilla sympathizer? And, by the way, what was going on out there? The memory of last night's encounter sent shivers down her spine.

When Jacinta left the house at noon, Sergio had come home for lunch. Off-season, the small city businesses closed their doors for two or three hours in the afternoon. They compensate for the extended after-hours schedule they had to keep with the tourist crowds in the evenings. Alicia and Sergio followed the custom, happy to oblige and enjoy a break during sunlight. They even drove to the slopes on some bright winter days and squeezed a couple of downhill skiing hours when the snow was fresh and the tourists were scarce.

Alicia opened the front door, and Sergio carried his cooler inside. He walked to the kitchen, opened the lid, and pulled out a beautiful Rainbow trout. It was already cleaned and wrapped in a thick plastic bag. He looked at her, beaming. Alicia whistled in admiration.

"Nice catch! What's the weight?"

"Over four pounds. Not bad, eh?" He was radiant. Alicia enjoyed cooking and eating the tender and delicate meat. Still, she did not want anything to do with catching the fish.

Her first and only experience not long ago had been a failure. Sergio prepared a line for her, taught her how to cast the fly, and she tried. By the end of the day, she got a nice trout. Alicia even got to pull the fighting, bright, and beautiful animal from the water. Although, when the moment came to remove the hook, she cowardly ran away and left the job to Sergio. She couldn't even look at the poor creature gasping for air. Sergio thought that it was a great catch and congratulated her. It went without saying that the experience would be the first and last for Alicia.

They had lunch, catering to Pablo, and kept a light conversation.

"I have a meeting tomorrow with Andrade at Huemul," Sergio said. "They have my project, and I hope they will approve it, and I'll get the financing. But still, they might not. The mortgage freeze on commercial lending is lasting too long."

Financing for sizeable construction work was almost inexistent. With a tight economy, things in the area had gone from bad to worse. And the effort to keep their livelihood afloat took much of their energies. Alicia saw the same exhaustion in the people around her at work. Meager salaries were not enough to survive with dignity. Still, both were aware that their situation was better than most.

"It's okay," she said with a sigh. "Let's hope for the best. It would not be good for us if this project did not come through. As you know, we are already behind on some payments."

"I know." His voice had an inflection that showed that he also was tired. The scarce money at the end of the month was a source of embittered discussions between them, and he preferred not to start an argument over that today. Not at the table.

Alicia knew well how much he hated when she got upset over their finances; she could go on, and he did not want to hear it. So the disagreements were always about what was a priority on their debtor's list.

"Things will get better. One payment at a time, we will get there. But sooner or later, things will have to improve. After all, what's important is that we are fine and that we are here. Everything else we can mend it."

Alicia turned to him, agreeing.

"You're right." Her eyes were watery again. "I'm such a complainer. We should be grateful for being okay." Then, after a pause, she said somberly, "I hope we can fix this country. I would hate to leave this mess to Pablo."

He sighed.

II

On Friday, April 2nd, the newspapers and radio flashes brought the news Alicia and Sergio had worried about for some time now. A surprise naval commando had landed on the shores of the Malvinas. The military junta, in power since 1976, upended the old conflict with the United Kingdom. The English actions regarding these islands had never been honest since the Brits had invaded them more than a hundred years ago. Nevertheless, the junta, albeit an unpopular government, managed to get the support of the majority of the public on this matter. Everybody now hoped to recover the islands, especially after the massive publicity campaign that the military had carried out in the media for months.

Alicia stared at the thick, black headlines: '*Argentina invades Malvinas Islands*' covering the top half of the front page. She felt a pang of anguish. Argentina had not been in a war in the Twentieth Century, and this decision felt like a bad omen. The mighty English Navy could tear the Argentines to pieces without considering the actions of eventual allies like the Americans.

The Falkland Islands, Islas Malvinas in Spanish, are two serrated shapes off the South coast near the lower part of Argentina's triangle. Much later, Alicia realized that those rocky islands on the way to Antarctica were no longer Argentinean, even if they belonged to the continental mass of land. Since the English took them over, it was *their* colony. It was a sad and unfair truth, no doubt. Although compared with the woes the country was suffering now, Malvinas' recovery was at the bottom of a long list of priorities. And now they were at war, courtesy of an unelected military junta. *Los Ingleses* would surely crush the Argentineans if only by sheer might.

She strolled to the kitchen. Sergio was pouring hot water on the instant coffee he had left ready in the breakfast mugs. Alicia kissed him lightly as she passed. He had made coffee every morning since they had moved in together, before marrying, years ago, when both were still students in Buenos Aires. She used to tease him: "You know that I'm a wife with breakfast not included." He would feign disappointment, but she knew he had assumed the making of the morning coffee ritual. He did many of the chores at home in a natural way that masked his traditional upbringing. He had always shared household chores. She did not even remember having to talk about it when they moved in together. It just happened.

Alicia paid attention and felt relieved that the kettle's whistle did not wake up Pablo, sleeping in his bedroom nearby.

"We are at war with England." She looked pointedly at him. "Did you see it?"

He had undoubtedly seen the paper; he brought it from the front porch earlier. He sighed. "Well, we knew this would happen. They have been preparing us for months with their propaganda."

His voice was calm, and this irritated her. At times, she hated his unwillingness to get upset over the unending stream of wrongful policies from the military junta in Buenos Aires. But at the same, she admired his self-control. Accepting facts, which happened so naturally to Sergio, was a struggle for her, usually ending in defeat and her anger taking over.

"It's crazy. Sure, the government propaganda prepared everybody all right," Alicia said, incensed.

He nodded, and she went on. "People fall for anything that appears on TV. How can they not see it? I hate how gullible the public is. The armed forces are taking us to hell in a handbasket, and nobody will do anything about it."

"What can they do? War is a good unifier, not to mention a great distraction. So, expect some cheers from the crowd."

"If it's true that the people have the government they deserve, this proves it. Don't they see the military is trying to hold onto power? So why do they buy this story about recovering the islands? Who cares when the economy is a mess, we are in a constant state of siege, and they're kicking our behinds with one thing or another?"

Sergio did not answer. He always fell silent whenever he wanted her to calm down. She went on with her monologue, but now her voice was calmer. "After a hundred and fifty years, suddenly we decide to take those islands back? How convenient!"

They finished their coffee in silence, hurried, feeling that this war was a matter that would be with them for a long time. Sergio picked up his jacket and car keys on his way out and kissed her briefly.

"Remember, Luis and Mary are coming after dinner," Alicia said. "Bring some homemade chocolate from La Abuela Goye for tonight. We will need some sweets to comfort us."

Anticipating the chat with their closest friends, she wished there was a phone at home. She would call them right now about the war, she thought with a sigh. It was one of the prices they had to pay for living in the still untamed Patagonia. The small town had an ongoing shortage of telephone lines. Most of their friends were also registered and waiting for the numbers to become available.

Still distraught by the disturbing news, she strolled into Pablo's room to dress the feisty toddler. The local National Radio was abuzz with armchair warrior opinions and patriotic calls. The sound of the military march preceding the war news bulletin brought haunting memories of previous coups, a succession of too many of them in a few decades.

People would not dare to complain openly, though. So she hadn't read one truthful political piece in the media in years. Instead, she treasured a box full of clips from the now-extinct *La Opinion*. Its editor, Jacobo Timmerman, was another exiled journalist. She knew that some of her colleagues at her newsroom felt the same way she did about the military. Glances were exchanged here and there, a word was said, a particular gesture caught. Those details showed that there was trouble brewing beyond the silence. Or wasn't there? Her hopes were not high. Nobody would talk candidly.

Alicia was nostalgic for her friends in Buenos Aires, still missing her student years and the spirited impromptu debates they held daily. But things were much more straightforward then. Even under military rule, during General Lanusse's presidency, there was still a free exchange of information.

About that time, she met Sergio. Soon they found they had many things in common, and being only children was one of them. But his rational, logical view of the world and how to deal with it captivated her.

His parents were a young European couple who had escaped World War II's ravages and came to make a new life in Buenos Aires. Franz Brauer, his father, hardly ever talked about the war, which was a common occurrence with most immigrants at the time. It was understandable, as many had suffered too much. He was a caring, affectionate father, though somehow overprotective. Sergio accepted his silence about the past while developing his own ideas, closer to what he later found in Alicia. Sergio managed the middle ground with ease, and she wondered how he did it. Was it strength or just denial? Alicia thought it was both a strategy for survival as good as any other. Survivors have to be flexible and negotiate everything.

They had traveled the world together, working and visiting places for several years. Sergio had been her friend, her lover, and resourceful companion. Also, mature and relaxed, so much so that at times seemed almost Buddhist in his calm measure and acceptance of the facts he could not change. Alicia realized that it was advantageous to be as adaptable as he was when adjusting to new circumstances.

The news from the war added to her unrest after encountering the men in the green Ford Falcon. In that context, a letter that she had foolishly mailed to the city mayor two weeks before distressed her in a way it wouldn't under normal circumstances. Her impulse had won over her good sense, and now Alicia regretted to have sent it.

It all started with an assignment she got to write about the new school in Barrio Alto, the most impoverished neighborhood in the city. The instructions were to commend the new heating system paid by the Municipal Council. There was considerable fanfare over the Council's good deeds. She had to interview the school principal and write a short piece with a couple of pictures. The City Council rewarded these rave reviews by purchasing advertisement space in the periodical's pages. It was routine and a necessary tradeoff called *chivo* in the newsroom's jargon.

"I'm always assigned these fluffy gigs to fill space between ads," she had complained to Sergio. "Only the guys get the meaty subjects. I wouldn't mind so much if some of them had a handle on their Spanish grammar. Then the discrimination wouldn't hurt so much. I'm the only one in that newsroom exposed to political science in depth at school, and here I am, writing about everything except that. Those are the subjects given to the guys in the newsroom."

"Talk with Carlos Alvarez. He's the editor in chief."

"It won't change anything. Everybody likes my work but the thought that men should do the meaty material prevails. Remember, he told me that, frankly, men should do the important work because they are the breadwinners at home and that we women work because we just want to do it. So I had to bite my tongue, not retort with the right answer."

The next day the teachers she interviewed were not interested in showing gratitude to the municipal authorities for the new heating system installed just before winter. They had other immediate, pressing concerns in their minds. "The Mayor and the Municipal Council just cut down the breakfast program, and most of the children go hungry till lunchtime," the principal said. She was seated at her desk, flanked by two teachers and looking at the tape recorder with determination. Alicia was astonished. She moved uncomfortably on the seat, and they seemed to understand that as a sign to go ahead with the matter, or they pretended to.

"You see, they need their milk and bread in the morning. Hungry children can neither concentrate nor pay attention to lessons." The other teacher added: "The kids fall asleep by midmorning in class. No food, no learning. It's that simple."

They told Alicia about the Mapuche Indian children, émigrés from the economically devastated Chile. They were brought to Barrio Alto by their unemployed parents looking for work near the international ski resort. Listening to these women, Alicia felt as if she came from another world. It was unexpected, and she did not like the vague, guilty feeling that assaulted her. So, although she guided the path of her interviews at the time, and maybe because of the sudden subject change, she politely let them go on.

"Most kids don't eat any dinner at home. They mostly eat *mate* tea and some bread," explained one of the teachers, looking hopeful to Alicia and talking to the tape recorder. "They don't get enough nutrition."

"That's why you see so many poor children that are short," volunteered the younger one eagerly, noticing Alicia's uneasiness. "They don't get enough proteins to eat. They never develop enough to reach an average height. Their brains do not develop fully either, and their IQ will always be lower than average too."

On her way out of the modest school building, Alicia noticed the children in recess, playing in the dusty, wire-fenced backyard. Red cheeks hit by the chilly wind, straight dark hair, slanted eyes, and big white smiles, oblivious to the hardships waiting for them ahead.

Back home, Alicia felt compelled to do something. She knew that the paper would not print anything on this subject. They were always in search of uplifting news. The lighter, the better. Unable to let the thing die just there, she wrote a mild piece, but predictably, Carlos Alvarez returned it to her with a dull comment.

"Of course, you will get paid in full for this job, Alicia, but I'm sure you understand. We can't print it." The smile was friendly and meaningful, almost saying, *"Alicia, you should know better. Don't complicate my life."* She was tempted to retort, but she took the article back without comment. Unwilling to just sweep the matter under the rug and believing a personal approach would be more helpful, she decided to write a letter to the Mayor. She mailed it the next day but never got a response.

The letter may not have been offensive enough to link it with the men from the green Falcon. Still, Alicia also signed a prominent open letter she wrote for the regional newspaper. It was about the slow and unreliable local hospital vaccination program for the children. That reader's letter had ruffled some big feathers in the local medical establishment not long ago. The hospital was, like everything else in the country, under military control.

So she had been treading on sort of dangerous territory lately. Each action she took seemed more and more like public defiance, and it made her more vulnerable. Still, something was missing. Were both actions enough to deserve to be threatened as those bullies did the other night? If not, then what was their real reason?

That evening Sergio put Pablo to bed. Alicia was washing the dinner dishes when they heard Mary and Luis's car in the driveway. She checked the water boiling for coffee and prepared the small cups, the sugar bowl, and opened the box of homemade chocolates that Sergio bought on his way home. Mary laughed when she came in and saw the box handing Alicia a similar one.

"No way to shed the pounds." She hugged Alicia and walked in. "I'll give Pablo a goodnight kiss."

Mary and Luis didn't have children yet and loved Pablo as their nephew.

Luis and Mary joined them many evenings after dinner for a coffee, a cigarette, soft music, and long conversations. After they sat at the table over coffee, the first topic of discussion was the military invasion's craziness and the consequences they would have to suffer.

"Did you guys see the flags? Everyone seems to be waving a flag all over the city," Mary said, shaking her head. "It is a big patriotic show. Nothing against flags, but they shouldn't need a war to start appearing all over the city."

"I couldn't agree more," Alicia said. "Everybody seems fascinated by the war at the newsroom, and they discuss the military toys that they watch on TV. All that expensive and outdated leftover junk these guys bought from other countries. And they are journalists; they should know better their history lessons."

"Everybody feels happy with the fantasy; they feel like winners sending other people's kids to war. But, do they really believe Argentina will recover the islands from England?" Luis wondered.

"I don't know. Who would dare to disagree?" Alicia asked. "People are scared. I wouldn't talk about it with anybody I don't know. Maybe many are scared to talk as I am."

"Well, *Argentina Trabaja y Avanza,* as the government TV propaganda goes," Sergio said. They all smiled faintly at the empty words: *Argentina works and goes forward.*

"Yeah, I wonder, where?" Mary asked with sarcasm.

"To hell, I guess," Sergio answered.

Alicia said, pensive: "The worst part is the poor soldiers. The troops are forced to go there."

"They are so young!" Added Mary, and then, with a worried voice, looking to Sergio and her husband: "You know, if this war lasts long, you guys may be called to serve. You are in the reserves."

Luis made a wink toward Sergio, and both crossed their fingers, smiling.

"Let's hope it doesn't happen," Alicia said. "Besides Jacinta's younger brother, Alcides, I don't think I know any other kid on the military service."

"Neither do I," Mary said.

They fell silent for a while. Sergio broke the silence. "Who wants another cup of fresh coffee?"

As was often the case, their chat lasted for hours, safe knowing that their friendship united them.

"This is our group therapy," Mary said at one point, and they all agreed, happy to have each other.

Alicia buckled Pablo at his car seat, piled her books, tape recorder, and notebook next to the toddler's tote, and geared toward the daycare center. The deep waters of the Nahuel-Huapi were dark and quiet. Cerro Otto's trees changed from autumn's fiery reds and yellows to a subdued brown, and the leaves fell. Everything seemed usual, but deep down, she knew that nothing would be the same from now on. *We are at war,* she thought with a shiver. So many Argentineans will die in combat –what a foreign concept for this country.

Alicia pulled into the driveway of the daycare's cabin facing the lake for the daily afternoon routine of leaving Pablo to socialize with other children. At the same time, she did her interviews and research work in town.

A few minutes later, heading south, she turned on the radio. "Tonight, General Leopoldo Fortunato Galtieri will address the country regarding the decision to invade Islas Malvinas." The familiar voice of one of her colleagues read the news bulletin. "President Galtieri's popularity has soared since the military action in the South."

The man continued talking, but Alicia's thoughts wandered off again. Galtieri, that drunken bully of a president, had been imposed on them at gunpoint, like the others before him. He was named the president by the current military junta, similar to many other previous military governments who had proclaimed themselves saviors of the motherland.

To think that by the end of the 1800s, just like New York, Buenos Aires was a powerful magnet for immigrants from Europe and the Mediterranean area. Argentina even ranked sixth in the world for its economic strength and bountiful natural resources. Then, in 1930, the first military coup against a constitutional president began the slow downfall of the underdeveloped Third World country that it had become. If the so-called revolutionary juntas kept asking for foreign loans to the International Monetary Fund, they would be indebted forever.

The lending conditions required increased cuts in the social net, and the working and middle class shouldered the payments. At the same time, the large corporations, primarily foreign now, were kept more or less safe through tax loopholes. So the public health, education, roads, and such were decaying and rotting. And this sacrifice was not even covering the *debt's service*, a fancy term for the enormous interest charged. At this pace, the capital borrowed would never be paid. Alicia felt they were doomed in a sea of maxed-out credit cards for generations to come. Still, there was more going on than greedy functionaries with hands in the cookie jar. Something was wrong, sort of a methodic disassembling of the country, but she did not have enough elements to grasp the whole picture. Information was too sparse and biased.

Ahead of her, a truck maneuvering in the narrow road stopped the traffic temporarily. The radio caught Alicia's attention again. The same voice said, "US Secretary of State Alexander Haig will travel to Buenos Aires in search of a negotiated settlement between our country and the United Kingdom." The newsman had been talking about Malvinas while her thoughts wandered. "We consider the US our ally in this matter, said a source from the military junta. Particularly reliable is UN Ambassador Jeanne Kirkpatrick, who was the guest of honor in a recent dinner at our embassy in Washington."

Alicia and Sergio agreed that the Americans wouldn't help Argentina this time. *They can't*, Alicia thought with a sigh. *They are, above all, English-speaking, and they will stick with the UK.*

The traffic moved again, slowly, following the huge truck. Alicia reminded herself to call Susana Machevsky later. Susana, the dear friend since childhood and buddy from journalism school, lived in Buenos Aires and was still looking for the man of her dreams. They shared the same distrust of the military coups and the love for democratic ideals. Their heroes were Mariano Moreno, the fierce

Argentinean intellectual voice of the independence from Spain, and Thomas Jefferson, the American forefather. They also shared a taste for dark chocolate, good-looking tanned guys, French cinema, and science fiction books; she reminisced, smiling.

About a week ago, Susana's last call differed from the brief long-distance greetings that they had shared for years, with an eye on the telephone bills. Leaving the main thoughts to their long, ten-plus page letters, they exchanged regularly. Susana said, and it was not the first time Alicia had heard of it, something about those phantom olive-green Ford Falcon cars. The ones suspect of discretely following people in the street, with plain-clothed, suspicious secret service or military men at the wheel. A car like the one that had stopped her on the road, she had thought with a shudder. It was not a subject to discuss by phone. Calls were often and randomly intercepted to hear what was said. For "national security" reasons, it was widely known. So she changed the subject.

"Pablo already is standing up in the cradle, holding the bars." She knew Susana would love to hear that.

"Already?" She asked, marveled, and from then on, the conversation went back to Susana's favorite subject, Pablo, to whom she affectionately called *my nephew*.

Less than two and a half months into the Malvinas War, it ended as hastily as it was declared. On June 14, Puerto Argentino fell under the pressure of the British military might. The sudden end of the war took all Argentineans by surprise. After deafening propaganda from the media, the anticlimactic news fell as a slap on the general public, who needed some time to digest it. Nevertheless, most people believed in the government-controlled media's message. They sincerely thought Argentina was not only gaining terrain against the enemy but had good chances of winning.

The next day, a few thousand people gathered in Plaza de Mayo to support the war. Also, they asked the government not to end it. They were trying to keep the delusion of a triumph alive. Twenty-four hours after the surrender, there was no more news or details on what was going on in the South Atlantic.

People had been pumped-up during these months to feel an

exalted patriotism against the British. Now, when things collapsed, there was a total absence of news from the government. It felt almost like a physical vacuum. Alicia tried to catch shortwave radio transmissions from Chile to find out the Argentinean troops' situation that most probably should have been taken prisoners by the Brits. A brief news flash told her that General Mario Menéndez, Argentinean commander on the islands, signed the surrender in Port Stanley, or Puerto Argentino.

Alicia switched the radio off. Then, unable to concentrate on her job pending, she walked to the window. The fall's pale sunlight bathed the last roses of the season and the bare branches of the trees. The light snow of the previous evening had melted, but some of the gray clouds were returning. Alicia thought of the pictures she had seen lately on the press from Malvinas. And felt deep compassion for those youngsters who had the bad fortune to serve their country just now. *And who knows what is truly going on there? It sure must have been hell. Pity the soldiers, stuck in those barren rocks, under the chilly winter wind blowing from Antarctica.* She sighed, invaded by a sense of profound sadness. Also felt guilt for the mainly teenage draftees, taken from their schools and homes and sent with minimum combat training to die or be maimed. And all at the whim of a bunch of macho men who seized power at gunpoint. A civilian government would never have done something like that. Or so she wanted to believe.

With a sigh, she walked to the laundry room where Jacinta was doing her chores. The young woman had her share of the tragedy: Alcides, her brother, happened to be on one of the first divisions disembarked on the islands. The family had not received news from him for a while.

"Have you heard anything from Alcides, Jacinta?"

The young woman turned to her, drying her hands on a towel.

"No. Nothing yet," she said somberly.

"I'm sorry, but I'm sure you will hear something soon." Alicia could not find anything else to say, and it was evident that some formulaic words wouldn't do.

"My brother is not much for writing. His last letter was dated two weeks before we got it. Anyway, it was short. About ten lines or so." She went back to her work, but not before Alicia noticed a choke in her voice.

Later that day, in the newsroom, she did not find more details on the sudden and unexpected end of the war. The staff looked as disoriented as everyone else. The only information available was rumors. That apparently was okay with the newsroom's editors. Alicia was sure that their weekly publication wouldn't touch the war's subject more in-depth than a brief reference if they mentioned it at all. So instead, everybody relied on radio or TV. The prominent Buenos Aires newspapers, flown to Bariloche every day, brought their regular quota of unreliable news. Chilean radio broadcasts told their story, but she distrusted the British propaganda content that it might carry. She called Susana long-distance, but her friend did not know much either. The intentions of the Junta were unknown yet, and the capital city was awash with rumors. Alicia hung up, still gloomy.

While Alicia was filling up Pablo's bathtub, that evening at home, Sergio appeared at the door.

"There are rumors that Galtieri has been asked to go," Alicia said. "Maybe the rest of the junta is blaming him personally as a way to save their skins," she wondered. "They have no honor. Not even between them."

"Nope, they don't. The only thing that you can count on is that the victims are going to be many. If the rumors circulating are true, there may have been a lot of criminal behavior from the top officers during the Islands' occupation," Sergio said. "Pity the poor draftees. Have you heard? Everybody calls them The Children of the War."

"Yes, and it's so right! Most of them are eighteen to twenty-two years old." Alicia nodded slowly, undressing Pablo. "There were so many killed when the General Belgrano sunk... what a waste of lives."

"Yes, well over three hundred guys." Sergio raised his voice while walking to the living room to drop the magazine and return to the bathroom. "That's a lot of losses for us. We haven't had a war in a century. This reminds me that none of our militaries have been in combat ever. How efficient could they be?"

"I don't know. So far, they have seemed useless except for

subjugating civilians." Alicia had undressed Pablo, put him in the tub, and tried to wash his head while he moved, spilling water around her. "How crazy was it to send that old ship, a floating classroom, to fight the English?"

"Unbelievable and criminal," Sergio said. "It was a relic from Pearl Harbor, a museum piece, and now is lost too with all those men."

Alicia kept on bathing little Pablo gently. Sergio stood against the small bathroom wall, helping hand back the soap and toys to Pablo, who enjoyed throwing them to the floor for his father to pick them up.

"On top of that, rumor says that the troops never got the donations of knitted garments, candies, and such that people collected," Alicia said, recalling the paper's commentaries the day before. She was Sergio's source of most of the confidential information, thanks to the newsroom wires and gossiping, so he asked, "Is that so? Where did they go, then?"

"Well, they say that a child went to buy a chocolate bar to a kiosk, and inside the label was a small slip of paper with a short note from another child to a soldier. That candy was meant for the troops, not to be sold in the market. If this is true, it's pathetic. How low can these guys go? It would mean that they have sent the gifts and donations to the black market, and somebody is making money out of it. Sickening!"

Sergio shook his head, but soon a warm smile erased his frown. He opened his arms, unfolding a warm towel to receive dripping, giggling Pablo from Alicia's hands.

Twenty-four hours after the surrender in the now renamed Port Stanley, the government was still silent. There was no reliable news about the war and the fate of the troops. In Buenos Aires, a spontaneous public rallied in Plaza de Mayo, asking for answers. Alicia went to the newsroom around nine o'clock to finish some items. Then, near midday, she got an unexpected phone call from Susana.

"I'm just writing a long letter to you," Alicia said, happy to hear her voice. "In several sections, so maybe in a couple of days, I'll mail it."

"Good, looking forward to it. Listen, you won't believe this." Her voice was excited: "I am heading right now to Plaza de Mayo with a group of people. I'm calling from a paid phone booth. There is a lot of anger here against the government, and there is a large rally going on now. The streets have been bursting with people since this morning. They had been coming downtown in buses and trains and walking all the way to Plaza de Mayo. They are asking Galtieri to resign." She sounded as if she had run and was out of breath. "I was downtown shopping, but now I am going to the Plaza too. Glad I have my flats on! I'll call you later."

"Be careful! Call me back, please!" Alicia said before Susana hung up.

She slowly put the receiver down, picturing in her mind the time-honored square in Buenos Aires, right across the government mansion. There, Argentineans showed their support or disapproval of the authorities. The Plaza had been the site to gather ever since colonial years, when the *porteños* stood forcing the dismissal of the last Spaniard Viceroy, one 25th of May, in 1810. They wanted answers, and the spontaneous act ignited the independence movement from Spanish control. It was sort of a Boston Tea Party for colonial Argentina. From then on, any rally of people in the square had deep meaning in their civic life.

Later, anxious for news and before leaving the newspaper's building, she dialed Susana's number. Fortunately, her friend was already back home.

"I'm glad you read my mind. I needed to talk to you," Susana said, excited. "I'm lying on the couch, feet up, getting my strength back. But, Alicia, you should have seen the people there, covering the Plaza."

Alicia moved a chair nearby and sat.

"I heard so many things," Susana went on in one breath. "I wish I had a tape recorder with me. This thing happened all of a sudden. I was downtown, shopping when I learned about the march and joined a group walking down to Avenida de Mayo."

After a brief pause, she added, now with dismay and frustration: "It's awful here, and at the Malvinas Islands, some rotten things happened. I heard the combatants are lying in the hospitals and telling horror stories from the front lines. It seems they left our soldiers without proper equipment or warm clothes. With rifles that didn't work, no munitions, and worst of all, they were hungry and debilitated because of their inept superiors. It seems there was no organized infrastructure to reach the combatants to distribute the food rations!"

There was silence. Alicia was stunned.

"The father of a soldier told me that two kids from his son's battalion were chained to a fence in the freezing weather. It was a punishment from their superiors for stealing bread. All the while, the officers were well fed and safe wherever they hid. How can you win a war like that?"

Alicia could not reply; she had a knot in her throat. What could she say?

Susana went on, now talking in a hushed voice. "The news is sketchy, but I can assure you that it isn't good at all. I heard that the English took our guys to their ships after the defeat, and they will be releasing them sooner or later. They do not want to keep prisoners, which is great. It seems they took the soldiers to different ports in the south, Trelew and Puerto Madryn," she said. Her usually clear voice was hoarse as if she had talked all day long. Or, better, as if she had shouted and sung along earlier in the day.

After a long pause, Alicia asked: "Did you ever, in your wildest dreams, think that this could happen to us?"

Another long silence ensued. Finally, Susana's voice came through in a hushed murmur. "No. I thought we lived in a safe world. But these things are happening now."

Alicia felt her heart beating at the memory of her own recent, shocking experience. She needed to change the subject. She did not want to tell Susana about her encounter with the men in the green Falcon.

"I wish you were here to talk more about all this," she managed to say.

"So do I. This is a mess. There is no official word or anything to reassure people. The casualties are not listed, neither are the wounded, and the combatants' families know nothing. It's a disaster, Ali. I'm so fed up with these abuses. I wish we did not live so far away from each other. We have so much to talk about." Her voice broke into another sob.

Alicia felt the knot in her throat again. She needed Susana near; she needed to tell her what was going on. Susana was the only friend that would understand her, the one Alicia could confide her inner thoughts. Then she had an inspiration.

"Susana, why don't you come down here to visit for a few days? You have postponed it for so long! It will be a good break, and you need it. We will hike, or walk if you want, or just sit and talk."

After a long silence in the line came the answer. "Well...I don't know...I have too many things going on here...."

"C'mon! You know you need this rest; better still, you deserve it. This is the least you can do for your health. And it will be beneficial for your love life too. By the way, how's it going with that guy, what's his name? Any better?" Alicia was referring to her friend's last passing romantic interest. Susana let go of a laugh that didn't sound happy at all.

"Yeah! Right. As if that would go anywhere! And you know it. There's no future there, at least from what I can see."

Her answer gave hope to Alicia, who insisted. "Get a bus ticket and come. You know that you will save money if you can stand the twenty hours of the bus ride. The buses are comfortable, and you can read a whole book! Remember when we went to Córdoba together? It was fun and cheaper."

It was a long shot. Susana always flew to her assignments, but she did not have a budget to spend on airline tickets for personal travel. Alicia knew her friend was on a tight budget, helping her parents, who were retired. Still, she sensed that Susana was tempted, so she kept pressing until she got half a confirmation. This lifted her spirit, and when she hung up, she felt happier than she had felt in a long time.

Alicia was one of the last people to leave the newsroom that evening. When she came out the front door, it was a cold, crisp night, and the moon was already high, lighting the darkness of the side street softly. She took the keys from her handbag and was about to leave when Carlos Alvarez, who was still inside the building, called her.

"Alicia, you have a phone call!"

She turned around, and a familiar nagging feeling hit her stomach again. Her heart was rushing when she picked up the line from a nearby desk. Upset with herself for not being able to take a sudden call without fretting, a common occurrence during the last week, she said tentatively, "Hello! Alicia here." To her surprise, Sergio greeted her from the other side of the line. His voice was gloomy.

"Alicia, can you pick Pablo up from the daycare? I'm still here, at Huemul's offices, and we are in the middle of a meeting that will go on for another hour, at least after past seven."

"Of course, no problem. See you at home for dinner."

"See you later, then." There was a silence, and he added: "I love you."

"I love you too… And whatever it is, take it easy, eh?"

"I will."

He hung up, and she had the feeling that things were not going well. If the project were not approved, they would have a hard time paying their fixed expenses. Sergio sounded tired too. It was hard to live from project to project.

"See you tomorrow. Drive safely," Alvarez said, bidding her goodbye.

"I will."

A shiver crossed Alicia's spine at the thought of the road by the lakeside she was about to take on her way home.

III

The telephone message that Alicia found on her desk the following day was a pleasant surprise. She thought her invitation to Susana was a long shot, but she did not expect her to accept it.

"*Leaving tonight for Bariloche. See you tomorrow evening. Arriving 18:30. Love. Susana.*"

Alicia organized her schedule, allowing extra time, and stopped by Sergio's office on her way to a press conference at the Chamber of Tourism.

Sergio shared a small room on the second floor of a downtown building with two contractors. They had to squeeze their drawing tables and cabinets to save rent, telephone, and expenses. It was a practical arrangement, as they were only acquaintances. Still, they shared a common interest in fly-fishing and a prized telephone line at the office. Alicia had met the families of Sergio's co-tenants, but they did not see each other socially.

Today he was working on the project that Huemul had requested to be budgeted down again. It meant hours of extra work and uncertain payment dates. She was disappointed when Sergio told her about it the night before. He had taken it with his usual calm demeanor, crabby but not anger. She knew Sergio was tired but wouldn't give up. Today he had left home earlier, ready to fight another round of a battle he desperately wanted to win. He would paddle upstream patiently, as much and as long as necessary until he would get to his goal.

Sergio watched her excitement, amused.

"We'll have to unpack the portable bed," she said. "We'll set it in Pablo's room. She is very accommodating; she'll appreciate whatever we put together. I wish I knew how long she's staying. She didn't say."

While she walked to the door, he kept looking at her, smiling.

"What? What are you laughing at?"

"I'm not laughing; I'm glad to see you happy." He blew a kiss. "It's been a long time since you looked so cheerful. I'm glad Susana is coming."

Alicia spent a significant part of her day getting ready for her friend's visit; she wanted to make the most of it. After several unsuccessful tries, she finally got through with the bus company. She found out that the bus from Buenos Aires would arrive earlier than planned. Sergio would pick up Pablo from the daycare. She had left everything ready for a quick dinner that he would start cooking before she got home with Susana.

Alicia got a few last-minute chores out of the way and arrived at the bus stop early. She sat in the spacious waiting room of COTAL, one of the two companies that operated between large Patagonian cities, watching the public and thinking of Susana and her sudden decision. No explanations; that was like her. It was okay with Alicia; that was another reason why they got along so well.

The waiting room people seemed to be mostly locals, but two tourist-looking couples and three noisy teenagers. Alicia saw a guy with a crew cut, clad in a thick, expensive jacket standing close to one of the couples. He was ostensibly reading a sports magazine. The man seemed focused on his reading, and after a few minutes, Alicia lost interest in him.

Bariloche didn't have a bus terminal. Two companies made the long-distance trip north and back from the country's main cities, Buenos Aires, Córdoba, Rosario, or Mendoza. Furthermore, there was only one daily departure scheduled for each route. As a result, the place was always busy at arrival and departure times. Long-distance buses have ruled the land lately. Air travel was too expensive, and the reliable, low-cost trains of years past were out of service due to negligence and lack of maintenance. Only one passenger train left making the trip from Buenos Aires, old and worn out, crossing La Pampa plains and half of Patagonia to end in Bariloche. Its customers were mainly students on tight budgets and locals unable to pay for airplanes or buses' fares.

Alicia always had this deep affection for trains. This particular relic from better times departed twice a week from the charming stone-and-log train station at the city's entrance, surrounded by tall pine trees and a lake view. The structure, built by the National Park System in the 1930s, sat right across the road from National Radio's austere building and seemed destined to obsolescence. Alicia took many black and white shots of the dwelling, admiring its sturdy beauty, reminiscent of Canada and the United States National Park System architecture.

The bus arrived half an hour early, as expected. Alicia jumped from her seat and went out, standing with others on the chilly and windy sidewalk, waiting for the doors to open.

They had forecasted snow, and she looked at the gray sky, weighing the possibilities. The chilly air brought the sweet smell of pastries baking nearby, mixed with the acrid fumes of traffic exhaust. She tightened the wooly scarf around her neck and ears, looking anxiously at the open bus door. Then, after several passengers came down, she spotted the blond curls and her friend's smiling face.

Susana was at least two inches taller than her, bony and athletic, compared with Alicia's slender frame and body. They embraced for a long time, in silence, holding each other, cheeks pressing hard against the other's hair. The joy of having her friend close again dispelled Alicia's worries and foreboding.

They stood on the sidewalk while the porter, donning a thick ski parka and wool gloves, took the luggage from the deep bus's underbelly. He deliberately checked the ticket numbers before handing bags over to passengers. Alicia looked around distractedly. She noticed the crew-cut man that had been reading the sports magazine now talking and laughing with a younger one, evidently the traveler he was waiting for. The brief thought that the other man might have been on the same bus with her friend for some specific and suspicious reason crossed her mind. Still, she dismissed it as a post-traumatic reaction to her terrifying encounter. There was no link between them, and she turned her attention to Susana, carrying her suitcase.

They walked toward Alicia's tattered Citroën, parked down the street.

"Aren't you tired after so many hours on the bus? Want to go home right away?" Alicia helped her place the suitcase in the small trunk.

"I'm tired, but I slept most of the time. The seats recline almost horizontally, and they are comfy. I don't need to rest now, thank you. On the contrary, I had enough coffee in the last three hours to keep awake an elephant." Susana opened the car door and got in, shivering in her light wool coat and flat shoes. Alicia got in the driver's seat.

"This town is always colder than I remember. Now to your question: Yes, I'd love a cup of hot chocolate." Susana's voice was more profound than Alicia's, and her Buenos Aires' *porteño* accent was strong.

"Let's stop at El Viajero before going home." The coffee shop at chocolate factory outlet was Susana's favorite. "It's early, and we won't have dinner before nine."

"Good idea. Do you still buy the fresh ground grains to make the Turkish-style coffee we like so much?"

"Yes. I knew you'd like to stop there."

After driving twice around the block, Alicia found a spot not far from the shop. They walked quickly toward the brightly lit store, its bright windows filled with elaborate, chocolate movable figurines and candies.

Inside, several glass cases displayed colorful boxes. A sizable bar counter with stools lined the right wall. Several locals sipped teas or coffee, and the sweet smell of fresh cocoa permeated the air. They sat at the bar and ordered. The large salesroom behind them bustled with tourists.

"I'm so glad you are here," Alicia sighed. "We have so much to talk about. But first, I need your advice on what's been happening here. Also, I want you to meet Martina Salgado, from the radio show."

"I'd love to. I like what you told me so far." She inhaled the steam deeply from her hot chocolate cup. "From what you've told me, you guys are having problems not talking enough about homemaking. This is a truly quaint little town disguised as a cosmopolitan tourist city."

"You got that right. Martina and I have our critics, and one of them is our main sponsor. Still, we have an audience that follows us, but we'll have time to talk about that later." Alicia paused to finish her espresso coffee. "How are your parents doing?"

"Mom is sending a little box with something for you and lots of kisses, and Dad always asks about you. You know, he loves you very much."

"Thanks. They are great parents...."

"They are, indeed, and very patient too. I'm grateful to have them."

"You should be; you should be." Alicia's voice was sad; she always had wondered how it would have been to have parents alive beyond her teen years. Hers had died young while she was in high school. That painful reality made her appreciate Susana's parents even more.

There was silence. Susana changed the subject.

"What do you think of Galtieri resigning? I heard it on the bus," she almost whispered. "He isn't the only one responsible for this mess. I don't think the new guy —what's his name? Reynaldo Bignone — is any better. They are just buying time."

Alicia lowered her voice too: "It's all the same crap. Do you believe that after the disaster in Malvinas, they'll call for free elections?"

"Don't know for sure," Susana whispered. "So far, they always lied to us. We'll see."

Instinctively, both friends were silent. They had a long habit of not discussing the government in public places.

"I will take a couple of pounds of chocolate with me on my way home," Susana said. "From the small factories, though. I prefer, what's its name? Yes, La Abuela Goye. The products of this store here are too commercialized. Too much-hydrogenated fat." And turning to Alicia, she said with a wink: "See, I pay attention to the research in your pieces."

Alicia laughed at the memory.

"That series about chocolate caused a stir at the newsroom. More than a few calls were complaining. Mainly, they came from the owners of this store, not to mention their withdrawal of ads in the paper, here and there. Still, their coffee is good. It was nothing personal; I only reported the results of my comparative research on the quality of their chocolate."

Sipping her warm cocoa with delight, Susana seemed pleased to be there.

Alicia asked, "What are your plans? Do you want to do anything in particular?"

"I want to spend time with you guys. I thought maybe a boat trip to Isla Victoria would be nice, but I won't spend a whole day on that. So let's stay around here. Or a hike or ride over by the Circuito Grande Route and the lakes. Whatever you prefer will be fine with me."

"We'll play it by ear, then. We'll have dinner with Mary and Luis one of these evenings. They'll be glad to see you again."

"Sure. I'd love that." There was a brief silence, and then she said, "Alicia, you'll laugh at this, but I'd like to take back home a few small items, a couple of ceramics from the area, and candles. I'm thinking of local products, but something good, maybe from El Bolson's artisans." She seemed almost embarrassed.

"Isn't that what tourists do?" Alicia laughed. "You are helping our economy. So, please spend as much as you want."

"I knew you would laugh. All the same, Mom wants a couple of things too. Do you still have here that boutique with hand-made products, Arbol?"

"We do, and it's more successful than ever. The owner expanded, adding two rooms. And they sell beautiful things, as always. I cannot afford those expensive hand-made sweaters, but I love looking at them in the windows."

'I'll go and check them out. I like to copy ideas here and there. I am knitting one of those thick wool sweaters. I'll show you when we get home. It's such a relaxing exercise when I'm going nuts on my assignments."

"I wish I could knit," sighed Alicia.

"Oh, please. You sew clothes that put my knitting to shame!" Susana laughed.

It was good to see her happy; her tooth-paste-poster-girl smile was the same Alicia remembered from high school. "Life can change us so much," she said with a sigh. "Would you have pictured me only eight years ago sewing my clothes and enjoying it? Unbelievable."

"It's as if all of our Mom's domestic lessons kicked in after we went on our own," Susana smiled and nodded.

"Well, yeah, except for the cleaning thing that I hate so much and the huge change in our married life when Pablo was born." Alicia sighed. "When you are pregnant, nobody tells you how much it takes to adjust."

"I guess you are the expert in this. But for me, the amazing thing is being able to control the panic of being close to thirty but feeling twenty inside."

The store got crowded. They looked around, and Susana said, "Ready to go?"

Alicia looked at the big and heavily decorated wooden Swiss clock on the wall nearby. "Gosh, almost an hour has passed. Let's go, but not before I pick a pound of fresh ground coffee."

They picked the coffee and walked toward one of the exit cashiers, where they stood in line. As she pulled out her wallet, Alicia heard a male behind her talking in a rather loud voice. She did not understand what he was saying, but something in the voice caught her attention. Turning her head, she saw, standing close to her, the man from the green Falcon. Alicia froze. He was looking away from her, talking to a younger man in another line. Still, she would recognize that voice anywhere. He spoke loud enough to be heard clearly from where she was standing. He did not seem to have noticed her.

For a few seconds, she couldn't take her eyes off him, his profile, the straight nose, the thick eyebrows, and the square face. Then, Alicia felt Susana's hand on her elbow. She turned, alarmed, to find Susana signaling with a nod to approach the cash register as the customer was leaving. The woman smiled patiently. Alicia apologized, let the woman pass, and shaking a bit, she approached the cashier.

"Here is the ticket. Please add the coffee," she said, turning her head enough to glance back at where the man was standing. He was walking away, still very much engaged in his chat with the other man. He mingled easily with the other tourists in his ski parka and mountain boots. It was different from the tailored wool city coat he was wearing the night of the encounter.

"Thank you," the young cashier said in a chirpy voice.

Susana grabbed Alicia's elbow as they walked away and whispered: "What's wrong? You look as if you've seen a ghost. What happened with that cashier?"

"Nothing happened with the cashier. Did you see the man a bit behind us, on the other line?" Alicia's voice choked, and she gestured toward the door.

"Who?"

"He left the store already." They stepped out, and Alicia looked around nervously, fastening her jacket. A cold wind rushed through Mitre Street, carrying small rain pellets. It was completely dark by now. Alicia did not move, and Susana looked at her, increasingly uneasy.

"Alicia, are you okay? Do you want to go back to the store, where it's warmer? What's with you?"

"I'm okay. Let's walk to the car. It's so cold." Alicia took Susana by the arm, and they ran, shivering. After starting the engine and setting the maximum heat, Alicia checked the street, searching for the man. She sighed and forced a smile.

"Tell me," Susana insisted, "pray to tell me what's going on with you!"

"Well, you see," she started, "there is one thing that I need your honest opinion about. Something I haven't told you yet."

Susana looked puzzled but kept silent, realizing that Alicia needed time to recover her breath from whatever it was that had shocked her earlier. Glancing at the sidewalks, trying to see if the man was still around, she drove through the center of town in silence. She took the road to Llao-Llao, with its meandering curves and beautiful sightseeing now invisible in the moonless night. Finally, Alicia said, "something happened to me a while ago. In fact, it was before the war started." She drove off the road, picking a spot in a parking lot next to a small candle factory, not far from where the encounter with the Falcon man had occurred across the road.

She turned to her friend, her face lit by the vehicles passing by and softened by the nearby mellow, constant amber gaslight lamp of the parking lot. She left the engine running and the heat on and told her the details of the worrisome encounter.

"That's what happened. That man scared me to death that day, and now I just found out he's still around."

Susana was silent while Alicia talked and now took an elastic band from her purse. Then, with a swift movement, she tied her hair back, looking absently at the cars' flashing lights before turning with a sigh her blue eyes toward her friend.

"What do you think about it?" asked Alicia wiping her tears.

She did not expect a strong reaction from Susana, who seldom showed her emotions. Still, she knew her friend was worried when she did not say anything for a long time. After so many years, Alicia could easily read her silences. Finally, Susana answered in a firm, calm voice:

"Let me tell you; it's good that you can cry like that and let everything out. I wish I could. My stomach ulcer would benefit." She patted Alicia's hand. "Now, you should know that you are in some shit if these guys appear in your life. It's no good, but it is all the same, in itself, a rare sign that the danger is not so great."

Now Alicia was the one with the silent questions. Susana went on.

"Well, first, if you were beyond doubt in trouble with any of the intelligence services, you would not have had a chance to see them coming. They would have broken into your home in the dark or caught you somewhere, even in plain daylight at the Civic Center. So, if that man wanted to have you, you could bet your life that he would have pulled you from your car that night by your hair and pushed you inside his car in less than a minute. That's what they do. They are very efficient. This guy probably is a small operator from one of the services or maybe an independent one. Who knows how many agencies are involved? I bet their world is pretty murky."

She took a chewing gum from her purse and offered one to Alicia, who accepted it out of the need to do something. She would gladly have lit a cigarette, but Susana had quit smoking a long time ago, so that she wouldn't bother her friend with the smoke in the confined space of the Citroën. The sweet mint-flavored gum dispelled the bitter taste in her mouth. Outside, the drizzle had become tiny snowflakes, still too light to accumulate on the ground.

"Second," Susana continued to explain as if she were talking to herself: "Why did he appear again today? I'm sure that he wants you to know that he is around. Otherwise, you would not have seen him again, believe me. They don't do any unexpected moves." Alicia was looking at Susana, impressed by her friend's certainty.

Susana went on: "These guys make art of torturing people in

many ways, psychological being one of the best."

Smiling sadly while looking at the darkness where the lake was, she added:

"That's why they push many wretched bodies from cars and trucks in the streets, in the bus stops, after finishing with them in the torture chambers. They *want us* to know. It's a show of power. I wonder how long it will take to clean this mess up when all this ends. Mutilated bodies are surfacing all over, particularly on the Rio de la Plata's coast. Nobody wants to talk about it. There are only whispers; they say the bodies are buried in unmarked tombs so nobody can find them.

Alicia was too disturbed, but she managed to ask, "What are you saying? If true, this is terrible..."

Susana turned again to Alicia: "Believe me, this nightmare will be over, sooner or later. It has to be. There must be many bodies, somewhere, in common graves, I guess. Few people return. The ones that do, you can bet your soul will not talk in the open."

"How do you know about the dead and bodies surfacing? Where did you hear this?" Alicia's voice was quivering. What Susana was saying was too horrible to accept, but somehow she had known that something was very wrong for a long time. Although I never guessed the magnitude. An incipient headache that she had vaguely noticed on leaving the chocolate store now was pounding her head.

"Well, people talk. Buenos Aires is a cauldron, reaching a boiling point now after this tragic war. These crimes had been happening since they took over in '76." There was a brief silence. "Why do you think that when they gave the Nobel Prize to Perez Esquivel in Europe, the press here cried that the world was against us?"

"I know. The press went berserk, calling him names. As they do with anybody that dares to complain openly." Alicia muttered.

"Do you remember the vile attacks against the human rights groups? Why is it, all of a sudden respecting human rights a bad thing? The press did not clarify. So, pray to tell me; what's the difference between the press in the USSR, Cuba, China, and ours?"

They stood in silence for a while. Susana looked at her watch, and Alicia did the same mechanically. It was eight-ten, and she had not felt the time passing. Susana was silent, and Alicia sighed.

"Honestly, deep down, all this is not news. Except that I didn't think it was so bad. I did not know. By the way, who are those *opposition* guys that you know? Are you talking about the Mothers of Plaza de Mayo? They say they're only a few weird women, a bunch of *locas*, who are the terrorists' mothers, who taught their children to be terrorists. Still, I give them credit. I wouldn't dare to parade around and be a target, as they are."

"If they had snatched Pablo from your arms, I bet you'd go barefoot to Buenos Aires to get him back," Susana responded with a voice full of emotion.

"Yeah, if you put it like that –I can't even bear to think that something like that is happening. How did we get to this point? Do you remember Anne Frank's story? I have been thinking about that book a lot lately. I was horrified that everybody in my parents' generation lived through that time and didn't do anything. And now *something* awful bad is happening here, around us!"

"Yes. I know. It scares the hell out of me. We are not talking only about people involved in anything illegal, no matter what they say. They say, 'sure, they were into something, and that's why they detained them.' But first, there are no 'detained' people. There are only kidnapped and disappeared people, that's it. And most may not even be involved in anything. Second, anybody doing community work is suspicious: students, even Catholic priests working with the poor, are gone. Jews like me are good targets. They consider us a double danger to the regime, not only because many don't agree with them, but because we are supposed to belong to a grand conspiracy to take over the world."

Alicia shook her head. "You have to be careful, promise me."

"I am. I am. Still, anybody can be picked up. You could be in the address book of somebody that they kidnapped earlier. Who knows? Others get denounced by people that hate them for personal reasons or have properties the government wants to confiscate."

"Just stealing?"

"Yes, you can call it that. Petty theft is a common thing. After one of these commandos invade your home and grab the person or persons they are looking for, they take all the valuables. They carry them in trucks, behind the cars that hold the kidnapped. They also take over their bank accounts and assets. They grab anything of value."

Alicia started crying in silence, and both remained silent. Finally, Susana put her hand on Alicia's and patted her tenderly.

"Don't worry; it will be okay here. I'm sure that Bariloche, like in so many other aspects, is a world apart. Here it's different than in larger cities."

Alicia blew her nose in the already wet cotton handkerchief. Then she composed herself in an automatic gesture, looking at her reddish eyes in the rear-view mirror.

"It sort of made sense when the military took over in '76, didn't it? We were tired of the terrorists of both sides' death squadrons killing left-wingers and leftist guerillas killing the military and planting bombs. It was such chaos when Peron's wife, that useless woman, Maria Estela Martínez, became president after he died. With her own Rasputin by her side, the sinister Lopez Rega. Still, I don't think anybody could have foreseen that the coup would raise the death squadrons to power."

"It was our fault! It was only our fault. We let them brainwash us that military coups and breaking the constitutional governments are the remedy to our problems. We admire and envy the Americans. Well, if the Americans deserve admiration, it's because their military would never dare to take over Washington at gunpoint as they do here. That's the secret to their success."

Susana spoke with conviction, and Alicia turned to look at her, nodding.

"You are so right...." She said. "We can't believe anything that the government says."

"Well, I guess we are paying the price of living in a fringe country. But, in my opinion, our destiny is to supply resources on the cheap."

"I don't believe Washington wants this," ventured Alicia.

"I don't know if it is even their intention, at least not the American people. This goes beyond nationality. It's a moneymaking machine, a historical tide. When corporations use up the Americans, they will let them hang to dry and go somewhere else. It's well beyond our means to stop it. This is a too big historical wave. In my opinion, the only thing that can change this situation is another tidal wave with the same strength against this one. Forget it. I don't think we will be able to change much, or at least, it will take a long time." Susana's voice was pessimistic.

"Not even with a new democratic election?"

"Be honest, Alicia. Do you *actually* believe that?" Susana looked her in the eye.

"I want to believe," Alicia replied, and she was sincere. "Otherwise, what's left?"

"Well, the kidnappings and the censorship could go away... but the country will be wrecked. I mean, it will take years to recover, pay that external debt, not to mention the deep-seated hatred we have built inside all of us."

After a while, Susana added, "I know I don't have to tell you this, but please, never talk about this with anybody except Sergio. Don't tell anybody else about your encounter with the Falcon guy, either."

"Don't worry," Alicia reassured her. "I wouldn't dare mention what you told me to anybody except Sergio. Thanks for your trust. Again, please, be careful with what you do or write. Please!"

"I will." Susana's voice was firm. "Believe me. Like you, I'm only writing light, superficial pieces for the magazine."

Alicia realized that her hands grabbed the steering wheel as if it were a lifesaver in the middle of the sea and let them loose. Then, after a silence, she said, trying to compose her voice, "We should go home now. We'll be much warmer and comfortable there than in this little box of a car I have."

Susana smiled, relieved as if she wanted to change the subject too. "That's my girl! You are right. I want to see the family. Let's go."

Alicia switched to first gear and slowly left the empty parking lot, entering the avenue toward Melipal. The snowfall had not coalesced into a full storm, but the wind was relentless.

Alicia turned on the radio. In the evening, they mainly broadcast soft music. She looked furtively toward Susana and felt grateful for having her nearby, even for a few days. Her friend not only shared her ideas, thoughts, and affection but was also a source of energy she needed very much.

They drove in silence, Susana looking at the trees that bordered the road. Alicia, attentive to the icy road ahead, couldn't erase the impression she had before. Her friend knew too much and probably had acquaintances that might be in danger. What Susana had said earlier about the Jewish people being under suspicion more than others sincerely worried her. People were supposed to have learned their lessons by now. This was Argentina, the open-arms country that received anybody and everybody.

She glanced again. Susana silently moved her lips to Billy Joel's *Just the Way you Are* now playing on the radio and looking through the windshield, deep in her thoughts. They had reached Bock Street, and she turned left, gearing uphill, toward her house, two blocks from the lakeside road. Susana now was whistling softly to a melodic Latin tune. Alicia smiled at her.

"I can't remember how many times I danced to this tune cheek to cheek with some awesome kid or other..."

"Same here," Susana said, nodding. "We had a lot of fun back then, eh?"

"We did, we sure did."

Ahead her small house placed on a corner had all the lights on. The reflection of the interior lamps on the wood-paneled walls glowed warm and cozy through the drapes. They pulled into the brick driveway.

Immediately the front door opened, and Sergio appeared, smiling broadly. He was waiting for them, and zipping up his duvet jacket, came out to help Susana with the suitcase.

IV

"Margaret Thatcher acts like a man and dresses like a woman," Luis said, picking up a menu from the white-clothed table. "There's not much to celebrate today."

It was the day after Susana arrived, and all of them were dining out.

"The woman is something, but our military heads aren't better." Then, still looking at the wine list, he added, pointing toward a line: "What about this cabernet? It's Mendocino and not too expensive."

"Yeah… It's fine with me." Sergio agreed and added, "About those warmongers, people seem to justify anything if they give them the right excuse."

"Lately, I've been hearing ridiculous things coming from people I thought were smarter than that," Susana commented.

"Same here," Mary said. "It's incredible what a successful brainwash this is."

Looking around her, Alicia felt excited and lost track of the conversation. She had hoped the sense of oppression and vague uneasiness would go away with Susana's arrival. Still, after yesterday's talk with her, the ominous feeling persisted. Nonetheless, no negative thoughts would dampen her delight in having everybody together. Sitting next to her was the adult people she valued and loved most, and a week ago, she would not have thought this encounter possible.

She watched Susana across the table chatting with Mary, sitting next to her, and felt a mix of apprehension and pride. She was always looking at Susana as an older sister, wiser, and more experienced, even though they were the same age. The comparison with a sister was an appropriate one. Alicia, as a blood sister would, had felt jealous of her at times. As a teenager, she had wished to have Susana's striking figure and the quick smile that always attracted the coolest kids before they even noticed Alicia's presence. Although in later years, things had leveled somehow. Now Alicia was less self-conscious of her bothersome girlish looks and skinny figure. After turning twenty-five, those hated traits had finally worked to her advantage. She enjoyed looking younger than her age.

Both women had spent the morning shopping downtown, exchanging small personal secrets, updating gossip on friends, and chatting about movies, books, and clothes. Namely, they did their best to enjoy the day, chasing the shadows away for a few hours.

Susana called across the table as if she were reading her mind: "Alicia, I was telling Mary what a great time we had downtown earlier today."

"Unbelievable." She agreed with bright eyes. "I was thinking about that just now."

"I read your mind! Didn't you notice it?" smiled Susana back.

"Well, you did." And turning to Mary, Alicia said, "I took the day off, and we went downtown at mid-morning with Pablo. The weather was snowy and nasty, but we had fun shopping and had lunch with Sergio."

While the others considered what to eat, Alicia looked around. Except for a few tourists, locals filled most tables. It was Friday night, and they had decided to try a new *parrilla*. A restaurant that cooked charcoal barbecue had just opened right outside the city's boundaries, where the Ñirihuau River flows into the Nahuel-Huapi Lake.

It was an ample dining room with all of the traditional Argentinean decorations of the gaucho and the *estancias*.

The Argentinean folk music playing in the background had the melancholic sound of the acoustic guitar and the percussion of the *bombos*, the drums whose beat gave an uplifting rhythm to the tune.

"Isn't that a gorgeous view?" Susana's voice brought Alicia back to the present. Everybody was looking through the window. They had a great view of the lake and mountains beyond through the wide glass panels. The river's surface reflected the sporadic moonlight like a silver ribbon on its way to the deep lake. Susana sighed.

"It's like living in a postcard all the time," she said, and the others agreed.

After they ordered barbecue and salads, the waiter turned around and walked toward the counter. Alicia distractedly followed him with her eyes when he came across two customers who had just entered the room and sat at their table. Alicia first looked through them, but something made her pay attention, and her eyes went back. The pair was the same she saw at the bus stop when Susana arrived. Something told her that it was an odd coincidence. Still, she tried to dispel her mistrust, reminding herself that Bariloche was a small town. It was not uncommon to find the same people at favorite hangouts more than once. Most tourists stayed an average of four days. Under the advice of their travel agents, they tended to patronize the most popular places. Again, Alicia told herself that this was just a coincidence. Sill, with so many traditional *parrilla* restaurants in town, her nagging wariness surfaced, and she turned toward Susana.

"See those two guys there, at the back of the room?"

"Yes. One of them is cute. The other barely looks like a twenty-year-old."

"The older one was at the bus stop when you came, and the young one came on your bus."

Susana looked again toward the table, frowning.

"Now that you mention it, you are right; he was sitting by himself in the back of the bus, I think."

Alicia thought she noticed a trace of nervousness in Susana's voice but immediately dismissed it. More than likely, her apprehensions made her expect some reaction from Susana. This thought was reassuring enough. The others were busy talking across the table, and only Mary had heard the exchange about the men. Everybody's attention turned to the expert waiter that brought the sizzling meats on the warmer, with a large bowl of greens and French fries on the side. The aroma of the beef was appetizing, and the women helped themselves first.

They ate mostly in silence, broken only here and there by observing the service's quality or the tourist season's weather. Then, they got back to the painful subject of the war.

"I hate the fact that those English beat us up like this. It's so hard to take," Alicia said, going for another helping of salad. "I guess they never forgave us for kicking their butts when they invaded Buenos

Aires twice, back in the 1800s."

"Yes. If the legend is true, the hot oil the colonial housewives dumped on their soldiers' heads from the roofs still hurts...." Luis said, alluding to the tales of civil defense tricks Buenos Aires neighbors engaged in twice against the invading English troops.

"They wanted to conquer La Pampa, and they wouldn't forgive us," Sergio said. "By the way, I don't know if it's true, but they say that during the first invasion before they were kicked out, the Brits managed to ship to London five tons of silver coins and other items. They sent it in a boat that sailed from Buenos Aires to Portsmouth. The cargo is supposed to be well documented."

"Well, it's not like they didn't seize anything besides the silver coins," Susana grinned. "Today, they own so many estancias that more than half of Patagonia is theirs. At least most of the lambs and wool industry is."

"You got that right," Luis agreed. "Who was that English Lord that said that it was way better to have economic power over the Spanish colonies than to seize them by force? The guy was right. We have been supplying them with excellent meat for pennies for over a century, with little investment from the English side."

There was silence while the table was cleared from dishes and serving plates. They checked the menu for dessert and ordered, adding coffee. Finally, they lit their cigarettes and remarked on their lack of will to quit smoking. Susana looked at Alicia in a meaningful way, reminding her that she had promised to stop twice before. Alicia smiled back sheepishly.

It was almost impossible to be together and not talk about the frustration and anxiety they had built during the last weeks.

Luis bent over the table and whispered:

"The rumor goes that the military Junta got a covert payoff from France's merchants who were very interested in putting the new Exocet missile in the world market. It seems they hadn't any conflict at hand in which to try it as a sales pitch. Nobody would risk testing a missile in the Middle East now, and our Junta would take money from anywhere." He shrugged, "That's the latest gossip."

"Hum... you know, that doesn't sound so crazy," Sergio said, cutting a piece of crepe dipped in *dulce de leche*. "Those Exocet are efficient, from what I read. I'd bet you that they are going to sell like hotcakes worldwide now, mainly in the Middle East."

Mary suddenly signaled to Alicia: "Check who is coming this way."

A small group was approaching on their way to the exit. Alicia saw Bruno Schneider, his wife, and another couple walking toward their table, coming from the room's back. She felt wary. She usually had this reaction whenever Schneider approached her since that day in the broadcasting room when he bullied her and Martina about their program's contents. But he and his wife only nodded, smiling politely and staying behind the other couple, Walter Fechner and his wife Regina, who stopped to talk to Sergio. Then, in a louder voice, maybe product of an extra glass of wine, Fechner said: "Sergio! What a nice surprise! How are you doing, son?"

Sergio smiled back at the couple, making a move to stand up. Fechner affectionately put his hand on his shoulder, "It's okay. Don't stand up. We're just leaving. Old people go to bed earlier than the young," laughing at his own words.

The Fechners were longtime friends of Sergio's parents, and he was a prominent local businessman. They owned and ran a traditional and prestigious Swiss-style hotel facing the lake. In addition, he was an associate of Schneider at the local Chamber of Tourism.

"This is my childhood friend Susana Machevsky; she is visiting us for a few days," Alicia said. Susana nodded and flashed her beautiful smile to all. Alicia noticed a slight gesture of recognition from Fechner when he heard Susana's last name, but she dismissed it as her imagination. They all exchanged greetings, and then Fechner turned toward Sergio again, "I just got the news that your parents are coming next August. I'm glad. Call me one of these days. We have to organize something; an outing maybe when your parents get here."

"Sure. We'll be in touch," Sergio said, smiling politely.

"Good night to all, for now. Enjoy your evening," Fechner said while the others muttered polite words. Then, the four walked toward the exit door, zigzagging unhurriedly between the busy, white-covered tables.

Sergio's parents had several acquaintances from the old country living in town. Each time Franz and Helena visited Bariloche, Alicia and Sergio had joined the group. They mainly were couples in their late fifties, all Central Europeans, and many of their friendships pre-dated WWII. They enjoyed dining out, skiing, or an occasional private party. The usual dining would be at any of the many German, Austrian, or Swiss restaurants in the area. They were always warm and very polite with Alicia. With guilt, she often imagined that maybe these innocent immigrants had a not-so-clean past, reading too much into bits and pieces of information. Although, as often, she thought the opposite.

After the group left, Alicia discreetly glanced to where the two men had sat earlier on. They were still there, and one of them looked briefly toward her table. When she turned around, she noticed Susana looking in the same direction, and now she was frowning, maybe involuntarily. Their eyes met, and Susana seemed embarrassed at having been caught looking at the man. Or was it Alicia's doubts about everything acting up again? Did Susana tell her everything when they talked in the car the day she arrived?

Around midnight, and after another round of coffee and cigarettes, they left the restaurant. Luis and Mary drove off in their recently purchased second-hand Fiat 600. They waved at the trio walking toward Sergio's station wagon, avoiding the small bright spots of frozen water on the asphalted parking lot.

Sergio dusted off the light snow on the windows and opened the doors of his Renault 12 Breck for Alicia and Susana, who hurried inside.

They drove in silence. Sergio took the lakeside road at the edge of downtown. Soon the tall, slender stone tower of the town's Cathedral sitting on a high slope across the street facing the lake was visible. Alicia could see the cross at the top of the tower, its white lights bright between the sequences of shadows from the cone-shaped pine trees surrounding the building. She turned around to look at Susana, sitting in the back, who smiled at her. Alicia looked again ahead and almost involuntarily said a prayer in silence for all of them.

Lydia, the young babysitter from the neighborhood, was dozing off on the couch with a book open on her lap. So she jumped when she heard the door opening.

"Is everything okay?" Sergio asked.

"Yeah." She looked tired and was relieved to see them. "Pablo is sleeping. He asked for the same Smurf story over and over, and he fell asleep early." Lydia grabbed her coat and books. She was ready to be taken home.

"I'll be back soon," Sergio said to Alicia, picking up the car keys from the table.

Lydia got in the station wagon, and Sergio drove out of the driveway. The house across the street was empty, and it had a "For Sale" sign in the front yard. Two generous trees on its sidewalk extended their branches in a canopy over the street. A car, parked below one of the trees, had the engine and lights on, and Sergio looked at it for a few minutes before stepping on the gas. Still, he could not see the faces of the two people inside, only two shadows, apparently engaged in a conversation, not looking at him.

Sergio maneuvered slowly, and the driver of the car across the street moved in the opposite direction. Again, Sergio drove very slowly until he saw the car disappear from his rearview mirror, turning uphill a block further north.

He looked at Lydia, who seemed not to have noticed anything.

"Did you see that car before?"

She turned and sleepily looked back over her shoulder.

"No. Now that I think about it, I didn't notice it. Was it there when you guys came home?"

"I didn't notice any car. I don't think it was there before. I was wondering if you saw anything through the windows while we were away."

"Nope," she said firmly. Then, thinking it over: "Well, I wasn't looking outside, at least not since early in the evening."

"It's okay. Don't worry. It was probably someone who got lost and was looking at the map for directions; tourists get lost all the time," he said as casually as possible.

When Sergio came in a few minutes later, he found Alicia and Susana in the hallway, talking in a low voice not to wake up Pablo, each on their way to their bedrooms.

"I'm glad you both are still up," he said. "This might not be important, but when I left to take Lydia home, I saw a car parked across the street, under the trees, with two guys. Even though they did not seem suspicious or anything, it struck me as odd at this hour of the night. Maybe they lost their way, or it was a couple fighting instead of two guys. Still…"

Both women looked worried, and he added, "I'm sure it's nothing. Maybe a tourist couple that got lost, like so many others."

Alicia whispered, "We are getting paranoid. I don't know if you realize it. If those jerks want to scare people off, they do it well. Maybe this car meant nothing, but we see shadows all around."

"Yes. Let's go to bed," Susana's voice sounded tired. "Tomorrow, we'll see things in a better light."

"Yes, you're right. Good night."

Alicia made a note to talk to Sergio about what Susana told her was happening in Buenos Aires. He should know, but not now. They were exhausted.

V

"Shh... don't wake him up," Alicia whispered, tiptoeing behind Sergio as they left their bedroom, where Pablo slept in his crib.

Around eight in the morning, she heard Sergio get up from the bed, and she followed him to the kitchen. He set the coffee maker, and she put the toaster on.

"How are you doing this morning?" he said with affection, putting his arms around her waist. She leaned on his chest.

"Fine, but still shaky about last night's mysterious car. I don't want to live like this." She lifted her head, looking at him in the eye. "Seriously, I'm talking to Martina today. All this is making me nervous."

She told him briefly what Susana had told her when she arrived. Then they sat down to eat breakfast. He listened in silence, and when she finished, he took her hand over the table.

"Try to keep things in perspective. We don't know, and we are alarmed, and we have reasons, but nothing concrete. What would you tell Martina? She'll ask you why you want to change the tone of the program."

"I'll give her an excuse: That Schneider is unhappy with our messages, and we cannot risk losing his sponsorship, so she doesn't need to know every detail."

"That's fine. Just don't say more than you need."

"Of course, I won't." Then she turned to him, a bit piqued: "This is not the first time you insist on it. Does it mean you don't trust me to keep a secret?"

"I didn't mean that, of course. But please, Alicia, let's not start another silly argument that won't lead anywhere, please." His voice was low.

"Well then, choose your words better. It did sound bad the way you said it," she whispered back, irritated.

He did not answer. They made an effort to focus on the newspaper and finished their breakfast. The recently nominated General Bignone took power, and rumors circulated about the political parties being allowed to function again. The muddled return of the troops from Malvinas was the other main topic, and both tried to mend the early verbal scuffle by exchanging short comments on the news in a low voice until they heard Pablo calling from his bed. Susana joined them soon, and after a quick breakfast, Alicia and her left for Martina's house.

The Salgados lived in a large, modern house in one of the new developments built on the soft slopes of the hills near Cerro Catedral. There was a car parked behind Martina's red Peugeot.

"They have a guest," Alicia said. "We won't stay long. I'll drop a draft for her to work on, and that's all. I want to return home by lunchtime."

"Fine with me," Susana said, getting out of the car.

Alicia looked forward to the afternoon off and knew that Martina's meetings with her could go on for hours. Martina opened the front door and led them to the spacious two-leveled living room. The white walls, sparsely decorated with native artifacts and pictures, had a warm and welcoming effect. Julio, Martina's husband, chatting with a guest, was sitting in comfortable leather armchairs around a small table.

As the three women approached the area, both men stood up and walked toward them. "This is Roberto Flores, a longtime friend of mine, who has just moved to Bariloche a few weeks ago."

Flores was tall, athletic, and he had short dark hair that emphasized his square jaw and light green eyes. He shook Alicia's hand firmly.

"Hi, nice to meet you," she said, smiling politely, "this is my old pal from Buenos Aires, Susana Machevsky."

Susana shook hands with both men and exchanged a few platitudes. Alicia noticed that the seemingly arrogant Roberto Flores was a little bit too eager toward Susana. There was something about him Alicia didn't like, albeit she could not pinpoint what it was. He had a mocking expression when he talked. They discussed movies and their merits, and then Martina excused herself, signaling Alicia to join her. They went to the kitchen, where they sat at the dinette table. Martina grabbed a folder marked LRA30, and Alicia opened her briefcase and took a draft out. They went over the material for the next day's program. When they finished, Alicia felt it was the right moment to tackle what was her primary concern:

"You know," she began, "I was thinking about what Schroeder told us. Maybe we should tone down our interviews and our exchanges on the air. I'm a little worried about him unhappy with us. He holds the money purse. If he cuts back on the funds, there won't be a radio broadcast for us any longer. What do you think?"

To her surprise, Martina agreed. "I was thinking of talking to you about this too." She shrugged and smiled. "We're chickens, I know, but as they say, better a coward alive than a hero dead. Frankly, I was concerned about all this shit about being branded as an extreme feminist. Soon not even the newspaper will give us work. It has happened to others."

Alicia sighed, relieved at not having to elaborate on her reasons. It was better than she thought, but, simultaneously, she felt she would have to pay the price for her cowardice at some point, and the thought bothered her. After they finished strategizing the new steps for the program's future projects, Alicia said, "I'm happy we are on the same wavelength, Martina."

"We better be if we are in the same radio show." Martina laughed at the double meaning. "C'mon, let's join the others."

Was Martina as unconcerned as she seemed to be? Alicia was sincerely relieved that they cleared out the thorny issue without too many explanations. Although a nagging inner voice still suggested this was unprofessional. This was not the journalism Alicia had aspired to do. Was she too idealistic? Why couldn't she be cynical about the whole issue, as the others seemed to be?

They returned to the living room, where the others had a lively conversation about a recent bestselling book. Susana seemed engaged in it, but she stood up, followed by the men when she saw they were coming back. Martina invited them to stay for lunch, but they excused themselves, alleging they already had plans for the afternoon.

Driving back home, Alicia asked with curiosity, "How did you like Martina and Julio?"

"She's nice, vivacious; I see why you get along with her. Julio is an interesting guy too. I didn't know he was a medical doctor. He seems to know a lot about art, but he has poor taste in literature."

"I didn't care much for their guest, Roberto," Alicia ventured.

"He seemed okay to me... perhaps a bit of a chauvinist in some of his opinion." Then she added, "He's a quite good-looking guy. He could be a fashion model, don't you think?"

"Yeah, but I didn't like how he looks you in the eye, insistent as if he's trying to read through you." Then she added as an afterthought, "Was he flirting with you, or did I misread it?"

"Yeah, at times, he was flirting," Susana admitted with a smile.

"I don't know; there is something about him," Alicia said.

"Yes, he has somewhat of a stare, but I don't think he realizes it. Listen; he has been in the Navy and retired young because of an injury, and now works for the Army here, not far from town."

"Hum... Is that right? That's why he lives near the Centro Atómico," Alicia said and then added, trying to keep her incipient paranoia under control: "Well, it doesn't mean anything."

"Nope. But we tend to believe that all servicemen may work for the intelligence services." Susana read her mind. "Even though this city seems to be a paradise under the radar, you happen to have proof they are everywhere."

"Yes. And I wonder if Martina worries about this matter. But anyhow, it isn't something she would discuss with me."

"Then again, there is always the possibility of us blowing this out of proportion."

"True. It's hard to know."

There was an uncomfortable silence. Then, after a while, Susana asked, "Does Julio lean toward the military?"

"I don't think so. He does not seem to like the government. You should hear him complaining about how the military in charge ruined the local regional hospital's system, which, they say, was working like clockwork before. It was organized years ago by a group of progressive young doctors. It's all dismantled now. The hospital is in a dire state, like most hospitals in the country. You have to bring your bandages, stitches, and disinfectant to get medical care. He hates that."

"All over the country, the same shit." Susana shook her head.

"Yeah... I believe the guy at the forefront of the hospital was fired right after the coup in '76; his name was Dr. Capellin. People talk about him with respect. Then the hospital was taken over by the military, like everything else."

They were almost home. It was around midday, and the wind of the previous evening had cleared the sky. The sun was shining, warming the cold breeze slightly. Nevertheless, it was dry and crisp. Sergio had taken Pablo with him to his office, and Alicia set the table for a light lunch.

"Let's make a couple of sandwiches," Alicia suggested.

"Good idea," said Susana, taking out the plates and napkins while humming a Beatles' tune. "I feel like going on a good, long walk after lunch. How about you?"

"A good long walk it will be, then."

"How about a hike around Cerro Otto?"

"It sounds great." Alicia's voice was enthusiastic. "It's uphill, though. You'll have to be patient with my legs. I haven't done it in a long time."

"It's not your legs. Nothing wrong with your legs," Susana retorted. "It's the smoking that holds you back, and those cigarettes will make you sick."

"Okay, okay, I know, you are right. So one of these days, I'll quit. I've done it before; I can do it again, and then it'll be for good. I'm sure."

"Hope so, but I won't hold my breath."

"This is all for today, dear listeners," Martina intoned in her professional address in front of the microphone. "Join us next Sunday at ten o'clock for another encounter with '*Women of Today and Tomorrow.*"

The rhythmic introduction to Jorge Benson's *On Broadway*, which opened and closed the program, followed. Martina looked to her right. The red light at the top of the window went off, and the young sound engineer sitting at the console behind the glass flashed the sign of OK. Alicia turned to Martina, and both sighed with relief.

"It was a good program; everything came out fine."

"Yes, I was a little worried at the beginning of the interview, particularly with the last woman, but she was fine." Martina stood up, lifting a pile of folders from the table.

"They all had good answers too...." Alicia said while gathering her papers and following her through the radio studio's heavy double wooden door. They hurried up; the next program's staff would come rushing in while the news of the hour was on the air, broadcasting from the second, smaller studio, invisible from the room they just left.

They walked to the foyer, entered a small dressing room, and picked up their coats and scarves before leaving through the building's main door to the blinding mid-morning light.

"Martina, I believe we had a good balance today. We did not bitch about anything, and the representatives of the artisan organization were very polite but clear on their points. They never said anything bad about the municipality, even though they could have. We should keep this approach. A chicken type of approach, I would call it."

"Yes. Chicken, honestly. But we don't have to give up everything. Just try to keep the balance, as you said." They walked briskly down the wooden stairs of the wide front veranda. "I meant to tell you, Alicia, thanks for bringing Susana home yesterday. I was glad to meet her. I can see why you both get along so well."

"She was impressed with you guys too."

"Roberto, Julio's friend, was asking about her," Martina said with a wink.

"Is that right?" Alicia feigned surprise.

"Yes, he was very interested. He's single. I don't know him well, but Julio has known him since grade school. They were neighbors for many years. He says he's a great guy. They reconnected again a couple of months ago when Roberto moved here from Bahia Blanca."

"I see you are helping him to find a girlfriend," said Alicia, amused.

"Well, I just thought, since he showed so much interest in Susana, that they may get to know each other. And, who knows?"

"I'll tell her. Anyway, she is leaving on Tuesday."

"I know. I'm just passing the message. They'd make a nice pair. However, Roberto is not planning to stay in Bariloche for long; sooner or later, he will go back north."

"I'll mention it to her."

"Yes. Just in case."

"I heard he was in the Navy and retired early?"

"Yes. Roberto had a car accident and got early retirement."

"What's his job here?"

"Some engineering position at the Army barracks. He says it's a short stint. Then he has to go back north, maybe somewhere around Buenos Aires."

"That's interesting," Alicia mumbled, with a distracted tone, while thinking how odd it was for Martina, so open-minded, so progressive in her ideas, to be sometimes so naive. Didn't she have any suspicions about this guy? Or was Alicia being too apprehensive, distrustful, and defensive? "I'm very fond of Susana, you know. I'm glad you like her. She's been my best friend for ages. She seemed to like you too. I'll mention Roberto to her."

"Well, let's plan something before she leaves. How about dinner tomorrow night?"

"That's nice of you, thank you."

Alicia drove straight home, thinking that the invitation would please her friend.

After lunch, Sergio excused himself and left for his office. He volunteered to take care of Pablo in the afternoon, but Susana insisted that the toddler come with them for a stroll outdoors. It was sunny, with that pale sun of the Bariloche winters. Only a few white, cotton-like clouds crossed the intense blue of the sky. Alicia took Sergio's station wagon, and they drove in silence west, toward Llao-Llao, paying attention to Pablo, who dozed off cuddled in his back chair. Finally, Alicia asked, "You haven't said anything about your last romance. What happened? You went out with him for two months. The guy seemed kind of okay to me, judging from your letters. Am I wrong?"

"There is nothing worth to say about him. As I told you, the guy was a loser." She sighed. "One more in the long list I am building."

"Hum... Not all men are losers, you know. The right guy for you is somewhere out there, and you will find him when you least expect it."

"It's okay with me. You know, I have enough friends to get along socially, and I have fun with them, considering the circumstances."

"I know. Have you seen anyone from the old gang lately?" Alicia had lost track of some of their friends in Buenos Aires, and she welcomed news from any of them through Susana.

"We had that dinner six months ago. Not everybody was there. You know, quite a few have already left the country; Amanda and Juan José to Madrid, Lina is in Brazil. They all got better contracts or jobs overseas. Let's see. Mariano was there, as well as Viviana and her fiancé, an incredibly handsome guy, I may add. I see them more often than the others."

"I wish I had been there."

"Everybody asked about you. Whenever you go to Buenos Aires, we'll organize something; I already promised that much to them. It's so hard to keep in touch over the years."

"You're right."

They drove in silence for a while. Then Alicia turned the cassette player on, and the soft sound of a violin solo, caught in the middle of one of Vivaldi's Four Seasons, filled the air.

"Talking about friends, have you seen... What's his name?" Alicia feigned forgetfulness, trying to see if Susana had his name ready. "The guy that lent me Vargas Llosa's *The City and the Dogs*...what's his name?'

Susana turned to her, smiling, and said: "C'mon, Alicia, I'd bet anything you remember well his name."

"Okay, yes... Gustavo Spinetti." Alicia conceded, smiling back.

Gustavo was perhaps the exception to that long list of losers. He was engaging, intellectually challenging, and a heartthrob. But when Susana met him, he was still too emotionally involved with his ex-wife after a messy divorce filed in Uruguay. Their relationship had lasted just over a year, and they broke amicably. It had happened over three years ago, but he had occasionally reappeared with postcards or unexpected phone calls. Alicia was almost sure that her friend still had feelings for him. The affair was intense enough, and Susana was distraught for months when they broke up. Alicia was relieved, though. Gustavo used to be an activist for the Juventud Peronista. The younger, left-leaning extension of the traditional Peronista Party and

Alicia thought that he would be in trouble sooner or later, as the polarization of the party's extreme factions now accelerated. After they split, Susana mentioned she was not interested in getting involved in politics.

"Have you heard anything from him lately?" Alicia insisted.

"I haven't. I believe Gustavo came back from Nicaragua some time ago. I heard somebody saw him in Buenos Aires, but he might be back in Managua. He got a good job as a systems engineer. You know, he specialized in this COBOL computer language. I guess he is doing something for a university there. Computers are a mystery to me, but he seems to love them. I wonder if those machines have a meaningful future, as he thinks."

"It's a field for brainy people. He was a sharp guy, I remember," Alicia conceded. "Bright and polite, sort of a quiet encyclopedia. He never said much. Too involved in risky politics. Wasn't he?"

"Yeah... You seem to remember him well," Susana smiled.

"I do. I liked Gustavo to tell you the truth. What I didn't like was the divorce and the messy situation he got in with his ex-wife. I don't think you would have ever gotten rid of that, Susana, if you pursued the relationship. I mean, with his ex and the family hanging like ballast on his life. And to tell you the truth, I didn't like his affiliation with the JP either. He was a true activist. That's bad now."

"I guess so." Susana was looking at the road ahead.

"I always thought he might get involved with *Montoneros* or some other terrorist group from that fringe of the party."

"C'mon, Alicia. Where did you get that outlandish idea from?" Susana's voice sounded annoyed. Her eyes were still on the road.

Alicia kept charging ahead with what she had to say. "I don't know. Don't get me wrong. It's a reasonable assumption, I guess. Then again, he probably is a Sandinista in Nicaragua now or a sympathizer. They are the black sheep of Latin America after Cuba. Unfortunately, they will hit them like hard from now on. Sandinistas won't get rid of the big powers, and they don't have much future in that path, the violence, I mean. With the Americans against them, they are done. Washington will not allow another Castro."

"You have a point there." Susana's voice was neutral.

"People do not want internal wars. We all want to live in peace."

Susana seemed to have lost interest in the subject. She turned toward the back seat to check on Pablo.

"He is napping peacefully," she said. "The drive makes him sleepy."

"Yes, it never fails."

Alicia understood that her friend did not want to talk about it, but she needed to say something else. So, although it was a delicate matter, she went on, "This is no news for you; somehow, I am convinced that he is trouble. You probably know this better than I ever will."

She glanced at Susana's face. A smile curved her lips, but she did not look back at Alicia, who continued: "First, he is married. Second, until divorce gets legally approved in this country, legal separations in Uruguay's courtrooms won't do here. So, for all we know, here he's still a married man, with a child to maintain and a wife who bugs him just for spite."

"Alicia, what's with you talking about him after such a long time? I haven't seen him in ages."

"I know, but if Gustavo goes back to Buenos Aires, I'm sure he'll contact you. He's handsome, with that look of a lonesome hero from a Far-West movie."

"I know, I know. I can't deny I think of him once in a while, but he doesn't have inner peace at all. His calm is just a mask. It's as if he were always looking for something, not his wife and not me. He carries something inside that doesn't let him rest. There is nothing for me there, Alicia. I'll never get back with him."

Susana's words gave Alicia the courage to go a bit further. "Good. Besides, he was very much involved with the JP," her voice was too forceful, and Susana glanced at her. "They are targets of the military now, and that makes you a target too if you ever see him or talk to him." Susana kept her eyes on the road ahead, silent. "See where am I coming from? Please, don't take it the wrong way. I don't want to intrude. I'm just worried about you."

"I know... but for goodness sake, Alicia, you can be persistent when you want! I already told you he hadn't contacted me, and I don't have the means to find out where the heck he is. So don't worry. He might not come back from Nicaragua or wherever he is now. And if he calls, I'll get rid of him right away. I promise. But he knows perfectly well what to do and what winds are blowing here."

"I hope so." Alicia seemed content with her answer, but as an extra measure of caution, she added, "I hope he knows better than putting you at risk."

"I'm sure he does. He's not that stupid." Susana's voice was impatient now as if she wanted to end the subject.

They drove in silence for a while, checking the back seat where Pablo was still sleeping and enjoying the lake and forest's view along the road.

Susana's words sounded convincing, but they did not dispel Alicia's fears. Lately, she seemed to worry about everything. She had this odd feeling that she should always be on alert. She wasn't sure where the hit would come from or why, or if it was only her feeble mind, which made her jittery.

At another turn of the winding road, the magnificent view of the Llao-Llao Hotel high up on the hill came in full view, with its green undulating golf course lawn surrounded by the two lakes' blue waters. Beyond, the rugged, snow-covered amphitheater of Cerro Lopez raised its serrated peaks to the blue sky. Susana sighed at the magnificence.

"That Cerro Lopez sure looks like a volcano that blew off half a mountain ages ago."

Alicia laughed, "You may be right. I never thought of that. Imagine what grandiose spectacle would have been at the time."

After a few minutes, Susana added, "I'm so glad I decided to come to see you guys. This place is so beautiful. If only I could have a hermit cabin on the top of the mountain and survive alone, I would move here."

"No, you wouldn't. It would be fine in summer, but you would take the next bus back to Buenos Aires in winter. Winters here in Patagonia can kill one's enthusiasm very quickly if you don't have enough amenities at home. You and I are creatures of asphalt, electric light, and hot tap water. Believe me. You could survive in downtown, but not on a cabin in the hills."

"I guess you are right." Susana sighed. "You know, this is my best Sunday in a long, long time. Thanks for insisting that I come over."

Alicia did not answer, but her words made her very happy.

On Monday morning, Alicia went to the *El Barilochense* early to drop a draft for editing and make a couple of phone calls. Then, she drove Pablo to the daycare center and took Susana downtown to walk and shop on her own. They would meet at midday with Sergio.

Alicia managed to finish her work early, looking forward to her break. She parked close to the café where they were meeting. Mitre Street was busy at lunchtime, with the locals and tourists strolling about carrying shopping bags loaded with regional products. It reminded her of Martina's plan for dinner; she would probably come by her office at the last minute before the end of the day.

The weather was good, and Alicia strolled, enjoying the sun. It was early, and she knew she would have to wait for Susana and Sergio, but it was okay. The day was gorgeous. She was the first to get to the cafe and managed to find a table by one of the large windows that sported flowers on the outside, aligned on wooden Swiss-style planters.

While watching the pedestrians, she noticed Susana chatting with Roberto Flores across the street. She recognized the crew cut and the tall figure. They seemed very engaged in the conversation, and she was laughing. Alicia smiled, surprised. After a few minutes, Sergio walked in the door, approached her table, and kissed Alicia, sitting in the chair next to her. Immediately he looked around and called the waiter.

"See those guys there?" she asked, motioning toward the window.

He looked, and after a moment, he said, "Isn't that, Susana?"

"Yes."

"Who's the guy?"

"That's Roberto Flores, the guy we met at Martina's. I told you about him yesterday."

"Is that right? What a coincidence."

"Yeah, that's what I was thinking. It's odd, Martina said she would see me today at work to organize something for tonight, but she didn't yet."

They saw Susana shake the man's hand, say good-bye, and face the street, waiting for the green lights to cross toward the café. Roberto paused for a few seconds, looking at her, and then turned around and sauntered away, blending in with the other pedestrians.

Susana arrived at the café and smiled from the door when she saw her friends. Then she collapsed in the seat and put her bags and handbag on the next chair.

"Hi, guys, have you been waiting long?"

"Not at all," Alicia said, smiling mischievously. "Only a few minutes, but we had some good entertainment across the street."

"Yeah, that was Roberto Flores," she smiled back. "We met about an hour ago. Isn't it a coincidence? He was shopping and sightseeing, and we bumped into each other."

"Hum… shouldn't he be working on Mondays?" Alicia said with a meaningful look.

"C'mon, Alicia," Sergio chided her. "Leave the poor woman alone. It probably was a coincidence that they met. Don't try to read more into it."

"Yeah, I suppose you're right. I shouldn't interfere," Alicia shrugged. "But Susana knows I'm a busybody, and she still loves me."

"I also thought it was a strange coincidence, don't worry," Susana said. "He invited me for coffee. Then we had a nice time walking and chatting. He'll be going to Buenos Aires soon. We exchanged telephone numbers, and he asked if he could call me to go out for dinner," then she added with her charming smile, "And guess what? I said yes."

"And why not? He's cute. Have fun; I didn't mean to pry into your business."

"Oh, of course not." Susana's voice was amused. She feigned not to like it, but Alicia's concerns were how to show love for her, and she appreciated that. "I never would think that about you, dear."

Sergio and Alicia laughed at Susana's obvious sarcasm, and they soon ordered lunch, happy to be sharing the moment. Tomorrow afternoon Susana would be ready to take the bus back to Buenos Aires.

Sergio's car was in the driveway, the engine on, warming up.

Luis and Mary had stopped earlier to bid Susana farewell, and after coffee and a brief, pleasant chat, they were going back to work.

"Come by tonight, after dinner, if you guys feel like it," Mary said, walking toward the car.

"Okay. See you later," Sergio answered, carrying Susana's luggage out the door and in the car's trunk. Pablo was strapped to his car seat, playing with a toy, ready for the ride. Susana hugged Sergio and got in the car. Alicia followed.

"Alicia, thanks for lending me the duffel bag. I didn't realize that I had bought so many things."

"You got chocolate and fruit preserves for the whole family, girl."

"If you need the duffel bag, I'll mail it to you," Susana said.

"Don't. I'll pick it up when I get to see you if we go to Carla's baby's baptism in less than a month."

"Okay, then."

The drive seemed too short, and they got downtown faster than they would have wanted. The bus was already in place, and some passengers were going in.

"Where did the time go? You are already leaving," Alicia lamented, carrying the duffel bag in one hand and Pablo perched on the other arm.

After dispatching the luggage, they sat for a while in the waiting room until the bus's departure. Then they walked in line with the other passengers toward the sidewalk, where the large coach was getting ready to leave. The big cargo trunk in the vehicle's belly was finally locked, and the driver took his place at the wheel. Susana and Alicia waited while the others got in.

"Don't let too much time pass without calling or sending a letter. Please." Alicia had tears in her eyes.

"I won't. Don't cry. I don't want you to cry. I truly enjoyed these days. Thank you so much for the wonderful weekend. I certainly needed it. You were right, as you always are." Her voice choked, and they embraced as tightly as Pablo's body allowed, in Alicia's arms. He moaned, upset for being enfolded for so long between his mother and Susana.

"We'll have it all over again when I get to Buenos Aires soon. It will still be more fun; we'll meet the gang for a big dinner."

"Yes, we will." Susana kissed Pablo's cheek. "Bye-bye, Pablito, you are a doll. It was a pleasure to see you so grown up and mature for your age." Then, looking at Alicia tenderly, she added: "You surely are doing a good job as a mom. He is such a great kid."

Alicia muttered thanks, watching Susana quickly climb onto the bus. Alicia stood on the sidewalk, trying to see what seat she was taking. Disappointed, she noticed that her place was not by the window, so they could not talk again. Alicia waved a kiss to her, and Susana smiled back. A middle-aged woman was sitting at the window, and she also smiled back at Alicia.

The bus was almost ready to leave, but it did not close the door yet. A clerk from the office came running. An exchange of words between him, the driver, and the young stewardess who would attend to the passengers during the trip happened. From where Alicia was standing, she could not understand what they said.

The woman sitting next to Susana stretched her neck out the window and said to a man standing close to Alicia, evidently her relative or friend, "It seems somebody is late, and we are waiting for him."

There was a lapse of two or three minutes. Then, suddenly, a car appeared and parked in a quick and unexpected maneuver in front of the bus. A man stepped out of the passenger seat, opened the back door, and pulled out a small suitcase. He closed the door and bent over the passenger window to speak briefly with the driver. Then the car moved fifty yards ahead and stopped, leaving space enough for the bus to depart.

The man walked toward the bus door with firm steps and tended a ticket to the clerk waiting for him. He got in, and the automatic double doors closed with a puffing sound. The bus moved ahead slowly and entered the traffic lane, turning right in the next corner.

Alicia stood there, looking at the intersection for a few seconds. Then, she shifted Pablo over to the other arm and walked on. Her eyes settled on the car that had brought the delayed passenger. She looked at the driver's seat, and her heart sunk. She held Pablo tight in her arms feeling stunned and confused. She could see the driver from behind, but as she recognized his head's shape as that of the green

Falcon man, the car swiftly moved away, preventing her from seeing his face. Although she wasn't sure, her heart was racing. If he was the man, what was he doing there? Who was the one that kept the bus waiting? Then she realized that she had been seeing this man everywhere. It was too coincidental that he would show up so often. It *had* to be a mistake. It was the only rational explanation.

Alicia kept walking, upset with what now seemed more and more like an obsession escalating to the point of playing tricks on her mind. She kissed her son's cheek and hurried toward where Sergio's white Renault was parked.

VI

"It was good to have had Susana here. I think she enjoyed it too," Alicia said with a satisfied smile.

"Yes. It was short but sweet," Sergio agreed, lifting his head from the newspaper. Two pieces of toast sprang from the toaster, and she placed them on a plate. Sergio had been preparing the rest of the breakfast.

"We talked a lot, she and I. I'm glad we had enough time to talk. Pity we cannot live closer. Or that the phone service isn't cheaper."

Sergio poured the coffee, and they sat at the table with the paper nearby.

"The bus should be halfway by now," Alicia said, "crossing La Pampa plains. And that's a long and monotonous journey."

"It's a hell of a long trip. Much easier to fly there."

"Yeah. If you can afford it. By the way, we should buy the tickets if we want to go to the christening of little Veronica. Do you think we'll be able to make it?"

"To tell you the truth, I don't think we will. I haven't heard anything from Huemul yet, and I don't think they'll soon pay my invoice. Not to mention the new project. No news about it, either."

Alicia remained silent for a while, and he went back to his paper.

"Sergio," she said suddenly, "yesterday, when Susana left, something weird happened. I don't know if I imagine things, but I could swear I saw the head of the green Falcon guy from the back, driving a car that brought a last-minute passenger to the bus. I don't know the man that got on the bus, but I thought I recognized the car driver."

"But you aren't sure."

"No."

"Then, maybe it wasn't him. Don't forget you're on edge lately."

"Yes. That's why I didn't tell you last night. I want to believe I was wrong."

He smiled. "I do believe you were wrong. Everything will be okay."

"I hope you're right."

"I'm always right," he said in jest.

"The sad part is I know you truly believe it." They laughed. Alicia knew it was very likely that she was not mistaken, but neither of them had any idea of what to do or what to expect.

On his way out, he kissed her longer than usual. She held on to him, and they stayed embraced for a bit longer, trying to fend off the ominous feeling that, they now realized, was always with them since the encounter with the man of the green Falcon.

As usual, the quiet morning hours while Pablo slept were productive. Alicia felt she had accomplished a good deal of work by nine o'clock when the doorbell rang, and she let Jacinta in. The young Mapuche woman's rugged and tanned face was impassive, as usual, while eyeing Alicia and exchanging a few greeting words. Rather tall and robust for a twenty-year-old, Jacinta had a straight nose that reminded Alicia of the North American Natives. She was almost sure this woman had Ranquel blood in her veins. Ranquel were the nomadic, slender Patagonian Indians, exceptional horse riders killed or forced from their fertile lands in the plains. Then, around the late 1800s, the army pushed them toward the Andes Mountains, the Mapuche tribe's ancestral home. The *Campaña del Desierto*, the local version of the North American Conquest of the West, was long due for historical revision, but that would have to wait for now.

Jacinta was short on words and efficient in her job. She had grasped her duties at home very quickly. After Alicia's previous experience with teenagers who did not pay enough attention to their work, she wanted to keep Jacinta for as long as possible. Unfortunately, they had to stretch their budget to pay her a higher than average hourly salary. Most of the women doing the low-paid housework in town were Mapuche, and Alicia was under the impression that their descendants living in the area did not acknowledge their heritage openly if they ever had the chance to learn it. Few spoke *la Lengua*, the tongue, as they called their ancient language. Mapuche families lived dispersed in all city areas, so it was hard to consider them as a group. Their music was a monotonous percussion beat, deemed not noteworthy or rich enough integrate the popular folk music, as other northern tribal sounds.

Alicia was curious about Jacinta's background. She read as much as she could about their traditions, and she had even bought a Mapuche-Spanish dictionary to translate the local names.

"I'm surprised Jacinta is not angry with the government for taking her brother to the front lines of the war," she had said to Sergio not long ago.

"Why would she? He was drafted into the military as any other Argentinean. Most people believed in the need to recover the islands."

"Well, they are being used. So many Indians perished when they conquered their land, and now they draft their descendants to fight for them in a war imposed by a self-appointed military government against a third country."

He took a while to answer, but he was assertive. "Those are two different things. Alcides was born in Argentina, and he feels Argentinean first, and then he may feel he's Mapuche. So if he feels he's a good citizen, as he learned, he will naturally want to defend the motherland if they ask him."

"Hum... seen from that point of view, maybe," she conceded, not convinced.

He added: "Alcides might question the reasons for the war, or why they wiped out his people long ago, but that's another thing altogether. In the war, they put all of us in the same boat, Indian or not. If they send you there, you have to go. That's why we have a draft."

"That's sad."

"People seldom question these things because security is involved. They are afraid. People don't ask the tough questions as you're doing. Besides, who wants to be anti-patriotic?"

She chuckled. "You're right. Fat chance anybody around here will question anything the government does."

"I believe it's better if we don't differentiate if they are Indians or not. We don't even think of the people around us as Indians, Europeans, Criollos, or whatever. When was the last time you looked at somebody's face or last name in this country and thought of their ancestry? Did you even care?"

"No. Not really. Nobody would ask me about that either."

"The subject doesn't even come up, and I, for once, am glad. Mapuche Indians may have lost their grandparents' identity, but in a sense, we all feel equally Argentinean, equally slapped around, equally impoverished. It is worse being identified and confined to a neighborhood, a ghetto, or a reservation, as some people are in other countries."

"You know, you would have made a good diplomat. You always understand the other side's way of thinking, the other side's reasoning."

"Thanks, but no thanks. I would be bored to death reading fat treatises."

She always enjoyed Sergio's natural common sense that made her rethink some of her long-established opinions. There might be some racist elements in the country, but she was proud of their racial integration, the ethnic mixture. It was one of the good things the Spaniards had brought, albeit inadvertently, with the colony. After their arrival to the American continent, Spaniard women and men married natives. The conquerors saw it as a natural integration to the colonial society. Alicia always felt hurt when people would blame all Latin-American countries' problems in Spain and its heritage, which she cherished, notwithstanding its colonial ills.

A sound coming from the laundry brought her to the present and, she joined Jacinta, asking with interest, "Did you get news from Alcides?"

The woman turned around, shaking her head sadly. Her pale looks this morning had already answered her polite question. "No, *señora*, nothing yet," she murmured.

"It's a matter of time," Alicia sighed. "I'm sure you will get word soon." It did not convince her, but she felt she had to say something reassuring. It was a miserable situation for everybody. "He'll be back home soon, you'll see."

The weekly staff meeting in the afternoon had already ended when Alicia got to the newsroom. Her coworkers were walking out of the meeting room.

"Alicia, you have to interview the guys from the Chamber of Commerce," Carlos Alvarez greeted her. "And I want you to write something nice and catchy for the gift shops at Patio Jardin. They are buying a large ad for the whole month, and I want several pictures. You know the routine."

Another *chivo* for the sponsors, Alicia thought, resigned. She would do another one of those uplifting, colorful double-page advertisements with a few words to fill in the spaces between pictures, published under the guise of news. She sighed. There were rumors about the mishandling of the disgraceful war adventure, but not in this newsroom. Everything had to be uplifting and inspiring here, and she needed her job, so that she would comply, mainly without a word.

Back at her desk, she checked, but there was no message from Susana. She had promised she would call as soon as she got home, but, instead, two days had passed without a word.

"Carlos, no long-distance calls for me today?" she asked with interest, anticipating the answer.

"No. We would have put a message on your desk."

She tried Susana's number twice. The short busy line told her that the phone seemed out of service. She would try once more before the end of the day. Resolving to shake away her apprehension, Alicia told herself that her thoughts were getting perilously paranoid once again.

A deadline was approaching; she had many pages to fill and limited time left. Moreover, the editors in Buenos Aires had no patience when the material was late at the paper's headquarters. Still, she got easily distracted by her thoughts while typing her pages.

Two hours later, she called Mary at work.

"Are you too busy now? Can I steal a few minutes from you?"

"Hey, you know that you can. What's on your mind?"

"I've been trying to call Susana, and her phone is not working. She hasn't called me as promised. I'm worried."

"Hum... Did you try her mom's?"

"Yes. Doesn't answer either."

"Well, try again." Mary seemed surprised by Alicia's uneasiness. "Is anything wrong?"

"No. Nothing is wrong. I'll try her mom again."

Mary offered to share a coffee on her way home. Alicia welcomed the suggestion with relief. She needed it.

"I'll be there around five-thirty. Will that be okay?"

"I have to be at the Chamber of Commerce at six-thirty."

"That gives us a few minutes for coffee then."

Alicia appreciated that Mary was close when she needed to talk. She was a loyal, trusted friend, and as soon as he arrived, they walked next door to a small sandwich and coffee shop. The smell of the tiny room was comforting. It had a nice feeling, reminiscent of a country kitchen, with only a few tables and a small counter. They ordered espressos and sat at one of the round, old-fashioned tables.

"I'm sure Susana is busy. Why are you so concerned? She doesn't call so often, does she? Most probably, she's busy after the weekend off."

"No, she does not call often, but this time she promised to, and I'm not sure if everything is okay with her... It's a long story." She tried to cut short the details. "Just don't mind my anxiety; I guess I am a control freak."

"That's not true. Susana will call you soon."

"I hope you're right. I got a bit jittery thinking about all the nasty rumors that go around. You know, with so many journalists that have vanished." Alicia thought of the green Falcon man, but she was not ready to tell Mary about it. Not yet.

"Don't worry. I'm pretty sure she'll call you soon."

Mary sounded just as Alicia did the day before, trying to comfort Jacinta over her brother's lack of news.

"I hope so." Then, after a pause, she added, "You might be right; maybe it's all in my mind. I'll call Sonia again. She should know about her daughter."

"That's a good idea." Mary patted Alicia's hand on the table and added, "Let me know as soon as you talk to her. Will you?"

"Sure. I will. Thank you, Mary, for being such a good friend and lending your shoulder for me to cry on."

"Never mind. You're free to use it whenever you want. You know that."

After the Chamber of Commerce interview, Alicia went back to the newsroom and tried to reach Susana. The line was always busy, still with the quick sound of an out-of-service line. The operator told her that some telephone lines were down because of the previous week's lousy *sudestada* weather, the wind, and rain from the Southeast, which always resulted in floods and interrupted services in Buenos Aires. Susana's mother still did not answer her phone. Susana should have arrived home yesterday afternoon, evening at the latest. The thought of her being at risk made Alicia's knees falter. Trying to calm down, she reminded herself that she did not know anything yet, and all these were simple panic attacks that she should control and go back to work. It's what Sergio would tell her too.

By Monday, Alicia was genuinely worried about Susana. What would she be doing so important that she wouldn't think of calling Alicia from another phone? When she dialed Sonia's number still, there was no answer. In the afternoon, Alicia called mutual friends. Viviana Ramirez was a financial analyst in a large company and had occasionally visited her in Bariloche. Viviana picked up her direct line. After a polite exchange of family and job news, Alicia mustered the courage to ask in the most natural tone she could convey, "By the way, Susana was visiting us not long ago. Did she tell you about it?

"Yes, in fact, she called me before leaving. We talked about meeting for dinner that same weekend, and she called me to cancel because she bought a ticket to Bariloche."

"Yes, she was here, and we had a great weekend. Did she call you after that?" Alicia tried to sound casual.

"No. I haven't heard anything. Did you call her at home?"

"The phone seems to be out of service."

"What else is new?" she chuckled. "Don't worry, if I get in touch with her, and it will be soon because we definitely will meet for dinner, I'll tell her to call you."

"Thanks, please, do." Then, she added as an afterthought: "I just found out she left a folder at home, and I wanted to know if it is important enough to mail it overnight to her. So write down my number and call me, please, and reverse the charge." The lie came out natural enough.

"Sure, don't worry about it. I'll call you as soon as I talk to her."

Alicia checked with another two common acquaintances, trying not to exaggerate her interest. Nobody had heard from Susana after the trip. Both friends promised to ask Susana to call her.

That evening Alicia conveyed her fears to Sergio. But as usual, if he thought that there was something suspicious, he didn't show it.

"Yes, it's odd. Then again, Susana may probably be busy with an assignment somewhere else and was unable or didn't have the time to call you. She used to go weeks without a word. Why would she change now?"

"Because she promised to call," Alicia answered impatiently.

"Well, you can always call her mom again. She'll tell you. Susana might well be at her parents' house, taking care of some family business or something."

"Yeah... That's what I'll do tomorrow. Sonia's phone kept on ringing, though. Weirdly, she does not answer her phone."

As soon as Alicia got to the newsroom the next day, she called Susana's mom again. After many unsuccessful attempts with unreliable long-distance lines, she finally was able to dial the complete number. Sonia picked up the phone right away.

"Hello?"

Alicia didn't expect her to answer so soon. "Hello, Sonia? It's Alicia here."

"Alicia? Hi, dear, how are you?" Sonia's voice sounded hushed. She was almost whispering. "I happen to be very busy now, dear; I cannot talk to you now. I'm busy, and I can't talk." She repeated herself, talking fast, as in a hurry. "I'll call you one of these days... I'm fine, though. Thanks for calling. Talk to you soon!"

She hung up the phone before Alicia had time to react. Sonia had shunned her on purpose, and her voice was tense. It was most unusual. Did she say she was busy? It sounded like an excuse and not a good one. Why wouldn't she take her call?

Stunned, she sat for a while at her desk, with her right hand on the receiver she had just put down, unable to do anything other than just look at it and try to figure out the short and odd conversation with her friend's mother meant.

It was not like Sonia. Something happened, either in her home or around her. Maybe she was not alone. She sounded tense and said she would call her back one of these days. She had never called before.

When she had a message for her, she would give it to Susana. Alicia even doubted Sonia had the newsroom number, unless she was trying to tell her something without spelling it out.

The disturbing conversation made Alicia panic. Her anxiety about Susana's whereabouts increased. Something was wrong, and she couldn't figure out what. Sonia had said she would call or contact her. But, when?

She dialed Sergio's office. He was momentarily away, and she left a message for him to call her as soon as he returned.

She had a meeting coming and an interview to do, but now she wanted to run away from the newsroom. What should she do now? She needed Sergio's input; she felt so upset that she could not think straight about what to do next.

Sergio did not call back, and she had to go to her appointment. It was hard to concentrate the rest of the afternoon on her interview with the Small Business Association's three executives. The issue was the upcoming tourist season. While the recorder registered their concerns, in her mind, she was playing over and over the brief telephone call with Sonia Machevsky, and each time her fears multiplied.

She made an effort to get back to the coming tourist season and the small business owners. Their economic worries seemed strangely remote to her now, and they shouldn't have been. Sergio still wasn't getting paid for home project jobs finished a couple of months ago, and her salary was meager despite the many weekly contributions she wrote for the paper. Her Sunday program was *ad-honorem*, for free, and the sponsor's ads hardly paid for the airtime. If the coming season was a failure and jobs were scarce, they couldn't afford their home fixed monthly expenses. Probably she would have to let Jacinta go, among other budget cuts.

When the interview was finally over, she drove home right away. When she got near the house, the snow was falling steadily, and her Citroën puffed slowly uphill, clutching on the patches of dry pavement as if complaining about the effort and the used tires.

She walked straight into the kitchen, where the warm aroma of roasted chicken welcomed her. She greeted Sergio with a kiss, and he followed her. Pablo was already sitting in the tall chair, ready for dinner.

"Wow, you look tired!" Sergio said. "Wash your hands."

Over dinner, Alicia poured out her feelings and told him every detail of the telephone conversation with Susana's mother early that afternoon.

He was puzzled and conceded that the situation was indeed strange. He knew Sonia. She was a calm person, not prone to exaggerations or theatrics. If she had been so mysterious, he agreed with Alicia that something was wrong.

After dinner, they put Pablo to sleep, and while Sergio read to him, Alicia prepared Turkish coffee, focusing on the preparation's ceremonial as an exercise in calming down. Then, he walked into the kitchen and affectionately put his arm on her shoulders.

"Are you done?"

He lit a cigarette for her, and she inhaled, enjoying every bit of it. She carried the coffee, and they strolled to the living room.

"Ah, I needed this. Thank you," Alicia said, picking up the cigarette. "You know, this thing will kill us. We should quit," she added.

They had quit smoking twice before but had lit a cigarette again a year later, and that was it; they were back smoking.

"The next time, it has to be the one. If I quit again, it will be forever, as the song goes," Sergio said. "I wouldn't quit now, though. At least not yet. I'm not ready."

"I know. Neither am I."

The late-night news was about to start, and Sergio was on his way to turn on the TV when two short and quick knocks at the door startled both of them. Alicia heard Sergio opening and greeting the visitors. Then, curious about who might have called so late, she peeked through the window and recognized the Fiat 600 parked in the driveway and rushed to the door to meet their friends.

"What's up? You guys look like there is something wrong. What is it?"

"Alicia, we don't know where to start..." Mary almost whispered, looking at them with apprehension. "Luis received a message for you today. Sounds unreal, but that's what happened...."

Luis took a deep breath and said, "I got this call, a long-distance call. A young man's voice asked me to identify myself. Then he demanded that I write down a message and give it to you as soon as possible. Then, he hung up. Here it is." Apologetically, he handed Alicia a folded paper.

Alicia reached for it eagerly. In Luis' familiar and clear printed handwriting, she read:

"Suzy has been missing for five days. I don't know where she is. Her phone is disconnected. Please, don't call me at home. Instead, call the number below and ask for Lita. She is a relative of mine. Leave your messages with her. Sonia."

Alicia read the words, and when she got to the last line, the letters started dancing in front of her eyes. At the bottom of the page, Luis had written a telephone number. She was sure of one thing: the message was from Sonia; nobody else called her friend Suzy. It was an intimate nickname between mother and daughter, and Sonia had used it on purpose. It was not a misapprehension she had. It was a nightmare, and it was truly happening. She had to make an effort to see straight and not to drop the paper.

Alicia quietly handed the note to Sergio and sat down, trying to grasp the real meaning. Her hand moved automatically to the pack of Marlboro Lights nearby, took out a cigarette, lit it, and inhaled deeply, not noticing that she had left a half-smoked one in the ashtray on the table. It felt warm and soothing. Mary and Luis were silent.

Sergio read the message, looked at her alarmed, and then at the others with an interrogative frown. Mary had tears in her eyes.

"Then, this explains the call..." he turned toward Alicia.

"What call?" Mary was anxious.

Alicia detailed every word of the call to Sonia.

Sergio poured coffee into the small cups, trying to do anything with his hands while taking turns with Alicia updating their friends. They listened in silence, sipping their coffee and looking at each other in disbelief.

"We never met Susana's mom." Mary shook her head, wondering. "How did she get Luis' work number?"

"Somehow, she got it," Luis said.

Alicia sat straight.

"Now, I remember. I gave Susana your number a long time ago, just if she couldn't reach me in the newsroom. She probably passed it on to her mom, just in case." Alicia was devastated, trying to think clearly, but she could only cry.

They stayed for another round of coffee, and the chat mainly was speculation around the same subject. The others made an effort to keep their calm. Nobody elaborated what everybody was thinking: Susana could be dead or worse, suffering physical torture, with no hope of returning.

Sergio vocalized part of the group's thoughts: "Let's be careful now. She is our friend, and if they kidnapped her, we might be at risk too. So keep your eyes open."

"None of us have done anything! I'm sure she hasn't either." There was anguish in Alicia's voice. "Oh, God, what are we going to do now?"

Mary turned to her, "I don't think we can do much."

Alicia felt suddenly ashamed for thinking about herself first, for being so afraid while her friend was in such peril. She felt hopeless, juggling fantastic ways to help her friend in her mind, none of them feasible. She reviewed every word of Sonia's message, trying to get a clue as to what to do. They stayed until late, considering the situation from different angles, their voices and ideas clouded by a palpable, discouraging certainty: there was very little they could do to help Susana. There were still too many unanswered questions.

That night, distraught and unable to sleep, Alicia counted over and over the lines of light that the windows' wood shades reflected on her bedroom's ceiling. She decided she had to do something and do it soon. It was more than a thought; it was a feeling with an almost physical root. The unbearable anguish that made her stomach a knot early in the evening became a tight hold, suffocating her chest until she realized that Susana was alone and, if she did not do anything for her friend, she could be lost. Alicia sat in bed, and suddenly her thoughts were clear. She knew what to do.

"Susana," she murmured, "I promise you, wherever you are, I will try to find you..." The knot broke in a well of tears, and she sobbed for a while.

Sergio woke up, turned around, and, noticing that she was crying, pulled her toward him. They stayed in a tight embrace until Alicia calmed down, and Sergio fell asleep again. Alicia kissed the arm that was holding her tenderly and closed her eyes. She knew what to do. She had a plan in mind and prayed in silence for its success.

VII

For several days, Alicia woke up during the night. The thought of Susana hurt or in pain made her jolt out of her light sleep, leave the bed and walk, shivering around the house with a physical feeling in her chest. Then, she would go back to bed, still nauseous, still crying, and fall asleep to wake up with a headache.

"I heard you last night. How are you feeling?" Sergio asked her the following morning after he saw her getting up from bed earlier than usual. Evidently, he did not know what to do or how to help her, and, in her pain, she appreciated his silent support.

Desperate to find out more through Sonia's relative in Buenos Aires, Alicia arrived at the newsroom the following morning earlier than usual. The extra makeup that she was wearing could not disguise her distraught face. Nevertheless, she invented a vague story about a fight with Sergio and an intense headache, which sounded reasonably authentic. Carlos Alvarez shook his head in understanding, and nobody else asked for any details, either.

"Carlos, I need to make a personal call to Buenos Aires from the conference room."

"Sure. Go ahead." He answered quickly, assuming it had to do with her marital fight. She took the crumpled piece of paper from her handbag and dialed the woman named Lita. Alicia had a list of questions written down that she would ask her if she had the opportunity. The telephone rang twice, and a woman answered.

"Yeah, I was waiting for your call," she said with a cagey voice that did not seem friendly. Maybe she was frightened about Susana's disappearance and not happy to get involved, and if this were the case, she wouldn't volunteer much information.

"I have a couple of questions."

"Yes."

"What happened to her?"

"A bunch of guys broke into her apartment, stayed there, and waited for her. When she walked in, there was a scuffle. The neighbors, an elderly couple, heard something and opened the doors across the hall. People in combat boots pushed them inside. The neighbors panicked and shut the door, so nobody was talking. Anyway, the armed men took her away. That much, I know. The apartment is a mess, Sonia says. They took everything of value, even her small safe box with jewelry. Everything else was knocked down or broken." The woman's voice died in a sob. There was silence for a few seconds.

"Was that on the day she got back from Bariloche?" Alicia asked.

"The same night. When she got back to Buenos Aires, it seems that she took a taxi from the bus stop. Other neighbors helped her with the baggage coming into the elevator. Later she went out to her parents' house. After dinner, she came back to her apartment, where they were waiting for her. That's what the neighbors and the concierge told Sonia."

"Have you found where she is now?" Alicia could barely talk, her voice choking and having difficulty breathing.

"No. We don't know. Sonia and Roberto are going around looking for help, pretty desperate."

"Please, tell Sonia I will be in contact with you again soon. Thank you very much for talking to me."

"I'll be careful, I promise," Alicia was firm. "Nobody will know I'm looking for her."

Sergio did not respond. He seemed busy, looking for something inside the refrigerator. Encouraged, she added, "The christening at Carla's *is* the perfect disguise."

"You don't even know what is going on there." He sounded annoyed and loud. "How come you are ready to go, just like that, to search for her? Can I ask where the heck you will start?"

He sounded irritated. Without taking anything from the fridge, he slammed the door and turned to Alicia. She hesitated. There was anger on his face; she seldom had seen him like this.

"Don't shout at me," she managed to say, concealing her

uneasiness.

"I'm not shouting." He lowered his voice.

Alicia and Sergio stood in the rectangular kitchen, glaring at each other across the aisle. Breakfast was on the small table, and the coffee in the green ceramic cups was getting cold, as were the toasts on the plate. Nearby, it was a bowl filled with the homemade blackberry jam that Alicia had canned at the end of summer. The argument began as soon as they were ready to sit at the table. They had been exchanging heated words for some time now.

Sergio seemed unusually furious, and his resistance surprised her. Still, she was determined not to flinch. Not on this matter.

As if looking for something to do, Sergio opened the fridge again and took out a pitcher of water.

"Alicia, please. Don't be naïve! I can't believe that I hear you say these things. You know they can follow you very easily if they want. They'll be on the lookout for anybody that has anything to do with her."

Sergio poured water into a glass and gulped half of it down. Then, with a nod, he offered the rest of it to her. Alicia smiled involuntarily. He was thoughtful even now when they were fighting, and she knew he acted without thinking, out of habit.

"Thanks." She sipped the water, realizing that her mouth was dry after the bitterness of the discussion. The water gave her strength. "I see your point, but you forget that Susana was vacationing, visiting us, in a tourist area, a National Park, for goodness sake, she was doing nothing wrong here! Not to mention I'm sure she did nothing wrong at all in Buenos Aires either. You know that. You know that they picked her up because of that son of a bitch, her ex-boyfriend. I was right not to trust him since the first day."

He did not reply. Alicia felt encouraged to go on. "It's only another trip to Buenos Aires. We go there often, and now there is the christening so I have a good reason to go. I'll be careful."

"You're acting like a child. Honestly, I don't want you to go."

"Want me? You don't want me to go? Since when do I follow your orders? This is too important for me, Sergio. I'll buy the ticket today, so be prepared."

He shook his head. "Susana has disappeared, and you haven't

even heard the details. Her mother seems terrified, and you're planning to go there, right into the eye of the storm. What do you want me to say?" Sergio's voice was angry again. Then, approaching her, he searched for the right words. "You know, I don't recognize you; honestly, you never acted like this before, so irresponsible."

"I never had my best friend disappear, taken away by a death squadron before! She's a sister to me. If I had a sister, I would do anything to help her. Wouldn't you?"

"You-can-not-help-her!! Don't you understand?" His breath was short and fast.

Alicia recoiled and then jumped at him. "Don't yell at me! Lower your voice. Pablo will hear you!"

"Ah, now you think of Pablo! He should have been your first concern!!"

Alicia looked at him with anger. She felt the tears welling in her eyes and made an effort to hold them; she did not want to cry. She felt his scheme to stop her had gone too far. He knew that touching her maternal feelings would hurt badly.

"How can you say that to me? That's unfair!" Her voice was choking. "You know how much I care for him! I'd never put him in danger; he'll be with you, safe. I have everything planned; the van from the daycare will pick him up every day, at whatever hour you ask, and drive him back at night if you want to."

He paced up and down the small room, then stopped, turning to her again:

"I'm not talking about who will drive him! What if something happens to you? What would we do? I love you, I love what we've worked so hard for, and I don't want to lose you!" His voice was almost quivering. He had finally been able to put into words what was at the core of his resistance to her plans, and she knew it. If she had been in his place, she would have done the same. So her anger dissolved into something close to guilt, although she did not want to let him weaken her decision.

"I'm sorry," she sighed, looking for a truce, moving a chair, and sitting next to the table. The coffee was cold by now, and she distractedly grabbed the toast, then the spread-knife and slowly, carefully, covered the golden surface of the bread with the bright purple jam.

He was still standing, waiting for an answer, buying time to compose himself.

Finally, she said, "I'm still going, Sergio." She looked at him. He nodded, but his eyes were saying something like, 'you must be crazy.' She went on: "I *have* to go. I want you to understand this clearly: I wouldn't be able to live with myself if I didn't do everything possible to help her. I know she is innocent. I'm positive she did not do anything wrong to deserve this... please, Sergio."

"That's not in question here. If Susana had done something wrong, whatever it may be, she would be detained and gone to jail and have her day in court in a normal world. Here it doesn't matter if you did something wrong or not." His face was red. Alicia had seen him like this only once before, and the sight made her nervous. She felt her legs shaking under the table. He continued: "These guys are criminals. They don't give a shit about the rules. Don't you understand?"

She did not answer. Her head was low; her eyes fixed absently on the toast she was holding.

After a few minutes, he nodded again, now forcing a grin that was almost an admission of defeat. His voice was calm: "I'll say this once more: I know for a fact that you'll end up doing whatever you want. I disagree with you, and I'm not going to do anything to help you with this crazy idea. It's unbelievable. You're willing to risk everything. You know that they might have you under surveillance." He walked out of the kitchen. She followed him, the whole toast still in her hand. Then, he walked toward the keychain holder on the wall and grabbed his car keys. "When those thugs threatened you on the road, you were scared, shaken, crying. Now, suddenly, all that is over, and you're playing Wonder Woman? I'm having a hard time relating to the person that lived with me all these years versus this new, irresponsible one you've become."

She was leaning against the open kitchen door, still in her pajamas and slippers, the toast in her hand, fruit jam on her fingers, her heart beating hard, and holding the tears that were pushing again. Something in Sergio's outburst hit the right chord, and she hesitated.

"Okay. You're right, but I've never been under this pressure before. I never thought something like this would come upon us, living in terror, afraid of talking, afraid of everything and everybody... I know I have to go to see if I can help her... find out more details. Somebody might know something."

He grabbed his down-filled jacket from the coat hanger that stood by the front door and turned to her. "That's a ridiculous idea. The worst stupidity I ever heard."

"You know me. I am not some risk-taking, idiotic woman. But I'm going, Sergio, no matter what," there was a determination in her low voice.

He opened the door. A chilly breeze blew in. The day was sunny and bright, one of those crisp, cold days of winter, with the sky's intense blue contrasting with the blinding white of the snow on the ground. Sergio slammed the door on his way out, and Alicia felt it as a slap in her face. She seldom saw him so enraged but could not be angry with him: she would have behaved much worse if she were in his place. He had a point, but she had a reason, a duty toward her friend.

Alicia turned around, got back to the kitchen, put the toast on the plate, wiped her fingers on a wet paper napkin, and mechanically took an empty mug from the top cabinet. Pouring hot coffee from the coffee maker, she felt comfortable with the brew's familiar morning smell.

There were many things to do in the coming days, minor chores she would have to finish before sitting on the long-distance bus to Buenos Aires. It was a pity that he wouldn't see her point. Her heart was still beating fast after the angry exchange with Sergio, but beyond the frustration of not getting him to understand her, she felt a liberating sense of purpose growing inside.

During all the years living in Bariloche, it had been easy to ignore reality. Now it had hit Alicia, and she felt compelled to fight back. In her humble and minuscule way, she needed to do something, not to surrender. Her decision to go to Buenos Aires gave her a new and empowering feeling. In her gut, she recognized that it was the right thing to do, not only for Susana but also for herself. No matter how slim the chances of making a difference were.

Pablo wailed from his bedroom, interrupting her thoughts. By the time Jacinta arrived, Alicia had taken care of him, and the child was in his playpen. The woman greeted him before starting her duties, and Alicia, immersed in her thoughts, did not notice anything unusual until later that morning.

"Is anything wrong, Jacinta? You don't look good today."

The young woman pulled a wrinkled, white cotton handkerchief from her skirt's pocket and blew her nose. She was crying, and her eyes were red and puffy. Alarmed, Alicia approached her and unsure what to do; she put a hand on her shoulder.

"Jacinta, I'm sorry, I didn't realize you were crying. What's wrong?"

"My brother is in the hospital, not in Malvinas. They told us that he's in a military hospital in Trelew. My mom is trying to find out how to get to him, find out more about how he is doing, and say they may move him to another city."

"I'm so sorry, Jacinta. When did you find out? Is it bad?"

Jacinta sobbed for a few minutes. Alicia pressed her hand on the bony shoulder.

"They told my mom. We don't know the details, but it seems he will lose his legs. At least one leg is gone, and the other may have to go too. A grenade, so they say. Mom is going crazy about it. We don't know what to do. They promised to let us know more details today. He was a POW until the English returned everybody. The wounded were the last."

"You shouldn't have come to work."

"I wanted to leave home. It's a mess. Everybody's crying and upset. I'm afraid for him, *señora*."

Jacinta sobbed again, and Alicia, in an impulse, put her arm around the woman's shoulders. Jacinta stood there, weeping, immobile, and almost embarrassed at being unexpectedly embraced. From up close, Jacinta smelled as if she had been in a camping site, a familiar mixture of food and firewood smoke that, for no reason that she could discern, provoked in Alicia a pang of compassion for her. The wood-burning cooking stove at Jacinta's home probably did not have a proper vent system, as it was so prevalent in her neighborhood's humble and precarious houses. The knot in her throat dissolved into tears that Alicia did not care to contain any longer. She was vulnerable for what she had heard, for Susana's fate, and for her domestic fight early in the morning. Alicia cried wholeheartedly. After a few minutes, she let Jacinta go, and both stood there, one in front of the other, sobbing in silence for a few minutes. Deeply hurt emotionally, they could not find words and shared their pain in silence for a while. Finally, Alicia managed to say:

"I'm so sorry, Jacinta. It's just such a miserable situation for everybody. I hope the news will be better later on. Hope it's all a misunderstanding about your brother, and he is not hurt so badly."

"Thank you, *señora*. Thank you very much." Jacinta was evidently surprised by the outburst of tears from Alicia and hesitated.

"I have a dear friend in distress," Alicia explained. "I'm worried about her too. That's why I'm so sad."

"Sorry to hear that."

"Let's pray for both your brother and my friend."

"Yes," Jacinta said. "I pray every day for him. But, I don't know if it helps."

"I'm sure it does," Alicia said with conviction, thinking that if God couldn't or wouldn't listen, or didn't exist, as she so often had suspected, at least the prayers would be a soothing, comforting exercise for them.

Before noon, Alicia told Jacinta to go home and take all the time needed to find out about her brother. Jacinta walked out after promising to keep her updated on what she knew about him by calling the newsroom and leaving messages. Her eyes still watery, Alicia looked at the now hunched figure, clad in the gray, worn-out, long stadium jacket strolling toward Bock Street, on her way to the down by the lakeside bus stop.

Alicia prepared a light lunch, and Sergio was back from work right before one o'clock. They did not exchange more than a few words at the table. Alicia finished the dishes and prepared the daycare bag while he busied himself with his work. She wondered if he had noticed her swollen eyes and if he cared at all. Pablo sensed the hostility between his parents and was weeping and moaning. Alicia felt mortified by Sergio's silence. On her way out, she said, "I will pick Pablo up at the daycare tonight, so don't worry."

"Fine," he answered, without lifting his head from his work. His coldness angered her. She felt miserable for not being able to convince him, but she was determined not to yield.

Holding Pablo in her arms, she slammed the door, and the child cried still louder. Alicia fastened him to the car seat and wiped his tears before sitting at the wheel. She had to stop the car two blocks ahead to soothe him, but he kept on weeping until she dropped him at the daycare.

On her way downtown, Alicia couldn't stop thinking about the reaction Sergio had to her plan. She expected to have some opposition from him, but this was way too much. Was she endangering herself by going alone to Buenos Aires? The strong drive overpowered every doubt she felt inside. She couldn't forgive Sergio's lack of trust in her ability to manage the situation. She was impulsive, yes, but not careless.

The only detail that worried her was the expenses she would incur. Sergio did not even mention the money, but Alicia was very conscious of it and ready to be as thrifty as needed. She had to tell Carlos Alvarez about the days she needed to take off, and the sooner he knew it, the better. The last thing she needed now was a job obstacle to her plans. Alicia went right to his office.

He welcomed her, as usual, with a smile, and she felt encouraged. Alvarez was in good spirits, scheduling the upcoming visit of the paper's owners. "I got an invitation to the baptism of my cousin's first child in Buenos Aires, and I would like to go, Carlos," she said convincingly. "I'm afraid I will need to take this coming week off. Hope it does not interfere too much with the scheduling."

He did not seem bothered: "I guess it's okay. You are not working on anything urgent, are you?"

"No. I'm not. I've been taking things day by day. I have no research going on now. Only a couple of items are on the back burner, but nothing will go out until late July."

"Good, good. Then, there's no problem. When are you leaving?"

"Well, either this coming weekend or Monday. I didn't get the tickets yet."

"You know how hard it's to get plane tickets. You should have bought them earlier."

"Well, I must say that I wasn't planning to go, but I feel I have to. Carla, my cousin, is so enthusiastic about this baptism, and she's my closest relative."

"Of course you have to go. Why weren't you planning to attend, if I may ask?"

"Because of money, for one," she ventured. "To tell you the truth, I'm not flying; I'm taking the bus."

"The bus?" He looked at her with surprise. "You'll waste two days on the road."

"Yeah, I know, but I can't afford a plane ticket, Carlos. We are a bit short of cash."

"Let me see..." He opened the top drawer of his desk and searched for something. "Let me see. I believe we have a couple of vouchers left from the last time we bartered ads with Austral... Yes, here, here they are. If you can find a seat, they are yours." He handed her two green airline tickets, the vouchers Austral, the domestic airline, usually gave in exchange for ad placements. Those tickets were used at the newsroom strictly on business trips, never for personal reasons, as far as Alicia knew. She was surprised; it was an unusual gesture from the frugal accountant.

"Are you sure I can have them?" Hesitant, she reached for the bright green pieces of paper that would take her to Buenos Aires in just three hours. "Carlos, I don't know what to say."

"You can say thank you if you want. And yes, you can have them." He winked at her. Alicia did not know what had surprised her more, his unexpected generosity or the fact that her pressing need was resolved as if by magic in less than five minutes.

"Oh, my goodness, Carlos, you are a lifesaver, believe me."

"I know. I know. Every penny counts. You deserve it, you work hard, and we are happy with you here."

His words moved Alicia, and maybe as a result of the emotional rollercoaster of that day, she felt her eyes watering: "Thank you. You don't know how important this is for me now."

He shrugged sheepishly. "Glad to help. Go ahead and enjoy your family in Buenos Aires."

Carla was elated at the news that her cousin was coming to her daughter's christening but was surprised that she wouldn't stay at her home. Alicia was calling from a public phone booth at the telephone company. After Carlos's generosity with the tickets, she did not want to impose o another long-distance call.

"Again, Carla, I have everything organized from here. The room is reserved. I told you I'd be working on interviews and typing notes."

"Doesn't matter, you still can stay with us; you know I have plenty of space here."

"I know, but I'm sure you'll be busy taking care of your relatives and the baby and getting everything ready. Think about it. Even if I'm there, we will not have much time to chat. So it is a perfect arrangement. I'll be close to you but out of sight, so you guys can go ahead with your chores."

"I *want* you to be in my sight."

"Look, you have to finish the Church's seminars with Veronica's Godparents and all that stuff that I cannot be of any help. Take it easy. If you need, I'll be close, only a few blocks away."

"Are you sure?"

"I'm positive. I'll have to do my own work too. It's only fair. That's why my boss is paying for the tickets and the hotel. Don't you think so?"

"If you put it that way... But I'm so disappointed not to have Sergio and Pablo here, with us too." She sounded truly sad. "I guess there's nothing I can do... What's the telephone number for the hotel you are staying at, again?"

Alicia sighed and read it to her. She was relieved that her lie was convincing, and her cousin hadn't suspected anything. How could she? There was no link between Carla's current family and Susana. Carla, on account of her younger age, was never a buddy of Alicia. She met Susana years ago, while Alicia was in high school, right after her parents died in a car accident, and she was already living at Carla's home. At that time, her cousin was only in junior high. Furthermore, she hadn't asked about Susana in years.

Carla insisted: "Then, when do you say the plane arrives?"

"At 7:30 pm."

"What about dinner after you arrive? I'll pick you up at the airport."

"It'll be late, don't worry. You have to take care of baby Veronica, and I guess your hubby will want to have some peace before his whole family gets here. So I'll take a taxi to the hotel and go to sleep. Tuesday morning, I have work to do, and after lunch, I'll go to see you," she lied again, but now she felt emboldened. From now on, she would have to get used to lying at a minute's notice. It was almost thrilling; she did not care at all.

Carla went on: "Okay. Dinner at home on Tuesday it is. You can come as early in the afternoon, as you want. We'll have *mate* tea and chat. I have nothing else to do that day except entertain you."

Alicia laughed: "Fine. It's a deal. Give my love to Aunt Marga and Guillermo. I'm looking forward to seeing both again."

"I'm calling Mom right now. She'll be so happy to know you're coming."

She hung up, still feeling a bit uneasy about the lies. She was truthful when she said it would be a pleasure to see Aunt Marga. She loved the woman, and she was the last connection to her mother Alicia had left in the world. She had not been truthful when talking about Guillermo, though. She had never liked him, and he seldom disguised his contempt for her. He was a rabid conservative in the process of climbing the ladder in his career. As such, he applauded heartily every democratic process break, benefiting from the insider knowledge that his job gave him ahead of time on the devaluations of the Peso against the Dollar. The exchange rate manipulations had impoverished many and brought a windfall on a few, such as Guillermo.

In her own words, her cousin had chosen a man with "strength of character, able to go ahead in life and make the best he could out of his circumstances." Alicia smiled when she remembered her answer to Carla's proud words. "Well, the ability to make money and win always is not the only attribute that makes a man worthy." Poor sweet and obedient Carla just ignored her cousin's comments.

Alicia convinced herself once again that it was her right not to tell them the truth about her trip. Her cousins would never understand what was important to her. Then also, having a family and loving them did not mean necessarily losing her identity. It was not easy, but the more she intensified her decision and plan to run and help her friend, the more self-assured she felt about managing the situation successfully.

With trembling knees, Alicia walked toward the door with the other passengers. In the small Bariloche airport waiting area, she had left little Pablo kicking and screaming in Sergio's arms. She felt torn between the need to go and her sense of duty toward her son. Sergio had kissed her on her cheek, still upset. He had not changed his mind, but ever the gentleman, he drove her to the airport and helped her with the small luggage.

"I shouldn't have to repeat it, but I will: be cautious. Please. Call me every day if you can."

There was affection in his voice, but she knew he was still upset. She did not blame him. In his place, she would have been panicky and probably not so gentle with him on departure.

The Austral Boeing 737 took off with a roar. It was a sunny and chilly afternoon. Alicia watched through the blurry window as the airport's small building with its familiar brick and log siding was left behind. The airplane went up on its way to Aeroparque, Buenos Aires's domestic airport, and swiftly reached the few and scattered cotton-white clouds over the bright white peaks of the lower mountains and the intensely dark blue surface of Lake Nahuel Huapi. The plane circled the lake, turned northeast toward the plains, and, leaving the hills behind, gained altitude atop Patagonia's vast plateau.

While preparing for the trip, she did not balk at her decision, but now she was not sure she should have acted against everybody else's advice. What if Sergio was right? It was too late for that now. She was not naïve and knew that some risk could be involved if she wasn't careful. Luis and Mary, whose opinion she always trusted, shared Sergio's doubts but could not convince her.

For the first time since she had known her, Mary had cried. It was the day before, and she hugged her without a word. Luis shook his head in disbelief and told her, feigning lightness, "Be a good girl in the big city, eh?" Alicia knew he did not approve, either. Pablo, sensing an imminent danger that he could not understand, acted up for three days, moaning and having unexpected tantrums. She had to do this, and now she needed to find back the confidence that evaporated after the departure.

After a polite nod, the man sitting next to her in the plane immersed his head in a book. As soon as the attendants finished the snack service, Alicia dozed off the last half of the three-hour flight. Then, finally, the voice from the cabin announcing the weather and time of arrival woke her up. They were about to land. Alicia rubbed her eyes and looked down through the small window.

There it was Buenos Aires. The evening was falling fast, and she could see the straight lights from the streets far down. An occasional dark area, a park maybe, or some bright-lit stadium broke the evenness of the view. It looked as if a bucket of shining crystals spilled on dark velvet. Farther to her right, a string of bright amber points, Avenida Costanera, followed the river margins. Beyond, it was the thick darkness of Rio de la Plata, carrying waters from the Brazilian jungle. A few lights from the sparse boats navigating the wide river titillated in the distance.

Buenos Aires centralized everything, particularly the country's transport system, modeled on the English companies that had owned Argentina's railroad lines until 1945: all points converged from the rest of the country to Buenos Aires. Seen on a map, it had the shape of a perfect semi-circle with the port of Buenos Aires as the central point, radiating to the West. The idea was to have a network of trains and interior roads to carry natural resources to the port and bring back products manufactured in Europe. Traffic between cities was irrelevant. By default, the airlines followed the same model: inter-city air travel was almost nonexistent, making routes expensive and contrived. Passengers were forced to commute to Buenos Aires and then go to their destiny, bringing hefty fees to the capital's Customs Office coffers.

The fierce independent regions fought these impositions in long and bloody battles in the 1800s. After the Independence from Spain, the provinces went to war against the Unitarian *porteño* government over policies that choked their prosperous colonial economies. Although the Provinces won and the system took the Federal denomination to all practical effects, the Unitarians established the rules. The economic grip of Buenos Aires over the rest of the country was still unquestionable. It was one of the several reasons the rest of the provinces had chronic financial woes and the capital's current colossal size compared with any other city in the country. Alicia sighed. Even though it was domineering, it was a great, unique metropolis.

They descended slowly to the chilly and humid air coming from the Rio de la Plata. The small transport bus drove the passengers from the plane's stairs to the new airport building, bursting with travelers walking in all directions. Alicia picked up her luggage from the carousel, enjoyed the busy hallways, and strolled leisurely to the taxi stop.

The loud sound of the telephone made Alicia jump, surprised. Then she realized where she was and grabbed the receiver.

The shrill voice on the line side said, "Good morning. It is seven o'clock."

The hotel was inexpensive, clean, and austere, not far from the intersection of Pueyrredón and Santa Fe Avenues, in Barrio Norte, close to Carla's apartment. It would fulfill Alicia's needs for the week. She mumbled a thank-you and hung up, collapsing back on the thin, thrifty foam-filled pillow.

Buenos Aires.

She had walked so many times through the streets of downtown, had ridden its small and speedy buses, had sat in its parks, sipped coffee on the many sidewalk cafés, loved and hated with a youthful passion. She had enjoyed the elegant Barrio Norte with its avenues and expensive boutiques as much as she had loved the old and decrepit beauty of Calle Lima with its condemned nineteen-century buildings. With her old Konica, she had shot the sooty, regal facades in black and white before the demolition that gave way to the two- blocks-wide Avenida 9 de Julio. In this city, Alicia delighted with the French New Wave foreign films in small movie theaters, endlessly analyzed over coffee with friends until dawn, browsed many magical and inaccessible editions in its mom-and-pop bookstores. This city had embraced her with the warmth and tenderness of a friend. It was an odd emotional support that emerged from bricks and cement, cobblestone, and tree-lined streets that Alicia felt almost physically every time she returned.

The night before, the taxi from the airport had left her at the hotel, and she registered hurriedly, carrying the two small suitcases to her room. She decided to dine downstairs in a small Italian restaurant across the street. It only had two empty tables. One could eat anywhere until well past midnight in Buenos Aires, and nobody would think it was odd. Sitting next to the window dressed with red-checkered curtains, with the view of the heavy traffic outside, she ordered fresh pasta and slowly savored the dish as well as her memories of the city, embellished by the years.

She had watched with friends the sun coming up across the expanse of Rio de la Plata while munching brown-bag croissants and coffee for breakfast. With Susana and their friends, she had shivered on their light evening clothes more than once, laughing in the chilly air of early mornings, sitting on the cold concrete benches of the old Costanera Sur, for the sheer pleasure of witnessing daybreak and being together.

It was the early 70's, and she was free, intense, and bold, quite a different creature than this one. Also, her city was other at the time. Now, most old independent bookstores were gone and replaced with disheveled outlets selling cheap imports, LP records, and cassettes. Gleaming, colorful neon-lit movie rental stores and pizza chains had sprouted over the formerly chic downtown streets. Only a few artsy movie theaters survived; strict censorship cut access to many artistic and intellectual currents. International tourists were gone. The imposed one-to-one parity of the American Dollar's currency was an incentive to travel abroad, so Brazil and Miami were cheaper and seemed more interesting than any local destination.

Florida Street, the cosmopolitan walking artery that a decade earlier bloomed with locally manufactured and fashionable products for tourism, now languished. Many of its stores had closed, and second-rate ones thrived. Trashy and cheap imports from Asian countries piled up in poorly kept windows. Alicia felt goosebumps remembering what Susana had told her about the death and torture happening right here. Her city seemed to be physically suffering the onslaught, and Alicia felt still more identified with it.

Over a dessert of *flan con dulce de leche,* she had even considered the possibility of a brief walk toward Avenida Santa Fe, but she was exhausted. Back in her room, she collapsed on the bed and grudgingly called Carla as promised. For the first time in days, she fell asleep right away and did not wake up until the telephone rang the following day.

She now glimpsed through the window that it would be a bright day. Planning her next move, she took a shower, dressed comfortably, and then stepped out of the hotel, eager to meet her city, a cherished friend again. The street was busy with pedestrians and vehicles.

She breathed the humid and familiar air from the river, walking firmly on the old, aged, and uneven, dear sidewalks.

VIII

The traffic was frantic, as usual, and after the long hiatus in the quiet, provincial streets of Bariloche, the sounds, smells, and speed of the wave of cars racing through the broad avenues were a breathtaking experience for her. Nevertheless, Alicia smiled pleased, standing in line with other passengers at the *colectivo* 60's bus stop on Avenida Callao, trying not to miss anything around her.

The popular "60" had the longest route of any *colectivo* or small bus line, and it ran from Plaza Constitución, one of the two commuting train terminals in the city, right north, to the delta of the Parana River, in the lush and green borough of El Tigre.

Alicia got on the bus and paid for the ticket. Immediately she took her change from the driver, who quickly and efficiently managed to hold the steering wheel with one hand while displaying between his fingers pesos bills sorted by value in a fan. The right hand dispensed the ticket, received the cash, and gave the change. Alicia had always marveled at the skill needed to do so many tasks simultaneously, as the maneuver involved driving and checking the traffic around as well. In her experience and the passenger's consensus, those young men were mainly moody, tense characters. But amazingly, the collisions and accidents were scarce considering the risks involved.

She sat in one of the few available seats; the trip to Plaza Italia would be short. There she was to meet Susana's mother. During the morning, after several phone calls to Lita from public phone booths, she had arranged to meet Sonia, who did not want Alicia to come to her home for security reasons. So it would have to be a furtive afternoon encounter at two-thirty in the Botanic Gardens, a public park in the neighborhood of Palermo that she had not visited since childhood.

Alicia got off the bus, strolled to the corner, and waited for the pedestrian light to cross the wide Avenida Las Heras. Palermo was a pleasant locale, home to several parks and wide-open spaces, wealthy households, and lately, ritzy apartment towers. It was only two-fifteen, so the extra time allowed her to enjoy the familiar places.

The Botanic Garden ground was just across the avenue from where she stood. Farther north, she could see the sturdy and understated entrance to the Sociedad Rural, where the proud *estancieros*, or cattle ranchers, showed and auctioned their best pure breed animals once a year. It was a renowned month-long fair, and she even got tickets more than once, on sunny Sundays, to visit the event with her friends, enjoy the traditional foods and hear more about the way of life in the vast cattle ranches, mostly placed on the fertile Pampa. A form of life that had defined the country's customs and traditions for over a century, elevating the rancher life and power to almost aristocratic status and dignifying everything that had to do with the possession of green, fertile lands and its maintenance.

Alicia sauntered, letting the other pedestrians pass her by. It was a good feeling to be at ease, not dreading that somebody would be following or checking on her. Sonia acted so secretively. Was she being followed? Maybe not, but it was natural that the whole family would be terrified after Susana's disappearance.

Looking over her shoulder, she crossed the imposing iron gates of the Botanic and walked a hundred yards by the shady and lonely park toward her right, as Lita had instructed. A woman clad in a wool hat and a grey coat came out from a side path to meet her. They stood briefly in front of each other, assessing their identities. Then, as soon as Alicia recognized Sonia, she walked briskly toward her. They looked at each other for a moment, and Sonia, shaking her head, opened her arms.

"Alicia, *hija*...."

Alicia ran to her embrace, and they stood there, weeping in silence for a while. Then, finally, Sonia let her go, firmly guiding her by the arm.

"C'mon, let's walk toward that wall over there. It's quiet, and at this time of the day, nobody comes through here. Office workers are back at their desks. Maybe a few children from schools, that's all." Her voice was confident and firm as Alicia remembered her. Not at all like the voice of the terrified woman that had answered the phone days ago.

They sat on a wooden bench, and soon a few pigeons flew around, waiting for food. Alicia did not know what to say and remained silent, overwhelmed with emotion.

"You know, it's pretty dangerous for you to be around us now. I mean, around the relatives of those who disappeared." Sonia was holding one of Alicia's hands, and her touch was warm and soft. Alicia's small and bony fingers felt comfortable in those firm and reliable hands that reminded her of her mother's. Sonia's eyes were red, and then Alicia realized that she looked old, wrinkled, exhausted. Yet, there were evident traces of her daughter's looks in her face; the bony cheeks, the still youthful mouth, the color of her eyes. She hadn't seen her for at least a year, but Susana's mother had aged remarkably, and she was sure that it all had happened in the last few weeks.

"How is Don Roberto doing?" Alicia always called Susana's father with the old, respectful *don* before his name. Twelve years older than Sonia, Roberto Machevsky was at sixty-five, an energetic, hardworking man that had retired only ten months earlier and was still waiting for his first check doing small part-time jobs. Alicia knew he would be devastated by Susana's disappearance.

"He had a mild stroke, and we had to rush him to the hospital, but now he is doing fine, back at home."

"I'm so sorry to hear that. You know how I love him. I hope he recovers soon."

"I know. It was hell; I had to take care of him while I was going around searching for Susana. Lita was a great help to us. I don't know what I would have done without her. Anyway, he is doing better, and it was only a mild stroke. He recovered well. He has been stricken by what happened, but we are going to be okay. You see, we have to focus on finding Suzy now."

They talked at length, mainly about how they kidnapped Susana and the people Sonia had contacted. Unfortunately, there were only a few clues to follow, and she had started knocking on doors early on with no results. Alicia had many questions about Susana, for which the mother did not have answers. Sonia pointedly asked many details of the last days she spent in Bariloche. Alicia gladly talked about it, mostly in tears, remembering how confident her friend had left for Buenos Aires. She also told her about their worries of being followed, which were never confirmed. Alicia pulled out from her purse an envelope with the pictures she took in Bariloche and said, "I thought you might want to have these."

Sonia slowly went through every picture, pointedly, crying quietly, and Alicia found it hard to watch her. So she stood up and slowly circled the bench, stretching her legs, while the pigeons fluttered about giving way as she walked. When Sonia secured the envelope in her handbag, Alicia returned next to her.

"Thank you, dear. I know how much you love her. Thanks for coming here, for your words, for your help. I'm just starting to understand what's happening. I'm learning where to go. I'm positive we will find her. and she will be back with us."

"Of course, Sonia, I'm sure of that. We will find her. She's not alone." Then, shaking her head, she added, "If I only knew what to do to help her. Tell me about you. You said earlier that you went to the police department and other offices."

"It won't be easy. First, we went crazy. We went everywhere, police, lawyers, and synagogue, anybody that could help us. To make a long story short, nobody would listen. One police detective even told me that my story could not be true because those disappearances were no longer happening in this country. He said that those things might have happened before, while the "special forces" were subduing the guerrilla, but not now. It wasn't happening any longer. That she most probably had eloped or run away for some reason I did not know. Or joined a guerrilla group and gone underground."

"Is that so? It's incredible."

"He even said something about parents that would not teach their children to abide by the law. I was so disgusted and insulted."

"Amazing. Did you present a habeas-corpus to the judge?"

"We sure did. That was the first thing, but the lawyer from the human rights group helping us told me not to expect miracles. The judges have to ask the military for information about the people kidnapped. Still, because the response from the Armed Forces Command is always that they do not have anybody in custody, the tribunals end up refusing to take the requests for habeas-corpus in."

"They don't have anybody in custody?"

"They have them somewhere, of course. But because the judges are friends of the military, there is no hope," she paused briefly to wipe her tears. "The newspapers don't write anything about it. These murderers keep denying any crimes are happening. The tactic of denying and lying has worked well for them. Still, the families should unite and fight back. I have joined a group of mothers, and we meet in Plaza de Mayo."

"I was about to ask you. I have heard many rumors about the mothers. Are they still working? We don't hear anything down there. At home, it's almost impossible to get news."

"I know. The Mothers are well organized, and they have helped me with all types of support and contact with human rights organizations. They are respected all over the world. Except here. We go every Thursday to walk, to demand our children's freedom."

"Sonia," Alicia sighed, choked with emotion, "You are brave. Some of the Mothers have been kidnapped and killed."

"It's not bravery. It's desperation. Who cares what they might do to me if I can help my daughter? I would give up my life a hundred times if I could if that brought her back safe. So we are not going to stop walking and demanding until they free them safe and sound."

They sat in silence for a few minutes, watching the few pedestrians strolling under the poplar and cypress trees on the central pathway.

"Have you tried your rabbi? Maybe the religious authorities can do something."

"Yes," she sighed. "They are afraid and do not want to get involved. They say that they will see what they can do, but they don't do much. The Catholic Church here doesn't do anything either. The military is killing priests, who minister to the poor, and the Church does not respond to our pleas. Either they are afraid or are friends with the government. I don't know."

"What an uphill battle, Sonia. Don't lose hope. I'm sure something will happen, and things will change," Alicia said, hating herself for not being able to muster more than formulaic sentences before a mother's grief. "This must be so hard on you, Sonia. Are you sure you want to keep talking about this?"

Sonia managed to smile briefly. "Dear, do you think there is anything else on my mind lately? I need to talk. Sometimes I think my head will explode, and my chest will burst into pieces. The worst part is not knowing what happened. It is killing us."

"Yes, I know." It was precisely Alicia's feelings, and she held her arm, placing her head on Sonia's strong shoulder. Then, after a few minutes, Sonia said, "I hope you're right. As long as she is alive," she said, bursting again into tears. It was painful for Alicia to watch her, and she did not say a word until she calmed down.

Sonia composed herself. She put her wet handkerchief in the handbag and took a clean one, and forced a smile, motioning her head toward a small pile of fresh, ironed cotton handkerchiefs.

"Lately, I travel with plenty of extra ones. I cry all the time, all over the city."

Alicia nodded in silence. Sonia stood up, and Alicia followed her. She strolled as if saddled with a heavy weight on her shoulders. Alicia took her by the arm, and they walked toward the park exit.

"Along with the things I gathered at Susana's apartment and took home, there is a navy blue duffel bag with your initials embroidered inside. I don't know why they did not take it too."

Alicia felt as if somebody was pushing on her chest.

"It's mine," she sobbed. "I lent it to her at home, to carry chocolates and gifts..."

Sonia patted her arm. "I know, dear. She brought them home that same day when she came to see us. I'll return it to you when we meet next."

"That's fine." They walked for a few minutes in silence.

Sonia sighed and said, "Alicia, I want you to come on Thursday to Plaza de Mayo. I don't want you to approach us. Just take a book or a magazine and sit close by the pyramid, as close as possible. I want you to witness a march. It will be good to have you near. Afterward, don't talk to me or wait for me. Just leave. We will meet an hour after the march breaks at the cafe on the corner of Rivadavia and Pasco. You can take the subway across the street to get there."

Alicia was overwhelmed by emotion. "Sure I will, Sonia. I'll be honored to be close to the march, close to you."

After she helped Sonia to the bus that would take her home, Alicia took a taxi to Carla's. While the expert and fearless driver zigzagged his way through the fast and noisy traffic, she recalled her encounter with Sonia. She never realized how similar both women were. Susana had her mom's keen mind, the quick analytical wit that Alicia enjoyed so much. She wished she could help Sonia to get her daughter back home safely.

The car rushed through the stately streets of Palermo toward Barrio Norte, avoiding the busy avenues. Once in the foyer of the elegant building, Alicia rang the apartment number. She answered almost instantly from the receiver on the wall. Then, looking at the camera in the ceiling, Alicia waved her hand.

"It's me!"

"Come in. Come in."

Alicia pushed the heavy glass door and entered the lobby. Crossing the plush seating area decorated with an oversized crystal lamp in the center, she took the elevator. Carla's apartment was an ample semi-floor, half of the third story of the expensive building. Her cousin had mentioned several times that she had a big surprise. Alicia wondered what it would be now. It was either another car or a trip to an exotic place. Guillermo was not thrifty and enjoyed an expensive lifestyle that was out of the reach of most people. Carla took pleasure in their newfound economic status and was thrilled at Guillermo's success, a man she met when he was an ambitious but penniless Economic Sciences student, dreaming big. She had quit her job and was absorbed mainly by a busy social schedule and tennis or canasta games at the exclusive club where they belonged. Alicia was curious to see how the arrival of baby Veronica might have changed her.

As it would an older sister, Alicia enjoyed the fact that her cousin was successful, that she had left behind the instability of the lower middle class where she was raised and now was reaching high. Carla was her closest relative, and she had refused for a long time to judge her lifestyle. But now, Alicia had mixed feelings about Guillermo's swift fortune at the financial enterprises. She had tried to remain neutral, but it was hard to ignore their callousness about the damage the so-called *Patria financiera,* the new upper social class to which they openly belonged, was doing to the country with its financial scams.

The elevator got to the third floor, and when she stepped out, her cousin was waiting in the hall, approaching her with open arms and a wide smile.

The subject of the evening was the surprise they had for her. They were moving soon to an entire floor they had just bought in an elegant new building with full balconies opening to Avenida Libertador across the Bosque de Palermo. It was one of the most expensive locations in town; they were delighted as children with a new toy, and Alicia tried to celebrate with them. At some point in the evening, Alicia felt guilty for being so judgmental. After all, seeing Carla happy made her happy too, because she loved her dearly. She felt proud looking at Carla managing her new maternal status with ease, and Veronica was a beautiful, healthy, and smiling six-month-old baby.

Carla insisted, so Alicia called Sergio from their apartment. He seemed glad and surprised to hear her at such an unexpected hour. They had a brief conversation. He updated her quickly: Pablo had been acting up in the evenings before going to bed, and now and then, he had a tantrum. Otherwise, everything was fine.

Since her arrival in Buenos Aires, Sergio had been polite but very curt, so she knew he was still upset with her. He had mentioned that Jacinta left a note in his letterbox at the office saying that her brother was not doing well, and after the double amputation, he was running a severe infection. Other than that, Bariloche was doing fine, the tourist season seemed good for business, and the snow was copious this year. They said goodbye, just courteously. His coldness hurt her, but she feigned not to notice.

After a carefully planned dinner, Guillermo drove her to the hotel. She went straight to bed, exhausted but proud of being able to manage a polite conversation all evening.

It was almost ten o'clock, but she decided to try Viviana Ramirez's home number. She wanted to find out if Susana's old friends had heard anything new that could help her. Viviana agreed to meet for lunch. Unfortunately, Susana's name did not come up, so she would have to wait until tomorrow to find out if her friend knew or heard anything new.

At twelve-thirty the next day, Alicia entered the spacious lobby of the building where Viviana worked. It was a well-known financial institution, and she was a middle manager with a bright future. She was planning to get married next year to a promising corporate lawyer, and she was, no doubt, the most successful member of the old gang of friends.

"You look great as always," Alicia said sincerely. Viviana's clothes and make-up were impeccable. She wore a business suit, her long red hair was as impressive as ever, and the freckles that had tortured her throughout all her teenage years were almost invisible.

"Thank you. You look fine yourself," Viviana answered courteously.

"Don't say that. I know you mean to be polite. I look awful."

"Not awful, not at all. Where did you get that? You look a bit tired, that's all."

They decided to have a brief lunch next door, in a crowded and noisy small cafeteria. Alicia did not mind. She needed to know, and she asked Viviana directly if she had heard of Susana. Her surprised look told her she did not know or suspect anything.

"Why?" Her expression changed. Her worried eyes said how alarmed she was to find out that Alicia was still looking for Susana. "Is anything wrong with her? You haven't heard from her since we last talked?"

"To tell you the truth, no," Alicia admitted.

Viviana's body language and voice showed how uncomfortable she was about what she was hearing. "I hope she's okay."

Alicia wanted to say that no, that their friend was not okay, and she did not know what to do or where to go to find out what happened but breathing deeply, she uttered a few sentences of excuses. However, Viviana did not buy her speech.

"Oh my gosh, Susana is in trouble. Isn't she?" She whispered with urgency, almost upset. Alicia nodded.

"I'm here for only five days, on a work assignment that doesn't give me much free time," she explained. "Nobody answers her phone or her mother's, so I figured I'd ask you if you have heard anything lately." She did not mention her meeting with Sonia or the kidnapping. She did not have the nerve to tell her, at least not yet.

After an uncomfortable silence, they changed the subject, and for a while, they both feigned interest in other matters. Lunch was almost over when Viviana, looking at Alicia in the eye, told her, talking very fast now, and in a low voice:

"I hope you don't take this the wrong way, Alicia, but I have to be honest with you. I don't know what has happened to Susana, and I sincerely hope she is fine, but if she's been jailed, or taken away, as may have happened to people involved in activities against the government, *I don't even want to know about it.* I don't want to be connected in any way to this. So I will deny that we ever spoke about it, and I hope she does not call me again. I have worked hard to get where I am, and I'm not going to risk my job and my future because a friend of mine has gone nuts and got involved in something."

Alicia was astounded, looking at Viviana's bright and cold eyes, could not believe what she was hearing. She had anticipated some denial or fear from her, but never this lecture, delivered in such a scolding way. She was a good friend of Susana, or so she thought.

"You are frightened," Alicia said, holding her stare. "I would say panicky."

Viviana shifted uncomfortably in her chair.

"I'm not." Lowering her eyes, she opened her purse and took out some money to leave as a tip on the table. She looked back at Alicia.

"Yes, you are scared to death, and I am too. We all are."

Viviana almost nodded while considering Alicia's words.

"To tell you the truth, I do not like this government either, but I'm not going around broadcasting it everywhere. I always thought Susana would end up messing up."

"Since when it's a crime to say that the government is a disaster? They work for us; we pay their hefty salaries. They are all our employees, after all." Alicia had many words at the tip of her tongue but decided not to say anything else. It wouldn't do any good, and if Viviana had taken sides on this issue, she wouldn't be able to change her views. Furthermore, Alicia did not have the strength to try it, and she felt wounded by Viviana's harsh words.

"Forget we talked today, please," Viviana stood up. "Nothing personal, mind you. I just don't want to have anything to do with this situation. I never thought Susana would be involved in something illegal."

"She is not involved in anything, and...." Alicia also stood up, answering rather loudly.

"Shh..." Viviana stopped her, alarmed. "Let's go out."

They left the cafeteria and walked back toward the big building.

"Where did you get the idea that she's involved in anything? Don't you know her?" Alicia asked, hurt. "You are her friend, aren't you?"

"I am. But now I see that all Susana's complaining about the government was more than words. She was always... how can I put it...." Viviana hesitated and then said in a hurried voice: "It's better if we just leave it, as it is, Alicia. What's the point? I don't want to get involved."

"Don't worry. You are not. I'm not involved either, but you're right. what's the point of talking any longer?"

They were back at the door of the large building.

"Honest, Alicia, I'm happy to have seen you again. Take care."

"Yeah. Same here. Glad to see you again."

After Viviana entered the building, Alicia turned around and walked away from the imposing front doors by the ample curve full of pedestrians. She paced fast, her head up while breathing deeply to calm down and hold back the tears.

IX

Alicia walked away from Viviana, deeply hurt, and went right back to the hotel to rethink what to do next. She had to plan carefully. Time was running short, and the information she had obtained so far was less than her lower expectations when she scheduled the trip. Alicia had mistakenly pictured the results of her investigation as immediate and valuable. So far, she had not been able to help Sonia with her daughter other than providing moral support. Worse, she had difficulties tracing Susana's steps and mapping out what happened.

The next name on the list was Mariano Ruiz. If it failed with Mariano, only one other friend was left to be comfortable calling, and he was the end of the list for her.

It took her a while to recover from Viviana's scolding words. After several calls and three cigarettes, she finally got hold of Mariano at the architectural firm where he worked. He sounded happy to hear from her, and when she settled for a drink after work instead of the dinner he suggested, he accepted gladly.

"In fact, it's good that you called me today. It's a rather quiet afternoon here. We can meet at five-thirty if you want. Is Sergio with you?"

He asked about Pablo, and after a brief exchange, Alicia hung up full of hopes. It could be that Mariano had heard something. He was part of the crowd who used to go out with Susana while still going out with Gustavo Spinetti. Mariano met Gustavo socially, so maybe he could shed some light on Alicia's suspicions about the elusive man. Otherwise, she would have to go back to Bariloche by the end of the week empty-handed. That perspective was too grim to think about it.

Mariano was already seated at a table when she stepped inside the old and traditional Café Tortoni, on Avenida de Mayo, not far from where she would go tomorrow to see Sonia walk with the mothers. He waved to her from afar.

He was already sipping a whiskey on the rocks and seemed sincerely happy to see her. She ordered the same, and they got right to the point. Mariano did not mince words:

"I think I know why you are here." He said with what she thought was a meaningful look.

"Do you?" He had caught her by surprise.

"It's Susana, isn't she?"

"Yeah." She was cautious. Mariano seemed so sure and laid-back about it, and Alicia was not comfortable giving away anything yet.

"Don't worry. You're in safe hands with me, Alicia. We think we know what happened to her, and I think we figured out why it happened too. We hope to help her from this site."

Alicia was taken aback, and it showed. Her heart was beating hard, and she managed to ask, "We? You said we. Who are we?"

He smiled apologetically. "Please forgive me. I should have been more specific to you. My friends don't have anything to do with any political group. I understand your distrust. Let me explain: My friends and I learned about Susana's disappearance through the grapevine, as they say, and we're trying to find out where they took her."

"How? How would you find that out?" Alicia was still uncomfortable with his casual tone after seeing Viviana cringe as soon as she suspected what was going on.

"We'll try several ways. As I said before, we learned that she was kidnapped." Mariano seemed to realize only then how much Alicia didn't know and quickly added, "I want you to know, before anything else, that I happen to attend a parish. Our priest is indefatigable, helping many people in the *villas miseria,* the slums. He has put his life at risk, I know, but you should see how many good-hearted people have shifted to his parish and now come to his mass. This small church is always full on Sundays. Catholic Charities has many ways to help. Our priest is a hands-on worker for Jesus."

"I don't understand the connection with Susana." Alicia was sure her friend would not be involved with a Catholic church, no matter what. She was a non-practicing Jew, and she wouldn't join a religious group of another faith either. Furthermore, Alicia felt a little uncomfortable with Mariano's open display of religious belief.

He continued, while looking at her, weighing her reaction: "Susana was working with a group of young lawyers that take *ad-honorem* individual cases of wrongful termination, job accidents, and the likes. She volunteered for them. That's a red flag nowadays."

"Was she?" Alicia was surprised. What else had Susana kept from her? Then, hurt at her friend's lack of trust and trying to hide her frustration, she reached for her handbag and took out the Jockey Club Lights. She needed a smoke and a good sip of whiskey.

He answered, "Yes, she is. She and a journalist co-worker of hers are volunteering. She may not have mentioned it to you. They type legal documents after hours. She's a hard worker."

He ordered another drink, accepted a cigarette from Alicia, and lit both.

Alicia was silent, watching the room while thinking. Why hadn't Susana been completely honest with her in Bariloche? She felt angry with her for risking her life. Finally, she looked back at him.

He managed a sad smile: "Alicia, I can see it in your eyes. You shouldn't judge her. She is doing what her conscience tells her to do. We all are. Sometimes you cannot turn your back on people in need." He paused, wondering if he had gone too far. Alicia watched him and thought about the school in Barrio Alto, the Mapuche children, and the letter she had sent to the Mayor. How could she pass judgment on anybody else?

"I know," she nodded.

Encouraged by her words, he ventured, "I'm a Christian. I was taught to love and respect humanity. Those guys that torture people go to church and talk about Christian values. How can they do what they are doing to a fellow human, no matter what? How can they go back to their churches and to their homes? I cannot think of doing that to an animal, let alone to a human being."

Alicia felt moved. Mariano was preachy, but he believed it sincerely; his voice denoted it. She was grateful to meet somebody who showed piety after her encounter with Viviana and the remarks that she could expect from her relatives.

"I totally agree." Then, trying to get the subject back to Susana, she added, "Why exactly do you think she was taken away?"

"Exactly? Who knows? First, I thought they decided to crack the lawyer's group, but none of them had disappeared, as far as I know, so there has to be another reason. She was discreet. Somebody else is involved here."

"What about Gustavo Spinetti?" She was cautious. "Do you remember him?"

He seemed to be waiting for the question. He nodded immediately: "Yeah. It's more likely that the thing comes from his side. He had been in hiding for long now. Somehow they may have found something about their old relationship."

"Do you know if he contacted her at all lately?"

"No. I don't think so. But, then again, Susana could have kept it to herself."

"Yes, she could." Alicia kept silent. Susana could have been lying to her in Bariloche when she said she did not hear from him lately. But why? Why would she do that? Alicia had thought she knew her friend well. Now she was not sure about it.

"Let's not prejudge," he said dryly. "The guy was in deep shit since a long time ago, and most probably he was taken away and gave Susana's name under torture, or they took his belongings and, her name was in his address book, or a piece of paper, whatever. That, and the fact that she was helping this group of lawyers is enough evidence against her."

"Mariano, I'm worried about her. Very worried."

"I know. I am too. I have contacts; they may be able to find out where she is. We may even find out how she is doing."

"Oh, my goodness. Will you let me know as soon as possible, please, if you hear anything?" She took a pen from her handbag and wrote quickly on a paper napkin. "This is the hotel number in Buenos Aires, and this is my work number in Bariloche. Just leave a message, and I will call you back. Leave your name and number, and I'll call you from a payphone."

"I will, I promise. But please, don't lose hope. She may come out soon. Who knows? Not many have been taken away lately. The worst was back in the early years of the Junta. So we hear of few people kidnapped lately."

"Yes, but by the same token, she may not be let go soon, and the thought makes me crazy." Then she asked, "Do you know how to reach Sonia, Susana's mom?"

He smiled. "Don't worry. We'll find her and let Sonia know if we learn anything."

"How can I thank you? And please, Mariano, be careful."

He made a dismissive gesture with his hand. "I'm very cautious. I know I am sometimes followed, but I don't think I'm important enough. I'm a rather boring person with a boring and methodical life."

"I mean, there is such a confabulation of silence about these things... it's a nightmare."

"Yes. It has to be over soon."

"That's what Susana said once. I wish you were right."

"You heard that popular saying, *every time it rained, it stopped*? It has to stop, and it will."

He walked her to the subway station nearby, and Alicia took the train A to Plaza Primera Junta, the end of the line, where after buying a light dessert for dinner in a coffee shop across the street, she would catch a bus to Flores, a ten-minute ride, to her aunt's home. A few days ago, on her arrival, Alicia had called Aunt Marga to say hello, and she had been invited to dinner today.

"So we can have a private get-together before the fuss of the celebrations at Carla's." Was she reading a trace of sarcasm in her voice? In Aunt Marga's opinion, she recalled, Guillermo was not the best candidate to marry her daughter. Alicia knew that she resented the way he controlled Carla in almost every aspect of her life.

She accepted the invitation gladly, looking forward to this evening. She loved Flores, the old neighborhood where she spent her early childhood back when her parents were still alive. She was sure her aunt would cook one of her favorite dishes; it was an affectionate gesture toward her that started long ago when she moved out to live near the college's campus and came to visit on Sundays and holidays.

After her parents' sudden death, Aunt Marga and Uncle Emilio received Alicia at their home with open arms. They were a soft-spoken couple, down-to-earth and uncomplicated. They had married in the early '50s, bought the large apartment on the eighth floor of a stately ten-story building right off Nazca and Rivadavia Avenues. They spent all their married life there. Benefited by the general post-war economic affluence of the middle-class during Peron's second presidency, they decorated it in what was at the time a fashionable style. The old decoration had a comforting, solid feeling of home for Alicia.

Uncle Emilio's job as an engineer for a foreign company allowed them the luxury of a small car for a few years and annual trips to the beach in Mar del Plata, a confirmation of their middle-class status. He, unfortunately, died not long after Carla, their only daughter, married Guillermo. Since then, her aunt had lived mainly alone. Nevertheless, the couple succeeded at being good substitute parents for Alicia, and she loved them dearly.

Feeling somehow responsible for her mom's loneliness, Carla had hired a woman companion who moved in with her to cater to her needs. Alicia was sure the dinner at Aunt Marga's would be short, as she was in the habit of going to bed early, and her interests were mainly domestic.

When Alicia rang the intercom from the small entrance to the building, Aunt Marga came down the first-floor hallway to greet her. A slim, agile petite woman in her mid-sixties, she had Carla's sharp voice, strong *porteño* accent, and inquisitive eyes. Alicia noticed with delight that her aunt had dyed her graying hair to a light brown.

"Wow, you look great, aunt, at least ten years younger. What a change," Alicia said with an admiring nod. The woman appreciated her compliments and hugged her again.

The table was already set, and she promptly served dinner, Alicia's favorite baked schnitzels, or *milanesas,* and mashed potatoes. After the required exchange of family news, her aunt talked about herself, how comfortable she felt living with somebody she trusted, as was the young woman who shared her apartment, who, coincidentally, was out for the evening. Alicia was sure her aunt had arranged things to have a private dinner, and she appreciated that.

"My only concern is that this new gal might marry and move out. She's in her late thirties. And I got used to having her around, she is helpful, a good listener, and she also talks, while photographs and furniture are totally mute." She turned to Alicia and laughed at the thought. Alicia smiled back, amused by the noticeable change in her aunt, who was unusually talkative. Alicia was surprised to find out that she was working in a nearby church now.

"I don't recall you going to church other than to Sunday mass to take Carla and me because the nun at her First Communion's class complained about our no practicing ways."

"Well, you know, when one gets older, things change, and one starts thinking in retrospect. Am I leaving something of value behind?" She paused, looking for an answer. "Well, I haven't done much in my life other than being a housewife and mother. So I thought that now with time to spare, I might as well do something useful. You know I get bored with TV shows, I hate soap operas, and lately, my eyes are too tired to read."

Alicia smiled. She loved this woman. Would her mom, if she had lived, be like Aunt Marga? Maybe not. Often siblings happen to be so different. How would her Mom have turned out as an older woman? Alicia's memories of her were the beautiful images of her childhood. She sighed.

"So, what are you doing there? I mean, working in the church."

"We are a group; about ten to fifteen. Some are retired women and other homemakers. We raise money for the parish. The priest needs the money dearly. We have a few projects going on."

"Such as?" Alicia welcomed the idea of Aunt Marga doing community work.

"Well, first we redecorated the altar, now we are going through his offices, making improvements and buying a couple of things. We organize raffles, monthly bake sales, and the likes. For instance, we sent packages to the troops fighting in Malvinas." She hesitated.

"Aren't you worried that those packages of donations may not actually have reached the men doing the fighting?"

Aunt Marga looked puzzled. "Of course not. Why would I? I'm sure they got there," and after a pause: "Oh... I see. You are talking about those rumors that have come out in the papers and radio lately. Aren't you?"

"Well, yes. In fact, I have heard..."

"Alicia, those are isolated events. But look, I'm sure those are all exaggerations or outright lies."

"I don't know, *Tia*. I'm not sure about that."

"What happens is that many do not like this government, and

127

they make up lies. But these men of the Junta had cleaned the country of bad people; they have brought peace and calm. Since they are in the government, there is no more instability. We are at peace."

"Yeah, we are at peace." Then Alicia couldn't refrain any longer: "The peace of the tombs, I would say."

"What do you mean by that?" There was no resentment in the woman's voice, just the impatience of a teacher talking to a child. Alicia understood she had gone too far, and it was useless to upset her aunt with a call to the reality that she wouldn't be willing to hear.

"Nothing, it's a way of saying we are at peace by force. You know that I don't see the breaking of democracy as a good thing or a peaceful thing. We have talked about this many times before."

"But you're wrong, dear. I know you prefer democracy with elections, but they not only saved democracy by getting rid of corruption. They even tried to recover the Malvinas Islands for us."

"Aunt Marga, honestly, how can one be democratic while taking power through a coup and seating a de facto government for over six years, without elections or Congress?" She knew she shouldn't, but Alicia needed to say it. "As for Malvinas, believe me, they knew it was a lost cause. They had to know it."

Aunt Marga was looking at her intently, waiting for her to finish:

"I don't think so, dear. Of course, you shouldn't listen to rumors, but, anyway, now things have settled down, and there aren't any more terrorists in the streets so that we can have elections again. Before that, it was too dangerous."

Alicia knew her aunt would not change her mind. Her only source of information was the propaganda broadcasted on television. She lived in a world constructed for her to accept and ignore reality.

Aunt Marga lifted her eyes from the serving plate and looked at her, "I'm sure we will vote next year, and then the civilians will mess it up again and run back begging for the Armed Forces to fix it. Just wait and see."

"You don't sound well," said Sergio after giving her all the domestic updates when she called him punctually at nine o'clock the next morning. "Are you OK? Did you catch a cold? You sound congested." He seemed concerned. She could not contain a hopeful smile. Today he had mellowed his cold and distant tone.

"No, I just overslept and had a headache. Yesterday was too emotional for me." Her deep conviction that no matter what happened between them, they would always be able to work out their problems seemed broken when she left Bariloche. But now, she had new hopes.

"Got any good news?" He seemed genuinely interested, so she gave him a brief, albeit general, description of what she found out.

His tone lifted Alicia's spirit only temporarily, though. When they hung up, she was not sure, after all. She had said: "I love you," and he had answered with an ambiguous "Same here."

She put down the receiver with a sigh. Sergio would never have said goodbye like this before. He would have told her he loved her and meant it in different circumstances with all the words. Too many things to mend were piling up between them. It would not be easy. Alicia's guilty feelings at failing her immediate family had assuaged her a bit. Pablo was doing fine. He would remember her and ask for his mommy or cry for a while, but Sergio said he was generally taking it better than expected. Sergio seemed to manage well by himself. It was comforting to know that he would be, besides an excellent father, a good substitute mother for Pablo if something happened to her. Undeniably, she loved that man dearly.

She turned the radio on while getting dressed, hoping for news or music, but the inane chatter and strident ads were intolerable, and she opted for silence.

The thought of going to Plaza de Mayo this afternoon had made her edgy. What should she expect? Would many onlookers be watching, like her? What if the police covered the area and disbanded the people? What if they got locked up? She pushed her negative thoughts away. The relatives of the victims faced that risk every day. She admired once again the inner strength that had guided those women every week, for years, risking their lives, demanding answers. If she were courageous enough, she told herself, today she would buy a white scarf and walk with them, in the name of her friend. But she lacked the guts. The thought made her feel ashamed of her weakness.

Later in the afternoon, Alicia was crossing the lobby when she heard the young concierge calling her. "*Señora* Brauer?"

She was not sure she had heard him correctly. "Yes?"

He bent over the counter and said, "Your last name is Brauer. I didn't know it."

"Yes, well, it's my husband's last name. I don't use it when I'm working."

"Ah.... "

"May I ask how you found out my married name? The ID card I showed when I registered only has my family name. I never changed it."

"Yes, that's the thing: you are registered here as Alicia Rivera, so... I mean, I wasn't sure it was you."

"I don't understand." Alicia tried to be as calm and polite as possible, but she was restless. Something was not right. He smiled absent-mindedly while shuffling a small pile of letters on the counter. Still, he was willing to provide more information because, per his training, the customer was always right.

He sighed, "Well, it's just that last night, this man was asking for you at the counter. It was not my shift, so I wasn't here. The employee that worked yesterday evening told me. It looks like you were out too, but he didn't want to see you. He was just verifying that you are a guest here. He gave the clerk your married name, and of course, he couldn't locate you on the list. But then, I believe he remembered your paternal last name, and only then the receptionist could verify that you are registered at the hotel."

"Who was this man? And why would the concierge give him any information at all?"

"I don't know. This man probably showed some type of ID to the night attendant. I didn't ask him. He just mentioned this to me when I took my shift, but I didn't think that was important." He ended the explanation with a look that said *it's as simple as that.*

"I can't believe you will give this information to anybody that asks... Don't you have rules here?" Alicia's knees became shaky.

"Yes, we do, ma'am. I'm pretty sure this person showed some ID, as I told you. We have to verify, and we do."

"What ID?"

"I don't know; the night porter didn't say."

The growing feeling was now full-blown nausea, and after

thanking him, she turned around and walked to the elevator. She needed a few minutes to recover. It was still early.

She tried a few of the breathing exercises Mary had recommended in her room, and somehow she could control her anxiety. It was clear that somebody had followed her. Was it because of her encounter with Mariano? He had mentioned that he was sure somebody followed him at some point. The thought of not going to Plaza de Mayo crossed her mind, but she dismissed it. She just was taken by surprise at the counter. She had not expected to be at risk in Buenos Aires. *How do mothers and relatives endure the constant danger looming over their heads for such a long time?* She wondered.

She felt ashamed of her weakness. Her reactions were the opposite of what she thought they should be if she were ever confronted with a real threat. She was a coward, as simple as that. Sitting on the bed, Alicia covered her face with her hands for a few minutes. When she recovered, her palms were soaked in tears, and she slowly walked toward the bathroom to splash cold water on her face before heading to Plaza de Mayo.

The thought of Susana and the ordeal she was most likely suffering and the horrible possibility of her death pulled Alicia out of her indecision. She had to go, no matter what. She wouldn't fail Sonia today.

Plaza de Mayo was busy at a quarter to five. Crisscrossed by administrative types hurrying back and forth and surrounded by dense traffic, nothing seemed to announce that it was a Thursday, and the mothers would be there. The various flocks of pigeons made their home in the elaborate moldings of the federal buildings, and the stylish Cathedral around the square fluttered around searching for food. It was a cloudy and chilly day. The breeze from the Rio de la Plata, two blocks down behind the massive *Casa Rosada,* the seat of the Executive branch of the government, was becoming uncomfortable.

Alicia walked from the subway exit at Calle Florida toward the old colonial *Cabildo* building in the corner and crossed the avenue with many pedestrians. She paced around the square's pathways slowly but with purpose and sat not far from the sleek pyramid, towering at the center. She chose a bench where a middle-aged couple talked and fed the birds. Further down, people were reading, chatting, or just waiting for somebody occupied several seats.

Her heart was beating fast, and Alicia thought the man near her would hear it, and with her stomach in knots, she prayed in silence a string of Our Fathers. Then, by repeating the words like a litany, she gradually regained control of her shaking.

She checked her wristwatch, looking sideways, feigning interest in the small flock of sparrows competing bravely for crumbs and seeds with the domineering population of the much larger pigeons. It was five minutes to five o'clock when, out of nowhere, the police appeared. Some of them were in uniforms, others were dressed in civilian clothes, but they were unmistakable. They positioned themselves in pairs and threes surrounding the pyramid.

At five o'clock, the bells of the Cathedral tolled with their sweet sound. In a matter of minutes, almost the length of one of the beautiful chimes, women of all ages, wearing white headscarves approached the police, went through their uneven round, and started walking around the pyramid. Their stride was steady, some were holding pictures in their hands, and others had them pinned to their clothes. It was a solemn march, an almost surreal image in the cold and breezy afternoon; the silent walk around the pyramid; the police occasionally exchanging words with each other, and the people who watched from afar, in small groups. Some passersby avoided the area and hurried, uninterested. An ostensibly foreign journalist crew, with two cameras and a reporter talking to one of them, were registering everything, tiptoeing around the marchers and guards.

Alicia felt suddenly at ease. It was as if this was a natural thing to watch, a reassuring image. Although it did not make sense to her, everything felt right, in place. At the same time, she knew the women were taking a chance. Some men in uniform looked like they would not flinch at shooting at the women right there, mainly if they were confident that their actions would go unpunished. The fact that those at the other end of the barrel —plain dressed housewives and mothers— were unarmed made this all the more striking.

Alicia looked sideways and noticed that the woman sitting next to her was missing from the bench. Had she joined the march too? She could not identify her among the others at the pyramid. The man kept on feeding the birds slowly, unfazed as if he had been alone all the time.

Nothing memorable happened for about half an hour. Then, as calmly as they met, the mothers walked away from the pyramid's area and blended with the pedestrians, taking their scarves off.

Alicia strolled toward the subway entrance and took the train to Pasco Street. Then, as agreed, she waited for Sonia inside the coffee shop to bid farewell to the anguished mother.

An hour or so later, Alicia walked away from the encounter holding a small package containing the duffel bag she had lent Susana to carry the chocolates and preserves back home, neatly cleaned and folded by Sonia.

Sitting in the subway coach, Alicia took the brown package out and stroked the ordinary paper tenderly for a few minutes on her way back to the hotel.

X

The baptism ceremony was on Saturday, and Alicia called Carla to meet on Friday, which happened to be the 9th of July, Independence Day.

"I've ordered *empanadas* and *locro* from El Ceibal," Carla said on the phone.

"Hum... It sounds delicious. I haven't had *locro* for a long, long time. Thanks." Alicia's mouth melted at the thought of the flavorful Northwestern native stew made with freshly grated corn, meat, and vegetables.

"I knew I would tempt you. We will enjoy the whole day chatting and organizing things."

"It's a deal."

"By the way, Mom won't be joining us, she has some big celebration at the Church, and she's volunteering there."

The days had slipped away, and it was already Friday. Alicia woke up very early, with a sense of urgency, reproaching herself of the many things she should have accomplished but hadn't.

Sergio called when Alicia just came out of the shower. He had planned a day out with Mary and Luis at the ski village at the base of Cerro Catedral. Considering Pablo's edginess, he thought the child might benefit from a day out. Sergio was in a hurry, and she noticed impatience in his voice when she tried to explain her views on her recent findings. She cut her comments short, hurt again by his lack of interest, and managed to ask him if there were any news on Alcides. Nothing yet, he said. He sent his congratulations to the family for the upcoming Christening, and she thanked him. They hung up the phone without her telling him about the man asking for her in the lobby. She felt frustrated and bitter against Sergio.

Her mission in Buenos Aires turned out to be far less successful than she had expected, but at least she got to spin one thread that may or may not bear fruits in the future. If Mariano's contacts did not produce results, she didn't know what she would do next. They had no other mutual friends in the city.

She could easily imagine Sergio's skepticism on her empty-handed return. He had changed so much lately. Either that or her perception of him had changed. Was he this cold person all along? Was it possible that she had never noticed that trait? She was feeling more and more isolated from her own family. How could this be happening? She had definitely expected more support from him, and that hurt her.

By nine-thirty, she finished dressing and left the hotel for what she knew would be a long day at Carla's home, with no possibilities of escape. Besides that, her schedule today called for a long-delayed visit to Susana's apartment. Sonia had agreed that there should be no danger at all if she visited the empty studio and offered to call Mateo, the live-in porter, and let him know about it. However, she declined to invite Alicia to her own home, knowing she was under constant surveillance for her connections with the Mothers.

Alicia had suppressed her anxiety, the urgency to see the place, to be near her friend's things once again as if by osmosis she would be able to fully attain the complete picture of her disappearance and a vision of where they held her.

She asked the taxi driver to stop two blocks before the building. It was downtown, and Susana loved the noise and the constant, lively crowd of passers-by, the shops and eateries, most of them open until one in the morning or later. She loved to have everything handy, readily available, whenever she fancied to go down the elevator and get a last-minute item.

Alicia strolled cautiously, stopping at several windows, feigning interest but checking through the reflection if somebody followed her. The building was on Santa Fe Avenue. It was a simple, ten-story plain facade, with a double glass door sandwiched between two small and classy stores, one selling women's shoes and apparel for teenagers. It was an exact copy of hundreds of other apartment structures in the city, and she pressed the porter's button in the intercom, feeling an urgent need for a cigarette, which was out of the question right now.

Rather than answering the intercom, the manager walked a few minutes later from a side hallway visible from the outside and approached the door crossing the small foyer. Alicia waved, and he seemed to recognize her.

"Hi, would you come in?" he said, his wrinkles marked by his smile while opening the door. Alicia walked into the hall, following his silent gesture.

"How are you, Mateo?" They shook hands.

"Fine, thank you, *señorita*. It's been a long time."

He spoke with a strong Spaniard accent, notwithstanding the almost three decades in Buenos Aires. Alicia followed him to the small apartment on the first floor, past the elevators, at the end of the hallway, where he lived with his wife.

Mateo opened the door, and Alicia stepped into the small but neat living and dining area. The wife, a plain woman with a round and maternal face that reminded Alicia of the Bolivian immigrants regularly arriving in Buenos Aires in search of work, approached her with a smile, and her hand extended. Both had recognized her, and they evidently knew why she was there. None of them seemed worried about talking with her, and that was a good sign.

They sat on the dining room chairs around the table, and the woman brought glasses and two bottles of Coca-Cola. Then, with a shy smile, she apologized and left the room to continue with her chores.

Turning to Alicia, Mateo asked, "I knew you would come here any day now. Mrs. Machevsky called me; she said you were in town and wanted to see the apartment. I haven't seen Mrs. Machevsky for a week, at least. She sounded sad over the phone. How's she doing?"

"She's frantic, but she's resilient and has a strong will to find her daughter."

He nodded, poured Coca-Cola into both glasses, and offered one to Alicia. She was grateful; her mouth was dry.

"No news from Miss Susana, I guess...."

"No. None yet," Alicia answered with a faint voice. They remained silent for some time.

He shook his head as if saying, what crazy and criminal world is this? But he did not say it. People did not talk lightly about these experiences.

Alicia ventured, "What exactly happened that day?"

He sighed and shifted in his chair, uncomfortable. "It all started early in the day. I was sweeping the curve in front of the building, as I do in the mornings. I saw two men sitting in a car parked in front of the building for a long time. I sensed something wrong; traffic police don't let anybody stop at the curb for long; too much traffic there. Miss Machevsky got home from her trip around two in the afternoon. I saw her coming in a taxi cab and another neighbor, a young man that lives upstairs in the 7th, who was just going out, helped her carry the bags to the elevator."

"Did you get to talk with her?"

"I welcomed her, yes. I was glad to see her, she's a nice girl, always happy and smiling, and so gentle with everybody. What a shame..."

He looked at Alicia with sadness. She was not sure if he was sad for the criminal act of kidnapping her, or, as many people did, he felt pity for the young woman taking the wrong turn in her life and getting involved in something murky. He finished his thought, "She said she enjoyed being with your family back in Bariloche, the only few words we exchanged. Then, later on, on her way out..."

"Around what did she go out again?"

"Couple of hours later, I reckon... yeah, no more than that. I didn't see Miss Machevsky. Fact is, my wife, she saw her when she left." He seemed to organize his thoughts. "Miss, if you ask me, I would say that something was not right that evening around here, and my instincts told me that I should be alert, but I didn't know what it was. After dinner, say ten o'clock, somebody rang the intercom repeatedly. I ran to the lobby and saw a bunch of men outside, one of them flashing a police ID through the glass door. When I opened, they barged in and asked for Miss Machevsky's apartment. I panicked and told them. Three of them ran to the elevator, and two stayed behind. One told me to go to my apartment and shut the door, and the other stood in the lobby. That much I saw before getting back inside and locking my door. My wife was crying, and I was scared to death, having never been so scared in my life. They were carrying heavy weapons."

He fell silent, and Alicia did not say anything; he needed time to recover from the upsetting memories. Then, after sipping more Coca-Cola, he said, "Then we learned that they pushed other neighbors inside their apartments too. They seemed to know that Miss Machevsky was coming home. She got here at around ten-twenty, I guess, and went up. When she got to her door and opened it, she was pushed inside by men that were waiting on the stairs nearby."

"Same guys you talked to or others?"

"Don't know. Maybe the same men, or a few more of them that came as reinforcement after I locked my door, I don't know for sure."

"And then?"

"This I was told by the neighbors across her apartment. They were also pushed inside and told not to come out, but the woman looked through the peephole in the door and saw the guys grabbing Ms. Susana and taking her out. She was screaming, and they slapped her, took her away, and then she watched how these men went in and out, making a ruckus, taking things from the apartment, until there was silence. This couple was too frightened to open the door, so they stayed inside for a little longer till later on when they called me on the phone. I told them to calm down and not to say anything to anybody, just in case." He shook his head again.

"Mateo, did they return at all?"

"Never saw them again. The first thing I did was to call her Mom; I have her phone number on file. The poor woman hung up, and soon she and her husband got here in a taxicab. It was awful. We were all scared; the neighbors saw the cars, and they heard the commotion. The men took many things away, broke others... Mrs. Machevsky called the police, and they came, looked around, and wrote a statement in a notebook. Nobody did anything else, though. We haven't heard from anybody else."

"Mrs. Machevsky went to the police headquarters. They took her deposition but never called her again." Alicia sighed and then added, "She said the apartment is closed now, and she wants to keep it that way."

"Yeah, she pays the rent, so until the contract is over, it's theirs. Nobody comes here except for Mrs. Machevsky. Sometimes she walks in there and stays for a while, then leaves. The neighbors and we were worried after that day, but nothing else happened in the building since the... incident."

"Is it OK if I see the apartment for a minute?'

"Yeah, sure, you are a close friend, and you used to come over all the time years ago..."

They went up in the elevator to the fifth floor, walked in silence to Susana's apartment door, and Mateo unlocked it, moving over to let Alicia go first. The place was as she remembered it but darker. The windows were shut, and only a faint line around the borders allowed the light to go through the drapes. Susana had always kept the windows open during the day. Now a smell of mold had invaded the tiny apartment, taking over the fresh air that was Susana's environment.

Mateo switched the lights on, and she felt her friend's absence tangibly. Furniture was missing, and the bookshelves were almost empty. Then, in a corner, she noticed the kitchenette in disarray with the refrigerator door open. It was a desolate image. Alicia felt a knot in her throat and could not utter a word, so she just looked around, taking mental note of the changes.

Mateo walked out into the hallway, leaving her alone, and she sat for a while on the convertible bed, still decked with the three large, beautiful cushions that she and Susana had purchased together a couple of years ago.

Alicia needed some time to recover after she left Susana's apartment. So she sat at a table in a nearby coffee shop for a while, sipping tea while doing her breathing exercises. Then, she took another cab to Carla's home. It was almost eleven, and her cousin was waiting for her with *mate* tea, gossip, and news on the family.

After chatting all morning, mostly around children's issues, Alicia was entirely updated with Carla's maternal feelings and experience. She was happy to see her cousin so involved and self-assured with the baby. Compared to her, Alicia had been an insecure mom from the beginning, questioning her aptitudes more than once and provoking Sergio's annoyance. However, he always thought she was fit and capable and ignored her doubts. At the time, he seemed more confident in her abilities than Alicia herself. That helped her gain confidence, albeit slowly.

Once she fed baby Veronica, Carla put her to bed, and the family sat at the table. The large color TV set, a regular guest at mealtime, was on in one of the ample family room corners. Guillermo preferred television to radio, and they had several distributed around the apartment so he could follow without interruptions whatever program he was watching. Alicia's dinner with Sergio was catching up on the daily news, so now the television non-stop talking in the background was a nuisance for her. She tried to ignore it and make a conversation with Carla.

"I'm glad to see what a good mom you are." She was sincere.

"Am I? Do you think so?" She seemed pleased with Alicia's praise. 'I hope *my* mom would see it that way too."

"I'm sure she does."

Guillermo sat at the table and turned the television's volume up.

"Shh. Listen, there is a news flash." They turned their attention to the pompous good-looking man holding a microphone. In the background, a ceremony was taking place, with many flags undulating on their masts. The military music receded. The man smiled broadly while announcing the Junta's wreath-laying homage paid early in the day to General José de San Martín, the hero of the country's independence from Spain.

Argentina, Chile, and Peru owed their freedom from the colonial yoke to the reserved and shy general that died poor and almost forgotten in an apartment house in Boulogne-Sur-Mer, France. It was the price he gladly paid for refusing to lead a fratricide civil war between Buenos Aires and the rebellious provinces in the 1800s.

"Imagine if San Martin could see this. What a joke," Alicia said, without thinking, and immediately regretted it.

"Why?" Guillermo turned to her, offended. "What's wrong with honoring him?"

"Nothing at all. I was thinking how sad it is that the military he so painfully created and organized and the country he liberated from the colonial tyranny... became *this*."

"What do you mean by *this*?"

"I mean this situation, the military constantly taking over and making the laws as they go."

"Alicia, I don't know if you have noticed, but these men just saved us from the *pinkos* that were planning to plant a red flag in Plaza de Mayo," he said as if the matter was an indisputable, well-known truth. Alicia felt her face turning red, and she tried to speak in a calm voice. Her fingernails were hurting her palms. She shook her head.

"Don't tell me that you believe that, please, Guillermo. You are a savvy man, a businessman, too intelligent to swallow that propaganda." She was proud of the calm and control in her voice.

"Oh, not now!" Carla jumped in, returning from the kitchen area with a plate. "You two won't start again on one of those political tirades, please, guys."

"Don't worry, Carla, we are just talking about what's going on. It seems that Alicia had a heavy diet of that leftist stuff that has ruined our country and still is poisoning our young."

"What leftist stuff?" Alicia was angry now. "Why is it when people expose the truth of what's going on here, others have such a hard time accepting reality and start calling names?"

"Others? Meaning me?"

"Well, yes, you. We are in a mighty screw up with the debt, and nobody cares. We started an unnecessary war that we lost. We have spent all our resources buying useless overpriced second-hand weaponry that the rich countries discard, and our local industry is gone. Gone. What leftist stuff are you talking about? These are facts, Guillermo."

He listened, smiling knowingly, waiting for her to cool down, but Carla stood up again, evidently nervous.

"Guys, please. Let's calm down, please!"

Looking at his wife, he said slowly, as a teacher would explain a lesson: "Dear, this is *not* a discussion. We are just exchanging ideas here. Alicia has these misconceptions that are so unfair to what this government is trying to do."

Carla left the table with a shrug. Guillermo turned to Alicia; she was evidently obfuscated.

"Well, you seem to have a short memory. Don't you remember the kidnappings, the bombs, terrorism on the streets?" Guillermo said.

"I haven't forgotten it, don't worry." She managed to say in a low voice. "On the contrary, I would say that the violence came well before those bombs and shootings. It came when these guys started taking over the government well before you and I were born. You know that, all that stuff of saving the homeland and all. They started the violence from the top down when they made those coups, choking our country with debt and selling everything out. From the very day when General Uriburu put a gun on President Yrigoyen's chest in 1930 on."

"Oh, come on! That's an old story now. Come on, don't bring that up again."

"Why not? You have to accept history if you want to understand what the heck is going on today."

"I remember the guerillas, and that was scary enough to justify a coup."

"The guerrillas came much later. The electoral fraud and military coups were first. Then, for decades, they never let a civilian government finish a term. All the while, they were selling out the country."

"That's not enough reason to kidnap or put bombs, Alicia."

"No. Of course not, but that's what happens when you push too much, and people have no way out. You get young hotheads anxious, and they take arms. Why didn't they put the guerrillas on trial in front of everybody? Then the thing would have ended right there, in a civilized way, not by kidnapping and death squadrons. It should never have happened."

He seemed sincerely disappointed. "You're so wrong. We needed to get out of our protectionism and open the markets to the world. These guys follow the free-market policies faithfully, they will succeed, and we will get out of this soon. We are improving. It's a given thing. Our industry will be back stronger."

"That would be true if our companies had the same strength and clout that the foreign multinationals have. But instead, they will chew us up and spit the rest. Those corporations are huge and hungry. Wait and see."

"Well, I don't think so. These are bright men. They have excellent advisors."

"Some are benefiting from these policies, but not the rest of the country."

"I hope you're not writing these things in your articles, Alicia. Everybody is going to laugh at you. Or misunderstand you for a *pinko*, which is worse."

"Don't worry. I only write fluffy stuff. Women are not supposed to have brains in this environment. So they would never ask me for an opinion piece, even if they could print it."

"Oh, yeah? You don't like anything that's going on in our country. Do you? You should move out; maybe you can write whatever you want in another place. This country cannot have freedom because people cannot manage it. They would go out of control. They need somebody to guide them."

Alicia sighed. She had much more to say, but it would be for naught. Guillermo misunderstood her silence for admission of his logic.

"Let's change the subject, you guys, please," Carla intervened again, trying to stop the fast exchange that was making her too nervous. "I'm bringing dessert. Did you enjoy the food? Let's talk about something else. I hate politics. Why do we have to talk politics at the table?"

"Sorry, Carla, I got a bit loud. You're right; the table is not the place to talk about this." Alicia helped her clear the plates from the table, feeling guilty for the lie. But she knew she had to say those words, or today she would explode inside.

Guillermo, ostensibly upset, tried to calm down. When they were back from the kitchen, he said, "It seems we'll never agree on this, Alicia. I'm sorry you cannot see the big picture as I see it."

"OK, Guillermo, let's make peace here." Alicia tried to talk slowly and calmly. "You have your ideas, and I have mine. Who knows what the truth is; maybe it's in between."

He did not respond, so she added, "I acknowledge I can get carried away sometimes."

"Yes, let's change the subject." He sighed and tried a forced smile. "After all, we are family and are allowed to think differently."

Docile, Carla intervened, putting down the plates: "By the way, guys, tell me how do you like these cakes. They're a sample of tomorrow's choice of desserts." She was eager to change the subject, and Alicia felt a pang of pity for her cousin, and he smiled at her with affection.

"They're delicious, Carla. Sorry that I didn't say it before. They will be a success tomorrow. Dinner was great too. You know I love this food. Thank you again."

In a spontaneous impulse, she pulled her chair closer to her cousin, kissing her on the cheek. Carla returned the tender gesture embracing her by her waist, and they stayed like that for a while.

XI

Alicia was careful to step on the plane with her right foot. She had a long-held superstition that stepping with the right foot would help to have a safe flight.

The direct three-hour flight was already packed with tourists and locals returning home. She sat in her narrow seat by the aisle and next to two apparent honeymooners. After being knocked in the head by passengers maneuvering with their overhead baggage, she was pleased when the plane took off.

Soon Buenos Aires was behind, and she had to confront the frustrating truth. She was not any closer to helping Susana than she was when she left Bariloche. She had gained a more in-depth insight into the situation, yes, but she achieved no tangible results, and her fears had not been assuaged during the trip. The presence of an unidentified man asking for her at the desk had conveyed the unpredictability of her predicament. Was she being followed? In Buenos Aires, she was careful to check her surroundings at all times, but she did not notice anything suspicious. If her worries happened to be accurate, and somebody was shadowing her, why would anybody want to do that? Who would spend money and resources on a terrified housewife-journalist that was no threat to anybody? Sure there would be more significant fish to catch if they were looking for "enemies of the State." Was it only her paranoia, then? It seemed the only rational explanation.

The passengers around her settled down for the three-hour flight, and the voices finally quieted. Alicia took out her book and opened it, but she could not concentrate. Instead, her mind wandered back to the past few days.

Saturday's baptism and the family reunion that followed were a respite for her after the busy week of meetings. Guillermo had been kind and cheerful with her during the party, so she returned the courtesy, happy for the truce he offered. Carla looked and acted like the perfect hostess, the baby behaved very well, and everything turned out as expected. The sun was out, which made for a balmy winter day. Alicia wished she could have sincerely enjoyed everything around her. That things were back to normal and that Pablo and Sergio would have joined her in the celebration.

The flight seemed shorter this time than a week earlier when she was anxious to get to Buenos Aires. The Patagonian sky was dark and starry, with a bright silver moon hanging atop the city as the plane approached the narrow, blue-lit landing strip.

She stepped out of the cabin and came down the stairs. The air was cold and dry. She walked with the other passengers toward the entrance of the terminal. As soon as she crossed the building's double glass door, she caught sight of Sergio, holding Pablo on his left arm and searching for her in the oncoming crowd. He smiled, relieved to see her coming in.

The following Tuesday, after her return, Alicia tried to catch up on several things at work while pondering a call from Mary early on in the newsroom. But again, her voice sounded hushed: "Alicia, let's have lunch today. I have something to tell you. Are you available?"

"Of course, I am."

"Good. Then I'll pick you up at twelve-thirty. I'll get a couple of sandwiches and something to drink at the deli, and we will go somewhere quiet to talk."

"Are you planning a picnic?"

"Sort of," she answered with a lighter tone of voice.

Alicia was intrigued by the unusual call and still wondering what Mary needed to tell her when Martina, in typical fashion, dropped by her desk like a whirlwind. She updated her at full speed about the latest gossip and the Sunday program that she hosted alone. Alicia had left material before leaving and a pre-taped commentary, so things went smoothly. Martina was satisfied with her solo performance.

"I'm glad everything went so well." Alicia was pleased.

Martina said, "By the way, I meant to ask you. How's Susana doing? Did she enjoy her trip here? When is she coming back?"

Alicia feared the half-expected questions and answered, trying to sound as natural as possible. "She's doing fine, busy with her job. She's fine, thank you." Then, looking down, she straightened a few folders, dreading more questions.

"Good. I don't know if I mentioned it to you, but Roberto Flores is moving back to Buenos Aires next month. I believe he was reassigned to La Plata."

Alicia did not know what to say. Finally, she managed to blurt out. seemingly distracted, "Is that so?"

"Yes. He was pretty smitten with Susana. They may see each other there. Don't you think so?"

"I don't know, I guess they might,"

"I'm sure they will. They make a handsome couple, both tall and athletic."

"Maybe. You know how these things are..." Alicia said, searching for a way to change the subject, but her friend did it for her.

"By the way," Martina said as if remembering suddenly: "I stopped here to tell you that I just got a message from Schneider. He wants to meet both of us. I'm very excited about it. Aren't you?"

"Well, it depends. What does he want to talk about?" She was suspicious.

Martina did not seem worried: "I don't know. The program is doing fine. He can't complain."

"Still."

Martina ignored Alicia's doubts. "When can we meet him?"

"Any day will be fine with me; just pick anytime after hours. Let me know when you schedule something. So far, I'm free after six every day of the week."

Martina turned around and walked into Carlos' office. Alicia tried to get back to her page, unable to summon the energy or the interest she used to have in her work. Lately, everything paled compared with the mission she had taken upon herself of helping Susana. The radio show came almost last on her list of current priorities. By lunchtime, she had finished one of her assignments and was ready for a break and the mysterious meeting with Mary.

The Fiat 600 was waiting for her at the door; she got in, and Mary drove in silence toward Cerro Otto, the nearby hill.

Alicia asked, "Well? What's the big news? Why couldn't you say it on the phone? I'm anxious to hear it."

"It's a long story. Last night, at your place, when you were telling us about what your friend Mariano said in Buenos Aires, I had an idea. I didn't mention anything then because it was just a remote possibility, and I wanted to talk it over with Luis beforehand."

She drove in silence for a few minutes. Mary seemed to be searching for the right words. Alicia was impatient.

"Well... Tell me. What's the idea?"

"Luis and I have these acquaintances, this family we met long ago when we moved here." They were on the slope of Cerro Otto incline, and Mary parked the car in a sunny spot, in a lookout area of the ascending road. She kept the engine running and the heat on and turned toward Alicia. "They descend from these old settlers; it's an old family. You have met them, but don't ask me their names. Long ago, I promised myself never to tell anybody. But this is different."

"That's fine with me."

"Well, this couple had a daughter that disappeared in Buenos Aires a few years back. She was a law student at the university in Buenos Aires. I don't know the whole story, though. Their youngest brother told us in confidence that they did not go to the police because they were frightened to death. The family did not want to call unwanted attention to them and become victims too.

"On top of that, they are very conservative; they were afraid to be dumped in the same old terrorist-sympathizer bag by the press, like all the others. So at that time, they contacted a priest, a Salesian, living in the area. Through him, they found out details of what happened to her. I know you don't want anybody here to find out about Susana, but at some point, you will have to talk about her if you find the right person to ask." Mary said, turning and grabbing the white paper bag from the back seat.

She handed one wrapped sandwich and a bottle of orange juice to Alicia.

"No problem. I'm OK with that, of course. But you know, I'm at the end of the rope."

"We'll get in contact with this family again."

"I'm thinking about what you just said. I wonder — how many

more families may be in this town suffering like this, and we don't know about it?"

"I don't know. These guys are the only ones I ever heard of. If people keep it a secret, it's hard to find out. Anyway, this happened almost five years ago. The girl was confirmed dead three years later."

"Imagine! Three years not knowing what happened."

"They learned that she probably was buried in a common or an unmarked grave, in a town outside Buenos Aires. We did not ask for details."

"It's horrible. You say I know this family? It's maddening. I pity them, whoever they are." Alicia held her sandwich, unable to take a bite.

Mary sighed: "What I do know for a fact is that they were terrified. Lately, we haven't seen each other as often as we used to, but Luis agrees with me. We should approach them and ask about that priest and find out if he still lives around here."

"Oh, Mary, I would be so grateful if you would do that. Anything will be better than not knowing."

"I'll try my best. And please, don't put your expectations too high. It may not take us anywhere."

"Then again, it might," Alicia said, hopeful. "I have this deep conviction; I can call it a certainty that Susana is alive, and if only we find out where we may be able to help her to get out."

"I hope you are right."

"I know I am. That's why I have to help her."

They ate their lunch slowly and quietly, both appreciating the scenery and the lake beyond.

After a while, Alicia could not contain herself any longer. "Mary, I don't know if you noticed anything, but Sergio and I are not doing well lately."

Mary did not answer.

"In fact, I believe we're pretty messed up. We're getting farther and farther apart. I thought things would get better when I returned from Buenos Aires, but they didn't. Mary, I'm losing him, and I don't know, for the first time, what to do about it. It's as if all my resources are dry. What's going on?"

Tearing bits of her sandwich apart with her fingers, Mary said,

"You're under tremendous stress; that's what's going on. These are hard times for you both. Give it a break. Everything will settle down soon, I'm sure."

"I don't know. I'm not so sure. He's not the same guy. Something has changed. The way we look at each other and our intimate life is currently dormant. The worst part is that I don't miss it. Isn't it a terrible thing to say?"

"Alicia, please. You know you two are in bad shape because of what's going on. Give it some time to heal. As soon as you find out more about Susana and this is resolved, things will be back to normal."

"I hope you're right," Alicia said without conviction. She wanted to tell her friend that things were not so simple. That she had a bad feeling about it, but she could not find the words.

"You'll see. Things will be okay. For starters, I'll find out about that priest. Be positive." She patted Alicia's shoulder.

"I'll try," Alicia said, turning her attention to the half-eaten sandwich she was still holding and wondering if the knot in her throat would ease enough to allow her to swallow a bite.

The instructions to the priest's home, hand-written on the small piece of paper that Mary handed her the night before, were clear. Alicia had to take the graveled narrow road that, unmarked, bent right two miles after the intersection of Route 258 and the unpaved road to Cerro Tronador.

It had been a long and anxious week for Alicia, but she finally got a thread to follow, and she was again hopeful.

The dwindling path disappeared ahead under a thick pine canopy. She followed it slowly and stopped in front of the locked-up entrance of a neatly stained log hedge. The log section ended at about thirty yards from both sides of the gate, and further under the forest, it continued as a tall, ten-foot barbed wire fence. Nothing was visible other than the thick pine trees and the naked rosehip bushes, dusted with fresh light snow. The place was inhabited because the road was clear of snow and ice, and the new gravel was well-shaped.

Her heart sunk. Alicia was not sure how to proceed from there. The fence was closed with a chain and a big lock. It was a dead end.

She was considering turning around and going back home when suddenly a *boyerito, a* dark-skinned teenage peasant boy wearing a thick duvet jacket, appeared from the trees inside the compound and ran toward the fence, waving his hand to her.

Alicia realized that nearby a security camera must have been checking the gate. The child probably belonged to a *peon's* family's house; peasants were also in charge of the gates in sizeable land properties and estancias. He quickly opened the lock, pushed the gate open, and showed her the road ahead, waving and smiling.

Alicia drove for a few minutes under the thick canopy until the gravel road became a broad, paved way. Then, after a sharp curve, she found herself in front of a large and impressive, two-story structure the size of a hotel. She stopped the car in front of the sizeable roofed entrance that covered a section of the driveway. The tall double front door opened almost immediately, and a young priest, dressed in a black winter coat, appeared and walked toward her car. With a quiet demeanor, he guided her inside the house.

"Father Johann will see you soon," he said without looking at her.

They crossed a spacious hall, and he opened the door to an austere, vast library with its window shades up, its four walls covered with books from top to bottom, and a gas fireplace burning in a corner. Alicia glanced appreciatively at the collection, wondering if all the tomes would be religious or maybe these pious men of faith had a worldlier reading at hand for their spiritual retreats in the forest.

The priest signaled to a cushioned side bench with a light motion, and she obediently sat, holding her purse in her lap, feeling like a teenager in the principal's office. Then, the young man nodded to her and walked out silently.

The place had a vague familiarity with it. It reminded Alicia of the plush military waiting rooms and offices in government buildings she worked at as a part-time typist in Buenos Aires while paying for her students' expenses.

The meeting had been arranged by phone after a series of back-and-forth messages, and Mary had told her that the priest was well aware of Alicia's identity and why she wanted to see him. Apparently, this meeting was a rare exception; Father Johann did not receive visitors. Currently, he dedicated his life to working in seclusion. There were no more details available. Not that she was interested in them.

Alicia sat tight, waiting, trying to calm the butterflies in her stomach. Would this meeting take her anywhere? All the roads seemed exhausted, and Susana was still in the hands of her unknown captors. There was no word from Mariano or Sonia other than an affectionate thank-you note from the latter that Alicia construed as a keep-in-touch gesture from the frightened mother.

The room was warm, and Alicia took her gloves and jacket off, folding them next to her on the bench. When she lifted her eyes from the coat, she saw a lateral door opening. An elderly and slightly slouched tall man appeared and walked toward her. He had white hair, and his face was wrinkled, weathered, maybe by the Patagonian winds, she thought. He smiled broadly, and she stood up, also smiling.

"Welcome to our home, *Hija mía*. Come on here," he motioned a slender and bony white hand out of his black robe toward a small set of chairs in the center of the room. "Let's sit in there; they're more cushioned." His voice was surprisingly firm for his looks and had a slight accent, maybe Nordic.

They sat on two stylish, antique chairs upholstered in burgundy velvet. Father Johann lifted a candy bowl from an end table and offered it to Alicia. She picked one of the brightly wrapped chocolate mints to soothe the dryness of her mouth. Father Johann put down the bowl and turned to her.

His inquisitive eyes resembled those of a much younger man, and he did not waste time. "Please allow me to be blunt and honest. I don't know if I can be of any service to you. I will try, though. This is a slippery slope for you and me. I want to be sure you understand that."

She liked his forthrightness. "I do," she answered in the same assertive tone. "Father, any hope will be better than nothing. Be honest with me. That's what I need. I'll do whatever is needed to find my friend and get her back home if I can."

His eyes were sharp, fixed on Alicia's as if he wanted to ensure that Alicia understood the message. "The first request from me is discretion. You've never been here or talked with me. As you can see, this house is a very secluded place, and we do not invite many lay people here. Our guests are from other provinces or other countries. Seldom, if ever, do our priests visit this house.

"I've never been here or seen you, for that matter," she repeated quickly.

"Good. Second, if I refer you to a third person at some point in time, you will never, under any circumstance, mention my connection to anybody. It is of utmost importance that neither my Order nor I will be connected to your research."

"I won't say anything. I promise."

He nodded and reached across the small table, picking up a pen and a small steno notebook. He opened it on a blank page and handed it to Alicia.

"Please, write down as many details as you can about this person you are trying to find. Even physical descriptions and whatever you know about the day she was taken away. Also, please, write down the number where to leave a message for you. If there is a message to you in the future, it will be from *the candle maker*."

Alicia complied, as clearly as her trembling hand allowed her. Then she scribbled the newsroom's telephone number and gave the notebook back to Father Johann.

"I beg you, Father. Help me." If he had asked her to kneel down right there, she would have gladly done it if that had helped her cause.

"I will do as much as I can," he said elusively.

"Anything. Please. I'm desperate," Alicia implored, unable to hold back her tears. She covered her face and sobbed for a few seconds. He remained silent, seated still. Finally, she made an effort and recovered from her outburst. "Sorry."

"It's fine. Don't apologize." He stood up and waited for her to put her handkerchief back in her purse. Then he extended his hands and took hers. His actions surprised her. After his distant formality, this was unexpected. His hands were bony but warm and stable. Alicia felt hers cold and small while he held them.

"*Dios te bendiga, Hija mía*," he blessed her, making a brief sign of the cross over her forehead without touching it.

"Thank you, Father," she muttered back, lowering her head. She saw herself as a child again, faced with the humbling mystery of the Catholic Church's representatives, the mighty nuns, and the priests, up there, next to the altar, and she felt a bit ashamed. It was incredible the power these images had over her after so many years of voluntary detachment from the institution.

When she raised her head, he had turned around and was leaving the room. She watched him close the door behind him, and then she took her coat and gloves. She was putting them on when the young priest reappeared and silently led her out of the library through the door they came in.

Once in her car, Alicia drove slowly toward Bariloche, a twenty-mile ride through one of the most beautiful lakeside landscapes of the area. She reenacted the conversation with Father Johann several times, switching her mood from hopeful to new depths of despair, depending on her interpretation of his words. Her head was hurting.

Hovering over her thoughts, beyond the hope the priest represented, was the unavoidable truth of a Church that covered a heinous crime being perpetrated to who knows how many thousands of people, under monstrous circumstances. In her eyes, the hierarchy's silence was unforgivable, and the private individual actions of regretful clerics would not wash the stain. She felt a mix of resentment and guilt, sorrow, and hopelessness. Torture and murder were wrong and despicable, a genuinely malevolent, evil behavior. Was it possible that the Church of her infancy knowingly justified and sheltered the devil?

History books testified to that dark trait back centuries in history. Maybe she should accept the Church's behavior to complement the nightmarish reality she was forced to acknowledge. Nobody in a position of power seemed exempt from that fact.

The sun was falling behind the top of the mountains, and when she reached home, it was dark. The whole afternoon had been like a dream, and she had glided through it in a daze. Finally, relieved, she pulled into her driveway and found out that Sergio was not home yet. She needed some time alone to sort out her thoughts and soothe the now-pounding headache that had started as soon as she left the mysterious and secluded house where she met Father Johann.

On Wednesday, the weekly meeting at the office had almost ended when Alicia walked in. She felt she should apologize.

"I had to take Pablo to the pediatrician early today, and it took forever until I got to see the doctor," Alicia said hurriedly to Carlos

Alvarez.

He dismissed the issue with his hand. "It's okay; you did not miss your assignments. But, Alicia, there is a message on your desk since yesterday, a woman called late last night." He seemed embarrassed and walked away.

Alicia knew she should allow a few days at least to receive news, but she had been waiting for Father Johann's message since Monday. Her hopes were high when she approached her desk, but it was news from Jacinta, who had been coming to work only twice a week since her brother had been admitted at the regional hospital with a bleak prognosis. With trembling hands, Alicia read the message dated the night before, after she left the office. "My brother Alcides died today. The wake will be tomorrow, Wednesday, at home. The funeral is on Thursday. Jacinta."

The healthy, energetic twenty-year-old man was brought back from Malvinas as a double amputee suffering a persistent post-surgical hospital infection contracted somewhere between Port Stanley and Bariloche. The local doctors had been unable to control.

Alicia sat down. She still felt angry about those lives lost for no reason. Malvinas Islands were farther away from being returned to her country by England, and they were in a worse position than before the war.

She hit the desk with her fist. "Shit."

"What's wrong? What's that face?" Martina walked toward her desk, coming out of the meeting room with other staff members. Alicia explained in a few words.

"What a waste. Poor kid. Those soldiers faced the English by themselves; most of the officers ran away. Did you hear that? Sickening. If you want me, I can go with you to the funeral. Let me know."

"Thank you. I will. Please, pass me the number of the flower shop we used last time here in the newsroom? I didn't write it down."

Martina opened her address book and gave her the number.

"Don't forget we have this meeting tonight with Schneider," she hesitated and then added, "I see you don't even remember."

"Ah, yes. I'll be there. My head is a mess now. I have so many things going on that I believe it's going to explode."

"Calm down. Everything will be okay."

Alicia suddenly felt annoyed with Martina's eternal optimism and upbeat mood. How could she explain to her that things were not as simple as she thought? It was impossible. She managed to smile blandly. "Thank you. You are such a good friend. Thanks for your concern. You are right; I'm tired."

"A good weekend with Sergio in a nice and secluded hotel somewhere will fix everything. You'll see," Martina said with a wink.

"You're right." Alicia stood up and feigned to be busy with a pile of files on the desk. "At what time was it, then?"

"At six o'clock in his office."

"I'll see you there, then."

Alicia dialed Sergio's number as soon as Martina left. He offered to go to Alcide's wake with her. He would be working late, and she could meet him at work at about seven-thirty.

"I'm glad you want to go with me. If Lydia is not available, I'll take Pablo to Mary's home for the evening."

"See you then."

Slightly before six, Alicia met with Martina in Schneider's building hallway, and both went up the flight of stairs in silence. They were ushered quickly into his office. He was short on words and to the point. He told them they would not renew the contract when it came due in August. The decision was final. Their last program with his sponsorship would be August 8. He was apologetic but firm.

"Tell us the truth," Alicia ventured. "What is the real reason you are backing from this program? I believe we deserve to know."

"Well, you know, I'm being hit by the same problems everybody is here, and until business doesn't get back on track again.....”

"Just tell us the truth," Martina's nervousness was evident in her voice. "We can handle it."

'This is the truth, girls, believe me."

Alicia grew impatient. Turning to her friend, she said: "That's fine, Martina, we'll never know for sure, even though we have a good idea. Don't we?"

He was again apologetic. "You may not believe it, but my finances are the real reason."

"Fine, it's okay, I guess. We'll find another way. Don't worry."

Martina stood up, and Alicia followed.

They left the office with their heads up and their spirits low. It was discouraging but predictable.

"It was a good experience while it lasted." Alicia was incensed.

"Yeah... at least we had the opportunity to talk about what our listeners are interested in." Martina was red-faced and upset. "What do you think of what this jerk told us?"

"That story of his finances troubles is a bunch of baloney. The truth is that he doesn't like our message. Neither does his wife and her friends. They are pissed off with anything that sounds too liberal for women. That's all."

Martina followed her down the steps.

"They're all frustrated, these old women, and they want the rest of us to follow the same fate. So they are full of resentment."

When they got to the bottom of the stairs, they hugged goodbye in silence, both afraid of a tearful outburst.

Alicia drove to Sergio's office, still floored by the experience. He was already waiting at the curb and hopped in the car. She did not feel like telling him right away about her last failure, so they stayed in silence, both smoking, absorbed in their thoughts.

The road to Barrio Alto was Calle Onelli, a busy local commercial street. It ascended the hill for a couple of miles before turning right in a broad curve that revealed the magnificent peaks of several mountains ahead, beyond the empty, flat extension of Pampa de Huenuleo. The most deprived outskirts of the city were taking hold there, advancing their precarious dwellings into the dry and grassy pampa's terrain with the background of a spectacular, post-card deserving panorama.

Alicia looked to her left. "Tomorrow, poor young Alcides Catriel will be taking residence there," she said dryly, signaling with her head toward the thick pine and cypress forested area of a few acres not far from the road. The local cemetery, swept by the wind, seemed like a green oasis inserted in the brown-colored surroundings. "It's so cold and windy here."

"I guess that when you are dead, it doesn't matter any longer," Sergio said drily. He seemed annoyed by her comment. Alicia did not say a word until she turned right on the neighborhood's dusty road where Jacinta lived. They drove past the school's square concrete building, where Alicia had the interview with the teachers.

"There is a map in the glove compartment," she said, and he snapped it open. It was a wrinkled piece of paper, drawn a long time ago by Jacinta. He took it out and unfolded it.

"Just in case we don't remember where it is. There are no street signs here," she said.

He shrugged. "That's because there are only a few streets and fewer houses."

"Do you want the map?"

He put it back in the glove compartment and locked it. "No. I remember the area well. Turn left here and right at the next corner. That one should be the house." He was right. It was a humble lodging, planted in a land surrounded by a rudimentary chain link fence. Groups of neighbors filled almost the entire front yard.

They parked in the front, behind two other cars. The house's lights were on, and they crossed the small gate and stepped on the uneven gravel pathway toward the open door. She peered inside before stepping on the concrete floor of the house. The pungent smell of wilted flowers and candles burning hit her.

Around the room, women dressed in dark clothes sat on chairs against the wall. Opposite the door and surrounded by flowers stood a large, shining coffin on a plain two-foot pedestal. It was packed with people standing still and silent. A group of women prayed the rosary out loud in front of the coffin. Alicia stood next to the door for a few minutes, looking for a familiar face.

Sergio whispered, "There she is, Jacinta."

She approached them slowly, avoiding the people, and extended her hand. Jacinta's eyes were red, and she looked older. They shook hands formally, mumbling their condolences.

"Thank you. Thank you for coming. The rosary just started," Jacinta murmured with a tired voice.

"We will stay only for a little while," Alicia whispered, not knowing what else to say.

"It's OK. My mother is praying there. I'll get you a chair." She moved away from them.

"The coffin is sealed," Alicia whispered to Sergio.

"Yes," he answered back also in a whisper.

A portrait of Alcides in uniform was on top of the coffin, standing proudly and smiling at the camera. Beneath the picture of the young man lay a small Argentinean flag. It looked almost like a headscarf. Next to the heart-wrenching and straightforward adornment was a modest homemade flower bouquet.

If it were not for the small light blue and white flag and the picture, nobody would say that a combatant veteran of a recent war was lying inside the coffin. Alicia doubted the people around her would miss the military homage if it did not come; Argentina was not at war for a century. They did not have a reference point other than the movies, and everybody knew that films were fiction.

She felt an urgent need to leave the place. The mixture of anger and frustration was so overpowering that she could easily have screamed. Inadvertently, she squeezed Sergio's arm. He put his hand on hers, and she forced herself to overcome her agitation. They moved over to a corner, where Jacinta somehow had found two empty chairs against the wall for them. They would have to wait until the prayers ended, so they sat still. Fiddling with her handbag's clasp, the voices' monotonous cadence took over Alicia's uneasiness, and slowly she joined the women's prayer. Murmuring the old soothing Hail Mary that she had learned as a child from her mother, it was as if she was holding a lifesaver in a high sea.

Santa Maria,
Madre de Dios,
Ruega por nosotros, los pecadores,
Ahora y en la hora de nuestra muerte. Amén.

Slowly, swayed by the cadence of the words repeated over and over, the unsettling thoughts vanished, and the buzzing and the monotonous murmur of the voices filled her mind, calming her down with the mild, soothing effect of an alcoholic beverage.

XII

Alicia finished cutting the vegetables for Saturday's lunch. When she lit the stove, she watched, with dismay, how the blue gas flame dwindled down and disappeared. She felt a wave of anger rising inside her.

"The gas cylinder is empty, again!" She exploded. He was working at the dinner table.

"I meant to order them," Sergio said, "Sorry, I forgot about it."

"When were you going to do it? They're almost empty, and you don't give a hoot about it. Soon we won't have food or hot water in this house." Alicia's voice was loud and angry. Pablo moaned in his playpen, but they didn't look at him.

"You can cook with the camping stove in the meantime," he said, taking the two-burner device from under a kitchen counter and placing it on top of the stove, evidently upset. "What's the problem now?"

She did not answer, suffocated by the tears and escalating anger directed at no one in particular now. Pablo was crying louder, and Alicia picked him up.

"I can't believe we are fighting like this over such stupid things," Sergio said, standing in the middle of the living room. "Seriously, you should do something about it."

"Why me?" she was still angry and ready for another round of recriminations. "What about you? You're the one who forgot to order the cylinders," she said, walking Pablo up and down the room.

Sergio called her to his side. "Alicia, please come here, sit down."

She obeyed in silence. He sighed, caressed the boy's head tenderly, and said to her in a soft voice, "It's not about the gas cylinders, I know. I understand what's going on, what's worrying you. The only problem is we have to do something about it. It can't go on

160

like this."

"Do something? About what?" She asked, putting a toy in Pablo's hands.

"About what's going on with us, we have to work together; we cannot go at each other's throats every two minutes. This is bad. I know, I know you're suffering, especially after the other day. In the wake, I know. It was hard to take on top of everything else, and now you need help. So why don't we figure out something and try to see a counselor?"

"A counselor? What do you mean? Do I look crazy or unbalanced to you?"

He hesitated. "No. It's just an idea. You need to talk with somebody. Obviously, to me, it's not enough. I don't know how to help you."

"That's because I cannot find a listener in you any longer. You used to be the person I always talked to. You used to be there for me, and you're not there any longer." She cried openly again, and he waited for her to calm down, taking Pablo to the playpen with his toy.

"You know that's unfair," he was hurt. "I'm always here for you, but this is a help I can't give you. You need a professional, Alicia, don't take it wrong, please."

"I'm not doing anything of the sort. You want to blame me for whatever we are going through, but I'm not taking the blame, no sir." Deep down, she knew that things were becoming uncontrollable for her, but she was not ready to admit it yet.

The feeling of losing the grip of things further and further was distressing enough for her. She just needed to get back to her usual self, and everything was going to be all right again. However, she loathed the idea of having to talk to a stranger about what she was going through.

On Monday, Sergio got tickets to a Camerata Bariloche concert, and they asked Lidia to babysit Pablo that evening.

On Friday, before leaving for the concert, Alicia noticed how happy her son seemed to be while playing with the babysitter. She was aware of the insufficient time she had dedicated to him lately, and to make matters worse, the child had changed his attitude; he was no longer cheerful around her, no matter how much effort she put. Pablo had taken to moaning and hanging on to her. Alicia did not know how to manage the situation, feeling suffocated by his constant attention when nearby. During the concert and moved by the music, she wept quietly. Sergio noticed her tears and held her hand firmly.

The days had passed without any news from Father Johann. A letter from Sonia, mailed through Lita, had deepened her sense of helplessness. She said they had not located Susana yet, and her husband's health was frail. Don Roberto had been admitted again to the hospital for a couple of days. Sonia continued to march with the Mothers every Thursday, but now with renewed hopes, she explained, because of the prospect of free elections in the future. Alicia felt moved by her relentlessness.

"We are asking the truth from the government," her letter said. "There will come the day when they, or some others in their place, will tell us the truth and return our children to us." It was followed by a detailed description of her customary heartbreaking peregrination through police and military offices. Alicia cried over the letter. She admired the woman's strength and energy but worried about her, and worst of all, for extensive periods, she felt her hopes of finding Susana were gone.

Sunday was no better. She had difficulties focusing on the program they had prepared and left Martina to do the talking. Knowing that it was condemned to end soon, she could not share Martina's enthusiasm for finishing the run "with a bang," as she put it.

"Is it worth the effort? I wonder," she ventured.

Martina turned to her, a bit annoyed. "Alicia, you have changed a lot lately," she scowled. "You keep denying it, but I know the woman that started this program with me last year, and she doesn't seem to be around any longer."

Alicia managed to respond with an unconvincing, "That's nonsense."

"Still, if you need to talk about whatever, you know, I'm here."

"Thanks, Martina." Alicia was sincerely sorry about what was going on between them. The radio show had been a source of pride before. Now it was a nuisance. She was giving up the fight, and Martina resented her for quitting so soon. Alicia left the studio after her friend, who excused herself right after the program had ended.

She drove home, feeling upset and miserable. The coastal avenue bordered the gardens of the Cathedral and, impulsively, she turned around and parked the car behind the church, under the tall pine trees. She needed a quiet place to sit and think, and a church always worked its magic on her. Her head in turmoil, she sat at the back, in a discreet place, ignored by the scattered parishioners that slowly came in for the noon mass and took their positions near the altar. Alicia searched for that inner calm she always used to find in her mind whenever she took refuge in God's house, but she realized that it was different; her chaotic state was unabated. After a while, she grew impatient and walked toward the door. This was the only instance she could remember when a church's silence and peace did not help her.

"The candle maker will call tomorrow at 11:30 a.m."

The handwritten telephone note left on Monday morning on her desk had been left in the open for everybody to see. Alicia quickly folded it and looked around to see if anybody had noticed anything out of order, but everybody seemed concerned with their own business.

"Who took this call?" she asked aloud.

From the back of the room, one of the reporters lifted his hand: "It was me."

Alicia approached his desk, and trying to sound natural, asked, "When did this person call? Did he say anything else?"

"It was the voice of a woman, elderly, I would say," he said, trying to remember details. "She called about an hour ago. By the way, Alicia, if you find a good artisan for candles, would you pass me the name and how I can find him or her? Some of the products they sell around here are crappy."

"I promise." Alicia was relieved to see that he did not suspect anything. And why would he? She walked back to her desk hurriedly. The phone rang, and she jumped on the receiver, half-expecting this to be the call that she knew would not come until the next day.

It was Mariano on the line, and she felt her hopes returning. He sounded enthusiastic.

"We're doing well with that job we talked about when you were here last time," he said with a positive inflection, masking the real subject of Susana.

She could not contain her excitement.

He continued, "Do you remember the products we were looking for? Well, I got word that there are some in stock. It may be stored in a warehouse not far from here. I'll put an order so we can be sure, and if so, I will start the purchasing process."

"This... this is great news," Alicia murmured. "Can you give me more details? What type of purchase process?"

"This is a prepaid call, and I have only a few minutes left. So we'll talk about this soon."

"Sure. Tell me when."

"Call me on the number you'll have in the letter I've already mailed to you. As soon as you receive it, please call me. Remember, late at night, after ten, I would say."

"OK. Mariano, thank you." Alicia's voice broke. When she hung up, she felt her face flush with emotion. Mariano and his friends had heard something. They knew or thought they knew where Susana might be. Could it be possible? It was great news. Still, she should be cautious. Hopeful but careful. She had to wait for Mariano's letter.

This venue and the call from the priest's contact were only two faint glimmers of hope, but at least it was something.

The morning flew by. Alicia was so backed up in the job assignments that she had to make an effort to concentrate on them. Completely uninterested in the subjects she had to write about, her head on the open possibilities, Alicia was anxious to get home and tell Sergio her good news. Today things had turned for the better. She even dared to hope that this turn of events helped her stop their relationship's progressive weakening.

Sergio received the good news with his customary calm at home while helping her set the table for lunch.

"Good. I'm sincerely glad you heard something. Don't expect too much, though, and you won't be let down."

"At this point, anything, any news will be good, compared with what we had until now."

"True. Call me at the office as soon as you learn anything. I'll meet you at any time during the day if you want me to."

Alicia looked at him. In his eyes, he had an affectionate look for her that she loved and had not seen since the day she decided to go to Buenos Aires by herself. For a few seconds, she just stared at him in silence.

"Thank you, Sergio." She did not want to go all the way and say what she was feeling for him. Her fear of rejection was too much to surmount, and she just watched him. Surprisingly, he was the one to make a move now.

He held her gaze and said, "Hey, we are in this together. Remember? You're not alone. Although sometimes it seems like you don't see anybody around you, I'm here."

"I know."

"By the way, I almost forgot to mention that I met Luis at the bank teller's line this morning. I told him we'd stop by for coffee at their house after dinner."

"Good," she said, pleased.

She was elated. The exchange she had with Sergio was natural, similar to thousands of inconsequential and kind conversations they had over the years. It was a bonus to the good news of the day, and she sincerely enjoyed it.

They ate in silence, but they both knew the ice was broken. He went back to his blueprints, and Alicia put Pablo down for a nap. She needed to relax too. She was exhausted. After finishing a few chores in the house, she finally collapsed on her bed and opened a copy of last Sunday's paper magazine. She fell asleep almost immediately.

When she opened her eyes, she noticed that Sergio had closed the curtains earlier. He was searching for something, and she looked at the alarm clock on top of the night table.

"Wow, it's almost three. I overslept for more than an hour."

He turned to her, holding some clothes in his hands. "You didn't say anything about needing to go anywhere early. Besides, it's so cold and windy outside, and you were sleeping so peacefully. Did you rest well?"

She smiled and nodded. Sergio left the clothes on the chair in the corner of the room: "Good. You needed it."

He approached the bed by her side and took her right hand, resting on the comforter. "You look much better now," he added with a wince and sat next to her on the bed, caressing her arm tenderly.

Alicia recognized the familiar electric jolt that she felt when he touched her skin in a certain way. By the time his lips touched hers, she knew the feeling that nothing could break the bond she had with him was back in full force, and it was exhilarating.

Punctually at 11:30 the next day, she was at her desk. Every two minutes, she checked the time, waiting for the call from the candle maker. Candle-maker. The moniker sounded corny, so unoriginal. Who would pick such a name? She couldn't imagine the aloof, princely Father Johann creating such a disguise for a contact. No, this person has to be totally different. A busybody woman married to a security guy? Quite possible.

Seated at the office now, waiting for the call, she could not avoid often checking if the phone was in good working order, and when it rang, she jumped from her chair.

"Is this Alicia Rivera?" asked the weak voice of an old woman.

"Yes. Who's this?" Alicia made an effort not to miss her answer.

"I have a message from the candle maker."

"Yes, yes, go ahead."

The woman took a few seconds before continuing in one breath, as if reading from a notebook, "Tomorrow night, eight-thirty, wait for your contact sitting at the café inside El Viajero, the chocolate store, on Mitre Street."

Alicia asked involuntarily, "El Viajero?"

"Yes. Sit at the counter by yourself. Go alone and be there on time."

Recovering from the emotional shock, she said eagerly, "Yes. I'll be there. Thank you."

The woman hung up, and Alicia held the receiver on her ear for a few seconds before putting it back on the hook. She felt relieved that the place the woman had picked was a familiar one. She would not have felt comfortable going to an out-of-the-way spot to meet somebody she did not know. That place was busy and safe.

Alicia had found reasons to be hopeful again. Either from Father Johann's or Mariano's side, she was sure something positive would come out of it. Nothing seemed too weird or too far-fetched now, and she felt safe, dreaming optimistic outcomes.

Mumbling an excuse and picking up some folders and her tape recorder, she left the newsroom and drove in a daze to Sergio's office.

"I'll go with you tomorrow," he immediately said after he learned the news.

"No. You won't."

"You don't know who this guy is. I'm not letting you go alone." He was firm, but she needed to negotiate this one.

"Sergio, please, I thought we finally understood each other. If she sees me with you, it might all be over. The woman said I should go alone, and I will."

"How are you sure it is a *she*? Did the woman say she was the candle maker?"

"No. Of course not, but I assume it's a woman. Now that you mention it, the person could easily be a he," she hesitated. "But it doesn't matter. If it's a contact from this respected priest, it can't be bad. Can it? Besides, it is a busy, noisy place to try to do something aggressive."

Sergio turned around, shaking his head in disbelief. "What's with you lately? It's so hard to reason with you. But, to be honest, I'm getting tired of the whole thing."

"Please, Sergio, I don't want another fight. Don't do this to me." There was anguish in her voice.

He walked around the drawing table twice before stopping in front of her. He made an effort to smile while holding both her forearms and looking at her in the eye. "OK. Listen, I have an idea. You will go alone, but I will be there too. I don't want to risk anything. Let me be there, from afar. I will not approach you under any circumstances."

"Are you sure? If you don't, you could ruin everything, and you know that. Everything is hanging by a fine thread here."

"I won't talk to you. Let me be there. I swear I won't approach you unless you are in danger or something like that, which I don't believe would happen there."

"See? You are contradicting yourself now; you said you don't believe I would be in danger?"

He smiled again and said, "Okay, you're right. But I'll be there, watching from afar, that's all."

Alicia knew he would do that anyway, so she preferred to set out the conditions beforehand.

"Fine, you go, but we will not talk at all to each other till we get back home. We'll get there separately."

"I'll follow you to make sure you're okay, I promise."

That evening Mary and Luis agreed over coffee that it was wiser if next day Sergio watched from afar, just in case. Alicia was not entirely convinced. She had not noticed any suspicious movement around her lately. After returning from Buenos Aires, the feeling that somebody was following her was slowly waning. In perspective, those thoughts now seemed somewhat paranoid.

"I'll pick up Pablo at the daycare center and take him home while you go to the meeting," offered Mary, always the volunteer.

After a rushed dinner in a nearby eatery, they strolled slowly toward the chocolate store. Sergio would go ahead and sit somewhere far from the counter; she would get there a bit later after walking around the block at least once.

Edgy, Alicia stepped inside the coffee shop where the warm, reassuringly familiar sweet smell of cocoa brought up intense memories of the recent past. The store was busy with customers, mainly tourists; four of the six stools at the counter were vacant, and she took the one that allowed her an empty seat on either side.

After ordering coffee, she checked the Swiss clock's time perched over the large mirror on the wall behind the counter. It was eight-thirty sharp, and she was growing increasingly nervous now. Her heart was beating fast, and her hands were wet and cold. She knew that nothing could happen to her in plain view of so many people. Still, she could not contain her anxiety. She had prepared a series of questions and requests from the person that would contact her.

While walking to the coffee shop, she had glanced at the tables in the back. Sergio sat in one of them. He looked at her and nodded. After that, she just kept on walking.

Alicia had not returned to El Viajero since the day Susana got to Bariloche. Now it seemed like an eternity had passed. She glanced at the customers' reflection in the mirror; the place was crowded with noisy tourist groups buying chocolate. Some of the youngsters still wore their ski attire, showing off their fashionable jackets and *après-*ski boots. They were loud and seemed to be enjoying their vacation. Fortunately, both stools next to her remained empty.

Impatient, Alicia looked again in the mirror, checking the people behind her, and then she noticed the man walking toward the cash register. She blinked twice, still doubtful. Was that the man from the green Falcon, by her right? Her stomach churned. He was not looking at her, but it was he. What was this man doing here at this time?

Approaching the counter, he leaned over the empty stool at her right, the one closer to the cash register. "Two small cups of coffee, black, to go. Thank you," she heard him say in a rather loud voice to the young attendant who walked away. Alicia froze. It could not be a coincidence. She was looking at him in the mirror, and he turned, smiling, also looking at her reflection across the counter. She heard him say now in a lower but clear voice, "Nice to see you again, Alicia." He glanced briefly toward the attendant pouring the coffee, half-sat on the empty stool, and then, without turning his head to her and looking at her image, he said with sarcasm, "So, looking for help from the candle maker, eh?"

The low voice, almost a whisper, made the northwestern accent more noticeable. Alicia even believed she saw him trying a sort of grin. She was looking up at his image in silence, and for a moment, she turned slightly to her right, glancing at him sideways and then to the mirror. Since his arrival, he had set the rules of not looking at each other directly. She knew that she should answer something, anything. If the guy could help, she did not want to snub him out without giving him a chance. At the same time, she was not sure about what to say. His tone had the same arrogant pitch that revolted her the first time they met.

"How –how can *you* help me?" she managed to utter, realizing that this was only one of the many questions she could ask him.

"Let's say it's going to have a price –financial and personal on your part. It won't be easy to get what you are looking for, you understand."

"What do you exactly mean?"

"Well, it will take research, personal contacts, money. It will be expensive," the man murmured, glancing again at the waiter.

"How much?" she managed to ask in a whisper.

He answered without hesitation to her image in the mirror: "Exactly forty thousand, in American Dollars, one payment, ten days from today."

"That's a lot of money!"

Alicia's heart was beating wildly against her chest. The attendant brought the coffee. The man handed a bill and received the ticket and the change back. Alicia sensed he was about to leave her with insufficient information and was desperate to grasp the details of his request. She had the feeling that the time was like water spilling through her fingers and implored with urgency, "How should we go about this?"

"Be ready; I'll contact you. I know some important people, but they are short on patience. So it has to be done soon," he said, turning his attention to the coffee cups that were on the counter now. He picked them up without looking at her image in the mirror again.

"Soon? When?" The pressure on her chest was suffocating. He was about to leave the counter, so she couldn't avoid it any longer and looked at him. He held her gaze.

"I told you. Come up with the cash; you have ten days. I'll send you instructions soon," the man paused for a second, and as an afterthought, he winced at her with a smirk, "Watch out for counterfeit bills, the twenties in particular," then he turned around, his back to her and walked away from the counter. She turned to the mirror, and with her eyes still fixed on his reflection, she saw him approaching another man standing next to the door, who took the second coffee cup from him. Immediately both stepped out of the store.

Alicia tried to find Sergio in the busy reflections of the salesroom. He had probably seen somebody leaning on the counter next to her, but he might not have noticed that they had talked. The man had stayed only a few minutes, waiting for the coffee, never close enough to have been seen from afar as having an exchange of words with her.

Unsure of what to do next, she sipped the rest of the coffee left in her cup. It was still warm. Everything had happened so quickly and unexpectedly. It was only seven minutes past eight-thirty, and the meeting was already over. She had a very different expectation of this evening. Who was this guy? Why did he keep appearing in her life like a shadow? If he was planning to endanger her in any way, shouldn't it have happened by now? What had he meant by money and, how did he put it? Personal effort? Personal endeavor, she thought he said. She could not recall exactly, but she was sure that he told her forty thousand dollars, and that was an enormous sum for them.

Her stomach was upset, either because of the coffee or the stress. She felt suddenly ill and left the counter, walking toward the restrooms at the back of the store. Looking toward Sergio's table, she noticed that he stood up and was about to leave his table when he saw her walking. She made a sign with her hand that everything was fine, trying to smile, and he sat again.

Alicia ran to the bathroom, knowing that she would not stop the vomit if she did not get to the toilet in time. When she recovered enough to return to the salesroom, Sergio stood by the counter, feigning interest in the cakes showcase, and seemed reassured to see her. She walked by, and he followed her to the door.

The chilly air outside was reinvigorating, and she looked around. Was the man still nearby? Probably not. She walked to the busy intersection and slowed down. Sergio walked behind her a few steps; then they turned left at the corner, out of Mitre Street's bright lights where the tourists strolled in groups.

"Are you okay?" he asked, a little confused, grabbing her arm. "Did you get to talk with anybody in there?"

She nodded, and when he saw her eyes welling with tears, he sighed.

"Let's go home," he said, lightly holding her by the arm. They walked in silence uphill toward the parking lot.

On their way home, Alicia recounted the meeting details, and he listened in silence, his eyes on the road. "Son of a bitch," he finally said, "he fooled me well. I saw a guy standing there, ordering something, but it didn't look as if he was talking to you, so I ignored his face on his way out."

Sergio agreed that the sum was high for them, and they devised a plan to get hold of the money. Their house was paid in full, but mortgages through the banks were unavailable except for very few new homes or government officials' friends. The only other option was feared but much sought-after, mortgage pawnshops. There were two private lenders in town: Pedro Uranga and Assaf Rosen. The first one represented several influential local investors, and Rosen was an independent operator.

"Well, many stories are going around. For example, they don't forgive debts, but they say both are fair in their dealings."

"We have no other way to get the money. So before we do anything, Sergio, I want to be sure you want to proceed with this. It's a lot of money. It's a big chunk of our house's value."

"Why, do you have any doubts?" he glanced at her.

"Oh, no, of course not." Her voice was firm. "I just want to make sure that it is okay with you."

"Didn't I suggest it?" he asked with a hint of reproach in his voice.

"Yes, you did, and I am very grateful for that," she said, conciliatory.

"We will contact Sonia and see if they can come up with part of it. They will do whatever is needed, I know, so we'll see."

They drove in silence and went straight to Mary and Luis' home to ponder repeatedly over the words of the man of the green Falcon.

"This is definitely a weird situation," Mary said after they debated exhaustively the short encounter later that night at her home. "It doesn't seem to be dangerous, though."

Sergio and Luis reluctantly concurred, but Alicia was still shocked by the dreaded man's unexpected surfacing and wondering what his words might mean. It was not clear to her yet.

Mary and Luis thought the mortgage pawn against their house was a risky solution, but they agreed with Sergio that it was the only way to get a significant amount of money right away.

"It's an acre of excellent land," Luis said, "Uranga and Rosen will salivate at the thought of grabbing it. You have to be careful, Sergio, and try to negotiate how to pay the money back on your own schedule. The interest will be high."

They left close to midnight, carrying Pablo sound asleep and wrapped in a warm blanket. They had talked only about the money, but Alicia knew that Sergio had many more concerns about the possibility of Alicia having another encounter with the shadowy man. They went to bed in silence, both immersed in their thoughts and uncertainties.

As usual, Alicia had trouble falling asleep, and for the first time since Susana disappeared, she dreamed about her.

They were younger, maybe teenagers, and walked by the same street where Susana lived when they first met at school. It was dark, and the tall elm trees that bordered the wide sidewalks of Villa Devoto, their old neighborhood, seemed like menacing presences in the night. Alicia could not distinguish the houses and was unsure where they were walking when suddenly, without a word, Susana sat down on the cobblestones. Alicia stood next to her. She noticed that her friend was sitting on the old tram's railway. After so many years, they still haven't pulled out these rails from the street; no trams are running through them any longer, she thought. *In fact, we never even saw one tramway on these tracks*. She approached her friend and extended her hand. "Get up, Susana. It's late. Let's go." Susana looked up and shook her head with a grin. Was she smiling? Or crying? It was dark, and now Alicia heard a sound similar to a train approaching. She panicked; she could not see it, but she knew, at that exact moment, that it was an old tram, and it could hit Susana. Alicia tried to scream at her to get up, but her voice would not come out of her throat while Susana stayed there, refusing to get out of the rails. Then, shaking and desperate, she woke up.

Sergio was sitting on the bed and had switched the lights on. He extended his arms and held her tight, stroking her hair. She cried on his chest, unable to say anything for a while.

On Thursday, Pablo woke up early with a high fever. Alicia took him to the pediatrician and called Carlos Alvarez to let him know she would be working from home the rest of the morning. Sergio agreed to work at home in the afternoon so she could go to the newsroom. Impatient, Alicia got there soon after lunch and checked her mail. Mariano's letter was not there.

The phone rang, and she heard the overly restrained, deep voice of Jacinta.

"I'm glad to hear from you," Alicia said. "We tried to contact you. We drove by your house, but nobody was at home. Are you okay?"

"I'm fine, thank you."

"How's your mother doing?"

"She's pretty ill."

"What's wrong?"

"I think it is sorrow. She's crying so much, lost weight, and is sad all the time. She's not the same person she used to be and doesn't want to accept Alcide's death. She visits the cemetery every day."

"I'm so sorry. Can I help in any way?"

"No. Thank you, I don't think so. I don't think nobody can help her."

"Don't say that. I'm sure your Mom would talk with somebody. Anybody she respects and listens to. Maybe a priest?"

"I don't think so. Mom doesn't like our priest."

"There has to be somebody else. Maybe a friend?"

"Maybe—a woman we know."

Jacinta hesitated. Alicia knew what she was trying to say, so she went ahead with it.

"Do you know any *machi* that can help her?" There was a silence, and Alicia thought she might have gone too far. Not everybody in town was respectful of the Mapuche beliefs and traditions, and she did not want Jacinta to misunderstand her when she suggested her mother see a tribal healer.

"Yes, maybe," she finally said, still hesitant. "Maybe a *machi* can help her."

"Jacinta, please, let me know if there's anything I can do."

"Well, yeah. I need my job back, if you don't mind, señora. Can I go back to work at your home, or have you already hired somebody else?

"Of course not! I wouldn't do that. You can come back whenever you want. In fact, my house is a mess without your help. We'll be happy to have you back."

"Thanks, señora. I need this break. If you don't mind, I will start on Monday."

"Good. See you on Monday then."

She hung up, and Alicia felt thankful that Jacinta would get back to her routine. At the same time, she was not sure how to afford her wages. Their budget would be strained to the limit. The Malvinas veteran's families were not getting any compensation from the military. They were now demanding a pension from the Junta, and she was sure it would be a long, uphill battle. Alicia did not have the heart to tell Jacinta that she might eventually have to let her go shortly, though.

Mariano's letter was in her mailbox the next day. She pushed the rest of the mail to the side of her desk and was about to open the light blue and white-bordered airmail envelope when Carlos Alvarez approached her.

"I meant to tell you, Alicia, I have just scheduled two great interviews with you." He seemed proud. "Guess with whom at the upcoming film festival? Say two big names. Go ahead."

With the letter burning in her hand, Alicia was not in the mood to be interrupted to play some silly word game with him, but she did not show her thoughts. He was a good guy, this Carlos, she could not complain. He had always backed her up at work. The least she could do was to be patient and polite. Mainly since she suspected that he had covered for her at some point with the Mayor's office after her impulsive letter about the primary school in Barrio Alto. That one was a delicate matter, and Alicia was curious to find out as soon as the circumstances were right, and she could feel comfortable asking him about it. But that would have to wait for now.

She smiled as nicely as she could. "I'm terrible at guessing, Carlos. Tell me. Please," she implored mockingly, knowing that it would delight him. He shrugged.

"Okay. You never would guess, anyway. I got you not one, but two exclusives with none other than Maria Luisa Bemberg and Fernando Ayala." Beaming, he stepped back, ready to appreciate the impact on her. In part impressed with the names and not wanting to disappoint him, she exaggerated her reaction. "They will be here in August for the closing of the Film Festival, and I got the interviews for Friday the 27th!"

"Ohmigosh, Carlos, I can't believe you got that exclusive for me!" she clapped like a child. But of course, it was what he expected.

Nodding with satisfaction, he said, "You will write two good pieces out of these interviews, I know it."

She fussed a bit more about it. She was in awe of the chance to interview these two directors, but Mariano's letter was still unopened in her hand, and she wanted to get back to it. After another exchange about the interviews, he finally walked away.

The letter was brief. It repeated what Mariano had told her on the phone and had his new phone number. He and his friends were convinced that the information the man just released gave them was correct. Alicia could hardly wait for the evening, hoping for more news about Susana than the few lines in the letter.

Alicia was glad when she finished her tasks for the day and returned home. Sergio had everything under control, as usual. After a productive working day at home, he had a roast in the oven, and Pablo was playing in bed, recovering from his fever. They exchanged news over dinner, and before ten, late as Mariano had suggested, she drove back to town.

Alicia worried about Pablo's behavior. Watching him and Sergio together, she realized that the child would act like a spoiled brat as soon as she appeared. It seemed he did this on purpose, and it made her feel incompetent in a field Alicia thought had mastered quite well. Pablo's uneasiness with her was another source of instability that she should, at some point, talk in-depth with a counselor if she ever got around to scheduling an appointment.

The downtown offices of the telephone company were open for business past midnight. Only two customers talked inside the cabins aligned against the wall, and the only employee behind the large counter looked bored.

"Cabin number 6," he said with a yawn.

Mariano answered immediately. Alicia was relieved to hear his voice.

"Good news, dear *flaquita*. We have good news. We know Susana is still there," he sounded happy.

She's alive, thank God, Alicia thought and sighed. "Where is she?"

"We don't know exactly where. We only know what this guy said. They took him to several detention places, and when he was released, he was dropped at a countryside bus station somewhere around San Nicolas, half-naked and beaten badly. He gave us a list of names he remembered from people held in those places. We hope his memory is good enough."

"So, what did he say about her?"

"He heard Susana's voice calling from another cell in the hallway. He did not see her. She shouted her name and other names for him to know. The place is at the northern tip of Buenos Aires. They held him in three other places, all of them around the area. He is not sure where exactly those places are, but we have a good idea."

"Is she okay?"

"She was, not long ago. He heard her again about two weeks ago."

"Thank God."

"Yes. Now we are working around the clock trying to find out where she is. They transfer the prisoners often in some cases, and we don't know why. We will find out something soon."

"You think so?"

"Yes, I'm very optimistic now. At least we know that Susana's been seen, and she was okay. This is good news." He hesitated. "You know, we believe this informer is afraid. He is not talking much. Probably he's been threatened with retaliation if he talks about anything. So he's giving only names. He's not specific about places, but it's enough. We are confident about finding her."

"Is this man reliable?"

"We don't know. It's hard to say. We hope he is."

"I've never prayed so hard for something in my life as I'm now praying for her."

"Well, you already got an answer to your prayers. Keep on praying. It helps." Mariano seemed convinced and candid about his faith in some divine intervention. Alicia was not so sure about it.

"I will, I will," she said, trying to convince herself that her actions had influenced the news he was giving her. "Have you guys talked about this with Sonia?"

"Yes. We update her constantly. She's okay. We make sure her parents have at least what they need."

"Thank you, Susana will appreciate your help so much. Do you think it is safe to exchange letters with Sonia about delicate matters? I don't want to bother her cousin again, and I have a couple of things I want to share with her."

"I don't see why not. Everything seems quiet around her. But you never know. Sonia is probably being followed by those guys, that's for sure."

"I wonder if her phone is safe."

"Hard to know. She's with the Mothers, don't forget that. They keep a close eye on them. So you just be careful."

"Thanks. I will. When should I call you back?"

"I'll call you at work if I have news. If I don't call in a week from today, call me back here, same time."

Alicia thought about telling Mariano about her own search for help through Father Johann and the upcoming meeting, but she did not say anything. She wasn't sure if it was entirely safe to talk. It was impossible to assess if they were using a safety line or not. Mariano seemed to believe so, but Alicia opted to keep the meeting to herself.

Returning home, she had mixed feelings. Was the man that heard Susana's voice a reliable source? She remembered the stories she had heard before. There were unanswered questions. Why some of the disappeared come back at all? Was there something they did or said that helped them over the others? What was it? Naming people under torture? Or were they freed so there would be a constant reminder of what was going on in the secret dungeons of the Dirty War if people refused to accept submission? Were these freed prisoners reliable at all? No matter what they had done while locked up, they would always be suspected. What a tragic destiny the military had designed for them.

The lonely road bordering the lake brought back unsettling memories of the night when the men in the green Falcon stopped her. She had the terrifying certainty that she was walking in circles, and she might never get out of this nightmare.

Shuddering, Alicia drove as fast as possible back home, trying unsuccessfully to dispel her doubts and soothe the familiar oppression taking hold of her stomach once again.

XIII

Sergio stood up from his drawing board and walked toward the window, glancing at the driveway. It was Saturday morning, and Alicia had come back a little while ago from the phone company's long-distance booths downtown and did not say a word. Since she returned home, she has been taking care of Pablo.

Sergio walked toward her and asked, "You haven't said anything about the call. Did Sonia mention how much they could get or when she might have it?"

"She has nothing yet," she answered, lifting her son and placing him inside his playpen. I hate to call her, even if I want to find out how she's doing. Last time, she cried for a while; she's in an emotional seesaw. Today she's thrilled, full of hopes again, and she's sure she'll get the money. I didn't ask for details, but probably they'll go to a pawnshop too. What else? Unless they have a relative that could come up with something—I don't believe they have any savings left by now." Alicia put Pablo's toys back next to him. "She said she would call me on Monday, or Tuesday, the most, with an answer."

They had been in a frantic race to get the forty thousand American dollars demanded by the man from the green Falcon, and Sergio was showing signs that he was worried. The ten days seemed too short now. To show their power, the potential lenders pretended not to be available at the first approach. It was their way of signaling that the interested party should make concessions to get what they wanted. Sergio had to call twice before he finally got to see them.

He answered the question he knew she was about to ask. "I think we should take Uranga's mortgage offer. We have no time to spare. Besides, it doesn't matter now how much Susana's parents can come up with. I don't think it will be as much as twenty thousand. We'll

179

have to get the rest."

"How much did you ask for?"

"I told both of them that I would need about thirty thousand, just in case."

"Good. Sonia seemed a bit surprised by the total amount, but she will do her best, I know." She approached the window and stood next to him in silence for a few seconds before adding, "About Uranga's offer if you think he offers the best deal, I'm okay with it."

They both knew the magnitude of what they were about to do. If late on the monthly payments, the punitive interests would be high. If they missed them, they would be evicted without consideration, and Uranga's company would become the legal owner of their home.

Sergio sighed. "You know you'll have to let Jacinta go."

She took a minute to answer. "Yes. I know. I already have the speech rehearsed in my mind. I don't want to hurt her, but I know that I will, anyway. She needs the money too, you know."

"Sorry, Alicia."

"It's okay. I know I'll have to do it," Alicia turned around, back to Pablo. "By the way, next week I will talk with Carlos Alvarez about some extra assignments. Plus, Diario Rio Negro may need freelancing articles from the area for their Sunday magazine. So I'll try there too."

As a skilled moneylender, Uranga had promised a better deal for the mortgage than did Assaf Rosen. The difference between them was only a few points of interest, and, in the long run, both were determined profiteers.

"It's going to be fine," he said with a calm voice. "We'll manage, you'll see. As long as we don't miss any more projects at Huemul and keep getting their contracts, it will be fine. I don't know how those guys do it, but they must have found a way to milk some cow or other in Buenos Aires, maybe in exchange for a bribe. I don't want to know, as long as the jobs keep on coming."

"Isn't it disgusting? We have to accept corruption because otherwise, we can't survive. How sad is this?"

"It would be sadder if we did not have any means at all. But, unfortunately, that's the way it is. It's a shame, but that's reality, Alicia. Don't feel guilty. You cannot change it."

She remained in silence for a while, playing with Pablo. "My only hope is to bring Susana back," she said, glancing sidewise, expecting his comment, but he was nodding toward the driveway.

"You were expecting Martina; she's already here."

"Wow, she's early. We have to prepare for our last program, and it will take a few hours of work. We haven't agreed yet about what the leading subject should be. Great."

"Have you got something for tomorrow's program?"

"Yeah, it's all done. We will review it now. But I hope we can make up our minds about the final one. That one will be hard to agree on," Alicia said, walking toward the door and opening it to welcome Martina in.

They worked for some time and then decided to take a break. While Alicia was in the kitchen brewing the coffee, Martina got a chair across the small table. Alicia knew she would talk about the subject she positively did not want to touch with her by her attitude.

"I hope you won't mind me telling you, but you seem almost happy that all this is ending. I never noticed before that you were so tired of the show," Martina started, hesitant.

Alicia did not answer, feigning to pay excessive attention to the kettle.

Martina finished her thought. "Maybe it is better this way, then."

"No. It isn't better," Alicia said with her eyes still fixed on the kettle. "They have kicked us out, tied our hands, they are shutting us down, it's not better, and it's a disgrace."

"I know. I was thinking about how you seem to be taking this, so... unlike you. I saw you fight for things that were far less important than this. What's wrong with you?"

"I'm just tired, so very drained."

It was a sincere answer, but Martina did not seem to believe it was enough. Alicia did not say more, and the subject was dropped there. They tried to tackle the program's final broadcast with energy, but they both knew that things never would be the same between them. Martina felt excluded, and Alicia felt frustrated because there was no way to explain what she was going through without telling her more than she should know.

The next day the program seemed monotonous and uneventful, and they sighed with relief when the red light went off. Now there was only one to go. So they departed ways without much talk, and Alicia drove off with a sense of defeat.

The hatred she felt for the unelected men running the country and all their underlings kept on growing inside her. It was as if it were poison invading her physically, obfuscating her mind. The less she talked about these feelings with others, the more asphyxiating they became. The pain in her stomach that had become an almost daily occurrence was back. She lit another Jockey Club while maneuvering to keep the car steady. After two puffs, she had to squeeze it, pushing other cigarette butts inside the small, almost full car ashtray. She felt disgusted by the bitter taste she now had to associate with the stomach pain and made a mental note to keep the cigarettes in check. She did not want to get sick just now.

On Monday morning, the phone rang twice on her desk, and Alicia picked up. When she heard Sonia's voice, she sighed, relieved.

"I'm so glad to hear your voice. I was waiting," Alicia heard herself saying.

"I have good news about the money we need. We got fifteen thousand. We would have gotten more if only we had extra time." Alicia noticed her voice was apologetic.

"This is great, Sonia. Have you arranged everything that you told me? Is still your friend coming here? Is she reliable enough?"

"Yes."

"Sonia, the important thing is that she be reliable," Alicia said, showing anxiety.

"Don't worry about it. Maria Luz is honest and responsible; that's why she is chaperoning these high school teens. The envelope is safe with her."

"I'm glad to hear that. I'm fretting about everything these days."

"I know, I know how much you are doing, don't think for a moment that we are not aware of it, and we are so grateful to you." Her voice broke into a sob, and Alicia waited until she recovered. "Can I ask you where are you guys getting the money from? Would that be a pawn shop?" Alicia hesitated, and Sonia added, "I knew that. I don't know how we could ever thank you enough for what you're doing, you and Sergio."

Alicia did not give her details. There was no point to it. Probably

Sonia and Roberto were going through the same painful process now. She sighed.

"Susana deserves it, and more. Let's hope everything turns out fine. Let's be optimistic and try everything we can. We'll get her back, you'll see, I have this hunch that everything will be okay," she said in a voice that did not mask the fear that there were no guarantees for their enterprise.

"I'm sure it will," echoed Sonia in the same uncertain tone. "This girl will contact you as soon as she gets there. From then on, it's up to you how you want to go about it."

"I will keep you posted. By the way, I meant to ask you. Have you heard from our friend Mariano lately?"

"Yes. He calls every week. We met with a group of mothers two weeks ago regarding paperwork and assistance. Those young men seem to be very helpful."

"Any news about where Susana is now?"

"No. We believe she is still at the same place. It's hard to know. We hope she's okay, but we don't know," she said, and her voice cracked. Alicia let her catch her breath. "Anyway, I have more hope now. I hope this man you are in contact with will help her to be released. He came well recommended, didn't he?"

"Of course. I trust he will help us," Alicia said, trying to assuage her own doubts.

A few minutes of mutual reassurances followed, and Alicia hung up, convinced that she had not lifted the other woman's spirits.

Later on, Alicia was working at the file cabinets at the end of the room when she saw Carlos Alvarez waving to her from his desk. A call for her, he signed; it should be Sergio, with news about the deal. She picked up the line on the nearby phone.

"Hi. Alicia. It's me." The deep, accented voice froze her, but she was relieved to hear from him. He did not wait for her answer. "Now listen carefully. You will leave the envelope at the public bus stop of Piedra Del Águila, inside the women's bathroom. There are five old cubicles there. Put the envelope atop the middle cubicle's water tank. It shouldn't show from below. Go there this Saturday afternoon, right after lunch. Let's say... one o'clock or so."

Alicia was feverishly trying to repeat to herself the instructions, not to forget any detail.

"Fine, I'll be there," she said and then added, quivering: "What if we need more time?"

"You haven't got more time. I told you that before. So don't mess it up."

"I won't. Listen, are you sure you can get my friend out?" she ventured, anguished.

"I know what I'm doing." He was more determined now. "Just do your end of the pact, and everything will work out fine."

He wants his money, Alicia thought, shuddering, uncertain that he would deliver as promised. If he did not, she would have no recourse left. No, most probably, this was the way these things got done. She was not used to shady dealings, and that was all. Maybe the personal part he alluded to was this, the trust she should put on him without any assurances.

"Okay. I will; we want Susana out soon, you know that" she said and instantly felt stupid, stating the obvious.

"Yeah, I know," he said before he hung up.

She was left shaking, trying to review mentally every detail he had given. She looked around, but nobody seemed aware of her or the call. Then, on an impulse, she took her handbag and picked up a folder at random, walking out of the newsroom with an excuse. Unable to wait for Sergio's call now, she would meet him at work.

He was on the phone with a client when she walked in. One of his co-tenants was in a corner, his head deep in a pile of blueprints. He waved to her, and she did the same. Alicia stood nearby Sergio's table, and when he finished his call, he turned toward her.

"I didn't know you were coming. I was about to call you. Uranga will have the money tomorrow morning for us. You'll have to come with me to sign the papers at his office."

She did not answer; her eyes puffed from crying while driving. Then, tears started coming down her reddened cheeks again.

He approached her and stroked her head softly. "Everything will be fine. Calm down."

She melted down and broke into a loud, uncharacteristic cry. Evidently taken by surprise, the other man tiptoed to the door and left without looking at them. Alicia did not care any longer; she let her wails out; she had lost all sense of embarrassment. Sergio pulled her gently toward him, his arm around her shoulders. She kept on sobbing on his chest, and none of them minded the traces of mascara and makeup her tears were leaving on the light-colored shirt.

The show had just ended, and Alicia walked inside the glistening and recently open movie theater. As she stepped in, the wooden double doors from the projection room opened. The public started coming out, dispersing in the lobby toward the exit doors.

She stood next to the ladies' room entrance, waiting for the woman who called her earlier and had Sonia's envelope.

"I have something for you from Sonia Machevsky," Maria Luz had said cautiously on the phone.

"Ah, yes. I was waiting for your call." Alicia was relieved to hear she was in Bariloche, and she brought the money on time. "Where are you staying?"

"Downtown, at the Cruz Del Sur hotel."

"Good. You are close to the movie theater on Moreno Street," Alicia instructed. "I'll be waiting for you in the lobby, near the ladies' room. I will wear a navy blue wool scarf over a grey tweed coat."

Maria Luz said she would wear jeans and a red duvet parka.

Alicia had been waiting for only a few minutes when an athletic-looking young woman, coming out of the bathroom, walked straight to her.

"Alicia?" She was smiling widely. "I'm Maria Luz." On closer look, Sonia's messenger was older than her first impression on the phone. Alicia realized that she could be easily her age. Was she a friend of Susana that she had never met before?

They shook hands and walked out of the building, blending with the other moviegoers. Maria Luz walked briskly, and Alicia, dressed for an official function downtown and wearing high heel boots, tried to keep her pace.

"Let's go to the hotel, across the street. I have Sonia's package for your there."

Alicia agreed and followed her through the lobby to the elevators.

"I share a room with another coordinator for this group. Fortunately, she's out but will be back soon," Maria Luz said.

As soon as they walked into the room, Maria Luz opened her oversized handbag. Took a bulky letter-sized, flapped plastic envelope with an elastic cord and button closure. She handed it to Alicia with a quick movement. Alicia opened the flap.

"Sit down, please. Here," Maria Luz said. "And count all of it. Sonia was precise about this."

Alicia sat on a chair next to a coffee table and took the hundred-dollar bills out of the envelope. Maria Luz stood next to her while she counted them.

"It's fine." Alicia finished counting.

"Good," Maria Luz murmured. "I was sort of nervous, traveling with so much cash."

Alicia put the bills back in the plastic envelope and looked up to her: "Thank you for helping with this."

"No problem," she said, and then hurriedly, "The girls are all over on my floor, better if they don't see us together, so I won't have to give explanations. My roommate is about to return too."

Alicia was ready to follow any instructions and stood up. Still, Maria Luz seemed embarrassed by sending her out like this.

"Sorry, Alicia, if I seem rude. I want to keep this encounter between you and me."

"It's fine," she said, sliding the thick envelope into her briefcase. Then, turning to Maria Luz, she noticed that the young woman tended her hand again, and she did the same. Now the woman did not shake her hand. Instead, she held it between her own hands and said, gravely, "I hope you can help bring her back. Please, do whatever you can." Her eyes were watery and bright in the dim light of the room. Alicia wished she could ask her more details; how long had she known Susana, even if they were friends. However, she did not dare ask; the woman seemed hurried.

"I'll do my best," she murmured back. "Thank you for being the courier here."

When she walked into the elevator, a group of chatty students got inside after her, laughing out loud.

"Lobby?" one of them asked her.

"Yes," she answered, fastening the briefcase lock in a mechanical gesture. Her mind was rushing. They had the money now, and things were moving in the right direction. She now would be able to deliver the forty thousand dollars on Saturday. It was another step closer to Susana's freedom.

The rest of the week was a rush of nervous activity. Alicia and Sergio did not get into arguments, as in a tacit pact. Instead, both avoided quarreling and tried not to talk about the challenges lying ahead if they could not comply with the terms of the deal. The lender seemed like a nice guy, unassuming and folksy, but they left the place as soon as the complicated paperwork was finished, and the money changed hands. Uranga was smiling, satisfied, while they went in silence.

"He has small pointy teeth, like a shark, doesn't he?" Alicia said after they had stepped outside the door. He laughed with a tense and loud laugh that prompted her to look at him, surprised. He was nervous; she could see it.

On Thursday morning, Alicia talked with Jacinta about letting her go. Looking at her dark brown, sad eyes, Alicia had unsettling thoughts. Visions of having power enough to physically knock the military junta and its enablers out of the country.

Her fantasies made her feel worse still, and when Jacinta was ready to leave, she handed her the last payment with an extra two weeks in it. They shook hands politely but awkwardly, and Alicia walked her to the door for the last time. She doubted she would see her again. They gravitated in such foreign circles that she was almost sure their paths would not cross once more.

Alicia stood by the window, looking at the young woman walking by the graveled street to the bus stop. She was sure that Jacinta would never know how much they had to scrape their budget to come up with the money she was carrying in that envelope. She knew that Jacinta was unaware that all of them were in the same predicament, only separated by a fictitious social status divide. That, one way or the other, everybody was tightly connected and doomed or saved almost in the same fashion.

"Do you think we will find snow on the road?" Alicia exhaled the smoke slowly while watching Lake Nahuel Huapi's last curves through the left window. The dark blue waters ended on the now almost white beach that she could see from the road, a half-mile down, beyond the snowed, soft hill that descended to the lake and in summer showed its bare pebbles, small rocks, and sand.

"I hope not. The road should be clear by now," he said. "So far, so good."

"I hope Pablo doesn't act up with Mary. He's been a brat lately."

He glanced at her sidewise. "Not only Pablo."

"Oh, not again, please." Alicia was not smiling. She would not start an argument now on their way to Piedra Del Águila, the town between the city of Neuquén and Bariloche that the man had designated for the delivery.

They were now crossing the impressive Valle Encantado, or Enchanted Valley, a natural monument with several miles of tall rock formations eroded ages ago by the elements. Today it showed a variety of shapes that could easily compete, if they were smaller, for the weirdest natural sculptures. The tall volcanic rocks still had the new dust of the previous day's snowfall, and the many cypresses that grew on the lower rises projected dark and velvety shades.

"Tall formations, aren't they?" Sergio said, glancing right and left.

"No kidding," she answered, trying to see the details and the big picture all at once. It was a beautiful leg of the journey just after leaving the Nahuel Huapi Lake area, the last remnants of the mountains before the beginning of the never-ending grasslands of the Patagonian plateau.

"These rocks always humble me. How many centuries of water work, from before we even appeared on this planet," he said.

"Yup… and they will be here long after our stupid fights and disputes are over. It's sort of comforting to know that they are something that will last. It's like watching the stars at night, on the beach of Lake Guillelmo."

"You got that right," he nodded.

They drove in silence again. The formations grew sparse, and lower hills appeared, green and velvety, descending to the Limay River, down below at their right.

Alicia wished that the beautiful landscape could, by some magical trick, influence her mind and soothe her pain. Lately, confusion and anguish was the prevailing mood inside her. That, and hate, a venomous feeling of hatred, overpowered her, and she tried to alleviate with fantasies of vengeance. Did Sergio realize how she felt? He would be horrified if he could read her mind. She was sure of that.

When they got to Piedra Del Águila, the gas station and the tourist service area had only a few cars. Mercifully, there were no tourist buses in sight. A restaurant attached to the building served the travelers going to and from Bariloche. The rest of the town was a line of buildings on Route 237, the main highway.

"It's quiet now," Sergio said, looking at his wristwatch. "We are on time."

"I won't find many women in the bathroom," Alicia said. "I'll go there right away before a tourist bus gets here."

She lifted the handbag from the back seat, with the forty thousand American dollars in an envelope inside.

"I will wait for you outside the building, parked over there," Sergio motioned toward the restaurant. "I'll put some gas in the car while you go inside."

She got out, and he added, "Be careful, please," before she closed the door.

She walked toward the central service area, clutching the handbag tightly. From the glass door, she saw the reflection of the car moving to the gas pump. She walked toward the restroom area. Three young women were chatting and combing their hair inside the ladies' room, ostensibly on their way out.

Alicia's hands were wet, and she felt the bottom of her feet wet also. Her heart was beating fast, and she tried to calm down before looking for the third booth from the left. It was empty, and she walked in, locking the door. She hung the handbag on a hook mounted on the wall. The bathrooms' booths were old but clean and freshly painted. Each one had an iron-cast water tank, painted in dark green, high above the toilets. A metal chain that came down almost to Alicia's head level was hooked to a handle on the tank's side to flush the water. Alicia realized that she would need to step on the toilet to reach the tank's top and secure the envelope there.

The three women had gone. Somebody else seemed to be using one of the other booths but none next to hers. Alicia knew she would not be alone for long. She took the envelope out of the handbag and stepped on the toilet, ready to maintain her balance using the booth's walls if needed. It was sturdy enough, and Alicia quickly slipped the envelope atop the middle of the tank, pushing it further until it did not show from below. Satisfied, she stepped down. To reassure herself that it was safely there, she pulled the handle and flushed water. Nothing happened.

Voices of women coming into the room reminded her that she should leave. She washed her hands meticulously while many more women walked in, chatting and evidently a bit wobbly from the long bus or car ride.

She left the warm service building and looked around for Sergio, parked nearby. He came out of the car.

"Do you want to have lunch here or somewhere else?" he asked.

"Not here, please. Let's try another restaurant, further north," she said, shivering from the cold wind and getting inside the vehicle. They drove slowly out of the area, heading north, looking for an eatery. In the warmth of the car, Alicia was still shuddering, and it was not from the cold.

"Are you sure he didn't give you instructions for after the delivery of the money?" he asked again.

They were in Sergio's office. Alicia had walked in after finishing an interview in a building nearby. She found him alone, and he had offered coffee. He was sitting on his stool at the drawing table, and she was on one of the three extra chairs for their clients.

"I told you, he said nothing about it. Seriously, Sergio, I'm freaking out. It's been four days already, and we haven't heard anything."

"We don't have a telephone number or an address to trace the guy," Sergio said, almost to himself. "We knew that, though. So we can't do anything but wait."

"I thought things would happen faster than this," Alicia said bitterly. "I called everybody, Sonia, Mariano; you name it, thinking that there would be news about Susana. What made me think that she would be freed just like that?"

"What about the forty grand we paid? That's a good reason, I would say."

She did not comment, and he added, "Then again, these things may take time. Please, let's not panic."

Alicia shook her head: "I thought we should have seen something after almost a week. I don't want to panic either, but I cannot stop wondering; what if it is a scam? What would we do?"

"Sooner or later, somebody will contact you. So let's think positive." Alicia knew that he was saying it only to calm her down; she could hear the nervousness in his voice.

"Yeah, we have done everything right. It has to work out well," she whispered while her stomach ached again.

The phone rang, and after talking for a couple of minutes with a client, he sat back at his table.

"By the way, my parents have a date for their trip. So they bought the plane tickets," he said, watching her reaction. "They called earlier today."

"We have agreed, haven't we? Not a word to them about this."

"Don't worry; they'll never suspect anything. Besides, it's none of their business."

"Yes, I know, sorry, I didn't mean that. It's that I am afraid that your parents will find out somehow. When are they coming, then?"

"September 10th, it's a Friday. They'll stay for two weeks, as always, at the hotel. There is a plan to go for a weekend to San Martin de Los Andes. Mom wants us to go. They're going with the Fechner."

"I don't know about that. Do you want to go?"

"Not particularly. If you don't feel like going, it's fine with me. My parents won't mind; they know we are working."

"We'll talk about your parents later and plan something for their arrival."

"Fine with me. Want a cigarette?" He was opening a new Marlboro Lights package. She shook her head.

"No, thanks." He looked at her, surprised.

"I have that old stomach ache again," she said dismissively.

"As soon as this is over, you will have to go and see a specialist for that problem. I have noticed that you hardly digest your food and you are eating less and less every day. You lost weight too, did you notice?"

"I told you I'd see a doctor. And I didn't lose weight. By the way, I'll pick up Pablo early and cook dinner tonight. It's a surprise. Hope you'll like it." They kissed for a long time before she pulled herself out of his arms. Then, on her way to the door, she looked back. He was smiling, and she winked at him.

On Friday, Alicia had a full schedule with the film festival, morning and afternoon, and the movie directors' anticipated interviews. She had bought empanadas in a deli downtown, and they had a brief lunch at home.

Pablo was scheduled to stay at the daycare until the evening. Distracted, she went through the motions of brushing her hair and dressing more carefully for the movie festival's appointments. Not every day, a modest journalist in a mountain town had the opportunity to interview prominent luminaries as these two movie directors. She should be more enthusiastic about this, she told herself.

"You look pretty today," Sergio smiled. "Saturday, I'll take you out for dinner, and I want you to dress up for me too."

She looked at him.

"Those interviews I have at the film festival," she chuckled. "That's the reason."

"Maybe you should dress like this more often."

"Yeah, you are probably right," she agreed, picking up her briefcase, ready to leave.

XIV

The reception of the hotel was crowded, and Alicia stood briefly in the spacious lobby. She looked around, searching for the registration table. Bariloche was busy with tourists attracted by the slopes' excellent ski conditions. In addition, both the local annual Snow Festival and Film Festival had brought numerous personalities from the arts and winter sports.

This year people seemed anxious to forget the disastrous war that had disappeared from the press as if by magic. Finally, the media was starting to tell the truth about the bleak reality of the military's regime, and some were elated by the possibilities opened by the promised election process ahead. In contrast, others felt weary of a civil government ascent and the accountability that would follow. It was, more than ever, a divided country. Two worlds that are distinctly separated sharing the same physical space.

Alicia approached a desk in the designated area for the festival, next to a large banner. She had pinned her identification card on the lapel of her coat. The young and busy assistant looked at her with tired eyes.

"I'm from the weekly *El Barilochense*," Alicia said. "I have an interview scheduled with Director Ayala and later on with Maria Luisa Bemberg."

Alicia sighed and waited patiently until the woman inspected a list of names she had on the table. Under different circumstances, Alicia would be looking forward to these interviews. Now it was more of a nuisance for her. She did not have the energy or will to follow the film screenings closely as before. Then the girl lifted her head and said, "Ah, yes, you are right here. Please, sit over there." She motioned her hand toward a pair of seats in a corner. "I'll get to you in no time."

"Thanks." Alicia took a seat, and after nodding to a few local people she knew, she centered her interest on the comings and goings of the festival staff.

"I'm sorry. We are a bit delayed with the schedule," the young girl approached Alicia, apologetic. "The director just started another interview. So it will be about twenty minutes, I would say. Half an hour, the most. Is that okay with you?"

"Well, I have no option, so I'll wait." Alicia tried to be as agreeable as she could with the overworked assistant.

"I will let you know as soon as he is ready for you," she said and walked back to the desk.

Alicia sighed and opened her briefcase. When Carlos handled her festival assignments, she barely looked through the page and quickly had put it away. With some free time on her hands, now she took out the brochure and browsed through it, trying to keep up with what was going on.

"Excuse me. Are you, Alicia Rivera, from *El Barilochense*?" the voice of a young man with a Public Relations ID card on his lapel startled Alicia. She had barely finished the first paragraph.

"Yes. It's me.'

"Please follow me to a meeting room right there. One of the assistants at the film festival will see you for a few minutes before the interview."

Alicia put the brochure back in her briefcase and followed the man. He opened a door and gave way to her, closing it from outside after she had entered. She was left alone, checking the meeting room. The furniture was sparse; only a traditional table for about ten people surrounded by comfortable-looking chairs, a large screen, and a telephone. In a corner, there was a couch and a TV set in front of it.

She approached the window. The lake was visible through the pine trees in the median of the avenue downhill. Suddenly she had the feeling that somebody had entered the room; she did not hear the door, but when she turned around, there was the man from the green Falcon, smiling at her.

"Hi," the man said with his trademark scornful smile. He seemed very amused at her surprise.

"You?" She heard herself saying. "Why are you here?"

Feeling uncomfortable, she rested her right hand on the back of a chair, trying to regain control, not knowing what was happening. Why was this man here? It did not make sense.

"I had some business nearby, and I found out you were waiting for an interview."

Alicia did not believe his explanation, but she was too shocked to react.

There was an embarrassing silence in which she just looked at him, face to face, trying to recover her nerve, overcoming her repulsion while he slowly changed his facial expression to something close to a smile.

"It seems that we have half an hour or so." He approached the table, and she moved back instinctively, holding the back of the chair that rolled with her. He stood there, smiling, two or three yards from Alicia. The scent of the aftershave imprinted in her brain hit her again.

"I don't understand. I am working. What are you doing here?" Her voice came out reasonably low and steady, embarrassed by the intimidating effect he had on her. "They told me I would see an assistant in this room..."

"I know," he chuckled. "The assistant is busy. It seems Ayala is pretty late on his schedule today." He shook his head. "All the same, now that you are here, why don't we take a few minutes to relax and chat a bit?" His provincial Northwestern accent was stronger and sounded more profound when he tried to be friendly.

"Nothing to talk with you, other than you owe me a full explanation. Where is my friend? Why your silence after I did my part of the deal? Why?" She blurted anxiously.

He lifted his palm open, still smiling.

"Wow, wow, before anything, I'm sure you will accept something to drink," he said, picking up the phone from the table. "What would you like? I'm having something strong if you don't mind."

She felt a wave of anger. He was in command. Alicia was still standing, and the man had moved his chair but did not sit. She knew she should react somehow. Later on, she would think of what she should have done, but she did not know what to do right now. It was the first time they were standing at the same level, one in front of the other. He was not as tall or as stocky as she had pictured him, but he was used to being in control.

"You didn't answer me!" She insisted.

"Please, Alicia," he said authoritarian.

She had to demand a response from him. There should be an explanation. She was not afraid; besides, he did not seem to be in an aggressive mood, somewhat in a conciliatory one.

"Sit down and relax. C'mon, sit here," the man motioned with a hand toward the seat in front of her. He held the telephone receiver in his hand and dialed, turning to Alicia: "What should I order for you? Maybe whiskey and soda too?"

"Fine," she murmured, gaining confidence. A sip of alcohol would help her. She had mints in her purse. They would mask any lingering liquor smell from her breath during the interviews. She walked around one of the chairs and sat on it. The man intimidated her with his sheer presence, and she hated that. The man nodded, seemingly pleased that she had calmed down and sat where she was told.

"A double whiskey on the rocks and a regular whiskey and soda, please," he said on the phone. The courtesy sounded like an order. He seemed used to barking commands even when saying *please*. Alicia feigned to busy herself with the briefcase. She was tempted to take a cigarette out, but she changed her mind; he did not seem to smoke, and she did not want to be chastised by him.

Was he a secret service agent or just a low-rank military? Maybe both, she thought. He was a bully. Not an officer, she was sure. Those officers she worked for when she was a student were gentlemen. So she was not surprised that he did not even give his name to the bartender. They probably knew at the bar that he would be calling. Who was this guy?

He hung up the phone. Turning around the revolving chair next to him, he sat facing Alicia, his right arm on the table. His fingers were tapping the bright lacquered wooden surface almost without making a sound. She noticed his manicured hands and the old-fashioned and thick gold ring with intricate initials carved on it. Like a mobster, she thought.

"I assume you have questions for me." He seemed to be waiting for her words.

"Of course I do," she said, encouraged. Now maybe the man would explain everything. For a second, she pictured herself coming back home and clarifying the situation with Sergio. They would be relieved that everything had a logical and clear explanation. "First, I want to know if you received the package I left in Piedra Del Águila," she said with a firm voice. "It was a lot of money for us to get a hold of."

"Well, you see, the money was not for me." She demurred. He added quickly, with a nod, "But don't worry. I know for a fact that it was delivered on time. It got where it was supposed to go."

She did not dare to ask where that place was.

"Then why my friend is not free yet?" For some reason, she said *my friend*, not naming her, as if to utter Susana's name out loud in front of him would be almost irreverent, an insult to her best friend. "Do you know when they will free her?" she almost implored, and he seemed concerned.

"Well, not really. See, it's not up to me. I'm only a messenger here. If I had the power, I would have let her go long ago." She wanted to believe it but couldn't.

"What now?" Tears were coming to her eyes, and she fought them. It was not the time for weaknesses. "Can't you do anything about it? Why did you ask for the money, then?"

"I am doing my part, believe me. It's not easy." He moved in his chair, bending forward, resting his elbows on his thighs, his hands clasped in front of him. He looked at her right in the eyes again.

"It looks like many things are going on in Buenos Aires right now, and it seems that your friend was in deep trouble from the beginning." He spoke slowly, and Alicia felt increasingly uneasy.

"I don't understand. What type of trouble?"

"Most likely, she has subversive friends. Terrorists are all over, and if she got detained, I'm sure there was a reason..."

He was interrupted by a sound knock on the door. The man stood up and gave way to the waiter, who put the whiskey glasses on the table, between the two chairs. He signed the slip, passed a tip to the waiter, and followed him, quickly locking the door after he left. Then, turning toward Alicia and smiling again, he said in a low voice, as if he were talking to a child, "It's better like this. We don't want to be interrupted. Do we? We only have a short time before your first interview." He sat again, moving his chair closer to hers.

Alicia was embarrassed for some reason she could not explain. The meeting had a surreal quality. He made her uncomfortable, no matter how politely he uttered his words. Maybe it was the memory of that evening on the road by the lake when she felt humiliated and threatened.

He handed her the glass and took a sip of his drink. He seemed to recover his thread of thought. Shaking his drink slowly and looking at her, he said, "Look, you're young. Your friend, this girl from Buenos Aires, is young too. Young people tend to be hot-headed about things, and later on, when years go by and experience sets in, they realize that those were only fantasies."

"Like...? What things?" she asked, grateful to be able to sip her drink, dispelling the dryness of her mouth. She realized they were not getting anywhere. He was not answering any questions. It was a waste of time, and she considered the possibility of leaving the room.

"Like believing in political causes and being influenced by foreign ideas," he was answering still with this didactic tone, like a teacher lecturing. Alicia felt offended by his words, but she would not fall into a discussion about politics with him. She knew where he stood, and he thought he knew her position too. Everything else was shallow chatter, but he went on lecturing her. Now his voice had warmer inflections as if his own words inspired him. Words that Alicia was not listening to. He had locked his eyes on hers, and she noticed that his irises were greenish, and his features were bony, square, a hint of an Andean native mixed with European blood. Overcoming a bout of disgust for the whole situation, she tried to concentrate on what he was saying.

"... So, as a result, they *had* to use a strong hand. There was no other way. You understand that, Alicia; you are a smart woman." He stopped his tirade, smiling at her. She was still looking at him in the eye, amazed at the conviction those eyes were reflecting. The man seemed to believe all this crap. It was so convenient even for him, maybe a small, insignificant fellow in the chain of command. He was enjoying the power he felt at delivering the message as if it were the gospel. She nodded involuntarily and sipped more whiskey.

"You may be right." She lied to him with her eyes fixed on the glass for a few seconds, unable to look straight at the man. Besides, she should be heading toward the door soon. Discretely she looked down at her watch. Unbelievable, only fifteen minutes had passed since she came into this room.

"Well, you see how well people can understand each other when they talk?" In his enthusiasm, he moved his chair closer to hers. He had almost finished his drink. She needed another sip of hers if she was going to keep calm. He went on. "I'm sure most of the young people that became political criminals are only misguided. They lack either a good role model or their teachers brainwash them. As a result, our universities are a breeding ground for all sorts of commie types."

She did not answer. She wouldn't know what to say. More precisely, she did not dare to contradict this presumptuous individual. This was not a conversation. It was a lecture, and she was there to listen. She should be leaving; the sooner, the better, and when she was about to stand up, he unexpectedly extended his hands and took hers. She recoiled involuntarily, but he held firmly, pulling her slightly toward him. Alicia shivered. He was too strong for her to resist. She tried to keep a calm appearance; she was not going anywhere, even if she wanted to.

"Your hands are fragile and cold," he said, caressing them. Alicia had to contain a look of disgust, still trying to free her hands and regret not leaving the room earlier. Then he added, looking at her hands, "Let me warm them up."

Now she saw it clear. She understood why the man was there. Why didn't she see it coming? He had said it would cost her a *financial and personal* effort. This was the *personal* part. He was a leech, and she was still struggling to come to terms with the situation. Was that what it would take to free Susana?

"Do I have a choice?" she asked, knowing the answer.

"We always do," he said, loosening the grip on her hands. She did not move. "You can walk away if you want." Now his eyes were again locked on hers, and she tried to control her nausea. "I'll open the door for you, believe me, and I won't stop you – but *I want you to stay*. Anyway, it's your choice."

What if she tried to leave now? What would be of Susana? She never would forgive herself if she had flinched at the last moment, and that meant her any harm. If this is what it took to save her, then she decided to go ahead and swim all the way to the other side of this dirty pool, where she would see the door unlocked, and she would walk out of that room. And pull Susana out with her.

"I'll stay. You know I have to," Alicia said, swallowing her pride. "I need you to do your part of the deal. I need my friend out." She stood up, still fighting with the instinct that told her to flee. He smiled, looking up at her as a winner. He was enjoying it, and she was angry: "You just do your part of the deal. That's it. That's all I ask."

"You see, Alicia, things are not like that at all. But if you want to believe it, how can I convince you otherwise?" He stood up, and now she was looking up at him, defiant.

"I want my friend to be freed." Her voice came out shakier than she meant to.

He shrugged and smiled again, with a knowing grin, pulled her chin up slowly, in a dominant way that sent chills down her spine. "C'mon, let me see those lips," he murmured, bending toward her.

Alicia sat on the couch where, at some point, the man had taken her. He was standing nearby, getting dressed. Noticing his satisfied glance as he straightened his shirt, Alicia realized that the pain she had often felt coming from her guts when she thought of guys like him was pure hate. A powerful, overwhelming revulsion toward the power that men like him exerted over her and everybody else she knew.

She breathed deeply, trying to control the tears and the urge to tell him what she thought, to curse at him, as he deserved. Still shaking and with her body hurting, she felt miserable and beaten while wiping herself clean with a few paper napkins.

This should be the last installment of Susana's ransom, she repeated for the umpteenth time since the man had pulled her against him, and she let him do it. They both knew that. Now it was his turn to honor the agreement; he should get Susana free. He must.

Now the man was standing with his back to her, turning his woolen sweater around. Alicia pulled her purse that had fallen on the floor nearby. Grabbing a cotton handkerchief, she finished wiping her legs, ashamed, humiliated, and not knowing what to do with the now wet and sticky piece of cloth. She grabbed a paper with an address written on it and wrapped the cotton. He was still moving slowly, allowing her time to finish tidying up. She grabbed her pantyhose from the floor and got dressed, breaking the silence. "When will we hear about my friend? When will they free her?"

He lifted his eyes from the leather belt he was fastening: "Honestly, I don't know. Soon you will find out; I'm sure of that."

"We are all waiting. Her parents—all of us," her voice was unsteady, and she wiped her tears with the back of her hand.

"I know," he said, straightening his hair with his fingers and walking toward her. She instinctively recoiled, but he got to touch her cheek lightly. "You are shy but every bit as delightful. I knew that from the first moment I saw you. I have a good eye for quality."

She felt queasy. Her stomach was acting up again, and Alicia did not want to get sick in front of this man. She breathed again deeply and finished with her clothes.

"Are you ready?" The man said, walking to the door.

"Give me a minute," she demanded. The man waited until she fastened her skirt and then unlocked the door.

"Bye, Alicia," he mumbled and left the room, closing the door behind him.

She checked her wristwatch. While they were there, almost forty-five minutes, nobody had knocked on the door or tried to come in. It was strange, considering how busy the hotel was with the festival. He must have had everything arranged beforehand.

Alicia sat at the conference table, took her cosmetics from the handbag, fixed her makeup, and combed her hair. Tears were coming to her eyes again, and she breathed deeply for a few minutes to calm down.

Then she collected her briefcase, put her jacket on, and took the wool coat lying on a chair nearby. Slowly she left the room, feeling increasingly sick. She was in no shape to have an interview. It was totally out of the question now. Still shaky, she approached the young girl at the festival reception table. "Did you, by any chance, call me? I had to leave the area for a while," she explained.

The girl asked for her name again and inspected the list. "Mr.

Ayala will be another fifteen minutes with the current interview," and lowering her voice, she said, "Those are the TV guys, you know, they take all the time. It's always the same. We are so behind on our schedules."

Alicia nodded. "Look, I'll have to cancel this interview. I have to go because I feel sick. I will call somebody else to replace me."

The girl drew back in her seat, alarmed.

Alicia confided in a low voice, "I may be coming down with the flu."

"Sure, go and take care of it. You look pale." She seemed relieved to see her leaving.

"Where are the restrooms?"

The girl motioned toward the end of the hallway, and Alicia ran, dodging groups of people and tourists lingering in the lobby, with a hand holding her mouth.

"How's she doing?" Alicia heard Mary's voice when Sergio opened the front door on Monday night. "Any better?"

"She's awake now. I think she's better," he said, closing the door. "It's hard to say, though." Then he added as an afterthought, "At least, the fever is gone."

"Good, good," Luis said.

"What was it, the flu?" Mary was interested.

"It looks like it. She's been very sick and weak all weekend. It may well be stomach flu or something like that. The doctor did not find anything other than a bit of a fever."

"Is Pablo sleeping?" Luis asked.

"Yeah. He had a rough time. He gets excited when something like this happens. He's not used to seeing his mom in bed all day."

"Well, glad to hear she's coming out of this." Alicia heard Mary's steps in the hallway. "I'll go to the bedroom."

"Please, go ahead."

Alicia had pulled herself out of bed, grabbed her gown, and was about to leave the room when Mary walked in.

"Wow, you are up. Are you feeling okay walking around?"

"Yes. I'm fine now. Sorry, I worried everybody."

"What do you think it may have been?"

"A virus, I guess. Who knows? There are so many bugs going around in winter, and we have so many tourists from all over here. But I'm better now, so don't worry."

Alicia was still pale and had puffiness around her eyes. She hoped her friend would not notice that it was mostly from crying.

Mary looked at her and said with her usual forthrightness, "You don't look well at all. I want you to see the doctor again tomorrow, just in case. Promise me. Do you want me to go with you?"

"No, please, Mary, this is already over. I can feel it, even though you may think I look sick. I'm fine."

"Yeah? Did you look at yourself in the mirror?"

Alicia felt uncomfortable. She would not talk with anybody in the world about what had happened. So she had to get over her sickly looks. If she knew her friend well, she was sure Mary would not leave the subject alone until things were cleared and resolved.

"Okay. I'll see my doctor again. I promise. Now let's change the subject, please. I smell fresh coffee. Let's go." She walked out of the room, and Mary followed.

She managed a reasonably cheerful attitude when their friends were there, and as soon as they left, she crawled into bed again. Sergio took a shower and tiptoed into the bedroom.

"I will sit in the dining room with my blueprints; I have to finish something. I'll put on some music with the volume down if you don't mind."

Alicia was awake in the dark. "Not at all, go ahead; I wouldn't mind some soft music."

She had slept most of the weekend and until late this morning. Sergio had called the doctor, worried about her unexpected collapse. It seemed that Sergio believed the virus excuse, but she couldn't be sure. He knew her too well.

"Call me if you need anything," he said, walking out of the room.

Cautiously, Alicia recalled what had happened on Friday, fighting the tears again. Nevertheless, she was determined to manage this situation, as she had managed others in her life. Tomorrow she would go back to work. She would wait for the phone call with the news of Susana's freedom. That was the only thing that mattered now.

She knew she would get used to the idea that she had lied to

Sergio and would be lying to him for the rest of her life about what happened that Friday. Nobody had to know, she said to herself over and over. Nobody will ever know. That guy was in her past now.

Susana would be free, and then she would be able to get on with her life. Concentrate on her family, and put that humiliating encounter in a sealed box in her brain forever. This weekend she had a deep, dreamless sleep, an encouraging sign that she was on her way to recovery. She felt rested and ready to start again.

The next day she got up early, before Sergio. Took a couple of aspirins to clear a vague headache and fussed with breakfast in the kitchen before waking up Pablo.

"It looks like you are much better today," Sergio said, walking into the kitchen. He was happy to see she had gotten out of bed. "The virus may have even changed you. What are you doing with the coffee pot in your hand so early in the morning?"

"I tried to surprise you. You deserve some attention from me after so many days of taking care of everything, don't you think so?"

They had breakfast, took care of Pablo, and left for work. He offered to drive the child to the daycare, so Alicia went straight to the newsroom.

She was early, the first one to get there. Anxiously, she inspected every piece of paper on her desk. There were no messages from the man and no messages from Mariano or Sonia either. What was going on? How long would it take?

She practiced her mental exercises for relaxation again. Finally, when her colleagues started arriving, she was calm enough to hit the typewriter and accomplish part of her workload.

Carlos Alvarez walked straight to her desk when he got in, concerned about her health. Before Alicia had time to apologize for not interviewing with Ayala, he said, "By the way, thank you for calling on Friday afternoon after you had to leave the hotel. We got to reschedule both interviews for Saturday morning, and Martina took care of them. She's working on the tape at home. Sorry. I know how much you wanted to cover the festival." He smiled supportively.

"I'm the one that's sorry. I felt bad for having to run away like that, but I was very ill."

"You sounded terrible on the phone. I'm glad you're feeling

better now."

The return to her daily schedule was comforting, and the rest of the week, things at home turned out to be easier than she expected. Sergio seemed to understand that she needed space. So she was not forced to pretend anything with him and was immensely grateful for his tactfulness. Alicia could not even think of being intimate again. Not yet.

He took her out for dinner, they visited their friends, and a semblance of normality gave Alicia hopes of getting her life back at last.

There was only one missing piece, and she prayed for that to fall into place too. Susana should be freed any time now, but she had to be patient.

The routine settled in, and her spirits went up. She felt energized by the news coming from Buenos Aires. The elections were a done deal for the following year. Whatever was left from the decimated ranks of the political parties was assembling to compete in the polls. They had only a year to rebuild their destroyed party structures after the relentless damage inflicted with incarcerations, kidnappings, and self-imposed exiles since 1976.

Another point, currently discussed in the media, helped Alicia to regain interest in the political process. The armed forces blatantly demanded pardons from the civilians for their so-called excesses in their fight against subversion during the recent "dirty war" if the elections were to occur.

It was a contested matter because those were euphemisms for the repression and the crimes committed against the opposition. Accepting would be equivalent to denying the missing people's victims and relatives the right to take the guilty party to justice. They were coaxing their safe exit. The armed forces felt they had saved the nation from the red menace, and they deserved to be honored and recognized as such. To them, it was a reasonable price to pay if several thousand innocent compatriot bystanders were killed in their concentration camps.

A week to the day she met the man from the green Falcon at the hotel, Alicia called Sonia. The worried mother had no news from

Susana's release yet.

"What does Mariano say? I haven't heard anything from him lately. Should I call him?" Alicia asked, increasingly anxious.

"I saw Mariano yesterday evening, after our march in Plaza de Mayo. He talked about a woman that was released a couple of days ago. The woman appears to be in miserable shape, physically and mentally. She probably met people who saw Susana at some point, or she met Susana. It's not clear yet. We'll see. I have a hunch that Mariano knows more than he told me. Maybe he wants to be sure before talking to me about it. I don't know."

"Did she say if other people were released lately?"

"No. Anyway, it seems like this woman was held in several places. The last one was at the Escuela de Mecánica de la Armada. Mariano says that they are trying to find out exactly what she knows.

"You mean ESMA? Did they hold people there? Right there, inside their school? In the middle of the city?"

"Yes, that's what it seems. It's crazy, isn't it?" There was silence. "I'll call you as soon as I learn something."

"Thank you, and please, tell Mariano to call me if he can."

"Sure."

"Sonia, I think that the military may let everybody go now, don't you think so? If the elections are truly coming, they may not want to keep people in concentration camps by next year."

"Yes, I hope so. Now they are covering their butts. Did you read the papers? I'm so upset. We will not negotiate with these criminals," Sonia was furious. "We want our children and relatives back alive. Like our banners read: *they took them alive, we want them back alive.* Now they are intimidating the politicians to agree to a full pardon for their crimes. They will have to let our children free or go to the justice to explain and pay for it."

"I'm with you on this; politicians should never accept to sell out the victims, but then again, don't set your hopes up too high. Remember that the judges we have now were put there by the military, and they're not precisely democratic. On the contrary, they benefited from the Junta."

"I know. But these judges are human beings too. They are Argentineans. Some of them may even be honest and decent enough to look at this and agree it's a crime against humanity what the military has done." Sonia had raised her voice.

"You're right, and we can't lose hope. Although, of course, it's a slim hope, but that's all we have, don't we? As long as they allow free elections next year... Let's hope for that."

"We're ready to keep on marching and asking and sending letters, and traveling, and will hassle everybody until they tell us the truth until they give us back our children..." Sonia broke into a sob.

Alicia was crying too and felt guilty for pushing her to the edge. This subject never came stress-free to them. Their dialogues were always interrupted with tears and outbursts of pain. Finally, she hung up the phone and went back to work.

Thirty minutes later, her next personal call came from Carla.

Carla had just returned from one of her trips to Miami with gifts for everybody. A box was in the mail for Pablo. The stark contrast between Sonia's and this call couldn't be more marked. Carla was exuberant and talked extensively about the trip and the short cruise they took to the Bahamas for the weekend while in Florida.

"I brought you some fancy lingerie too... they have this store called Victoria's Secret... believe me, Alicia, I would have bought one piece of everything they have there."

"Is that right?" Alicia tried to sound interested.

"Oh, yeah, shopping in Miami is great. Well, except for leather goods, leather is not at the level of Brazil or Argentina; we have more of a European taste, you know. But for everything else, it's a shopping paradise. You have to go there, believe me. You'll love it. And the beaches? Oh, my goodness, they are gorgeous."

"I'm sure we'll visit there someday."

"You and Sergio work too hard, dear; you should take it easy and go somewhere. When we go away, it's always like a honeymoon again. It's great. As I was saying, I had so much extra weight in the luggage that we had to pay a bundle of money at the airport. You should have seen Guillermo's face. He was upset with me, but let me tell you that he bought a lot of things for himself too, not to mention the tons of electronic gadgets he carried in those bags. Mostly expensive junk. And heavy to carry too. Clothes are lighter; you know that."

Alicia had a soft spot for her cousin, as she would for a younger sister, and she was sincerely glad for her happiness. If only she had not called right after Sonia.

The first sign that she was not healing yet came as a shock to Alicia. She had sincerely thought she succeeded in storing away her pain.

On Saturday, the day she dedicated to cleaning the house, Alicia found herself immersed in the memory of the evening of the encounter at the hotel as she sorted out her laundry. Then she experienced increasing doubts about what she should have done when he walked into that room. Maybe she should have left, but that was not an option since she had questions for him. He had made it clear it was part of the ransom. She had tried to leave, and the man wouldn't let her. Did she, in fact, attempt to escape? Why didn't she run off that place, exactly? She could not recall the whole incident with details. For some inexplicable reason, parts of it escaped her recollection.

Still, she now had a distinct impression that she was not able to leave. Had the man pushed her onto the couch? Why couldn't she remember what happened there? Her mind was foggy, and there were gaps in her memory. She did remember distinctly sitting on the couch, feeling physical pain, getting dressed, and afterward, feeling dirty. Standing next to the washing machine, with laundry clothes in her hands, now she felt goosebumps and, with repulsion, sensed his hands again on her skin. It was an instant, but it shook her to her bones. She recalled that she was forced to lie back on the couch, and he was all over her, suffocating her, while she was trying to suppress the nausea bouts.

She stood there trembling, her legs weak, her heart pumping madly, soaking wet. For a second, she had to lean against the washer, and then, slowly, she sat on the wooden top of the sturdy wicker box where she kept the clothes for the laundry. Alicia did not know how long she had sat there. It was a frightening experience. Then, slowly, her pulse went back to normal, and she remained there, surprised and afraid, clutching a towel that should have gone into the washer.

Pablo walked in, holding a toy, and gave it to her. She took it distractedly, and he asked her to pick him up, so she sat him on her lap. He wanted to play, but Alicia, feeling his hands on her face, started to cry. She felt miserable, and he was so beautiful, so young, so helpless.

"Mommy, Mommy," he called anguished. He hated to see her cry, but she could not stop. She was crying because she did not want him to be there. Alicia could not bear the fact of being around her son any longer.

Pablo cried too, and she felt a profound sadness for this child who was expecting her to be the mom she used to be. And here she was, a confused woman that did not want him there, that wanted him gone so she could leave and be at peace somewhere else.

Pablo was increasingly upset now, and she put him back on the floor. She stood up and took his hand, guiding him out of the laundry room toward his playpen. If her sense of duty was not so deeply ingrained in her, and Alicia could have followed her urges, she would have walked right to the front door and left her house for good at that very moment, leaving him with his toys.

"What's wrong?" Sergio asked, coming in from the back door, carrying a heap of logs for the fireplace, and surprised to hear Pablo scream. He looked at Alicia, standing there, next to him, as if she did not know where she was. "Alicia, what's wrong?"

He dropped the logs in the basket next to the fireplace and walked, shaking off the dust from his hands, to pick up Pablo, who was still pulling Alicia's sweater, demanding attention. She was looking at Sergio with a distraught stare.

"Nothing is wrong. I don't know what the heck he wants," Alicia said in frustration. "I have a splitting headache; can't listen to him screaming at me like that," she lied. Why does she suddenly feel like this? Why this urgency to push them both aside and run away? The fact of not knowing, not finding an answer, truly frightened her.

On Sunday, Martina and Alicia broadcasted their last radio show. They felt sad saying farewell, and they took the opportunity to talk about all the previously censored subjects. Time flew, and their compatibility and sync were at their peak, even though Alicia still felt sad. Martina kept her sense of humor through the end, all the while exalting the positive impact their enterprise had on the public while it lasted. Both departed after a brief chat at the building's entrance, and Alicia drove home, feeling defeated.

The next day it was already dark when Alicia got to the house's driveway. She had no news about Susana and felt increasingly worried that all that they had done might, after all, get any results. The very idea was maddening, so she tried to dispel the thoughts every time they came up.

She left the car open and walked toward the back door of the house.

"Would you help me with the groceries?" she called out to Sergio. He got his jacket on and helped her move the bags from the car into the house.

"I have the *mate* ready," he said, closing the door after their last trip to the car.

"Great!"

He filled the mate gourd and handed it to her. "You know, you don't have to go to the airport on Friday. If you want to stay with Pablo, it's okay. It's only a silly tradition for all of us to welcome them at the airport. My parents won't mind."

"Of course, we will all go to the airport, as always. I'm staying home Friday morning. I'll bring work here, so we won't need to take Pablo to the daycare that day."

"Are you sure?" Sergio was doubtful but continued to put the groceries away in silence.

"All this is because you think I'll be in a bad mood on Friday, isn't it? Well, I won't. I'll be polite and smiling, don't worry. See, I'm much better today. So you should trust me now and then."

"It's not a matter of trust," he said, looking at her. "Let's sit down."

She finished rearranging bottles in the refrigerator and turned around. Sergio was filling the mate gourd with more *yerba,* and she sat next to the table, looking at him while he poured the hot water and handed the mate to her.

"I just want to suggest something to you. It may be a good idea, now that you feel better, to do something to help you stay this way." He seemed encouraged by her silence while sipping the mate tea. Then, cautiously he added, "You know what I'm talking about, don't you?"

She handed the mate back to him and said with a shrug, "Yes. I know, and I told you already what the problem is. I don't feel comfortable talking with anybody in this town about my personal life. I meet these people socially all the time. We can stumble upon them in a restaurant or a public function. I wouldn't dare look at my counselor's face socially. Honestly."

"Any of the doctors that you may choose for treatment have an ethics code. Do you think they will go around broadcasting their client's secrets? Does Doctor Jimenez walk around talking about our illnesses?"

"Doctor Jimenez has been our family doctor forever. We know him well. I wouldn't feel comfortable with a counselor. That's all. This is not a physical illness."

"Alicia, please. Will you think about it?"

"If this is so important to you, I will try. We will talk next week after your parents go to San Martin de Los Andes. By the way, please don't send Mary again to try to convince me. That was too much."

"I didn't send her. If she talked to you, it was all on her own. How could you think I would *send* anybody?"

She shrugged. She wasn't going to go to therapy no matter what he said, so it would be better to delay the subject for a while until Sergio got tired of asking. "Okay, but let's leave it aside for a little while. Please? I have to think about this."

Alicia took refuge in her work, but the lack of news about Susana's release had her on edge. Every day that passed was a new disappointment.

The next day she took the morning off from work to tidy up the house and finish downloading an interview from her tape recorder. Since she let Jacinta go and started feeling ill and tired, her house chores had piled up. House cleaning was the least of Alicia's worries now, but with Sergio's family coming, she wanted to show a semblance of normality.

Lately, she has had this persistent stomach pain. Doctor Jimenez had thundered about the diet and the cigarettes and had given her some pink stuff to take. The sticky cream helped her, and she did feel better even without quitting. Alicia needed her cigarettes too much to think about that now– that, and alcohol. Alcohol was the little secret that she would not share with Doctor Jimenez. She had at least one double whiskey before dinner and two or three glasses of wine at the table. Sergio frowned, but she ignored him. Those drinks made her feel better, and she was not ready to give them up.

As soon as Alicia walked into the newsroom that afternoon, she saw the yellow telephone message on her desk from afar.

"Call me tonight. It's urgent. Mariano." She almost danced around her desk, celebrating the good news. It was about Susana, she was sure. She was released. It had to be that. It was the news she had been waiting for and fretting about all these weeks.

"I got a message from Mariano to call him today." She told Sergio on the phone right after reading the message. "I'm so sure they have let her out. Oh, Sergio, this is so great I can hardly wait. He wants me to call him tonight. Are you driving with me to the phone company?"

"Of course, I will. This is great news. Sure, I'll go with you," Sergio said, relieved. And after a pause: "At last. It took so long."

"Yes, it did," she echoed, her voice choking.

XV

Alicia hesitated while stepping out from the bright telephone company's offices to the street's penumbra and got into Sergio's car. He pushed the door open for her.

He listened to soft music, with Pablo sleeping and fastened in the back seat while she talked with Mariano.

"What happened?" he said, lowering the volume of the radio when he saw her face. She sat, looking at him as if waiting for him to say something. He asked again, now with concern, "Alicia, what's wrong? What did he say?"

She shook her head, still looking at him with dry, wide-open eyes.

"She's dead. She's dead. They killed her, Sergio, they've killed her!" Her voice was low and distraught, "She's dead... He said she's dead, drowned..."

"Now, calm down," Sergio demanded. She hesitated. He took a half-empty bottle of soda from the car's cup holder and handed it to her; obedient, she took a sip. "Start all over again. Did Mariano say that?"

"Yes, he told me they killed her. He said that she is dead, that the woman said so, this woman that I told you about, the one that was released or got free. She said that the guards killed many people; she identified Susana and saw her in one of those groups. The woman said she probably drowned, Sergio, they tortured her for weeks, and then they killed her." In shock, her voice had a hysterical pitch.

He asked again: "Tell me; tell me exactly what Mariano said, tell me all the details of the conversation. You were in that telephone booth for a long time, more than thirty minutes." He motioned to the telephone company's windows that let him see the booths from the car. "Alicia, did you realize that?"

She ignored his question and began the story as he asked. "As soon as Mariano answered the phone, I noticed his voice was not the same as always. Something was wrong, I felt it, Sergio, and I swear, I felt it in my bones. So I asked him directly, 'is something wrong?' and he babbled something like 'you take it easy, please, we are not hundred percent sure about this, but it may well be true,' so I pushed on, and finally he told me."

She paused for a couple of seconds and then, suddenly, with fists clenched, hitting the dashboard several times, she cried, "Son of a bitch! Fucker son of a bitch! He tricked me, he tricked me, the jerk!" and covering her face she burst into tears.

Pablo whined loud in the back seat. Sergio, surprised by her reaction, instinctively turned to check on him and then turned to her. "Shh... Who tricked you? Mariano?"

She did not answer, still crying.

He insisted, "Alicia, are you talking about the ransom we paid to that guy?"

Relieved that he would never guess what she was thinking about, she took the lifesaver he threw at her. "Yes, yes, all that money! He didn't have anything to give us back. He lied, he cheated us..." and she cried again, mainly for the memory of her private humiliation, a price far higher than the money extorted from them. Sergio seemed unfazed by the cheating, and she knew it was his particular way of dealing with what was happening and compensating for her emotional outburst.

"Okay, let's calm down now, please. We'll deal with that later, not now," he said in a slightly loud voice. Alicia uncovered her face and made an effort to control the tears.

After a minute, he sighed: "What else did Mariano tell you?"

Calmer now, she reclined her head back on the seat.

"When he told me about the woman that saw Susana carried away almost unconscious, drugged up, I believe I fainted right there in that seat. I don't remember hearing anything for a while until I heard his voice again, 'Alicia, Alicia, are you there?' and then I asked, 'what did you say? I don't think I understood', and he told me again, and I was there, listening, listening, and not knowing what to do! I still don't know what to do."

She stopped the tirade, looking at him, expecting something from him, maybe to help take her out of what was going on in her mind. Instead, he was silent for a few seconds.

Finally, he asked, "You said that Mariano *thinks* this is what happened? How can he be so sure? The woman may be wrong."

She hated it; Sergio always would do this to her. She would say something significant enough, and he instantly would lower its impact by reaching ridiculous conclusions.

She shook her head, angry. "How can he be so sure? Well, the woman was there, didn't I tell you that?"

"Drink some more." Ignoring her words, he handed her the bottle that she had put back in the holder. He waited for her to finish and then said, "Now go on. Slowly."

"Okay, Mariano said that this woman knows a lot. That they think she's for real. They are almost sure this woman is telling the truth. They know that because they know the names of people that disappeared, know the detention places, have other witnesses, and they can compare notes." Alicia was again coherent in her speech, and Sergio seemed at ease now, with her coming out of the panicky state in which she was a few minutes ago.

He lit a cigarette and passed it to her in silence. She lowered the window on her side to let the smoke out. Sergio glanced back to check again on Pablo.

Alicia took the cigarette and, holding it in her right hand next to the window, kept talking, looking at the blue line of smoke rising to the opening and going out. "It's crazy, uh? I just found out that they killed her, and I don't feel anything. Nothing at all. It's weird," she shrugged. "The woman had a long list of people that she met in different places of torture. She says she was transferred to the ESMA several months back, and she saw many people passing through there. They mainly were twenty-somethings. She's about forty years old and was doing some type of domestic work by the end of her time there. She saw many people in her ins and outs in the hallways. One of them was Susana. She identified her..."

Alicia inhaled again from the cigarette and remained silent for a few seconds, looking outside. Tears were running down her cheeks.

"The woman said that now and then they would inject something, maybe a drug, to a bunch of these guys that looked like college students to her, and they would be pushed out, piled up, half-drugged, in the back of a truck. The rumor was that they were taken to a plane. They drove them at night. She mentioned a DC-3 or a plane similar to that. The prisoners would be groggy so that they would be thrown out of the plane in the air in the open sea, without clothes..." She turned to Sergio and asked, "Isn't it too weird to be true?"

"It's totally outlandish. You can't believe this, just like that. It could be rumors. Who knows?" He seemed more worried about her state of mind than about the horrific story she was telling as if focusing on her angst would relieve him from the need to consider the truthfulness of the account, the horror of the whole thing.

She went on, "Mariano says they heard stories like this before, so he believes her about the plane and the dead... Sergio, the woman said that Susana was in one of those groups. Her little cell was empty the next day, like the others. If this is true, Susana is gone."

"We will see about that; nothing is for sure. You have to think about that, promise me." He paused until she nodded. "Does Sonia know about this?"

"Yes. Mariano says she's in denial. Sonia didn't want to believe the story. She says she'll keep looking for her daughter because she feels she's alive and will try to get her out. I don't have the guts to call her. I don't know if I can talk to her about this now. I can only imagine how she must be suffering."

She put her cigarette out with small, methodical movements and then pushed the ashtray closed. They remained in a silence filled by the car engine's hum and the voice of Joan Manuel Serrat singing in Spanish on the radio. They seemed to be wondering what to do next.

Alicia said, turning up the volume, "Listen, is Joan Manuel, singing Machado's poem. *Caminante, no hay camino, se hace camino al andar.* Susana loves these verses." She moved toward Sergio. He put an arm around her shoulders, and she reclined her head against him. "You're right. That woman could be wrong. We don't know for sure."

"No, we don't," he reassured her. "So, let's keep hoping for the best..." then his voice cracked, and he sobbed for a second. Alicia, surprised by the unexpected emotional outburst of his usually tightly controlled self, lifted her arm around his shoulder and they stayed

216

embraced for a while.

The next day the mood was somber at dinner. They had invited their friends to share a pizza at their home. As usual, Mary brought a box of chocolates, but now there were no laughs about their diet.

Alicia had slept only sporadically the night before. She went through her day as if somebody had taken over her brain. It was functioning independently from her, on automatic pilot. Her eyes were swollen and red, and her friends hugged her in silence.

Mary and Luis listened, munching their pizza and exchanging meaningful glances between themselves while Alicia and Sergio took turns talking about the phone call with Mariano.

"The question is: Is this woman reliable?" Sergio wondered. "Mariano and his friends seem to believe her."

"Sonia has a hard time accepting it," Alicia had tears in her eyes but was calm. "I do too."

"Of course," Mary said, patting her affectionately on the arm. "Nobody knows for sure."

"Mariano believes that this woman is telling the truth, though," Sergio said again, putting back the bottle of wine on the table after filling everybody's glasses. "I tried his number today until I got him to answer. His group has been busy trying to verify all the information this woman gave them, and it seems she's legit."

They ate in silence for a few minutes. Pablo moaned in his chair, half-sleep.

"I'll take him to bed," Alicia said. Sergio lifted the sleepy child, carried him to bed, and switched off the light. Alicia stayed with him a few minutes to be sure he was sleeping and then returned to the dining room where the others sat. Getting back to her chair, she broke the silence. "It seems this woman knew too many details that Mariano had from earlier witnesses about what's going on at the ESMA. Who would have thought? A military school, now it's a torture center. Right there, in the middle of the city."

Alicia was crying again, and they remained silent for a while. Her serving got cold on her plate, but she did not seem to notice. Instead, she went ahead with her story. "Mariano talked about *holocaust methods*; I don't know what he meant because he did not elaborate, and to tell you the truth, I didn't dare to ask."

"You don't go worrying about things you don't know," Mary jumped quickly, attempting to reassure her. "He may have been talking in figurative terms, not meaning what exactly he said."

"I'm sure of that," added Sergio, happy that somebody helped him take Alicia from her brooding thoughts.

Alicia shook her head. "No. Let's not kid ourselves. Those seem to be real concentration camps. He said so not in so many words, but I know he meant it because of his voice." She paused for a few seconds. "Mariano told me about systematic torture that there are uniformed men, priests, and worse, there are medical doctors that control the torment sessions, so people don't die."

"So much for the Hippocratic Oath," Sergio sneered. "Incredible."

"What do they care? They are fanatics." Alicia's tone rose in an angry outburst of impotence.

"What is most disgusting of all is that they say they have priests assisting the people that are dying from torture sessions?" Mary blurted, "Doing what? Sending them to Paradise or Hell? That's sickening."

Luis put words to everybody's thoughts. "What's wrong with these people?"

"It seems like a bad dream," Sergio said. "This sordid story is happening under the radar. Most people don't know about it."

"What would they do if the public knew?" Luis asked. "Would they care, perchance?"

They looked at each other, and they all thought they knew the answer. There was a long silence. After a while, Sergio said, "Guys, my parents are coming tomorrow. We agreed with Alicia not to mention anything about Susana or the money we paid."

"That goes without saying," Luis answered, and then, "By the way, what happened with that money?"

"To tell you the truth," Alicia said, "when I told Mariano about it, he said, 'how could you fall for that trick?' He believes these crooks make a flourishing business from the property they steal and the real estate they grab from the people they snatch. I did not know what to say; I was having a hard time grasping what I heard from him. He also asked me how much money we put there, and he told me he was sorry that we fell for it."

"I'm sure they are doing good business," Sergio said. "That's what they did at Susana's apartment. They took her electronics, and Sonia said that a jewelry box with her gold earrings and chains was missing, as well as a roll of dollars she kept for emergencies stashed in her first aid kit. Didn't they?" He asked Alicia.

She nodded. "They didn't miss anything, the thugs."

"Do you guys think Alicia should ask Father Johann about the green Falcon guy?" Mary ventured. "After all, he was the contact."

"I thought of that too," Alicia said, looking at Sergio. "We even talked about it."

"Yeah, we wondered if we should try to contact him, but they did things in a hushed and anonymous way that does not leave room for claims or anything like that," Sergio said, shrugging.

"Besides, he made it clear; nothing should be connected to him or the church in the future. I don't even believe this priest knows anything about what's going on. He seemed to be acting in good faith." Alicia's voice was choking. After a pause, she added, "This man... these thugs operate without any accountability."

Sergio put his glass down and said, "Yeah, well, for the same token, we should then send word to him that this was a fiasco, and if he is honest, he will not use that contact in the future."

"Maybe a discreet note through the parish?" Luis suggested, and Alicia agreed.

"Come to think of it; I should let him know. It's the honest way to go about this mess; I still believe the priest acted in good faith, and they are using him."

Mary said with regret, "I'm sorry about that. I thought I was helping. I shouldn't have tried."

Sergio and Alicia reacted at the same time. "Please don't. How could you know?" he said.

"Don't say that. You meant well, and I'm grateful for your help," Alicia added and kept on weeping quietly, unable to stop her sobs. She felt cheated twice, and the pain was almost unbearable, mainly because she could not share it with anybody else. Also felt physically sick with the man's memory and his unfamiliar, hungry hands on her body. For some inexplicable reason, this unsettling memory was fresher in her mind as time went by, instead of it fading away as she had expected, increasing her guilt about her lying to Sergio.

Mary followed Alicia to the kitchen. "I've noticed that you're smoking twice as much as you did before. Don't do that," she said. "You don't want to get sick. Come on now. Try to manage this without hurting yourself, eh?"

Alicia turned to her, exaggeratedly rolling her eyes, but her smile was sad.

"Mary, I appreciate that you care, but I will survive this, don't worry. I have to prepare for Franz and Helena's visit; it will be hard for us, though, to put on nice faces for two weeks, but we'll manage. I need cigarettes to help me through."

"I'm sure you'll do fine. But then, when they're gone, you will have to take care of yourself. And do it soon. Promise me." She helped Alicia straighten the kitchen and washing dishes and glasses.

"Okay. We'll see. After Franz and Helena leave, I promise."

"Again, I don't have to tell you that I'm here if you need me."

Alicia was fond of Mary and her unwavering affection, the fact that she could count on her if she needed. Still, she had decided that Mary was never to find out the complete truth about her anguish. She was determined never to utter a word about how she had willingly and knowingly submitted to his manipulation. Alicia shuddered out of nausea and guilt.

Franz and Helena arrived, and, as Alicia's courtesy manners dictated, the three of them drove to the airport to welcome them. She felt sincerely happy that they would be around them for a while. She wished to be able to open up to them, but it was impossible. Sergio was the one that had a cautious structure built around him and his private life that was seldom let down before his parents. Alicia trusted him on this matter, feeling, nonetheless, a vague nostalgia for some ideal parent-child relationship that she could not clearly define.

They had reserved a hotel room and rented a car to move independently while Alicia and Sergio worked. In the evenings, they expected to share time together, which meant dining out almost every day.

"Pablo is ready," Alicia said to Sergio, walking into the bedroom where he was finishing getting dressed to go out again. "I'll put on some foundation and lipstick, and we'll be ready to go. I have to cover up with makeup these nasty bags I have under my eyes now."

"Alicia, before we leave— I wanted to tell you something all day and did not find the right moment," he said, lifting his head from the shirt he was buttoning and looking at her. "My parents came by the office today, before lunch, for an informal visit."

"Oh, yeah? That's nice. Had you invited them to lunch?"

"No. It was a surprise visit, and like everything else my father does, it was not random. They had something to tell me."

Alicia stopped almost at the door, holding the cosmetic bag in her hand on her way to the bathroom.

He continued. "Remember last night they told us about their plans to move to the United States, and his friend calling him to join his company there, and all that?"

"Yes, and the news was that they set a date to leave the country," she said, not very sure of what he wanted to say.

"Well, it seems dad wants to test the waters with us too... he frankly asked me if I would consider joining them in the company up there, in Fort Lauderdale."

"What do you mean, join them there? Do you mean to go to live there?"

"Well, yes. The fact is that dad will go there as a partner and take his capital with him for investment; it opens the door for the company to call me to work there. They would set up a job contract for me. It's the opportunity to get a green card after some time."

"But for how long would we stay there?"

"I don't know," he looked at her, and she could read in his eyes that Franz had sold the idea to his son. She panicked for a few minutes, standing there, in the middle of the room, not knowing what to say. He added, "It may be for as long as we want. It'll be up to us."

Sergio waited for her response, and she did not want to hurt him. She did not want to leave her home or her country, but she felt genuinely guilty. He had always been trustworthy with her, and she had failed him. His own wife. The cheap liar, the cheater. He did not deserve it.

"We could think about it. What did you tell him?" Alicia knew she would not have the nerve to stop him if he wanted to go ahead with it.

"Exactly what you are telling me. That I would talk with you, and we will think about it." He was cautious.

"What else did they say? Your mom asked me last night in the bathroom if I felt okay. Do they suspect anything?"

She knew that his parents had noticed something the night before, over dinner with the Fechner at Club De Caza y Pesca, down by the Nahuel-Huapi coast. The restaurant was famous for its energetic Tyrolese ethnic show, complete with leg slapping dance and traditional German tunes. Fortunately, the dancers kept their attention, but Alicia found Helena's eyes on her several times during the night.

"To tell you the truth, she interrogated me this morning, with her police-style questioning, about you," he confessed.

"I knew it," Alicia said. "Sorry, I don't want them to notice anything is wrong. What did she say? I thought I was fine, even happy last night, wasn't I?"

"My parents agreed that you don't look well. So I told them you are coming down with the flu." He shrugged. "It's the best excuse I could think of, but she pressed on, so I had to say something credible. So I told them that our finances are not too good, and you were worried."

"We decided not to talk about it with them, Sergio. Didn't we?"

"It was fine; they believe we are sad because we don't have enough assignments in our jobs. That took them out of the personal issues, so it was okay. Then dad insisted upon us deciding to follow them to Florida. He painted it in a way that, well, I know you don't want to hear this, but it made a lot of sense to me."

"He sold you on the idea, I know." Pablo walked into the bedroom, bringing a book for his mother to read to him. She sat on the bed and picked him up, holding him on her lap. He quietly started playing with her necklace, sensing that the conversation was heating up with children's extra perception of their parents.

"Don't jump to conclusions," Sergio said quickly. "I'm only saying that we probably should give it a thought. This country isn't going ahead. It's going backward, if anything, and we are stuck here."

"Don't say that. If the military allows a civilian government to come in, things may get better, and we will be working to recover whatever these jerks destroyed," Alicia said without conviction.

Sergio shook his head. "No. You know that's not so. That's our illusion, a new government, and a new start. For how long? Until another big landowner convinces the next generation of uniformed macho men to take over the government at gunpoint? Or a foreign bank hits us with the invoices for the loans? Alicia, I'm tired of this."

She was silent, not knowing what to say; he was right.

"Let's take it easy, let's think about it. Please," Sergio was almost pleading. "Think of Pablo's life. What's ahead for him? He will go to college, get a degree, and then drive a taxi because there are not enough jobs available. Look at us, struggling day by day to put food on the table. How long since we took a real vacation?"

She did not answer right away.

He had an inquisitive look. "Well, what do you think?"

"Wow, you can be convincing whenever you want. I'll give you that much," she said, nervously trying to diffuse the intensity of the moment. "We will talk about it with your parents, of course, and ask for more details too."

"Good." He turned around, smiling, and picked up his jacket from the closet.

Franz and Helena's presence in Bariloche meant Alicia's time with Sergio and Pablo was reduced considerably to her relief. Her son enjoyed daily attention from his grandparents, who took him all over on their strolls, shopping, and sightseeing in the afternoons. He was fascinated with their interest in him, and Alicia felt vaguely guilty because it relieved her of her duties, and she welcomed the break. It meant more opportunities to be absorbed by her work or sleep and forget everything for a few hours.

Lately, she had called Sonia often, out of respect for the grieving mother, but every time they spoke, it required an emotional exertion that left Alicia drained and depressed. By the third call, she realized that they were repeating the same dialog with different words. Still, she was unable to cut down or skip her phone calls.

Sergio had noticed her somber moods after each one of those

calls, but she invariably answered, "I know. But if I were in Susana's place, I would appreciate it if she would call my mother too. It's the least I can do. It's such a hardship for her and Don Roberto."

They did not join Franz, Helena, and the Fechner in their three-day San Martin de Los Andes visit. They did not insist or ask questions.

On their last evening in Bariloche, Franz made reservations in a charming small Swiss restaurant nestled in the forest near Llao-Llao, just for the four of them. The place was warm and cozy, and Alicia knew the main subject of the evening. Franz and Helena would not leave without making it clear, in her presence, that they wanted their son to follow them to Florida. She was ready for their pitch and as ambivalent as ever.

Over an excellent wine and a perfectly blended cheese fondue, Franz steered the conversation toward politics. Alicia did not take the bait, and she knew he would be mystified; she had shared, and very much enjoyed, debating the pros and cons of the national politics before.

He asked her pointedly, "What's your take on these coming elections?"

"You mean if they ever allow us to vote," she snipped, and he laughed. "Then, how many parties will be on the ballots? How many handshakes are under the table to let the Juntas go free of scrutiny? There will be too many questions to answer before we go to the polls."

"Maybe the worst part won't be dirty politics, but the dirty economy."

"What do you mean?" Of course, she knew what he meant and where he was going, but she let him try to sell his product anyway.

"You know this government has bankrupted the country. They don't put a number on the external debt and the national debt. It's because the figure will be larger than anybody wants us to know. The boys from the *plata dulce* entities will be in action with their financial scams for a long time to come."

"Sure. I'm sure it will be a huge debt, but we are not the first or the last to have one. When the military decides to leave, the civilians may clean up all this crap." She had doubts that a civil government would succeed, but it was too hard to admit it openly to him.

"Well, do you believe any civilian government, no matter who wins the elections, will be able to govern? I don't think so. They will have to tighten the middle class and take such extreme economic measures to govern that people won't let them finish the term. You'll have the unions in the street right away."

"You know," Sergio intervened, "I believe dad is right on this. I know you want to dream about how we will reconstruct and recover. I'm sorry, but I don't think it's realistic."

Franz seemed pleased with Sergio's agreeing with him. It was not often that they coincided on political matters. He turned to Alicia. "As soon as the holders of the debt want, they will come with their notes to cash, and we won't be able to eat and pay the credit cards these guys have spent in our name. The international banks will cry foul, and we will be in a crunch to pay the interests and survive."

"So you mean it's over for us. I mean, for the country," Alicia said, remembering Susana's words.

"Yes. That's what I believe. If anything, we are going backward, and it will take many decades to recover if we ever do fully. But you already know that, because we have talked enough about this before. Haven't we?"

Alicia nodded. "Yes, you're right."

Helena, silent during the whole exchange, now said eagerly, "We all love this country and know that when you were away traveling, you guys had missed it, but please think about the future. We made a good life, Franz and I, twenty-five years ago living here, and now we feel that we can do it again, in a place where there is stability to work. No military in the streets, no devaluations, no unemployment."

"A place where you can speak your mind," Franz added with a meaningful gaze to Alicia, who smiled widely to his barrage of tempting points.

Encouraged by her silence and by Sergio's agreeing with them, they explained their plan to invest in the construction business in the South Florida burgeoning economy. Franz was excited about the prospects. "There are many investors there, from all over the world, Alicia. You would be surprised. Trying to salvage whatever they have and make a future. In less than twenty years, listen to what I tell you, by the year 2000, Miami will be the capital of Latin America not only financial but cultural."

"Yes, and like they used to say in Uruguay during the Tupamaros craziness, 'the last leaving, please switch the lights off of their country,'" Alicia said, saddened.

"I wish things were different. We'll miss our home, all of this. There's no better place to live than this country," Helena said with moist eyes, "but they have made a big mess out of it."

Alicia thought all of us had, and nobody here was without blame. We all have contributed to this, for commission and others for omission, but she did not say anything.

On their way home, Sergio was silent. They had put on music, and both were looking ahead, at the lines in the road and the pine trees, suddenly brought alive from the darkness by the car's headlights.

"It's a good offer," Alicia said, lighting two cigarettes and passing one to Sergio. "We are fortunate to have an offer for a way out. Even though it will be no picnic for us here, we were overseas once, and we know the feeling and the cost of leaving everything behind."

"Yeah."

"Besides, if everybody would leave, what would become of these countries? In all Latin America, it's almost the same."

"People have emigrated for millennia, Alicia, and no country went down the drain because of that. Look at Europe, they sent millions to Australia, North, and South America, and there you have them, stronger than ever, forty years after that war."

They did not talk again. Alicia was, as usual, annoyed with his certainty. He would go to the end of the world convinced that the path he chose was the one, while she would doubt and question her own at every turn of the road.

She decided to give the idea rest for a while. This one was too big of a decision for her to take in one evening. She needed more time and thought. And she was so tired.

After Sergio's parents left, what used to be a fluid dialog between Alicia and Sergio became an exchange of basic sentences, and they pointedly avoided talking about Susana. He never mentioned her, and she was grateful for his silence. The thought of her friend being tortured and drowned was too vivid for her. Alicia could not get over it or try to forget. She had an immense reservoir of hatred inside, and she did not know how to deal with it. It was like a cesspool that was poisoning her from inside. She was sure it was better for everybody if she did not talk about it.

The stomachaches worsened, and waking up in the mornings seemed at times an impossible task. She often felt lethargic and had an intense need to curl on the couch and sleep. Trivial things would elicit tears and feelings of despair, and she felt embarrassed and confused about that. Classical music, a delight before, now made her cry for no reason. The only thing that took her mind out of her misery was writing, and she tried to do as much of it as possible, taking assignment upon assignment, a pattern that Carlos Alvarez made fair use of. While her overwrought state lasted, she would write non-stop until exhaustion. Then she would revert again to apathy, and her body would be as exhausted as her mind in the mornings.

She dreaded the mere thought of intimacy with Sergio. The closest she had allowed him to get was cuddling together before sleeping, and she knew he was increasingly resenting her rejection and her excuses.

"I think you have to do something about these moods and your constant crying in the corners, Alicia," he said one evening after once again she broke into tears when he attempted to caress her. "This is not you. And this has been going on for too long now. You cannot get over what happened with Susana all by yourself."

"Don't say that."

"Well, you need help. You have changed. You don't talk any longer about your feelings, as you used to. My goodness, you don't even complain about the government anymore!"

"This from Mr. Buddha himself," she laughed nervously. "When did you let your feelings pass through that thick barrier you have?"

"Don't change the subject. I'm not in question here." He was annoyed now.

"Who knows. Maybe the government finally shut me up. They did you a favor, though. You won't have to hear my rants any longer." She meant it as a joke, but he was not laughing.

"You will have to face the fact that we haven't been together since... what... I don't even remember, and you don't seem to care or be interested. So if it's something I did, I want you to tell me, right now, honestly."

"Honestly? Well, honestly, it's not you, nothing to do with you," she said, regretting what was happening, wishing she could erase from her mind the flashbacks she had so often now that made her cringe with guilt and disgust. "I will do something about it. This time I will." But she knew she was not ready to talk about it with a stranger.

"You know what you should do. Go and get help for once and for all."

"I will, I will," she sighed. If that would make him happier, she was ready to see a counselor and follow the charade.

The next day she randomly picked an unknown name from the list of their medical insurance's brochure, and she hoped that he would be a total stranger, a face that she never had crossed before or met in town. She couldn't bear to talk to somebody she knew.

"Psychologists.... let's see, this one seems good enough," she said over breakfast, pointing to one. "If he's booked, this other one has a good ring to his name too."

"Okay. You call one of them today. And stop acting like a wise girl because you will go see one of them, and you will start working on getting out of your depression or whatever you have now."

"Yeah, just like that." Then, regretting her words, she added, avoiding Sergio's eyes, "No. But seriously, I promise I will try."

Alicia's hands were wet, and her heart was pounding while she sat on the comfortable chair. It was her first visit to the counselor, a young and friendly enough psychologist. His room was cozy, with an ample window to the backyard treetops. He welcomed her, closed the door, and sat at his desk. That was almost thirty minutes ago, and she was increasingly nervous. First, she had to beat the urgency of leaving the office before even seeing him. Now, she had answered his questions with monosyllables but trying not to be impolite. There had been long silences between the exchanges, and she was praying for the meeting to be over. Finally, she felt compelled to be honest with him. "This is embarrassing for me. I'm not used to talking about my personal problems with anybody except maybe a couple of friends. If that." Her voice was strangled by emotion, and she hated it.

He looked at her again, smiling: "It's fine. You don't have to talk if you don't feel like it. It's up to you."

"To be honest with you, I don't want to talk about me."

"Then don't. We can talk about any other issue that comes to your mind."

Alicia's impulse was to leave right away. She did not know this man. Why would she want to talk about anything else with him? She did not want his help. It was an expensive waste of time for her and the health insurance. She made a civilized effort to stay there and be polite.

"I am here because he asked me to, and I promised to do it."

"Who asked you to come?"

"Sergio, my husband. He's worried about me. He says I work too much, I don't rest enough, and I'm edgy lately."

"Are you?"

"Well, yes. I'm exhausted and don't sleep well." She did not add what was bothering her: the frequent nightmares, the panic attacks at home and in the street lately, her tantrums about minor domestic inconveniences, and the aversion to intimacy with Sergio. But, overall, the unexplained and shameful rejection she felt for her son did not mean she loved him less. She made it a point not to mention her flashbacks about the man from the green Falcon, her loath, this deep hatred for him that consumed her every day.

The counselor asked, "Any particular reason?"

"For what?"

"The sleepless nights."

"None that I can think of. Other than the fact that I'm overworked and short of time for most of the things I want to do. I can't get to sleep, and when I do, I often wake up during the night." she interrupted the sentence; she was too close to handing him the opportunity to ask about her tortured dreams.

"We can help you with medication to sleep better. We'll need a consultation with one of our psychiatrists. Do you believe you will need it?"

"You mean sleeping pills? No, thanks. I'm not too fond of drugs.

I don't take even aspirin unless I need it badly." She recoiled, and then, smiling dismissively, she added, "It's not that bad... I'm not sick or anything, believe me. I'll manage with chamomile tea."

Amazingly, he approved with his head. Doctor Jimenez would have smiled at her words.

He had suggested a psychiatrist. Was he trying to extend the exposition of her problems to yet another professional? At this rate, soon, she would be broadcasting her personal life on the radio.

All in all, he seemed agreeable enough and not pushy, but right then and there, Alicia decided to cut these sessions short. He wanted to see her twice a week, but she declined, "I'm sorry, but I will only be able to come once a week if that..."

The counselor leaned forward slightly in his chair and said, in an earnest tone that made her feel a bit at fault for acting so dismissively with him, "That's fine. I'll be here if you feel like talking at any other time."

She punctually attended the weekly sessions, but things at home did not improve. She did not have the energy to care any longer. She felt detached from Sergio and Pablo, but they seemed to keep tugging at her for attention to the point in which Alicia exploded. Finally, after another of the daily confrontations over domestic issues, Sergio vented his resentment, almost shouting at her.

"You don't have a clue as to how tired I am of your attitude. You act as if nothing were important anymore. We have so many things to do. Yet, you don't participate in anything. Can't you at least show a bit of interest?"

She shrugged and tried to ignore him, shuffling some papers on the table.

He went on, "Don't do that. Please, don't do that to us all, Alicia. Are you going to therapy when you have appointments? Are you truly doing anything positive there?"

"What do you mean? You wanted me to sit once a week with a complete stranger and talk. I'm doing it. It's up to me what I talk about with him. That's all."

"Okay, I know you're doing your part." He sounded conciliatory. He knew that antagonizing her would be worse. She seemed to be always on edge.

"I try, Sergio, you know I'm trying."

"I know. I know it's hard on all of us. But I meant to ask you, please try to be more patient with Pablo. He's not a happy and easygoing kid anymore. I worry about him; he's the one who suffers the consequences. I honestly believe all of us are hurt by what happened."

"Yeah, you bet we are." Then she added, trying to appease him, "I'm nervous about this trip to Buenos Aires for the Consulate interview; I'm afraid to sell everything we have and leave for good. I dread packing our books and photographs in boxes and sending them overseas. It makes me nervous."

He walked toward her, but she did not seek his embrace, as she would have months ago when they were a completely different couple under the same roof. Instead, he stood there, next to her.

"Alicia, I promise everything will be all right, you'll see. Yesterday, when I spoke with mom, she told me all the details they are preparing for our arrival. They're thrilled that we are joining them. Fort Lauderdale is supposed to be beautiful, always sunny, with waterways. We will get there. We'll take one step at a time, and we'll get there. But I cannot do it by myself; I need you too, I need your enthusiasm, your attention. I need the Alicia you used to be."

She took his hand in hers and hard-pressed it for a few seconds while looking at him through the tears. "You may find it difficult believing me, Sergio, but I love you. I'll do as much as I can. But I also want a new start after what we had gone through."

He smiled and kissed her hands. For a moment, it seemed as if they had reconnected. But Alicia knew better. Her words were sincere, but she had the clear perception that a light went out inside her. She seemed unable to find the will to reignite it, trying less and less to regain that energy, feeling a vague, twisted comfort in the fact that she was letting herself go, letting this deep sadness take over her. She was abandoning her self-control to this other overpowering, invasive sensation of despair and hatred while she curled, protected, in a warm and comfortable corner of herself.

XVI

Early February 1983

Alicia heard the steps coming from behind her and turned around, smiling at Mary, who was punctual as always. They had arranged to meet at the park behind Centro Cívico, next to the sun-drenched playground, and Alicia sat on a wooden bench facing the deep blue Nahuel Huapi waters right beyond the road. She had been drowsily keeping an eye on Pablo, who was busy playing with other kids in the sandbox.

"Hi. I bought two coffees," Mary said, sitting next to her friend and offering a cup. "Did you wait long?"

"Not too long. Pablo's having a great time. It's such a beautiful day, warm and calm." Alicia turned to her friend smiling. "I love this season."

"Spring is the best season here," she said, sitting next to Alicia. "Pablo is growing fast and changing so much. He'll be quite handsome."

"I know. Soon he will be two years old. Unbelievable."

"He's going to be tall like his father; you can see that." Mary waved and blew a kiss toward Pablo, who smiled broadly at her. "He's so cute, and talking about cute; you look much better lately. How are the sessions with the therapist going? It's been what... over three months now?"

"Thanks for the compliment, but I haven't noticed any change... I don't know if this guy is of any help to me, to be honest with you."

"Give it some time; these things take longer to heal. You were struck, but you will recover. Just keep on trying."

"Yeah... we'll see. This treatment is going to end soon, though.

Yesterday we got a letter from the Embassy. Everything went fine in Buenos Aires, the medical checkup at the Hospital Británico, and the Consulate interview. They have approved our visas to emigrate, I guess because we have no criminal records. We were told that's a must for the Consulate."

"Hey, congratulations!" Mary was excited. "This is great news."

"Yeah. We'll be leaving soon. In fact, we have to set a date to leave and buy the tickets to Miami." Then, turning to her friend, "I can hardly believe we are almost through with all this...it was such a mess. We ended up so tired. The garage sale was exhausting," Alicia sighed. "I know there is still more to come, and it scares me because I don't feel I have the energy to go ahead any longer."

"I'm sure you will. You guys managed to work while organizing things; I give you credit for that."

"The worst part was this trip to Buenos Aires, so close to the holidays. Meeting Sonia and Roberto and saying goodbye to them drained us. I felt like a deserter when I convinced myself so easily not to go to Plaza de Mayo when they marched while we were right there, a few miles away, in the hotel. I worried that if somebody saw us, they would label us as socialists or something, which would screw up our application at the Consulate. Afterward, I felt awful for being so scared."

"Sonia knows what's going on; she knows you guys and all you did for Susana."

"All the same... it was painful because she hopes that Susana may still be alive and may be released when the civilians... Do tell me, do you think that there is a possibility that everybody was wrong and she is still alive somewhere? That she may come back one day?"

"I don't know. How can we know?"

Alicia murmured, "What's better? Not to lose hope and wait forever, or try to find closure when you still don't know what might have happened to her?"

"I don't know. But honestly, I wish I knew."

"Ah, Mary, I hate these guys so much. You have no idea."

"I know you do, but what's the point? It's all over now; they will be gone soon, I hope."

"No, this won't be over just like that. People still talk about the consequences of the war in Europe forty years ago; imagine how long it will take for us to get over this. Do you actually believe that if we don't clean the house, things will be okay? No way... This is going to fester forever if they sweep it under the rug. I know it. I can feel it in my bones."

After a brief silence, Mary changed the subject. "I meant to ask you about the house. Did anybody answer the ad for a tenant?" She was ostensibly eluding her friend's eyes, and Alicia did not mind. She preferred not to delve into painful subjects any longer.

"A couple of calls. We'll see. The best solution would have been to sell it, but nobody is buying now with the elections coming. Another bitter pill was to admit to Sergio's parents that we needed a loan to pay off Uranga's mortgage. We'll pay them back as soon as we start working in Florida."

"You'll be okay on that front. I haven't been there, but I know their economy has nothing to do with this mess we have here... at least the salaries there are worth something from one year to the next."

Alicia shook her head. It was so odd. She felt uncomfortable talking with Mary about leaving, and she was the one that changed the subject. "You know, this weather is so nice, and this place is so peaceful. I wish we could stay sitting here forever."

Mary turned to look at her. "We'll miss you guys so dearly. Life's a bitch."

"I know. We'll miss you too. A lot."

Both remained silent for a long time, sitting next to each other, watching the children play.

More people than they expected attended the farewell dinner organized by their friends. Alicia and Sergio were overwhelmed by the gesture of affection.

Alicia and Martina left the table before dessert time, and dodging seats crossed the humming restaurant room. Alicia meant to ask Mary to come along, but she was too busy immersed in a conversation with another colleague, so she kept walking.

"Martina, this is a wonderful dinner. Thank you so much for helping organize it. I know that you were behind the whole thing, taking the time to gather so many friends." Alicia was blushing, excited, and with one-too-many glasses of wine that slightly slurred her speech as she walked next to Martina to the ladies' room. She added, "This is a great farewell dinner. I'm going to miss all this so much, the people and the city."

Martina took her arm and affectionately pressed it. "I know. We'll miss you too..."

They walked into the restroom and stood there behind two other women, waiting for their turn to use the toilets.

"So you have all packed already. You know, you were lucky to find a nice couple to rent your home while you find a buyer."

"Yeah, they seem nice enough. I hope they take care of the house. If we get a buyer, it will be a good excuse to come back for a visit."

"It will take time, but you will find a buyer. It's a nice piece of property, large enough and in a prime spot."

"We'll see. I cannot think about next month, let alone next year."

"Everything will be fine, you'll see. Besides, you guys are moving to the center of the world, so to speak. The United States *is the center* of the world in many aspects. So you'll be okay, I'm sure–ah, by the way, I almost forgot to tell you about Roberto Flores, Julio's friend."

"What about him?" Alicia answered, surprised. Her recollection of that man always made her feel uncomfortable, for no specific reason that she could point out.

"Well, listen to this," Martina continued, "It so happens that he moved to the United States too. He got a job with some big corporation, and he's living in a suburb near San Diego."

"Is that right?" Alicia did not know what to say. "Across the map from Florida, though."

"Yes, he's been hired by a security company with a good salary and benefits. There's a work contract included and the residency papers. Lucky guy."

"Good for him," Alicia muttered.

"Yes, he wrote a long letter to us with all the details before leaving. I'll give you his phone number before you go. You never know if you'll travel to the West coast. You guys could meet him."

"Yes, that would be nice."

Martina went further, making mental connections as she spoke.

"By the way, how's Susana? Have you heard of her lately?"

"Oh, yes, she's okay." Alicia lied without hesitation. "She's working hard on her assignments. I did not get to see her in Buenos Aires, though. She was traveling on business."

Martina meant to say something back, but a woman walked out of one of the stalls. "Oops, it's your turn. Go ahead."

Alicia complied gladly and walked away. The slight veil that blurred her senses after the wine had vanished. The mention of Roberto Flores brought memories of the last days with Susana, and as it was often the case when she had an extra drink, she burst into tears, unable to stop for a few minutes. When she calmed down, she left the toilet and walked to the sink to wash her face. She should have followed the counselor's advice and taken something to help her cope with all of this, she thought, but then again, she wouldn't be able to drink even a glass of alcohol, and that was inadmissible for her.

"Let me fix this a bit," she said apologetically, pulling makeup out of her handbag. Martina laughed, coming back from the toilet. "My goodness, you are totally drunk," she said, holding her by the arm to leave the room. Alicia let her believe that she was intoxicated. In fact, she needed another drink to ease the pain and bury the memories. Alcohol didn't have the same punch lately. She needed to increase her intake to get the same soothing effect. Then, as she had in the last month when she got numb by drinking, Alicia would concentrate on the sweet fact that May in the northern hemisphere means Springtime, sun, and warm weather. So she would skip altogether the coming Bariloche winter and all the winters that will follow.

XVII

Fort Lauderdale, Florida, USA
June 1984, 14 months later

Sergio stopped his Ford Escort by the curb, the motor still running, and checked the rearview mirror to confirm that no cars were coming from behind. The street was narrow and slightly shaded with beautiful palm trees. He turned to Alicia with a satisfied and inquiring look. "Well? Should we go inside now?"

Alicia glanced at the details of the sizeable ranch-style house, the lovely tended garden in front, and the paneled windows. It was a stately but unpretentious house. It would be their first own house in this new home that was America. She knew what Sergio was expecting from her, and she complied with as much enthusiasm as she could muster. "You are dying to open the door all by yourself, aren't you? So let's go for it."

He parked the car in the ample circular driveway, right in front of the house's double entrance door. Alicia stood in the paved way leading to the front steps.

"It's like the huge, lovely American houses of the fifties and sixties that I used to envy in magazines when I was a child," she said. "With a basketball hoop on the side... sort of like that nice Brady's home...."

"Brady's home?"

"The Bunch's, of course... you didn't watch enough TV in your childhood."

"Ah, yeah, but I got bored with the Brady Bunch. Did I miss a lot?" he said, laughing and unlocking the front door with a satisfied look. "Let's walk into your new home."

They went in cautiously as if expecting somebody to come to the

237

door. Alicia should feel dizzily happy; she owed him that much. Why was she unable to join him, not even in this marital joy that he deserved? What a disgusting individual she was, full of guilt and hatred. It had not always been this way, though. For a few seconds, she had a flash memory of the Alicia she used to be, spontaneous and sincere. Not any longer. Did Sergio notice the extent of her change? She was sure that he should know, deep inside, he was only holding a shadow of that long-ago woman. Twice, during shouting matches over domestic things, he had threatened her with ending what he called a *parody of marriage*. But then he had calmed down and never acted upon that. Could it be that he loved her, or the memory of her, so much that he would gladly take whatever was left? If so, she, a liar and a cheater deserved him even less.

He was inspecting the details on the walls, windowsills, and floors intently. "It has great potential for improvements. We'll make it a neat place, you'll see."

She followed him. "I like it as it is, but I know you will improve it," she said sincerely. He kissed her forehead, and they walked through the hall to the open living room area.

"It's huge. Carla will be thrilled when she sees this house. By the time they come back in a couple of months on their way to New York, we may be living here." Her cousin was coming here so often lately that Guillermo searched for a small apartment to buy in Manhattan. "They can stay at home, too."

"Sure." He seemed pleased and proud. Then, after a pause, he added, "This house is the second property we ever owned. It's much larger than anything we could have afforded in Argentina."

She nodded. Sergio had accepted his father's co-signature for the mortgage application. They recently arrived and did not have enough credit history to get a bank loan, although Sergio's salary was high for a newcomer.

The purchase of this house confirmed Sergio's success in the new country. She knew she had to celebrate. So she forced herself once again. They walked the spacious, luminous rooms one by one. The windows were immense, and the view of the waterway from the living room caught her attention.

"It's so nice to have a view of palm trees and water," she said appreciatively. "I can hardly see the house across the water from here."

He walked toward the window, looking at the view. "You're right. It's a nice view of the water. You will be happy here, I promise you, Alicia. Things will improve, you'll see." His voice had an inflection that made her look at him. "I love you so much, and I'm so happy to see you getting better by the day. Even my folks noticed that you don't seem so sad lately. I'm glad you like Florida. Pablo seems to like it too. He even likes his babysitter."

"What's not to like? It's warm all the time; it is all green, the sea is gorgeous… we are spoiled here, Sergio. Aren't we?"

"Don't we deserve it, after all?"

She took refuge in his arms, and he held her tight for a few minutes. Then, as it usually happened when they were close, she felt the urge to break the shared emotional moment.

"This is getting too mushy," she said, moving away from him.

"I like mushy," he murmured, letting her go. "I'm always available for mushy."

Alicia remained silent. Then Sergio walked away from her before she would leave him. "Let's check the rest of the house," he added in a neutral tone.

Living in Florida had turned into a curious experience for Alicia. Her persistent nightmares regularly returned after a brief, peaceful interval in which she hoped they had gone for good. Not only did they not go away, but they became recurring. At night, she inhabited a parallel world in the twilight; the objects and people were well defined, but the surroundings were blurry and dark. Sometimes the images were in color, but the colors were gloomy, and they added to the menacing, suffocating atmosphere of the dreams.

During the day, she made an effort to comply with her self-imposed routine, forcing her to do typing, housekeeping, and Pablo's care. However, the painful memories of Susana and her own unfortunate personal attempt at helping her followed her all the time, and she found refuge in a weariness that allowed her to grieve in silence.

They had followed the news from Argentina, first in the Spanish press and later in English newspapers. In December, President Alfonsín decreed the creation of the *Comisión Nacional Sobre la Desaparición de las Personas,* a committee to investigate the disappearances during the military years. Also, the laureate writer Ernesto Sábato was named its head, and they were working to gather the information that eventually would serve to administer justice.

An international team of pathologists had converged in Argentina after many common graves were opened. Also, there was a coordinated search for victims' corpses in tombs marked *"NN"* all over the country. The team was in the process of identifying the remains. It was a gruesome and ghastly task, and Alicia could barely read the articles that reached her. Susana's body was not found yet, and Sonia hoped it was because she was alive somewhere, maybe amnesic and that one day she would surprise her returning home. Alicia was sure she was dead, and the drowning version was the most feasible. If so, her remains almost certainly would not be found, and it would always be an open wound for all of them. The lack of a tomb where to place her remains would be forever an unfinished family duty.

Resentful at her aloofness, Pablo seemed to read her mind and detect her brooding moods, reacting with anger and pain against her indifference and detachment. She knew that he was suffering but, not knowing how to help him, ended up resenting his constant interference on her self-imposed busy schedule.

Franz and Helena gladly shared their free time with their grandson, and Pablo had a bedroom of his own in their home. Lately, he seemed happier with them than around his parents. Soon after moving to Florida, Sergio's parents embraced the old family tradition of meeting for dinner on Sundays. The couple had remodeled the cozy condominium they had bought while still living in Argentina. Resilient as real survivors, they had adjusted almost immediately to the new environment, and now they were learning English. They even asked Sergio and Alicia to chat in the newly acquired language to help them practice.

Alicia admired their determination and drive. Franz and Helena started from scratch in another place and took pains and joys with the same enthusiasm. The Fechners, their old-time friends, had followed a similar path. Now they were neighbors again, as they had in Europe during the war years.

It was Sunday, and the family was sitting at the table. Sergio had picked a few tango CDs, and the soft, well-known music played low in the dining room. Alicia brought coffee cups from the kitchen.

"So, what's the name of that machine again, Alicia? Word processor? It seems interesting, such a modern typewriter," Helena asked while cutting a cherry pie she had baked that same morning for dessert. "Sergio says it has a computer too. Isn't it too complicated?"

"Not at all. The brand is Amstrad, and it's both a word processor and computer; Sears imports it from the UK. I don't understand anything about computers; it's just technical gibberish for me, not that I need a computer. But the word-processing part is very convenient and fast. I love it. It has a small device called a disk, and if you insert it one way is an electronic typewriter. Inserted the other side up, it is a computer, and you can play a game, besides other uses that I didn't bother to explore in the manual, a real mysterious book. If I get a supply of regular manuscripts to type, it can be a good stay-at-home job. I believe I have a niche here. They need bilingual typists." Alicia was proud of her verbosity today, her ability to pretend, mainly because it was a feat she seldom was capable of reaching. Sergio seemed pleased with her high spirits too.

"To start, it's okay, but are you sure you want just a typist job?" Franz asked, trying to feign disinterest. Alicia did not answer. She knew he did not buy into this new Alicia, anxious to stay home and avoid people. But then again, he was not privy to the whole story.

Helena seemed happy for her. "That's great; you already have one client. I'm sure you will do okay; your English is excellent."

Sergio intervened. "Soon, Alicia will feel confident enough, and she will be back to writing for a publication. Won't you?"

Alicia smiled at him as she would to Pablo when the child said something cute that she would ignore. "Maybe, we will see about that."

It was not a secret that she had not written anything since leaving Argentina and had refused to make friends. Their social life was limited to the family and Sergio's acquaintances at work, and she did not seem interested in anything except reading and being alone. Her recent purchase of the word processor was the first timid approach to change, and Sergio saw it as a good omen. He had high hopes of Alicia overcoming the on-and-off depression that she refused to admit but was ostensibly leading her to alcoholism. He had agreed to her plead not to talk about her drinking problem with his parents. Nevertheless, she knew that Franz and Helena concealed their anxiety about their son's family adjustment to the new country, so she felt compelled to go along and show a reasonably steady façade lately.

Both parents avoided talking about the political news coming from Argentina, and Alicia was thankful for that. She did not know if Sergio had something to do with their silence, but it was apparent they eluded a subject that they knew would upset her.

"By the way, this coming Friday is the tenth-anniversary dinner at the club," Franz said, playing with Pablo, sitting on his lap. "You guys haven't forgotten, have you?"

"Of course not. We'd love to go," Alicia said. "It'll be nice to dress for a formal party after such a long time. Also, it's a good excuse to go shopping."

"I'm amazed at the number of Argentineans that have moved to Florida in the last year." Franz seemed happy about it. "The club is already ten years old, but it's just starting to grow now. I'm glad they are adding a gym. You should become members."

"We will. In the meantime, we are looking forward to this dinner," Sergio said.

"I'm sure you will enjoy the party and the atmosphere. I'm buying the tickets tomorrow for all of us."

"We have *canasta* tournaments and weekly barbecues, and boating is now popular there, being next to the water and all," Helena said with a wink to Sergio. "What about buying a boat to dock at your new home? It would be great..."

"Mom, don't hold your breath. That's something for the future. Far ahead, I may say..."

Alicia did not intervene; she was busy helping clear the table, feeling tired, wishing to go home and rest. If only she could sleep well. She had tried over-the-counter valerian pills from the health store, several vitamins, and her often-reliable chamomile tea without results. Glad to get away from the chatting, she carried the dishes and started to clean the kitchen.

The Saturday of the anniversary dance at the club was an opportunity to break the monotony and isolation that worried Sergio more than Alicia. He insisted on buying a complete outfit for the party and even volunteered and helped her pick the dress.

"You look beautiful," he said when she walked into the living room, ready to go. She had mocked a grand entrance, and he had applauded. Now they were driving to the Argentinean club's dinner after leaving Pablo upset and crying because he was left behind with his babysitter.

"The waiting was worthwhile, and the color suits you well," he said, smiling.

"Thank you." On an impulse, she had bought the dark burgundy gown with a sleek bodice and a v-neckline that plunged in the back. Sergio had strongly approved. It enhanced her figure, and Alicia felt different as if the dress could cover her true self for a while. However, nothing could be perfect for her; she worried about Pablo's aggressive behavior this evening. Her guilty feelings would inevitably seep through and get to her. Fortunately, she had reinforced her will with two strong margaritas while getting dressed and dropped an adequate supply of mints in her purse.

"Do you think he's calmed down by now? At least Melissa seems to know what she's doing, and he likes her."

"I'm sure he is. We'll call home from the club. I bet he's fine; he knows we feel bad about leaving him, but I promised to take him to the Independence Day picnic next week. He likes the fireworks."

"Yes, he told me about it." Then she added, "Sometimes I don't know what to do. I never knew parents could be this helpless. I'm relieved you are such a good dad. He loves you so much."

"Well, thanks, you are a great mom yourself," he seemed pleased. "But take it easy. Coming here was a big change for us. I'm sure we'll make it, but it will take patience."

"I know," she sighed. Sergio believed in the healing power of positive thinking, even though he would never have described his attitude as such. She felt a pang of envy. It seemed so much relaxed for him.

They drove in silence and parked in the ample, graveled open space next to the building used as a parking lot. Twenty or so cars were already lined in. Small groups walked toward the old, sizable two-story house that was the club's proud acquisition. Sitting on a recently manicured lawn by the river, the building had belonged to a prominent Florida family. A decade ago, the club bought it as a fixer-upper for a reasonable price and is now restored to its old splendor.

They followed the others to the entrance as Alicia tried to tiptoe on the graveled ground to protect her stiletto heels. He showed the tickets at the door, and they entered the ballroom, looking for their place not far from the entrance.

Franz and Helena were already at their table, chatting animatedly with the Fechner and another couple they hadn't met before. They seemed friendly enough, and the conversation took a turn from the food they had on the menu to gossip about the other club members.

Alicia got bored with their continuous chatter and looked around, paying attention instead to the decorations hung from the ceiling and the orchestra, placed in a corner, alternate playing European-style tangos and traditional melodic Argentinean folk tunes.

The hall was composed of two long rooms, evidently the mansion's former living and dining areas now linked by an archway with columns. Three rows of tables had been placed near the walls, leaving the arch free and a sizable dance floor in each room. The tables were mainly occupied by now, as the salad was being served.

Alicia had methodically built the courage to face the evening from early in the day, and now she felt comfortable enough almost to enjoy being there.

The dinner was nearly over, and she made an effort to pull herself out of her thoughts, turning her attention to what Sergio was saying to the others. "...So, I don't think the President will give in to anybody. He promised to clear the air. That's why he won the election. He cannot afford to pardon the torturers just like that..."

"Alfonsín is not as strong as you may think," Fechner cut him short. "He's going to be kicked out of office anytime now if my sources are right. He turned out to be a lousy president if you ask me."

There was an uncomfortable silence. The Fechner common defense of the military juntas' dirty war methods was a sticky point for

Franz when Sergio was present. He tried to steer the conversation in a different direction whenever possible. Finally, Alicia, needing to act upon her disgust for the guy, took Sergio's hand, and standing up, she said: "This is lovely, let's dance." He looked at her, surprised, and at first, he resisted a bit but noticing the pleading in her eyes, he stood up swiftly.

"Yes, let's dance," he said, and, turning toward the table, he muttered an excuse. He followed Alicia to the open area in the room where two or three couples were swirling to the tune of a *valsecito criollo*, a folk version of a waltz.

"No spinning, please. I'll get sick," she panicked at his first fast turn.

He laughed. "You mean you are not already sick from the conversation?"

She smiled, and he slowed the pace. They danced for a few minutes in silence. He was a good dancer, and she enjoyed that. He had a good sense of rhythm, and his slim and muscular body guided her effortlessly. While dancing, he made subtle changes, created new steps, and invented swirls, all without missing the music's beat. She had forgotten how much she enjoyed their bodies locked like this, just following the rhythm in unison while his strong hand held her by the waist.

"I'm glad we came tonight. Maybe we need to go out more often," Alicia ventured.

He looked at her, surprised. "Wow, I'm glad you said that. You read my mind."

"We should do something about it," she said when the music stopped and the melody of tango filled the air. "Maybe take those tango lessons we once said we would take."

"I'm in. Just go and book the dancing classes." They danced in silence for a while, paying close attention to their unpracticed tango steps and occasionally glancing at the other tables. He waved hello to a noisy group.

"Coworkers," he explained.

Alicia focused on Sergio's shoulder, right at her eye level. She always had loved the soft curve of his neck, the elegant lobe of his ear. Why was she feeling so attracted to these intimate details again? She hadn't experienced this for a long time; daring to look at Sergio closely, even enjoy his company. It felt so good to dance with him this tango tune.

"We should learn some more *cortes y quebradas*," Alicia said. "Fancy steps like the dancers in Buenos Aires do. Not those outlandish rigid twists that some professionals do in shows. Tango should be subtle and elegant, not crude sexual moves or marionette-like dancing."

"Yes, but still, this is deeply sensual music, you know that."

"I know, but I resent it when they make a mockery of it all over the world when this music is so much more than that."

"It's just a business, people are buying that, and they sell it," he said.

The music ended, and they stood for a few seconds scouting the crowd that was joining the dance floor after dinner had finished. Then, at the sound of another tango, they started dancing again.

And then she saw the man.

First, it was just a glimpse of a head. Her eyes were distractedly looking at the people sitting at the tables when she saw the familiar shape. It was the same haircut and outline she had seen a long time ago, and under the light of passing cars, turn around and walk toward the darkness of a green Ford Falcon crossed in front of her car. Alicia shivered under the silky burgundy evening gown, and Sergio felt it.

"What is it? Are you cold?"

"No, no," she said, looking around, trying desperately to find the man again, locate where she saw him. Maybe her eyes were playing a trick on her? Punishing her for daring to enjoy a moment without bad memories or guilt?

She thought she had seen this man in a crowd before. As in the day they landed at Miami International Airport when Alicia would have sworn, she saw him going up an escalator while waiting at the carousel for their luggage. Now her stomach tightened with a bout of nausea. Was this, again, a creation of her mind to terrorize her and then vanish? Another panicked flash?

No. This time it was different. Alicia saw him again in another turn. The man was still there. As they danced, she looked at him from afar, reassured now by the distance; a couple was swirling on the floor and two rows of tables. The steps of the dance took them closer. Now she could see him from the side. It was he, no doubt about it. She shivered again, and Sergio stopped dancing.

"Are you okay? Let's sit." He guided her around the other dancing couples to their place. "Are you sure you're okay?"

"Yes, it's only a dizzy spell, maybe too much dancing. Maybe the food," she said, trying to find a proper excuse. "I need some water."

They reached the table, and Alicia saw, relieved, that it was empty; the others were probably dancing. Sergio poured a glass of sparkling water from a bottle, and she sipped slowly, sitting in silence, doing her breathing exercises. He knew her too well to ask her again how she was doing. He let her recover. On occasions, she had collapsed for no apparent reason in the last year. When she felt her legs strong enough, she stood up. He followed.

"I'm going to the bathroom," she said, smiling faintly. "It'll be a minute."

"Are you sure? I'll walk you there." He said, motioning toward her.

"No. I'm okay." Her voice had a harsh tone, and he stood there, looking surprised as she added, apologetically, "Don't worry, I'll be back in a minute." She patted his arm and walked away.

Earlier in the evening, she noticed that the restrooms were at the end of the second open area, which was not far from where she saw the man. The music now was a romantic *bolero,* and many couples were walking back to their seats. She scouted the room. The best path would be next to the right wall, close to the windows. The dancing floor was at her left. She walked parallel to the wall, reached the arch and around the column, and entered the next room. The man was still sitting in the same place. She cringed. Now she was right in front of him, across several tables. He was not looking in her direction, and she stepped cautiously, ready to turn around if needed, hoping he would not notice her.

The man seemed deeply involved in a conversation with the others. He was next to a blond and ostentatious middle-aged woman and a man. Another couple was sitting across. Alicia realized that he was too involved in the chatting to care to look around. She passed close to his table without being noticed. It was him, enjoying the evening. Trembling, she entered the restroom to find Helena at the lavatory, washing her hands, the last person she wanted to cross paths with at this moment.

"Hi, there, Alicia," she greeted her. "Go ahead. I'll wait for you, dear. I'll fix my makeup in the meantime, and we'll go back to the table."

Alicia leaned against the wall of the cubicle for a few minutes to recover. Her mind raced. She felt nauseous and weak. What was that man doing here? It was not a nightmare any longer. Here of all the places, in a country as big as this one. It was hard to believe this was happening. She thought she would never see him again. Not that his shadow had not followed her night and day since the shameful encounter at the hotel.

"Are you okay?" Helena's voice called from the other side of the door.

"Yes, I'm fine. I'll be right out." She flushed the toilet, quickly put a mint in her mouth, and opened the door. "I'm a bit tired. I haven't danced in years," she apologized.

"You'll get in shape in no time if you come here often. It's excellent cardiovascular exercise." Helena talked about health and diets while Alicia tried to fix her mascara and looked at her face in detail. She found it pale and exhausted. Her eyes were red, and she looked older than she was. Worse, she needed another drink. Soon.

"Well, you don't look well," Helena said, her inquisitive eyes on Alicia, who tried to conceal her face, turning around. "But I'm glad you were dancing earlier."

"I feel worn out to tell you the truth. We should leave soon if Sergio doesn't mind," she said while they walked out. Helena waved to several people on their way back, naming them for Alicia's benefit. She wondered if Helena would know the man and his entourage.

Helena smiled while talking, scouting the crowd. "Sooner or later, you get to know everybody around here. Same faces come up in most parties."

"Helena, do you know those guys back there, in the third table?" She motioned toward it without turning her head; she did not want to be seen or identified by him. "Over there, where the tall blond with the shining blouse is sitting."

"Ah, those three are big shots here, members of some committee or other. They are around together all the time. One of them, the guy with the reddish hair, is the son of one of the club's founders," Helena said while walking. Alicia did not notice any redhead. The man she was interested in had a dark brown short crew cut.

"What about the others?"

"I don't know their names." Then she added, "I know they're organizing the picnic. You know the big event next month, the picnic on the 4th of July. Maybe the Consul will be here too, and there will be fireworks on the water. So it will be something, two independence celebrations in one, the following week is our own on the 9th of July, so that it will be a blast."

"Yes, I know. Sergio told me about it, and Pablo is very excited."

"Franz bought the tickets for you guys too. I'm sure he told Sergio. Sure, Pablo will be thrilled; he used to love the New Year's fireworks at home." Helena always called Argentina *home*.

They had reached their table now.

"I'm sure we will be here. Thank you." Her voice came out choking, and Helena looked at her, smiling as if she thought Alicia was moved by her grandmotherly interest in Pablo's wellbeing.

"You are more than welcome, dear."

"Are you better now?" Sergio asked, moving the chair for her. She collapsed there and sipped some water.

"Yes, I'm fine, thanks," she motioned him toward the others. "Please keep on with your chat." He smiled and turned around to answer a question from Fechner.

Alicia's heartbeats now were deafening in her head, as if broadcasted through a loudspeaker. Yet, all the while, her thoughts had the certainty and clarity of printed text in front of her.

In an unexpected turn of events, the opportunity to act upon what she had fantasized for so long in her feverish dreams was just served to her on a silver plate, and she was ready, better still, anxious, to take it.

"You didn't sleep well last night," he said, pouring coffee into her cup. "I heard you tossing and turning and even walking out of the bedroom twice. Are you okay?"

She was taken aback by his words. She thought he was sleeping, and she tried to be silent as much as she could.

"Oh, yeah… I'm okay now. I just woke up, that's all."

He smiled, not convinced. Alicia grabbed the Miami Herald copy from the kitchen table and opened it, feigning interest in the news. She would not ruin the precarious harmony that they had reached the previous evening at the club. It lasted only two or three songs, but it was enough for the memories of better times to come back, almost suffocating her with nostalgia. She was determined to let him relive whatever they had had before and make him happy; whatever he had, for no fault of him, lost forever, albeit for a brief moment. She owed him that much.

He left for work, and she took care of the daily chores with her mind working feverishly on what she had decided to do. It would take some crafting and many a drink, but she was up to the task. Now that the energy had returned, and there was a purpose in her near future.

During the following three weeks, the time had the unique quality of running slow, at a measured pace. Alicia had never lived time in this continuously deliberate, purposeful manner before. She weighed every hour, deciding her actions, evaluating the consequences of proceeding one way or the other, even over small domestic things that otherwise would not have caught her attention.

She devoted herself to Pablo, who mostly ignored her, used as he was to her aloofness and impatience, which had forced him to create his own world when at home. Still, Alicia dutifully followed him around. She even took the time to dust off a long-forgotten notebook which, when he was born, had been meant to be a diary written for him, with details of his birth and early years, that she had abandoned in a drawer after the Malvinas War hit them.

She penned several pages of hand-written notes for him during the four hours a day he was away at kindergarten, eager by the sudden need to open her heart to the man he would be in the years to come. She wondered how he would judge her, what questions he would ask, but foremost, to what extent she was willing to tell him about her inner feelings, the turmoil, dark fantasies, and frightening indifference for everything.

Since arriving in Florida, she had maintained a regular exchange of letters and pictures with Mary and Sonia, especially Mary, whose company and camaraderie she missed dearly. Now she sat and wrote a long, affectionate letter to each of them, and while doing so, she had the odd feeling that she was writing messages to her past, more than updates on her present. They would understand. She knew that.

The short notes to Aunt Marga and Carla were the hardest to write. Nonetheless, Alicia put herself to the task dutifully. She even wrote letters to Mariano. Alicia felt grateful; he regularly informed her about the civil government's perils under another impending military coup's perpetual Damocles sword. He detailed the unbearable news on the forensic jobs of identification on the countless common graves opened after the elections. Although she skipped those lines lately, unable to read more grisliness or conjure up more macabre images in her mind.

Sergio had made her promise not to read any longer the clips and newspapers that Mariano and Sonia mailed. One afternoon he found her crying and gloomy, sitting in their back yard's lawn, surrounded by the horrific news articles and inner pages pictures spread.

All that was over now for her; the letters she painstakingly wrote this week were peaceful and affectionate, reflecting her new state of mind. No anger, no complaints, just letting them know how much she had valued their friendship and their support while walking that thorny road together. In every envelope, she attached a recent photograph of Sergio and her hugging Pablo, all of them smiling happily for the camera.

XVIII

"Wait here, I'll be down in a minute," Alicia said, rushing up the flight of stairs to her bedroom. The new house will not have stairs, she thought. It would be so much easier to move around. She had dreamed of a ranch home, like the one Sergio had just bought. Well, no regrets at all. Things happen, and she learned to take things as they came, and today, the big day finally had come. She shouted from the top of the stairs, "As soon as I finish my makeup, we'll leave."

"Okay, hurry up. We are already late," Sergio yelled back from downstairs.

She rushed to the bathroom and turned her attention to the colorful mixture of eye-shadow boxes, pencils, and brushes neatly arranged in her makeup case. She needed more color in that pale face of hers, and she was about to pick one when she changed her mind and took the sleek margarita glass from the countertop. She gulped down with pleasure the lemony, acidic drink. It was the way she liked her margaritas. No salt.

Deciding on a dark grey eye-liner, she searched for the train of thought she had right before going downstairs to bid farewell to Pablo, leaving for the 4th of July picnic with Franz and Helena. Where was she? Yeah, she was thinking again about Bariloche. It always amazed her how much misery people would be able to endure for years and years without saying enough, without turning like a cornered wild animal and seeking retribution. She had seen people around her accepting things, cursing their destiny but licking their wounds, healing, and recovering. Was that strength or a character flaw? Well, it did not matter now. As far as she was concerned, all that was over. Another gulp of margarita, and she focused again on the mirror. Thank goodness for alcohol. Today she needed the welcome comfort of her favorite drink, smoothing her senses, steadying her pulse. It was her third, and she hoped Sergio had not noticed. Let's do a bit of color on the cheeks now. That was much better.

The Instrumental Beatles' CD playing in the background had ended, and now it was a selection of Piazzolla's tangos swirling in the air. Her perception of music always improved after a couple of drinks; she could detect subtleties that she had not noticed before, as in this version of Adios Nonino. Ah, the sweetness of the bandoneon— it channeled right to her soul from the cobbled streets of Buenos Aires, darting straight on Alicia's oldest memories and pulling them up, all of them, without discrimination; the cherished as well as the painful ones. What? No. No tears today, definitely not. She wiped carefully around her eyes and slowly applied dark brown mascara on her eyelashes, fluttering them a couple of times. That's enough. It shouldn't be overdone. She wanted to look natural, even a bit coquettish; the opposite of how she sees herself. She may have been a little depressed lately, but that was also over. This Alicia was now a very poised and calm woman.

The sound of the bedroom door opening startled her. Sergio walked into the dressing room and stood by the bathroom door. He was, as every time, tired of waiting and ready to go. She could see it on his face.

"I just checked the oil in your car. It needs change. I'll do it tomorrow." Then, looking appreciatively at her, he added, "Wow. You look stunning. Men will turn to look at you and will envy me."

She forced a smile. "Thanks, it's nice of you, but I'm not buying it."

"Hmm… those jeans fit you well."

She tried to smile again. "They better. They cost a mint."

"Pity, because you don't need clothes…"

She shook her head, smiling. "Sergio, I'm trying to finish my makeup here. Please, wait downstairs."

Alicia made an effort to keep her voice natural, feigning a casual tone. Her hands were wet now, and her heart was beating as if she had run a mile. He was referring to the night before, in which they had, for the first time in ages, great sex. And she had been sincere, spontaneous, pretending for a short while that things could get back to what they had been a long, long ago. But it was not so simple as it seemed. She knew well all that was gone.

Now she had to lie to him again, and she was not good at it. Sergio meant well, but she wished he would leave her alone.

"Alicia, that's your second drink today, and it's only past noon," his tone was admonishing but without bitterness. "You promised me." She smiled sheepishly. He is sweet, she thought, always trying so hard to help me. He means well, dear Sergio; he does not want to accept it is over, and neither do I, in a way. She sighed and lied again. "No more. This one is the last. I won't drink again until the evening. You had your beer. I had this glass. That's all, promise."

He shook his head. For a split second, she felt weak. She thought of telling him everything, lifting her heart's weight, and running to his arms, and the thought made her lose her balance. To regain her composure, she pretended something was wrong with her sandal, and she looked down. What was this weakness now? Pull yourself together. When she looked back at him, he still had a hint of skepticism. It was evident he did not believe her promise not to drink, and he was right.

"By the way," she managed to say with a straight face, "do you think this blouse is okay for this weather? Have you been outside?"

"It's just right. Outside is warm but dry; a perfect Independence Day afternoon." He stroked her chin lightly, smiled, and turned around. "Hurry up," he warned in a loud voice before leaving the room. "It's getting late. The barbecue starts at one."

"I love you," she said.

"Love you too... hurry up."

She knew he had come upstairs to check on her, to see how she was doing, he meant well, and he aimed to protect her. She walked out of the narrow bathroom and locked the bedroom door that Sergio had left open. Then calmly, she went to the walk-in closet, opened a top drawer, and took out a bundle wrapped in a soft wool scarf. Carefully Alicia deposited it inside the large, fashionable handbag that she would wear today and was already open on a chair. On top, she placed the two small plastic toys that Pablo had left behind earlier, and Alicia knew he would want them sooner or later. Taking her time, she closed the top zipper of the bag.

Before leaving the room, she approached the wall mirror and checked her image from head to toes. She looked slim and at least ten years younger than her age, almost attractive. Not bad. Much more sophisticated than when she was living in Bariloche. She wondered if he would recognize her at first sight or if she would have to identify herself, as Edmond Dantès would do upon confronting Ferdinand Mondego. The thought brought a smile to her face. She had always loved Edmond and his single-minded persistence through three volumes.

Reaching up, she got a bottle of perfume from a shelf and sprayed it all around her. Today she wanted to be at her best.

Lifting the handbag with care, she slung it over her left shoulder. Her forearm touched the soft leather, and she pressed it against her side.

While leaving the room, she noticed the melancholic bandoneon sound still floating in the air behind her and coming again from the tiny speaker in the hallway. Sergio always left the music on until right before leaving the house.

Lunch was almost ending. Pablo swallowed his food in a hurry and over the clean picnic plate; he begged in English, with a marked American accent, "I wanna go back there." Then he wiped his face and hands with a soiled napkin, looking at his parents. Sergio was still halfway through his beef ribs, so Alicia jumped at the opportunity.

"I'll take you, dear, and then I'll pick up some dessert," Alicia said and stood up. Then, lifting Pablo from the chair, she put him down on the graveled ground with a swirl that made him laugh. The family was sitting at one of the tables lined under several tents behind the club's building. The terrain was soft on a slope that ended in the water edge where patrons docked small boats. The day was bright, and the club teemed with members and guests.

"I'll take Pablo to the other kids."

"That's fine," Sergio nodded. "See you."

"Does anybody want any sweets? Franz?" she asked politely.

"No, thank you," Sergio said.

"Thank you, dear. Helena and Regina are already bringing some to us," Franz answered smiling, motioning toward his friend Fechner, seated next to him.

Alicia picked up her heavy leather handbag from under her chair and took the toys out.

"Do you want them now?" she asked Pablo. "Want to take them with you?"

He shook his head. "No, I wanna go now..." he said impatiently. Alicia left the toys on the table and bent over toward Sergio, kissing him on his forehead.

"I love you so much," she murmured in his ear, "you are the best man in the whole world, and I want you to know it."

He turned to her and murmured back, "Well, you are pretty good yourself."

She walked away, holding Pablo's hand, toward the grassy area where the babysitters watched the younger children under the trees. Pablo was excited and pulled her ahead. Then, trembling and with her eyes blurry because of the tears, she bent over and kissed him several times. The child fought to loosen her grip and ran toward the kids already playing in the enclosed area. She stood there while one of the teenagers closed the fence from inside, and Pablo joined the others. Then she turned around and walked toward the large building.

She left behind the busy tents where people were sitting, enjoying the meal, or walking to or from the area where the barbecue pit sent long streaks of smoke up beyond the tall trees that bordered the club's property.

Walking as steadily as her shaking legs allowed her, Alicia approached the building, focused on breathing rhythmically. Engaged on her breathing, as she had carefully planned, each inhalation was as deep and relaxing as possible. Her heartbeat sound was now a drum in her ears, and Alicia felt she was ready for this. She knew every reaction of her body when in danger, so she had anticipated the possibility of a panic attack. She wiped her cold, wet hands on the side of her jeans. She could feel the adrenaline rushing through her veins, her throat dry, but the steps firm. Her mind had only one definite purpose.

She stepped inside the house and scouted the first room. A group of men was standing around a table, busy talking. The windows were open, and the full daylight gave the place the same discretely elegant look it had had that night, during the dinner and dance a few weeks ago, when she saw the man again.

Alicia looked carefully at every person in the room and walked past the arch to the next, where people sat on sofas around coffee tables at both end corners. She stood still near the arch that separated both rooms, with her back to the narrow dividing wall. The group in the left corner was engaged in a card game of *truco*, which provoked laughs and vociferous expressions from the players. The opposite corner was more discreet. There, five men were quietly smoking and chatting, looking at what seemed to be travel brochures from Argentina opened on the coffee table. And among them was the man from the green Falcon, as she had expected. Earlier on, she had seen him walking into the clubhouse with others, and she had hurried to finish her light lunch, to be able to leave the table soon. Now she felt relieved, the search was over, and the adrenaline rush was almost thrilling.

He was facing her across the room, sitting, relaxed against the back of the seat, saying something that must have been funny because everybody laughed at once. A dirty joke, maybe? What else other than slime would come out of that man's mouth? What else but filthiness out of that brain? The deep revulsion she felt all these years for him, and his kind was there, intact, powerful, and she mined out of that negative energy with glee. She paused to gather strength.

She glanced around. Nobody seemed to have noticed her. Good. She opened the leather bag and, holding it with one hand, with the other, she searched inside for the gun, wrapped in the scarf, carefully packed at home before leaving her bedroom. She reached and touched the cold surface. She took it out, halfway to the top of the bag. Mercifully, the handbag was outsized, and nobody would see it yet. She should get near the group before taking it out completely. The gun felt familiar in her hand. She knew that, after everything had passed, Sergio would feel responsible for having taught her how to use it and even celebrated her startling right eye at shooting a target on her first try.

Sergio bought the gun about a year ago, influenced by Franz, she was sure, for self-defense, just in case, and she had held this gun many times at home in the last weeks, gauging its shape and weight, rehearsing how she would pull it out and how she would carry it. Now she should get closer not to miss her target, but with enough distance to prevent the others from jumping at her before she did what she had to. Her mind was working fast, though strangely clear and calm. If she approached the group near the wall to her right, she would be shielded from the back, and nobody would be behind her.

She felt reassured now that she had her movements planned. She knew exactly what to do and turned her attention to the group. The man was listening attentively to another guy, sitting at his right, so he had his head turned away from Alicia. She took the hand out of the bag and wiped it on her jeans once more. She needed her hand dry and steady. Then, with her eyes on him, she searched the handbag. When she held the gun again, she knew it was the right moment to step ahead.

Walking firmly toward the group she stood right in the place she had planned, close enough to the man. He noticed her presence and turned quickly. With a firm hand, she took the gun out of the bag. "Get up, *hijo de puta!*" she shouted at him, and he looked at her, trying to register what was going on and who this woman was. Then, in a voice that came out shriller than she had planned, she shouted again, now nervously, "Get up, I told you, fucker! Against the wall, you dirty pig!"

"*Qué*...What??" He said, looking at her, and she realized, with a sort of demented glee, that he had recognized her and that he just knew what was going to happen.

The other men, taken by surprise and slow to react after a heavy dinner and wine, just watched in disbelief. Two of them stood up but did not move from their places. Alicia's eyes were fixed on the man that slowly backed sideways from the couch, near the wall, with his hands half-up, in an involuntary defensive movement because she had not asked him to do so.

She locked her eyes on his. She knew that he was calculating what to do and how to grab her gun. But the distance was too much to jump on her. With a shriller but firm voice, she said the few words that she had been rehearsing from when she saw his hated face again in that same room. "This is for Susana and all the others like her."

And just like that, with a steady pulse and an internal strength that could have moved a mountain, she shot at him once, twice, three times, aiming at his chest. The man looked bewildered when he realized the extent of what was happening. In a futile gesture, he put his palms up to stop her and looked down to his chest, where three red marks started growing on the spotless white polo shirt.

"*Yegua de mierda, qué hacés, hija de puta...*" he mustered with difficulty. Then he silently leaned against the wall and slipped down, very slowly, in what Alicia thought was an eternity. Finally, he reached the floor, half seated, pathetically disjointed. His head hanging at the side, the eyes open in a glazed, empty stare, resembling a marionette thrown from above.

The room swirled around Alicia for a moment, but she regained her balance quickly. Her heart was beating madly; she had not noticed it before. The others had jumped closer after she shot the man, but nobody reached for her or tried to grab the gun.

She stood there, looking at everybody, in a daze, and then glanced at the man on the floor. Had he moved? No, he did not move. She sighed with relief and lowered the gun, realizing suddenly that the onlookers would worry about her sanity and wonder if she was about to shoot the others. She also noticed now that the room was full of voices, even though she could not make up what they were saying. She had to calm them down.

"It's okay, it's okay, it's over," she said clearly, to nobody in particular. "Call the policeman. He's outside; I saw him there before."

She bent over carefully, leaving the gun on the wooden floor in front of her. She kicked it forward, and then, finally relieved of her burden, she looked up, crossing her hands behind her neck, as she had seen lawbreakers surrender to police in so many movies.

Acknowledgements

To my husband Tomás Jakovljevic, for his unconditional support, his continuous interest in my work and his invaluable insights.

To writer and poet Rebecca Byrkit, who guided me at a UCLA workshop where I wrote the short story *Malvinas*, later to became this book.

To my daughter Adriana McCormick, a thoughtful and supportive reader.

To the first readers of fragments of the novel's first drafts: The writer and teacher Norma Watkins and my fellow writers at the MDC literary workshops and reading groups.

OTHER BOOKS BY THE AUTHOR

DEL MEDITERRANEO AL PLATA   (Spanish)
A novel

This is the engrossing and dramatic real-life family saga about the immigration experience of the author's grandparents and great-grandparents that comprises a century. Is the true story of two families, one Italian and the other Spanish, who decided to migrate to the bountiful and promising Argentina of 1900s

> **Nominated Finalist in Genealogy/Heritage/Ancestry at the 2012 Dan Pointer's Global e-Book Awards in Santa Barbara, CA**
> **www.globalebookawards.com**

LA CASA VIEJA Y OTROS RELATOS (Spanish)

A collection of short stories

> **Awarded Gold Medal - Spanish Category at the 2017 Florida Book Awards Organized by Florida State University, Florida**

> **Awarded Honorable Mention Best Popular Fiction-Spanish or Bilingual, at the 2016 International Latino Book Awards, organized by Latino Literacy Now in Los Angeles, CA**

EL RECADO
DE LA MUJER HOLANDESA
(Spanish Version)

Un diario íntimo que aparece en Buenos
Aires después de medio siglo.
Una historia que nos mantiene cautivos.
Una aventura romántica que trasciende
el tiempo y las fronteras.
Un recado que nos llega desde la distancia
con una misión
que la tragedia dejó trunca.

UNA HISTORIA INOLVIDABLE

http://www.Amazon.com/isabel-garcia-
cintas/e/

Página Web de la autora:
www.isabelgarciacintas.com

**Bronze Medal Best Novel-Mystery
2021 International
Latino Book Awards**

EL RECADO DE LA MUJER HOLANDESA
(English version forthcoming)

An intimate diary that appears in Buenos Aires

after half a century.

A story that keeps us captive.

A romantic adventure that transcends

time and borders.

A message that comes to us from a distance with

a mission that tragedy left truncated.

AN UNFORGETTABLE STORY

www.ingramcontent.com/pod-product-compliance
Lightning Source LLC
Chambersburg PA
CBHW031217020726
47499CB00002B/614

* 9 780983 852308 *